PENGUIN POPULAR CLASSICS

TWENTY THOUSAND LEAGUES UNDER THE SEA

JULES VERNE

Translated by
Mendor T. Brunetti

PENGUIN BOOKS

PENGUIN BOOKS

Published by the Penguin Group
Penguin Books Ltd, 27 Wrights Lane, London w8 5tz, England
Penguin Books USA Inc., 375 Hudson Street, New York, New York 10014, USA
Penguin Books Australia Ltd, Ringwood, Victoria, Australia
Penguin Books Canada Ltd, 10 Alcorn Avenue, Toronto, Ontario, Canada m4v 3b2
Penguin Books (NZ) Ltd, 182–190 Wairau Road, Auckland 10, New Zealand

Penguin Books Ltd, Registered Offices: Harmondsworth, Middlesex, England

First published 1869
Published in Penguin Popular Classics 1994
3 5 7 9 10 8 6 4 2

Printed in England by Clays Ltd, St Ives plc

TWENTY THOUSAND
LEAGUES UNDER THE SEA
BY JULES VERNE

JULES VERNE (1828–1905). Often overlooked by English critics, Verne was a prolific writer whose work combined a vivid imagination with a gift for popularizing science and travel. He remains among the classics of nineteenth-century French literature.

Born in Nantes in 1828, Jules Verne was the eldest of five children. His father, Pierre Verne, a successful lawyer, was known to write occasional verse but encouraged his son to follow the family profession, which Verne duly did, studying law in Paris. His schooldays proved unexceptional and, apart from an unrequited love he cherished for his cousin, happy. After successfully completing his *baccalauréat* at the Lycée in Nantes in 1847, Verne went to Paris in order to study for the bar. For the next ten years he devoted himself to his real interest, writing, living an artist's existence in a succession of gloomy lodgings. During this time he achieved moderate success with his plays, and it is thought that about seven of his works reached the stage or print. Alexandre Dumas *père* and *fils* were instrumental in this. In 1856 Verne attended a wedding where he met his future wife, Honorine de Viane, a widow with two daughters. After his marriage in 1857 Verne became a stockbroker and for a time his interests vacillated between the *bourse* and the theatre. It was not until the success of some of his traveller's tales which he wrote for the *Musée des familles* that his true talent for imaginative travel stories emerged. The success of *Five Weeks in a Balloon* (1862) led to a partnership between Verne and the publisher Hetzel that lasted for forty years and was intended, in Hetzel's own words, 'to sum up all the geographical, geological, physical and astronomical knowledge amassed by modern science, and to rewrite the history of the world'. Between the publication of *Journey to the Centre of the Earth* in 1864 and his death Verne wrote a staggering sixty-three novels, including *From the Earth to the Moon* (1865),

Twenty Thousand Leagues under the Sea (1869) and *Around the World in Eighty Days* (1873). Verne himself travelled widely in Europe, North Africa and America and was a keen yachtsman. He divided his time between Paris, Amiens and his yacht, but for reasons which remain a mystery he suddenly sold his yacht in 1886 and never travelled again. A month later he was shot twice by his mentally unstable nephew, leaving him permanently lame. Jules Verne died at Amiens in 1905. After his death several posthumous works appeared, but it has since been discovered that Verne's son Michel wrote large chunks of them.

Twenty Thousand Leagues under the Sea was first serialized in 1869, although it wasn't published in English until 1873. The story of Professor Aronnax's terrifying undersea journey and encounters with the brilliant but maniacal Captain Nemo remains one of the most enthralling adventure books ever written.

CONTENTS

Conversion Table

LIKE MANY technical-minded—and especially nautical-minded —persons, Jules Verne would use either the "Anglo-Saxon" or the French measure, depending on which was more appropriate or practicable at the moment. We have taken a similar liberty in translation, using, at any given point, either the English or the metric system, depending on which would provide figures easier to work with and to remember. Often we have supplied the equivalent figures because that too is typical of Verne's virtuoso style.

The reader will find it profitable occasionally to flip to this table for quick definitions and equivalents until, as will inevitably happen, he will have mastered the terms he needs.

LEAGUE: Roughly, two to three nautical miles; when Verne wants to be more exact, he himself gives the equivalent in English miles.

FATHOM: An English measure equivalent to six feet (approximately the maximum distance a man can span by stretching out his arms horizontally in a continuous line with his shoulders).

CABLE: One hundred fathoms, or 600 feet; in some navies, a cable's length has been set officially at 720 feet.

METER: The basic unit in the French metric system, equivalent to 39.37 inches; in rough conversion, one English yard.

CENTIMETER: One hundredth of a meter, or 0.39 inch.

CUBIC CENTIMETER: .061 cubic inch.

KILOMETER: One thousand meters, or .62 miles.

LITER: 61.02 cubic inches, or 1.057 quarts.

PART ONE

Chapter I

A SHIFTING REEF

THE YEAR 1866 was marked by a strange occurrence, an unexplained and inexplicable phenomenon that surely no one has forgotten. People living along the coasts, and even far inland, had been perturbed by certain rumors, while seafaring men had been especially alarmed. Merchants, shipowners, captains and skippers throughout Europe and America, naval officers of many nations, and governments on both continents —all were deeply concerned.

The fact was that for some time a number of ships had been encountering, on the high seas, "an enormous thing," described as a long, spindle-shaped object that was sometimes phosphorescent, and infinitely larger and faster than a whale.

The facts concerning this apparition, which had been recorded in the logs of the various ships, agreed more or less as to the shape of the object or creature in question, the incalculable speed of its movements, its surprising power, and the strange life with which it seemed to be endowed. If it was a cetacean, then it exceeded in size any that science had so far classified as such. Neither Cuvier, nor Lacépède, nor Duméril, nor de Quatrefages would have admitted the existence of such a monster—unless they had seen it with the trained eye of the scientist.

Taking an average of the observations made on various occasions, rejecting the hesitant estimates that gave this object a length of two hundred feet, and discounting the exaggerated opinions that made it out to be one mile wide and three miles long, it could, nevertheless, be stated that this phenomenal

13

being was far bigger than anything that had been confirmed to date by the ichthyologists—if indeed it existed at all.

But the fact that it did exist was no longer deniable, and seeing that the human mind is always hankering after something to marvel at, the stir created throughout the world by this supernatural apparition will be well understood. As for relegating it to the realm of fable, that was out of the question.

On the 20th of July, 1866, the steamer *Governor Higginson* of the Calcutta and Burnach Steam Navigation Company had met this moving mass five miles off the east coast of Australia. At first Captain Baker thought it was an unknown reef. Just as he was preparing to establish its exact position, two jets of water, projected by the mysterious object, rose hissing 150 feet into the air. This meant that unless this reef had a geyser within it, the *Governor Higginson* was confronted by some sort of aquatic mammal, thus far unknown, which was capable of spouting columns of water, mixed with air and vapor, through its blowholes.

The same thing was also observed on the 23rd of July of the same year, in the Pacific, by the *Cristobal-Colon* of the West India and Pacific Steam Navigation Company. Apparently, therefore, this extraordinary cetacean was able to move from one place to another with surprising speed, since, within the space of three days, the *Governor Higginson* and the *Cristobal-Colon* had seen it at two points on the map separated by a distance of more than seven hundred nautical leagues or about 2,100 nautical miles.

Fifteen days later and about six thousand miles from the last-given position, the *Helvetia* of the Compagnie Nationale, and the *Shannon* of the Royal-Mail Company, sailing in opposite directions in that portion of the Atlantic situated between the United States and Europe, signaled to each other that they had sighted the monster at 42° 15′ north by 60° 35′ west of the meridian of Greenwich. This joint observation, then, estimated the minimum length of the mammal at more than 350 English feet, since it was longer than either the *Shannon* or the *Helvetia*, both of which measured over 300 feet from stem to stern. Moreover, it had to be borne in mind that the hugest whales, those found near the Aleutian, Kulammak, and Umgullich Islands, have never been longer than 180 feet, if that.

These reports, coming in one after the other, with fresh observations made by the transatlantic ship *le Pereire*, news of a collision between the monster and the *Etna* of the Inman line, an official memorandum drawn up by the officers of the French frigate *la Normandie*, a highly objective survey made

14

by the staff of Commodore Fitz-James on board the *Lord Clyde*—all this greatly aroused public interest. In countries of volatile temperament, the phenomenon was the subject of many a joke, but serious-minded, practical countries, like England, America, and Germany, took the matter very seriously.

In all the commercial centers, the monster was fashionable! It was sung about in the cafés, made fun of in the papers, and even represented on the stage. Reporters of the yellow press took the opportunity to invent all sorts of wild stories about it. Some newspapers—short of something to write about—raked up all the gigantic imaginary creatures they could find, from the white whale—the terrible "Moby Dick" of the hyperborean regions—to the huge kraken, whose tentacles could enfold a five-hundred-ton ship and drag it down to the bottom of the ocean. Even the accounts found in ancient writings were revived: the opinions of Aristotle and Pliny, who admitted the existence of such monsters; the Norwegian tales of Bishop Pontoppidan; the reports of Paul Heggede; and lastly, the reports of Mr. Harrington, whose good faith may in no way be considered suspect when he says that in 1857, on board the *Castillan,* he saw that enormous serpent that had, until then, never been seen in any waters except those once "navigated" by the now-defunct newspaper, the *Constitutionnel.*

Then an interminable controversy between the credulous and the incredulous exploded in all the learned societies and scientific journals. The "question of the monster" inflamed all minds. Journalists professing knowledge on scientific matters, at odds with those laying claim to intellect, spilled gallons of ink in the course of this memorable campaign; some of them even drew a little blood, for, from talking about the sea serpent, they shifted their ground all too easily to the most offensive personal slurs.

For six months the battle was waged to and fro with varying fortune. To leading articles by the Geographic Institute of Brazil, the Royal Academy of Sciences in Berlin, the British Association, the Smithsonian Institution in Washington; to discussions in the *Indian Archipelago,* in the Abbé Moigno's *Cosmos,* and in Petermann's *Mittheilungen;* as well as to scientific articles in the more important newspapers in France and abroad—the popular press retorted with endless wit. Their humorists, parodying a remark of Linnaeus, quoted by the adversaries of the monster, to the effect that "nature does not make fools," adjured their contemporaries not to give the lie to nature by admitting the existence of krakens, sea serpents, "Moby Dicks," and other lucubrations of delirious sailors. Finally, to cap it all, in an article in a much-feared satirical journal, the most celebrated and popular of the editors struck at the monster as a legendary Hippolyte, and dealt him a death blow amidst a universal chorus of mirth. Wit had vanquished science.

During the first months of the year 1867, the question seemed to have been buried for good and never likely to be raised again, when new facts were brought to the notice of the public. It was then no longer a question of a scientific problem to be solved, but a real and genuine danger to be avoided. The question took on quite a different complexion. The monster again became a small island, rock, or reef; but if it was a reef it was a shifting one, indeterminate and incomprehensible.

On March 5, 1867, the *Moravian* of the Montreal Ocean Company, which was sailing in a latitude of 27° 30′ and a longitude of 72° 15′, struck with her starboard quarter a rock not marked in any chart of that part of the sea. Under the combined efforts of wind and four-hundred-horsepower engines, it was going at the rate of thirteen knots. There is no doubt that but for the superior quality of her hull, the *Moravian* would have broken up under the impact and gone down with the 237 passengers she was bringing back from Canada.

The accident had occurred at about five o'clock in the morning, just as day was breaking. The officers of the watch hurried aft, where they scanned the sea with the greatest attention. But they could see nothing except a choppy area about three cables' lengths away, as if the carpetlike surface of the water had been violently agitated. The exact bearings of the place were taken, and the *Moravian* continued on its course, without apparent damage. Had it struck a submerged rock or an enormous piece of drifting wreckage? No one could tell. But later, when the ship's bottom was inspected, they found that part of her keel had been broken.

This incident, which was extremely serious in itself, might well have been forgotten like so many others, if the same thing had not happened three weeks later under identical circumstances. However, because of the nationality of the ship that had been a victim of this latest collision, and because of the reputation of the company to which it belonged, the occurrence had enormous repercussions.

Everyone has heard the name of the famous English shipowner, Cunard. In 1840 this farsighted industrialist founded a postal service between Liverpool and Halifax, with three wooden paddle steamers, each of 1,162 tons and powered by 400-horsepower engines. Eight years later, the company's fleet was increased by the addition of four 650-horsepower,

1820-ton boats, and, two years after that, by two other ships, both superior in power and tonnage. In 1853 the Cunard company, whose privilege of carrying the mail had just been renewed, added successively to its fleet the *Arabia*, the *Persia*, the *China*, the *Scotia*, the *Java*, and the *Russia*, all first-rate ships and the biggest, after the *Great Eastern*, that had ever ploughed the seas. Thus, in 1867 the company owned twelve ships, eight of them paddle steamers and four of them propeller-driven.

I have supplied these very brief details so that everybody may be well aware of the importance of this shipping line, known throughout the world for its intelligent management. No oceangoing shipping concern has ever been so well run, and no business has ever been crowned with more success. Over the past twenty-six years, Cunard ships have crossed the Atlantic two thousand times without as much as a voyage ever being missed, or any delay being recorded, or a letter, man, or ship being lost. Moreover, in spite of the strong competition offered by France, passengers continue to choose the Cunard line in preference to all others, according to a survey of official records of recent years. When all this has been said, nobody will be surprised at the stir caused by the accident that happened to one of the company's finest steamers.

On the 13th of April, 1867, the sea was calm and the wind moderate, and the *Scotia* was situated in a longitude of 15° 12' and a latitude of 45° 37'. Her thousand-horsepower engines were driving her along at a speed of 13½ knots. Her paddles were treading the water with perfect rhythm and regularity. Her draught was twenty-two feet, and her displacement equal to 233,924.35 cubic feet.

At 4:17 P.M., when the passengers were enjoying lunch in the great saloon, a slight shock was felt on the hull, somewhat aft of the port paddle.

The *Scotia* had not struck, she had *been* struck, by something with a cutting or perforating edge. The collision had seemed so light that no one on board would have been alarmed but for the coal-trimmers, who rushed up onto the bridge shouting: "We're sinking! We're sinking!"

At first the passengers were very frightened, but Captain Anderson hastened to reassure them. Indeed, there was no question of any imminent danger, for the *Scotia* was divided into seven compartments by means of watertight bulkheads, and was thus able to withstand any leak.

Captain Anderson immediately went down into the hold, where he found that the fifth compartment had been flooded and the water was coming in so fast that the leak must be a

17

considerable one. Most fortunately, this compartment did not contain the boilers; otherwise, the furnaces would have been extinguished at once.

Captain Anderson had the engines stopped, and one of the sailors dived down to ascertain the extent of the damage. A few moments later, he found that there was a large hole, two meters, or almost seven feet, in diameter, in the bottom of the steamer. Such a leak could not be patched, so the *Scotia,* then three hundred miles from Cape Clear, had to continue her course with paddles half submerged. After three days' delay, which caused considerable concern in Liverpool, she reached the company's shipyard.

The engineers then proceeded to examine the *Scotia,* which was put in dry dock, and they could scarcely believe their eyes: for there, some eight feet below the watermark, was a rent shaped like an isosceles triangle. The break in the iron plates was so clean that it could not have been more neatly done by a cutting machine. Obviously, the instrument that had produced such a perforation was not of a common stamp! Moreover, after having been driven home with prodigious force to pierce iron plating 1½ inches thick, it must have withdrawn itself by means of a reverse motion that was utterly inexplicable.

This new incident enflamed public opinion again. From then on, all accidents at sea that could not otherwise be accounted for were blamed on the monster. The fantastic creature had therefore to shoulder the responsibility for all shipwrecks; moreover, the number of these is unfortunately considerable, for of the three thousand ships whose loss is annually recorded by the Bureau Veritas,* the number of craft, both steam and sail, presumed lost with all hands in the absence of any news, is never less than two hundred!

And now, of course, it was the monster who was, justly or unjustly, accused of their disappearance. As a result, travel between the continents was becoming more and more dangerous, and the public therefore demanded that the sea be purged of this dread cetacean, at all costs, once and for all!

* The French equivalent of Lloyd's of London. —M.T.B.

Chapter II

PRO AND CON

AT THE TIME when these events occurred, I was returning from a scientific expedition to the badlands of Nebraska in the United States of America, to which the French Government had assigned me in my capacity of Assistant Professor at the Paris Museum of Natural History.

After six months in Nebraska, I arrived in New York toward the end of March, laden with valuable collections. My departure for France had been fixed for the beginning of May. Thus, at the time of the *Scotia* incident, I was classifying my mineralogical, botanical, and zoological specimens.

Of course, I was well informed on this topical question. How could I have been otherwise, having read and reread all the American and European newspapers without having got any further toward an answer? The mystery intrigued me; and since it was impossible to form a definite opinion, I drifted from one extreme to the other. That there *was* something, there could be no doubt, and doubting Thomases were invited to put their hands into the "wound" in the *Scotia*.

By the time I got to New York, the discussion had reached the boiling point. The hypothesis of a floating islet, or an unapproachable reef, which had been supported by people incompetent to judge, had now been completely abandoned.— And indeed, unless this reef had an engine in its belly, how could it possibly move from place to place with such prodigious speed?

The existence of a floating hull, a gigantic shipwreck, was rejected for the same reason.

There remained only two possible solutions, and these created two distinct parties: on one side, those who believed in a monster of colossal strength; on the other, those who believed in a "submarine" vessel of enormous power.

But this second hypothesis, plausible as it sounded, would not stand up to inquiries in both the Old World and the New. It was not likely that a private individual could have such a machine at his command. Where and when might he have had it built, and how could he have kept its construction a secret?

19

Only a government could possess such a destructive machine, and in these disastrous times, when man is daily striving to multiply the power of weapons of war, it was quite possible that some state was trying out this formidable contrivance unknown to all the others. After the Chassepot breech-loading rifles had come the torpedoes; after the torpedoes, the submarine rams; and then—the reaction. At least, so I hope.

But the idea of an engine of war faded as one country after another issued a formal denial. Since the public interest was involved and oceanic communications were affected, the honesty of the governments in question could not be doubted. Moreover, how could the construction of a submarine craft have escaped public notice? For to keep the secret under such circumstances would be very difficult for a private individual, while for a country whose every act was jealously watched by rival powers, it would certainly be impossible.

Therefore, after inquiries had been made in England, France, Russia, Prussia, Spain, Italy, America, and even in Turkey, the hypothesis of a submarine *Monitor* was definitely rejected.

So once again the monster came to the surface of the debate, in spite of the endless jokes to which it was subjected by the popular press, whose imagination very soon began to run riot with the most absurdly invented sea creatures.

Upon my arrival in New York, several people had done me the honor of asking me for my opinion. In France, I had published a two-volume work on *The Mysteries of the Great Ocean Depths,* which had been particularly well received in the world of science, thus turning me into a specialist in this rather obscure branch of natural history. So my opinion was sought. As long as I was able to ignore the facts of the case, I took refuge in absolute skepticism; however, very soon I found I had my back to the wall and was forced to make a definite statement. Even "the Honorable Pierre Aronnax, Professor at the Museum of Paris" was called upon by the *New York Herald* to venture some sort of appraisal.

So I spoke out. I did so because I was unable to hold my tongue. I discussed the question in all its aspects, political and scientific. Here is the peroration of my article, which was printed in the issue of the 30th of April:

"Therefore, after examining the various hypotheses one by one," I said, "all other suppositions having been rejected, we are forced to admit the existence of a marine creature of enormous power.

"The deepest parts of the ocean are completely unknown to us. Soundings have been unable to reach them. What goes on in those remote depths? What creatures can live twelve or fifteen miles below the surface of the water? What sort of organism do these animals possess? It is almost impossible to imagine.

"However, the solution of the problem put to me is obviously affected by the shape of the dilemma itself.

"Either we know about all the varieties of creature that inhabit our planet, or we do not.

"If we do not know them all, if nature still holds secrets for us in the field of ichthyology, nothing is more reasonable than to admit the existence of fishes or cetaceans, or even of new species or types, living in a special environment at the bottom of the sea at depths inaccessible to our soundings, and that some incident, some fantastic occurrence or, if you will, some whim brings up to the upper surface of the ocean from time to time, and at long intervals.

"If, on the other hand, we do know all the living species, then we shall have to look for the animal in question among the lists of marine life already catalogued. In that case, I should be inclined to decide on the existence of a *giant narwhal*.

"The common narwhal or sea unicorn often attains a length of sixty feet. Multiply this by five, or even ten, give this cetacean strength proportionate to its size, increase its offensive weapons accordingly, and you may have the animal we are looking for. It would have the proportions established by the officers of the *Shannon*, the instrument needed to pierce the *Scotia*'s side, and the power necessary to damage a steamer's hull.

"The narwhal is armed with a kind of ivory sword, or halberd, as some naturalists call it. It is a sort of main tooth, or tusk hard as steel. Some of these tusks have been found embedded in the bodies of whales, which the narwhal* al-

* The order of Cetacea includes all marine animals—the whales, the dolphins, and the porpoises. Verne deals only with whales—the whalebone, the narwhal or narwal, and the cachalot or the sperm whale.

The whalebone is the largest living animal. It may reach a length of about 100 feet and may weigh about 150 tons. These whales have no teeth but have plates of baleen in the upper jaw that form a fringelike sieve to collect and retain food.

The narwhal is marbled gray or white in color, has no dorsal fin, and attains a length of twenty feet. It is sometimes called the unicorn of the sea, because the male possesses a twisted, long, pointed tusk or horn, which may attain a length of six or seven feet and which furnishes ivory of commercial value. Verne exaggerates the size of his narwhal, but then he is talking of a giant mammal.

The cachalot or sperm whale attains the same dimensions as the whalebone whale, but it differs from the latter in that it possesses strong teeth in the lower jaw. The cachalot is carniverous and feeds on large game. It has a large closed cavity in the head containing a large quantity of oil and a blubber weighing five tons and yielding oil of superior quality. A pathological secretion of its intestines produces ambergris, used as a fixative in perfumery.—M.T.B.

ways attacks with success; others have been extracted, not without difficulty, from the bottoms of ships that they had pierced right through, as a gimlet pierces a barrel. The Museum of the Faculty of Medicine in Paris has one of these weapons, which is seven feet long and eighteen inches wide at the base!

"Now, suppose the weapon to be ten times stronger, and the animal ten times more powerful; launch it at a speed of twenty miles an hour, multiply its mass by the square of its speed, and you will obtain an impact capable of producing the damage in question.

"Thus, until we have fuller information, I would opt for a sea unicorn of colossal dimensions, armed not with a halberd but with a real spur, similar to the armor-plated frigates, or the 'rams' used in war, possessing both the mass and the motive power of the latter.

"This would be an explanation for this inexplicable phenomenon—unless, of course, there be something else, beyond anything that we have ever surmised, seen, felt, or experienced—which is still possible!"

These last words were somewhat cowardly on my part, but up to a point I wanted to preserve my dignity as a professor, and not give the Americans a chance to laugh—for when they laugh, they certainly do it in style. So I was leaving myself a way out. After all, I was, in effect, admitting the existence of the "monster."

My article was hotly debated, which meant that it caused quite a sensation and gained a number of supporters. The solution that it proposed at least left plenty of scope to the imagination. The human mind delights in grand visions of supernatural beings. And the sea is their very best medium, the only environment in which such giants—compared to which land animals, such as the elephant and rhinoceros, are like dwarfs—can be produced and developed. The sea bears within it the largest species of known mammals, and perhaps it also conceals mollusks of incomparable size, crustaceans too fearful to contemplate, such as three-hundred-foot lobsters, or crabs weighing two hundred tons! Why not? Long ago, in distant geological ages, land animals, birds, apes, quadrupeds, and reptiles were developed on an enormous scale. The Creator had cast them in a huge mold, which time gradually reduced. Why should the sea, in its unknown depths, not have conserved some of these gigantic specimens of the life of another age—for apparently the sea never changes, while the earth is continually undergoing mutations? Why should the sea not conceal, within its bosom, the last of these titanic species, for which the years are but centuries, and the centuries millennia?

But I have allowed myself to be carried away by dreams that I ought no longer to indulge in. Enough of these fantasies that time has now changed for me into terrible reality. I repeat: opinion thus crystallized as to the nature of the phenomenon, and the public acknowledged, without dispute, the existence of a prodigious creature that had nothing in common with the fabulous sea serpents.

While some people saw this as posing a purely scientific problem, others, who were more practical, especially in America and England, were of the opinion that the ocean should be purged of this redoubtable monster, in order to ensure the safety of transoceanic communications. Industrial and commercial journals dealt with the question mainly from this point of view. *The Shipping and Mercantile Gazette*, the *Lloyd's List*, the *Paquebot*, and the *Revue Maritime et Coloniale*—all papers dealing with insurance companies, which were threatening to raise their premiums—were unanimous on this point.

Thus, public opinion had spoken, and the United States of America was the first to declare its intentions. Preparations were therefore made in New York to fit out an expedition to pursue the narwhal. A high-speed ice-breaking frigate, the *Abraham Lincoln*, was made ready to take to the sea as soon as possible. The arsenals were opened to Commander Farragut, who hastened to arm his ship.

However, as is often the case, once it had been decided to give chase to the monster, the monster failed to reappear. For two months it was not heard of. No ship encountered it. It seemed as though the sea unicorn knew about the plots that were being hatched against it. After all, there had been so much talk about it, even over the transatlantic cable! Some wits alleged that the crafty creature no doubt had intercepted a cablegram and was now reaping the benefit of it.

Thus, the frigate was armed to fight a long-distance campaign and equipped with formidable fishing equipment, but no one knew where it should go. Impatience was growing when, on the 2nd of July, it was learned that the *Tampico*, a steamer of the San Francisco-Shanghai line, had sighted the animal, three weeks before, in the North Pacific.

The news caused the greatest excitement, and Commander Farragut was given less than twenty-four hours to get ready. The ship was laden with food and provisions, and the holds overflowed with coal. Not a member of the crew was missing from his post. All that needed to be done was to kindle the furnaces, stoke up, and weigh anchor. Half a day's delay

23

would have been unforgivable—although it must be said that Commander Farragut asked nothing better than to get going.

Three hours before the *Abraham Lincoln* was to leave its Brooklyn pier, I received a letter couched in the following terms:

To:
Monsieur Aronnax, Professor at the Museum of Paris
Fifth Avenue Hotel, New York

Sir,
If you wish to join the expedition of the *Abraham Lincoln*, the Government of the Union will be pleased to see France represented by you in this enterprise. Commander Farragut has reserved a cabin for your use.

Yours very cordially,
J. B. Hobson
Secretary of the Navy

Chapter III

JUST AS MONSIEUR WISHES

THREE SECONDS BEFORE receiving J. B. Hobson's letter, I had had no more thought of chasing the sea unicorn than of finding the Northwest Passage. Three seconds after reading the letter of the Honorable Secretary of the Navy, I realized that my true vocation, my life's only aim, was to pursue this annoying monster and rid the world of it.

However, I had just come back from an exhausting journey, and was dying for a rest. I had wanted nothing better than to return to my country, my friends, my little apartment at le Jardin des Plantes,* and to my beloved, precious collections. But nothing could hold me back now! Now I forgot everything: my fatigue, my friends, and my collections, and I accepted the American Government's invitation without another thought.

"After all," I reflected, "all roads lead back to Europe, and the unicorn will surely be obliging enough to take me towards the coast of France. This worthy animal will doubtless let itself be caught in European waters—just to please me— for I want to bring back not less than two feet of his ivory spur for the Museum of Natural history." However, in the meantime, I should have to go and look for this narwhal in the North Pacific, which meant going to France via the Antipodes!

"Conseil," I called out impatiently.

Conseil was my faithful servant who accompanied me on all my travels, a fine Flemish lad whom I liked as much as he liked me. Phlegmatic by nature, punctual on principle, zealous from habit, he was seldom taken by surprise by any of life's unexpected incidents. He was also very clever with his hands, ready to perform any service required of him, and in spite of his name, he never gave advice—no! not even when he was not asked!

Through rubbing shoulders with learned men in our small world at the Jardin des Plantes, Conseil had picked up quite a bit of information. In him I had a well-versed specialist in

* Another name for the Paris Museum of Natural History—M.T.B.

the classification of subjects of natural history, for with the agility of an acrobat he would run up and down the whole scale of branches, groups, classes, subclasses, orders, families, genuses, subgenuses, species, and varieties. But there his knowledge came to an end. To classify was his whole life, but he could do nothing else. Since he was very knowledgeable about the theory of classification, but not about the practical side, I doubt if he could tell the difference between a cachalot and a whale! But what a fine, good fellow he was!

For ten years Conseil had followed me wherever science had led. Never once had he complained of the length or hardships of a journey. Never once had he objected to packing his bags and leaving for whatever place it might be, whether China or the Congo, regardless of the distance. He had always gone, as he was about to go now, without question. Moreover, his health was good and he had a good resistance to disease, solid muscles, not the slightest hint of nerves—and he was very ethical, of course.

This lad was thirty years old, and his age was to that of his master as fifteen is to twenty. —May I be forgiven for this roundabout way of saying that I was forty?

But Conseil had one fault. He was formal to the point of excess, and spoke to me only in the third person—so much so, indeed, that I sometimes found it quite irritating.

"Conseil!" I repeated, as I began to make feverish preparations for my departure.

Of course, I was sure of this boy, who was so faithful, and so normally I never asked him whether it was convenient for him to follow me on my journeys; but this time the expedition might last indefinitely, and the enterprise, consisting of hunting an animal capable of sinking a frigate as easily as a nutshell, might well be dangerous. There was good reason to think the matter over, even for the most impassive man in the world. What would Conseil say?

"Conseil!" I shouted for the third time.

Conseil appeared.

"Did Monsieur call me?" he said as he came in.

"Yes, my lad. Get my things ready, and get yourself ready. We leave within two hours."

"Just as Monsieur wishes," Conseil replied quietly.

"There isn't a moment to lose. Pack everything into my trunk: traveling kit, suits, shirts and socks. Don't bother to count anything. Just stuff in as much as you can, and hurry!"

"But what about Monsieur's collections?" asked Conseil.

"We will take care of that later."

"What! Monsieur's archiotherium, his hyracotherium, the oreodons, the cheoptamus, and all the other specimens?"

"They will keep them at the hotel."

"And Monsieur's live babirusa?"

"They will feed it while we are away. Anyway, I will give orders to have our whole menagerie sent to France."

"Then we are not returning to Paris?" asked Conseil.

"Oh yes . . . of course we are . . ." I answered evasively. "But we shall be making a detour."

"Whatever detour Monsieur wishes."

"Oh, it will only be a short one, just a less-direct route, that's all. We are sailing on board the *Abraham Lincoln*."

"Whatever suits Monsieur best," Conseil replied calmly.

"You see, my friend, it's been because of the famous monster, the narwhal. We're going to rid the seas of it! The author of a two-volume work on *The Mysteries of the Great Ocean Depths* can't afford to miss the chance of sailing with Commander Farragut. It will be a glorious mission, but a dangerous one too. We don't know where we're going. These animals can be very temperamental. But we will go all the same. Our captain is a very courageous man."

"Wherever Monsieur goes, I go," Conseil replied.

"But give it a little thought! I don't want to hide anything from you. This is one of those journeys from which people don't always come back."

"Whatever pleases Monsieur."

A quarter of an hour later our bags were packed. Conseil had done everything in the twinkling of an eye, and I was sure that nothing was missing, for that boy could classify shirts and suits as well as birds and mammals.

The hotel elevator took us down to the mezzanine, and I walked down the few steps to the ground floor. I paid my bill at the front desk, which always seems to be besieged by a large crowd of people. I gave orders for my packages of straw-wrapped animals and dried plants to be sent to Paris. Then I deposited enough money to take care of the babirusa, and with Conseil following me, jumped into a cab.

The carriage, available at a fixed fare of four dollars, went down Broadway as far as Union Square, proceeded along Fourth Avenue as far as its junction with Bowery Street, turned into Katrin Street, and pulled up at Pier 34. There, the Katrin Ferry transported us, men, horses and carriages, to Brooklyn, that great suburb of New York, situated on the left bank of the East River, and in a few minutes we arrived at the wharf where the *Abraham Lincoln* was belching clouds of black smoke from her two smokestacks.

Our luggage was immediately carried onto the deck of the frigate, and I hurried on board. I asked for Commander Farragut, and one of the sailors led me onto the poop, where I

27

found myself in the presence of a good-looking officer, who held out his hand to me.

"Monsieur Pierre Aronnax?" he asked.

"Yes, indeed. Commander Farragut?"

"Welcome aboard, Professor. Your cabin is ready."

I bowed to the captain, and leaving him to attend to his equipment, had myself conducted to the cabin assigned to me.

The *Abraham Lincoln* had been perfectly chosen and fitted out for its new job. It was a fast frigate, equipped with high-pressure engines able to get the steam pressure up to seven atmospheres.

Under such pressure, the *Abraham Lincoln* could attain a mean speed of 18 3/10 miles—a considerable speed, but not enough to deal with the gigantic cetacean.

The ship's interior matched her nautical qualities. I was very pleased with my cabin, which was situated aft and opened into the wardroom.

"We will be comfortable here," I said to Conseil.

"As comfortable, if Monsieur will permit me to say so, as a hermit crab in the shell of a whelk."

I left Conseil to attend to our luggage, and went back on deck to watch the preparations for casting off.

At that moment, Captain Farragut was ordering the men to cast loose the last mooring ropes holding the *Abraham Lincoln* to her Brooklyn pier. Thus, if I had arrived a quarter of an hour later, or even less, the frigate would have left without me, and I should have missed this extraordinary, improbable expedition, whose truthful account may even now be greeted with incredulity.

For Commander Farragut was unwilling to lose any time in heading for the seas where the beast had just been sighted. He sent for his engineer.

"Have you got up full steam?" he asked him.

"Yes sir!" replied the engineer.

"Go ahead," the captain said.

The order was transmitted to the engine room by means of a compressed-air signaling device; the engineer started up the wheel, and the steam whistled as it rushed into the half-open slide valves. The long horizontal pistons creaked and pushed the rods of the shaft. The blades of the propeller threshed the water with increasing speed, and the *Abraham Lincoln* advanced majestically into the midst of a hundred or so ferry-boats and tenders, loaded with well-wishers and acting as an escort.

The piers of Brooklyn and all that part of New York bordering on the East River were lined with curious spectators.

Three cheers burst from 500,000 throats and echoed through the air. Thousands of handkerchiefs waved above the packed crowds bidding farewell to the *Abraham Lincoln,* until she reached the waters of the Hudson, at the point where that elongated peninsula forms the City of New York.

Then the frigate, following the New Jersey coast along the right bank of that wonderful river, studded with villas, sailed between the forts, which now saluted her with their big guns. The *Abraham Lincoln* replied by hauling down and hoisting the American flag three times, and thirty-nine* stars shone splendidly from the mizzen peak. Then, reducing speed to negotiate the narrow channel, marked by buoys, in the inner bay formed by Sandy Hook Point, she coasted the long, sandy stretch, where crowds of thousands gave her another cheer.

The escorts of boats and tenders were still following the frigate, and did not leave her until they came abreast of the lightship, whose two lights mark the entrance to New York Harbor.

Six bells (three o'clock) sounded, and the pilot went down into his small boat and returned to the little schooner that was waiting for him to leeward. The boilers were stoked up; the propeller pounded the waves more quickly; the frigate skirted the low yellow coast of Long Island; and at eight o'clock in the evening, after the lights of Fire Island had faded away to the northwest, she ran full steam ahead into the dark waters of the Atlantic.

* At the time of which Aronnax speaks, the Stars and Stripes comprised only thirty-seven stars; in the nineteenth century, when states were added so frequently, even American writers lost count.—M.T.B.

Chapter IV

NED LAND

COMMANDER FARRAGUT was a fine sailor, worthy of the frigate that he commanded. He and his ship were as one, for he was its very soul. And on the subject of the monster there was no doubt in his mind, nor would he allow anyone on board to question the existence of the animal. He believed in it as certain good women believe in the Leviathan—as a matter of faith rather than reason. The monster did exist, and he had sworn to rid the seas of it. He was a sort of Knight of Rhodes, another Dieudonné de Gozon going out to meet the serpent that was laying waste his island. Either Commander Farragut would kill the narwhal, or the narwhal would kill him. There was no middle course.

The ship's officers shared their captain's view. You should have heard them talking, discussing, arguing, and calculating the chances of an encounter, as they scrutinized the vast expanse of ocean. Some of them, who would have cursed such a chore under different circumstances, took up a post in the crosstrees. As long as the sun was in the sky, the rigging was alive with sailors, who found it unbearable to stand on their bare feet in the scorching heat of the wooden deck. And still the *Abraham Lincoln* was not yet ploughing the suspect waters of the Pacific.

As for the crew, they asked nothing better than to encounter the sea unicorn, harpoon it, hoist it aboard and carve it up. They surveyed the sea with rapt attention. Commander Farragut, incidentally, had spoken of a certain sum of two thousand dollars, which would be given to anybody, be he cabin boy or ordinary seaman, sailor or officer, who sighted the monster. So you can well imagine how eyes were strained aboard the *Abraham Lincoln*.

I didn't lag behind the others, and I would have delegated my daily watch to no one else. There would have been a hundred good reasons for calling the ship the *Argus*.* The only one of us who showed his indifference to this matter that oc-

* In ancient mythology, Argus was a monster with one hundred eyes. —M.T.B.

cupied all our thoughts—and whose attitude contrasted with the general enthusiasm on board—was Conseil.

I have already said that Commander Farragut had carefully equipped his ship with devices suitable for catching the gigantic cetacean. No whaler could have been better armed. We possessed every known apparatus, from the harpoon thrown by hand to the blunderbuss with its barbed arrows and the duck gun with its explosive bullets. On the forecastle there stood the perfect breech-loading cannon, thick-walled and narrow-bored, like the model displayed at the 1867 World Exhibition. This excellent weapon, an American invention, was capable of firing a nine-pound conical projectile an average distance of ten miles without any difficulty. So the *Abraham Lincoln* had every sort and kind of destructive weapon. And better still, she had on board Ned Land, the prince of harpooners.

Ned Land was a Canadian with a rare swiftness of hand, who knew no equal in his perilous trade. He possessed the qualities of skill, coolness, daring, and cunning to a higher degree than most, and it was a wily whale or a singularly shrewd cachalot that could escape the thrust of his harpoon.

Ned Land was about forty years old. He was a big man—measuring more than six English feet—and strongly built; he looked serious and spoke but little, although he could be violent sometimes, and became very angry if someone crossed him. His physique attracted attention, and the strength and sternness of his expression gave a strange emphasis to his face.

In my opinion, Commander Farragut had done well to recruit this man. His keen eye and strong arm made him worth all the others put together. The best way of describing him would be to liken him to a powerful telescope that could double as a cannon and was always ready for action.

Whoever calls himself Canadian calls himself French, and uncommunicative as Ned was, I must admit that he took a liking to me. My nationality attracted him to me, no doubt. It was a chance for him to talk, and for me to hear the ancient tongue of Rabelais, which is still spoken in some of the Canadian provinces. The harpooner's family originally came from Quebec, and were a hardy tribe of fishermen when that town still belonged to France.

Gradually Ned began to enjoy chatting, and I loved to hear him telling of his adventures in the polar seas. In a naturally poetic manner, he recounted his fishing expeditions and his fights; his account would take an epic form, and I felt as though I were listening to some Canadian Homer, reciting the Iliad of the Far North.

31

I have described my fearless friend as I know him today. For we have become old friends, united in that unshakable friendship that is born of mutual experience with the most awful perils. Ah, my good Ned, I ask nothing better than to live another hundred years just to have longer to remember you!

And what did Ned Land think about the great sea monster? To tell the truth, he did not believe in the unicorn and was the only man on board who did not share the general conviction. He even avoided talking about the subject; so I felt it my duty, finally, to broach the question.

One magnificent evening, on the 30th of July*—that is, three weeks after our departure—the frigate was off Cape Blanc, thirty miles to leeward of the coast of Patagonia. We had crossed the Tropic of Capricorn, and the Strait of Magellan was less than seven hundred miles to the south. Within a week, the *Abraham Lincoln* would be in the Pacific.

Seated on the poop, Ned Land and I chatted of this and that as we looked out over those mysterious waters whose depths have so far remained inaccessible to human scrutiny. Naturally, I brought the subject around to the giant unicorn, and began to examine the chances of success or failure of our expedition. Then, seeing that Ned was letting me talk without saying much himself, I came to the point:

"Ned," I asked him, "how can you possibly doubt the existence of the cetacean that we are pursuing? Have you any particular reason for appearing so incredulous?"

The harpooner looked at me for a few moments before answering, thumped his forehead with his hand in a gesture that was typical of him, closed his eyes as though to collect his thoughts, and then finally said:

"Well, Monsieur Aronnax, perhaps I have."

"But Ned, you are a whaler by profession; you know all the great marine mammals; so you ought to find it easy to accept the idea of an enormous cetacean. Considering all the aspects of this situation, you should be the last one to have doubts!"

"That's exactly what misleads you, Professor," replied Ned. "Let ordinary people believe in extraordinary comets that travel through space, or in the existence of antediluvian monsters that populate the bowels of the earth, if they want to; but astronomers and geologists don't believe in such fantasies, and the same goes for the whaler. I have hunted many cetaceans, I have harpooned a large number of them, and I have

* Aronnax is sometimes forgetful about such details. Here the date should be the 23rd or the 24th.—M.T.B.

killed several; and although they were powerful and well armed, neither their tails nor their weapons could have damaged the iron plates of a steamer."

"And yet, Ned, there are cases cited of ships whose hulls have been pierced right through by the tusk of the narwhal."

"That's possible with wooden ships," replied the Canadian, "but I've never seen any. So, until I see evidence to the contrary, I'll deny that whales, cachalots, or sea unicorns are capable of doing such damage."

"But listen, Ned—"

"No, Professor, it isn't possible. It could be anything you say except that. What about a gigantic octopus?"

"That is even less likely, Ned. The octopus is only a mollusk; the very name indicates that its flesh is anything but solid. Even if it were five hundred feet long, the octopus, which does not belong to the vertebrates, would be unable to damage ships like the *Scotia* or the *Abraham Lincoln*. We have to reject as imaginary the prowess of krakens, and other monsters of that species."

"So, Monsieur le Naturaliste," Ned Land went on in a somewhat impish tone of voice, "you insist on saying that the animal is an enormous cetacean?"

"Yes, Ned, I say this with a conviction based on the logic of the facts. I believe in the existence of a powerfully organized mammal belonging to the vertebrates, like whales, cachalots, or dolphins, and equipped with a hornlike spur of great penetrating power."

"Hm," said the harpooner, shaking his head with the air of a man unwilling to be convinced.

"Bear in mind, my worthy Canadian," I continued, "that if such an animal exists, if it lives in the depths of the ocean, and if it frequents the liquid strata miles below the surface, then it must of necessity possess an organism whose power defies comparison."

"And just why must it have such a powerful organism?" asked Ned.

"Because it would need it to be able to live at such depths and resist the pressure of the water."

"Really?" said Ned, winking at me slyly.

"Really. And I can easily prove it to you with a few figures."

"Oh, figures!" replied Ned. "People can do anything they like with figures!"

"That may be true of business, Ned, but not in mathematics. Listen to me. Let us say that one atmosphere is equal to the pressure exerted by a column of water thirty-two feet high. Actually the column of water would not be as high because we are speaking of seawater, whose density is greater than that of fresh water. So, when you dive, Ned, as many times thirty-two feet of water as there are above you, so many times does your body have to bear a pressure equal to that of the atmosphere—that is to say, about fifteen pounds for every square inch of its surface. So it follows that at three hundred and twenty feet this pressure equals ten atmospheres, at thirty-two hundred feet one hundred atmospheres, at thirty-two thousand feet—or about six miles down—one thousand atmospheres. That means that if you could attain that depth in the ocean, each square inch of the surface of your body would have to bear a pressure of about fifteen thousand pounds! Now, my good Ned, do you know how many square inches there are on the surface of your body?"

"I have no idea, Monsieur Aronnax."

"About twenty-six hundred."

"As much as that?"

"And since the atmospheric pressure is, roughly, about fifteen pounds to the square inch, your twenty-six hundred square inches are at this moment carrying a pressure of . . . about thirty-nine thousand pounds."

"Without my being aware of it?"

"Without your being aware of it. If you are not crushed by such a pressure, it is because the air penetrates inside your body with equal pressure. Owing to the perfect equilibrium created by the inside and outside pressures, they neutralize each other, which permits you to bear them without discomfort. But in the water, it's a different matter."

"Yes, I can see that," said Ned, who had become more attentive, "because the water surrounds me but does not penetrate me."

"Precisely, Ned. So, at thirty-two feet below the surface of the sea, you would have a pressure of thirty-nine thousand pounds; at three hundred and twenty feet, ten times as much; at thirty-two hundred feet, a hundred times as much, or three million nine hundred thousand pounds; and at thirty-two thousand feet, thirty-nine million pounds. So you would be flattened as if you had just been removed from the plates of a hydraulic press!"

"The Devil!" exclaimed Ned.

"So, my worthy harpooner, if a vertebrate several hundred yards long and with a proportionate width, the surface of whose body therefore consists of millions of square inches, can live at such depths, the pressure it can stand would amount to billions and billions of pounds. How enormous must be the power of resistance of its bone structure and the strength of its organism to be able to bear such pressure!"

"Why," said Ned, "it would have to be made of iron plates eight inches thick, like an armored frigate."

"Indeed, Ned; and just think what damage such a mass could inflict if launched with the speed of an express train against the hull of a ship."

"Well, yes, quite so—perhaps," said Ned, who was dazed by these figures but did not want to give in.

"Well, have I convinced you?"

"You've convinced me of one thing, Monsieur le Naturaliste; and that is that if such animals do exist at the bottom of the sea, they must of necessity be as strong as you say they are."

"But if they don't exist, you stubborn harpooner, how do you explain what happened to the *Scotia?*"

"Perhaps . . ."

"Yes, yes, go on!"

"Because . . . no—that isn't true!" His answer, although he did not realize it, echoed the celebrated reply of Arago.[*]

But this answer merely proved the harpooner's obstinacy and nothing else, so I did not press him any further that day. The damage to the *Scotia* could not be denied. So real had been the hole in her side that it had had to be repaired, and I should not have thought that the existence of a hole could be proved more conclusively than that. Now, that hole had not happened without a cause, and since it had not been caused by rocks below the surface, it must have been made by the perforating weapon of an animal.

Therefore, according to me, and for all the reasons I have just given, the animal must belong to the vertebrates, class of mammals, group of pisciforms, and, finally, order of cetaceans. As regards the family to which it belonged—whale, cachalot, or dolphin—the genus or species in which it was to be included, that was a question to be elucidated later on. In order to solve it, the unknown monster would have to be dissected, and in order to dissect it, it would have to be caught; in order to be caught, it would have to be harpooned—and that was Ned Land's concern. But in order to harpoon it, it would have to be seen—which was the business of the crew —and if we were to see it, we should first have to meet it— and that was a matter of luck.

---

[*] Dominique François Jean Arago (1786-1853), French physicist, discovered the principle of development of magnetism by rotation.— M.T.B.

Chapter V

FORWARD TO ADVENTURE

FOR SOME TIME, the voyage of the *Abraham Lincoln* was marked by no particular incident. However, there was just one incident that threw into relief the marvelous skill of Ned Land and showed how right we were to have such confidence in him.

On the 30th of June, off the Falkland Islands, the frigate met some American whalers, and we learned that they had heard nothing new about the narwhal. But one of them, the captain of the *Monroe*, hearing that Ned Land was on board the *Abraham Lincoln*, asked for his help in hunting a whale that had been sighted. Commander Farragut, who was anxious to see Ned Land at work, authorized him to go on board the *Monroe*. The Canadian had good luck, for instead of one whale, he harpooned two in quick succession; one of the whales was struck through the heart, while the other one was caught after a few minutes' chase.

I decided that if the monster ever met Ned, I would not bet on the monster.

With great speed, the frigate skirted the southeast coast of America. On the 3rd of July, we reached the entrance to the Strait of Magellan, off Cape Vierges. But Commander Farragut would not follow such a tortuous passage, and altered his course so as to sail around Cape Horn.

Unanimously the crew agreed with him. After all, was it likely that they would meet the narwhal in this narrow strait? A good number of the sailors said that the monster could never get through that passage: "He is much too big for that!"

About three P.M. on July 6th, the *Abraham Lincoln*, now fifteen miles farther south, rounded that solitary island, that lost rock at the extremity of the American continent, to which some Dutch sailors had given the name of their native town, Cape Horn. The course was set northwest, and the next day the frigate's propeller was at last churning the waters of the Pacific Ocean.

"Keep your eyes peeled!" the sailors of the *Abraham Lincoln* kept saying.

36

And indeed all eyes were kept wide open, for both eyes and glasses, to tell the truth, were a bit dazzled by the prospect of a two-thousand-dollar reward, and did not rest for a moment. Day and night, all kept a close watch over the sea; those who could see better during the day and those who could see better at night were competing equally for the prize.

Even I, for whom money has little charm, was by no means the least attentive man on board. Taking only a few minutes off for my meals, snatching a few hours' sleep, and indifferent to sun and rain, I was up on deck all the time. Whether I leaned on the forecastle rail or on the taffrail, my eager eye took in the downy foam that whitened the sea as far as the eye could see. How often I shared the feelings of the captain's staff and the crew when some capricious whale suddenly showed its dark back above the waves! In a moment the deck would be crowded. The cabins would pour forth a stream of sailors and officers, each with heaving chest and anxious eye, all watching the movement of that animal. I stared and stared until I was nearly blind, while Conseil, phlegmatic as always, would repeat calmly:

"If Monsieur would not strain his eyes so much, he would see better."

How frustrating it was! The *Abraham Lincoln* would alter its course and make for the animal, a simple whale or a common cachalot, which would soon disappear amid a hail of curses.

However, the weather held good. We were conducting our search under the most favorable conditions. It was the bad season in the Southern Hemisphere, whose July corresponds to our January in Europe; but the sea remained calm and could be easily scanned for a great distance.

Ned Land continued to be stubbornly incredulous; he even pretended not to watch the sea except when he was on duty —unless of course a whale had been sighted. His marvelous sight might have proved very useful to us. But eight hours out of twelve the obstinate Canadian would be reading or sleeping in his cabin. Again and again, I reproached him for his detachment.

"Bah!" he would reply, "there's nothing here, Monsieur Aronnax, and if there were some animal, what chance should we stand of spotting it? After all, aren't we just looking at random? We're told that the elusive animal has been sighted again in the Pacific, admittedly; but two months have already passed since then, and judging by the temperament of your narwhal, he doesn't much like hanging around in the same area! On the contrary, he has an extraordinary ability to move from one place to another. Now, Professor, you know better than I do that nature doesn't do anything contrary to good sense, and it wouldn't give a naturally slow animal the ability to move quickly if it had no need of that ability. So, if the beast exists at all, it must be far away by now!"

I did not know what to say to this. Obviously, we were sailing blindly. But how else should we proceed? True, our chances were very limited, but as yet no one doubted that we should be successful, and there wasn't a sailor on board who had not laid odds on the narwhal and on its appearing soon.

On July 20th, we cut the Tropic of Capricorn at longitude 105°, and seven days later, on the 27th, we crossed the equator on the 110th meridian. Having taken these bearings, the frigate now followed a decidedly western course and scoured the central waters of the Pacific. Captain Farragut felt, and with good reason, that it was better to stay in deep waters and keep clear of continents and islands, which the beast itself seemed to avoid—"probably because there wasn't enough water for it," as the boatswain said. After refueling, the frigate sailed past the Tuamotu Islands, the Marquesas, and the Sandwich Islands, crossed the Tropic of Cancer at longitude 132°, and made for the China Seas.

At last we were in the area where the monster had last been reported, and truly, we no longer lived normal lives. The hearts of all aboard palpitated so wildly that we all risked developing some incurable aneurism. The entire crew were in a state of nervous excitement that I can scarcely describe; they would not eat; they would no longer sleep; and twenty times a day some error or some optical illusion suffered by a sailor perched up in the rigging would get us all worked up into a sweat. Such sensations, repeated twenty times, kept us in such a state of tension that there was bound to be some reaction soon.

And the reaction did set in. For three months, during which every day seemed like an age, the *Abraham Lincoln* ploughed the waters of the North Pacific, running at whales, deviating sharply from her course, veering from one tack to another, stopping suddenly, putting on steam, or backing up again at the risk of wrecking her machinery. Not a single area between the coast of Japan and the coast of America did we leave unexplored. But to no avail! For we saw nothing but a vast expanse of deserted sea, nothing that resembled a gigantic narwhal, or a submerged island, a piece of wreckage, or a shifting reef—or indeed anything at all that was out of the ordinary!

And so the reaction came. First of all, despondency set in, and this led the way to incredulity. A new atmosphere developed on board, consisting of three-tenths of shame and seven-tenths of fury. The men felt that they had been "bloody fools" to let themselves be taken in by something utterly fantastic, but their anger was even greater. The various lines of argument that had been built up over the past year collapsed like a pack of cards, and all that anyone could think of was of making up for all the time that had been so stupidly sacrificed, by eating or sleeping as much as possible.

The natural fickleness of the human mind led from one extreme to the other. The most ardent supporters of the enterprise thus became its most fanatical opponents. The reaction mounted and spread throughout the ship, from the coal-trimmers to the wardroom, and certainly, had it not been for the resolute determination of Commander Farragut, the frigate would surely have turned south again.

However, the useless search could not go on. The *Abraham Lincoln* had nothing to reproach herself for; she had done her best. Never had an American crew shown more zeal or patience, and they could not be blamed for the failure. Even so, there was nothing to do but to turn back.

Such, then, were the arguments presented to the captain. But he resisted them, and the morale of the men, who made no attempt to hide their discontent, deteriorated greatly. I will not say that there was a spirit of mutiny on board, but after holding out for a reasonable period, Captain Farragut, like Columbus before him, asked the crew to be patient for just three more days. If within three days the monster had not appeared, the man at the helm would give three turns of the wheel, and the *Abraham Lincoln* would make for the Atlantic.

This promise, made on the 2nd of November, had the effect of rallying the crew, and each kept scanning the ocean with renewed enthusiasm. Every man hoped to cast that final glance that would give a final touch to his impressions. Spyglasses were used with feverish activity. This was the supreme challenge to the giant narwhal, who could not now reasonably fail to appear and defy that challenge.

Two days went by. The steam of the *Abraham Lincoln* was at half pressure; we tried a thousand tricks to attract the attention of the animal, to arouse it from its apathy, in case it was roaming in that area. We trailed enormous slices of bacon in our wake—but only the sharks derived satisfaction from this, I must admit. Small craft radiated in all directions from the *Abraham Lincoln* as she lay to, and left not one corner of the sea unexplored. But the night of November 4th came and this mystery of the deep was still unsolved.

The next day, the 5th of November, at midday, the three

days' delay requested by Farragut was to expire, and the commander, faithful to his promise, would have to set his course for the southeast and abandon the North Pacific for good.

The frigate was then in latitude 31° 15′ north and longitude 136° 42′ east. The coast of Japan was still less than two hundred miles to leeward. Night was falling. They had just sounded eight bells; large clouds hid the face of the moon, which was then in its first quarter. The sea rippled peacefully under the bow of our ship.

I was leaning over the starboard rail. Conseil, standing next to me, was looking straight ahead. The crew, perched in the ratlines, were scanning the horizon, which was gradually contracting and growing darker. The officers were scrutinizing the gathering gloom through their night glasses. Now and again, the somber ocean glistened as a ray of moonlight darted between the fringes of two clouds. The next moment, all trace of light would be shut out by the darkness.

Looking at Conseil, I realized that the good fellow must be feeling something, however little, of the general excitement. At least, so I thought. Perhaps, for the first time, he was intrigued and his nerves were tingling.

"Come on, Conseil," I said to him, "here is your last chance to pocket two thousand dollars."

"If Monsieur will permit me to say so, I never counted on getting the prize, and if the government of the Union had promised me one hundred thousand dollars, they would have been none the poorer for it."

"You are right, Conseil. It has been a silly business after all, and we got involved in it too lightheartedly. What a lot of wasted time and pointless excitement! We could have been back in France six months ago."

"And we should have been in Monsieur's apartment," he added, "in Monsieur's museum! By now, I should have classified all Monsieur's fossils! And the babirusa would be installed in a cage in the Jardin des Plantes, arousing people's curiosity and attracting many visitors."

"Just as you say, Conseil. But not only that; now we will probably be made fun of into the bargain."

"I don't think there's much doubt about that," Conseil replied quietly. "I imagine they *will* make fun of Monsieur. But may I say . . . ?"

"You may, Conseil."

"Well, Monsieur will only be getting what he deserves!"

"Really!"

"When one has the honor of being a learned man like Monsieur, one should not expose oneself to—"

40

Conseil did not finish his compliment. Amid the silence all around a voice had just rung out. It was the voice of Ned Land, and Ned was shouting:

"Ahoy! There it is at last! Abeam to leeward!"

Chapter VI

FULL STEAM AHEAD!

NED'S SHOUT brought the whole crew running helter-skelter in the direction of the harpooner: the captain, the officers, the boatswain, sailors, cabin boys, and all, right down to the engineers, who left their engines, and the stokers, who abandoned their furnaces. The order had been given to heave to, and the frigate was just drifting to a stop.

It was pitch-dark by then, and although the Canadian's sight was very good, I wondered how he had managed to see what he had seen. My heart was beating like a sledgehammer.

But Ned Land had not made a mistake, and now we could all see the object he was pointing at.

Two cables' lengths away from the *Abraham Lincoln,* on her starboard quarter, the sea seemed to be illuminated from below. It was no mere phenomenon of phosphorescence, and there was no mistaking it. The monster was submerged a few fathoms beneath the surface and was radiating that intense but inexplicable light that had been mentioned in the reports of several captains. This magnificent radiation must have been produced by some enormously powerful source of light, for the luminous area formed a huge elongated oval, the center of which was intensely bright, and whose brilliancy gradually decreased in the distance.

"That's only a mass of phosphorescent organisms," said one of the officers.

"No, sir, certainly not," I replied. "Pholads or salpae never produce such a powerful light. That brightness definitely has an electric quality. And besides, look! It's moving! It's swerving! It's coming straight at us!"

A chorus of cries rose from the frigate.

"Silence!" shouted the captain. "Helm alee, reverse engines!"

Seamen and engineers hurried to their stations, the engines were reversed, and the *Abraham Lincoln,* beating to port, described a semicircle.

"Right helm! Go ahead!" cried Commander Farragut.

These orders were carried out, and the frigate moved rapidly away from the blinding light.

Did I say "moved away"? I should have said "tried to move away," but that mysterious and uncanny animal came toward us at a speed that was twice our own.

We gasped for breath! Amazement more than fear rendered us speechless and motionless. The animal was not only gaining on us, but seemed to be playing with us. It circled the frigate, which was speeding at fourteen knots, and immersed it in a brilliant glow of what seemed to be luminous dust. Then it withdrew two or three miles, leaving behind it a phosphorescent trail resembling whirlwinds of vapor streaming behind a fast-moving train. Suddenly, out of the dark circle of the horizon, where it had gone to gain momentum, the monster rushed with incredible speed toward the *Abraham Lincoln*, stopped short within twenty feet of it—and vanished —not by plunging beneath the waters, since its brilliant glow did not diminish gradually, but instantaneously, as if the source of its dazzling light had been suddenly cut off. Then it reappeared on the other side of the ship, having either sped around it or swum underneath it. At any moment a collision could have occurred that would have been fatal—for us.

I was astonished, however, at the maneuvers of our frigate! It was fleeing and not attacking. It was being pursued instead of pursuing.

I called Commander Farragut's attention to this. His usually impassive demeanor had changed to one of indescribable astonishment.

"Monsieur Aronnax," he replied, "I do not know what terrible creature I have to contend with, and I do not want to run foolish risks with my frigate in this darkness. Besides, how can one attack the unknown or defend oneself against it? Let us wait for daylight, and the roles will be reversed."

"Have you any longer any doubts as to the nature of this monster?"

"No, sir. Obviously, it's a gigantic narwhal, but an electric one, too."

"Perhaps," I suggested, "we can get no closer to it than we could chasing a numbfish or an electric eel."

"That may well be," replied the captain, "and if it possesses the power to electrocute, then it is certainly the most terrible animal ever to have been fashioned by the hand of the Creator. That's why, sir, I must be on my guard."

No one thought of sleeping, and the crew were on their feet all night long. The *Abraham Lincoln*, being unable to compete as regards speed, sailed slowly with reduced steam. The narwhal, on the other hand, imitating the frigate, was

43

just riding the waves, and seemed to have decided not to abandon the area of the conflict.

However, toward midnight, it disappeared, or, to use a more appropriate expression, it "went out" like a big glowworm. Had it fled? This was more to be feared than hoped for! But, at seven minutes to one in the morning, we heard a deafening hiss, like a jet of water gushing forth with great force.

Commander Farragut, Ned Land, and I were on the poop, peering eagerly into the inky darkness.

"Ned Land," asked the captain, "you have often heard whales roar, haven't you?"

"Very often, sir, but never a whale the sight of which earned me two thousand dollars."

"Of course, the prize is yours. But tell me, isn't that the noise that cetaceans make when they blow water out through their vents?"

"It's the same noise, sir, but that's very much louder. But there's no mistaking it. That's certainly some kind of cetacean nearby. With your permission, sir," added the harpooner, "we'll have a few words with him tomorrow, when daybreak comes."

"If he is prepared to listen to you, Master Land," I replied, feeling somewhat unconvinced.

"If I could just get within four harpoon lengths," retorted the Canadian, "he would have to listen to me!"

"But to approach him," went on the captain, "shouldn't I put a whaleboat at your disposal?"

"Certainly, sir."

"But wouldn't that be risking the lives of my men?"

"Yes, and mine too," the harpooner replied simply.

At about two o'clock in the morning, the luminous glow reappeared, just as intense, five miles to windward of the *Abraham Lincoln*. In spite of the distance, and in spite of the noise of wind and sea, one could distinctly hear the formidable threshing of the beast's tail, and even its panting breath. It seemed that when the enormous narwhal came to the surface of the ocean, air poured into its lungs, like steam being sucked into the vast cylinders of a two-thousand-horsepower engine.

"Hm," I thought, "a whale with the strength of a cavalry regiment would be some whale indeed!"

So we remained on the alert until daybreak, preparing for the fight. The fishing gear was laid out along the rails. The second-in-command loaded the blunderbusses, which could fire harpoons as far as a mile, and the long duck guns, which could fire explosive bullets capable of inflicting mortal wounds on even the biggest animals. Ned Land had sharpened his harpoon, a terrible weapon in his hands.

Day began to break at six o'clock, and with the first crack of dawn the narwhal's brilliant light went out. At seven o'clock the day was fairly bright, but a dense morning mist was gathering on the horizon, and the best spyglasses could not pierce it. So everyone was disappointed and angry.

I climbed up on the mizzenmast; some officers were already perched on the mastheads.

At eight o'clock the fog, lying heavily on the waves, began to rise little by little in thick scrolls. The horizon grew wider and clearer. Suddenly, just as on the day before, we heard Ned Land's voice:

"There it is! On the port quarter!" cried the harpooner.

All eyes turned in the direction he had indicated.

There, a mile and a half from the frigate, a long black body emerged a yard above the surface. Its tail, threshing about violently, was causing a considerable turmoil. Never did a tail whip up the waters with such force, and as the animal moved, it left in its wake an immense, brilliantly white, foamy furrow.

The frigate approached the cetacean, and I studied it calmly and dispassionately. The reports by the *Shannon* and the *Helvetia* had somewhat exaggerated its dimensions, for I estimated its length at only 250 feet. As for its width, I found this difficult to judge; but as a whole the animal seemed to me to be admirably proportioned in all dimensions.

As I was watching this phenomenal creature, two jets of steam and water shot up out of its vents to a height of about 120 feet, which enabled me to ascertain its means of breathing. I reached the definite conclusion that it belonged to the vertebrates, class of mammals, subclass of monodelphians, division of pisciforms, order of cetaceans, family of— Here I could not make up my mind. The order of cetaceans consists of three families: whales, cachalots, and dolphins, and the narwhals belong to the last of these. Each of these families is divided into several genera, each genus into species, and each species into varieties. So the variety, species, genus, and family had yet to be established, but I did not doubt that with the aid of Providence and Commander Farragut I should complete my classification.

Impatiently the crew were awaiting orders. The captain, after having observed the animal attentively, sent for the engineer, who came running up.

"Sir," asked the captain, "have you got up steam?"

"Yes, sir!" replied the engineer.

"Good. Then stoke up your fires and full speed ahead!"

45

Three cheers greeted this order. The hour to join battle had struck. A few seconds later, the frigate's two funnels were vomiting forth clouds of black smoke, and the deck trembled with the vibrations of the boilers.

The *Abraham Lincoln,* driven forward by her powerful screw, made straight for the animal, which, with apparent indifference, allowed the ship to approach to within half a cable's length. Then, disdaining to dive, it pretended to flee—but it moved only fast enough to maintain its distance.

This pursuit lasted about three-quarters of an hour, without the frigate's gaining as much as five yards on the cetacean. It was obvious that at this rate we should never catch up with it.

Commander Farragut, enraged, tugged at the thick tuft of hair that bristled beneath his chin.

"Ned Land!" he cried.

The Canadian came running up.

"Well, Master Land," asked the captain, "do you still advise me to put out the boats?"

"No, sir," replied Ned Land. "That animal is going to be caught only with his permission."

"Well, what shall we do, then?"

"Put on more steam, sir, if you can. With your permission, I'll post myself under the bowsprit, and if we get within a harpoon's length, I'll harpoon it."

"Go ahead, Ned," replied Commander Farragut. "Engineer, more pressure!"

So Ned Land went out under the bowsprit. The fires were stoked up even higher and the propeller accelerated to forty-three revolutions per minute, so that steam was shooting out of the valves. Heaving the log, we calculated that the *Abraham Lincoln* was making 18.5 knots.

But the accursed beast was also moving at 18.5 knots!

For another hour the frigate kept up this pace, without gaining as much as a fathom! This was humiliating for one of the fastest ships in the American Navy. The sailors angrily cursed the beast, which, however, did not deign to reply. The captain was no longer twisting his beard; he was chewing it.

The engineer was summoned again.

"Have you reached maximum pressure?" the captain asked him.

"Yes, sir," replied the engineer.

"And your valves are charged at . . . ?"

"At six and a half atmospheres."

"Then charge them at ten atmospheres."

A typical American command if ever I heard one! —A

steamboat captain in one of those competitive races on the Mississippi couldn't have done better to shake off pursuit.

"Conseil," I said to my faithful servant who stood by my side, "do you realize that we will probably blow up?"

"As Monsieur pleases," replied Conseil.

However, I will admit that it was a risk I was prepared to take.

The valves were charged. Coal was poured into the furnaces. The fans blew torrents of air into the braziers. The *Abraham Lincoln*'s speed increased. Her masts trembled to their very steps, and the billows of smoke could scarcely shoot through the narrow funnels.

The log was heaved again.

"Well, Mr. Helmsman?" asked Commander Farragut.

"Nineteen and three-tenths knots, sir."

"Stoke up the fires!"

The engineer obeyed. The pressure gauge was now showing ten atmospheres. But it seemed that the cetacean was also "getting up steam," for without straining itself, it too moved off at 19 3/10 knots!

What a chase! How can I describe the excitement that made me tremble all over? Ned Land stayed at his post, harpoon in hand. Several times the animal allowed us to approach it.

"We're catching up on him! We're gaining on him!" the Canadian would cry.

Then, just as he was getting ready to strike, the cetacean would steal away at a speed that, in my opinion, could not be less than thirty miles an hour. Even when we were going at full speed, it actually taunted us by circling around us. A cry of fury broke from the crew.

At midday, we had got no further than at eight o'clock in the morning.

Commander Farragut therefore decided to employ more direct methods.

"So this animal can go faster than the *Abraham Lincoln!*" he said. "All right, we'll see if it can move faster than these cannonballs. Mate, man the forward gun!"

The forecastle gun was immediately loaded and aimed. The shot left the barrel, but passed a few feet above the cetacean, which was about half a mile off.

"Someone with a better aim!" cried the captain. "Five hundred dollars to anyone who can pierce the hide of that infernal beast!"

An old gray-bearded gunner—I can see him now—with a steady eye and a calm expression, stepped up to the gun, swung it into position, and aimed slowly and deliberately.

There was a great *boom*, followed by the cheers of the crew.

The shell hit the target, striking but not penetrating the animal. Instead the shot had glanced off the beast's rounded surface, and was lost in the sea two miles away.

"Well, what d'you say to that?" the old gunner exclaimed angrily. "That thing must be covered with six-inch armored plating!"

"Confound the thing!" cried Commander Farragut.

So the chase began again, and Commander Farragut, leaning toward me, said:

"I'll go after that beast till my ship blows up!"

"Yes," I answered, "and you're quite right to do so."

We had some hope that the animal would tire itself out and that it would not be insensitive to fatigue like a steam engine. But it was no use. The hours dragged on without its showing the slightest sign of weariness.

However, it must be said in praise of the *Abraham Lincoln* that that fine ship was putting up a tireless, determined fight. I reckon that she had traveled at least three hundred miles that unlucky day of November 6th! But eventually night fell and enveloped the choppy sea in darkness.

I thought that our expedition was now over, and that we should never see the fantastic animal again. But I was mistaken.

At about 10:50 P.M. the brilliant light reappeared, about three miles to windward of the frigate, as clear and as bright as the night before.

The narwhal seemed to be motionless. Perhaps he was tired after the day's exertion and was sleeping, letting himself drift on the waves. Here was a possibility that Commander Farragut intended to take advantage of.

He gave his orders. The *Abraham Lincoln* was held at half steam, and advanced cautiously so as not to awaken her adversary. It is not unusual to encounter whales sound asleep in mid-ocean that can successfully be attacked, and Ned Land had harpooned more than one as it slept. The Canadian returned to his post under the bowsprit.

The frigate approached silently until it was two cables' lengths from the animal, stopped its engines, and drifted gently forward. On deck one could have heard a pin drop. We were not a hundred feet from the luminous patch, which was growing brighter and dazzling us.

At that moment, leaning over the forecastle rail, I could see Ned Land below me, grasping the martingale in one hand and brandishing his terrible harpoon with the other. He was barely twenty feet away from the motionless animal.

Suddenly his arm straightened, and the harpoon shot out. I

48

heard a deep, ringing tone, as though he had struck a hard surface.

Immediately the dazzling glow went out, and two enormous jets of water landed on the frigate's deck. The water swept like a torrent from one end of the ship to the other, knocking men over and breaking the lashing of the spars.

There was a fearful jolt and—unable to retain my balance —I was flung over the rail out into the sea!

Chapter VII

AN UNKNOWN SPECIES OF WHALE

ALTHOUGH MY PLUNGE took me completely by surprise, I nevertheless have a very clear recollection of how I felt.

At first I was dragged down to a depth of about twenty feet. I am a good swimmer, although I cannot claim to be the equal of Byron or Edgar Poe, who were masters of the art, and so my dip did not cause me to lose my head. Two vigorous kicks brought me back to the surface.

My first concern was to look for the frigate. Had the crew noticed my disappearance? Had the *Abraham Lincoln* veered about? Was Commander Farragut putting out a boat? Could I hope to be rescued?

The darkness was impenetrable, but I could just make out a black mass disappearing eastward, until its riding lights faded away in the distance. It was the frigate. I felt utterly lost.

"Help! Help!" I cried, striking out toward the *Abraham Lincoln* in desperation.

My clothes clung to my body, impeding my progress and paralyzing all my movements. I was drowning, I was suffocating . . . !

"Help!"

This was the last cry I uttered. My mouth filled with water. I struggled wildly as I felt myself being dragged downward into the abyss. . . .

Suddenly my clothes were grasped by a strong hand, I felt myself being hauled to the surface, and I heard—yes, I really did hear—these words being spoken close to my ear:

"If Monsieur would be obliging enough to lean on my shoulder, he might find it easier to swim."

With one hand I seized the arm of my faithful Conseil.

"It's you," I said. "It's you!"

"Yes, it's I," replied Conseil, "at Monsieur's command."

"Did that jolt throw you overboard at the same time as me?"

"Not at all. But I am in Monsieur's service. I had to follow Monsieur."

That splendid boy seemed to think his action was entirely natural!

"What about the frigate?" I asked.

"The frigate!" replied Conseil, turning on his back. "I think that Monsieur will do well not to count too much on her!"

"What do you mean?"

"When I dived into the water, I heard the men at the wheel shouting, 'The propeller and rudder are broken.'"

"Broken?"

"Yes, broken by the monster's tusk. I don't think the *Abraham Lincoln* has suffered any worse damage than that. But it's a bit of a nuisance for us, because she won't steer anymore."

"Then we're lost!"

"Perhaps," Conseil replied calmly, "but we still have a few hours, and in a few hours a lot can happen."

Conseil's imperturbability gave me strength. I swam with more energy, but I was so impeded by my clothes, which clung to me like a leaden cape, that I had the greatest difficulty in keeping afloat. Conseil noticed this.

"Will Monsieur permit me to cut his clothes away?" he said, and sliding an open knife under my garments, he ripped them open with one rapid stroke. Then he pulled them off briskly, while I swam for both of us.

I, in my turn, did the same for Conseil, and we continued to "navigate" side by side.

However, the situation was no less desperate. Perhaps our disappearance had not been noticed, and even if it had, the frigate was unable to come back to leeward toward us, since she had been deprived of her rudder. Our only hope, therefore, lay in the boats.

Conseil assessed our chances coolly, and made his plans accordingly. What an extraordinary lad he was! This phlegmatic young man was absolutely at home in this kind of situation!

Thus it was decided that our only hope of salvation lay in being picked up by the *Abraham Lincoln*'s boats, and hence we ought to prepare to wait as long as possible. So I decided that we should divide our efforts so that they should not be used up at the same time, and this is what we resolved to do: one of us, lying on his back, would remain motionless, with his arms folded and his legs outstretched, while the other would swim and push him along. This towing procedure was not to last more than ten minutes, so that, by working in relays like this, we should be able to keep it up for some hours, perhaps until dawn.

It was a slim chance, but hope is so strongly rooted in the heart of man! Moreover, there were, after all, two of us. I might add—however improbable it may seem—that I tried to destroy all illusions, I pretended to give up hope; but I just couldn't!

The collision of the frigate and the cetacean had taken place at about eleven o'clock in the evening. I could therefore reckon on our having to swim for eight hours before the sun rose. By working in relays, this should be possible. The sea was fairly calm, and so it was not too tiring. Sometimes I tried to penetrate the coal-black night, broken only by the phosphorescence of our movements in the water. I watched the luminous wavelets breaking over my hand, all flecked with silvery patches. It seemed as if we had been cast into a pool of mercury.

At about one o'clock in the morning, I was seized with acute fatigue. My limbs became stiff and I was suffering from violent cramps. Conseil had to hold me up, and our preservation depended upon him alone. Soon I heard the poor boy panting; his breath was becoming shorter and quicker. I realized that he couldn't hold out much longer.

"Leave me! Leave me!" I said to him.

"Abandon Monsieur? Never!" he replied. "I would rather drown first."

At that moment the moon appeared through the edge of a large cloud that was billowing across the sky in the east. The sea glittered in its rays, and its kindly light gave us new strength. I looked up and surveyed all points on the horizon. Then I saw the frigate. She was five miles away, a dark, barely perceptible mass. But there were no boats in sight!

I wanted to shout. But what was the good of shouting at such a distance! My swollen lips would produce no sound. Conseil, however, was able to utter a few words, and I heard him repeat several times:

"Help! Help!"

We stopped swimming for a second and listened. Was it the buzzing in our ears, or was it really a cry answering Conseil?

"Did you hear that?" I murmured.

"Yes, I did!"

Conseil gave another desperate cry.

This time it was unmistakable! A human voice responded. Was it the voice of some other wretch, abandoned in the middle of the ocean, some other victim of the collision? Or was it one of the frigate's boats calling to us in the dark?

Conseil made a supreme effort, and resting on my shoulder

52

while I made one final effort to remain afloat, he raised himself half out of the water and then fell back exhausted.

"What did you see?"

"I saw. . . ." He murmured, "I saw. . . . But we mustn't talk . . . we have to save our strength. . . ."

What had he seen? Then, I don't know why, for the first time I thought of the monster! . . . But where had that voice come from? . . . . The times are long past since Jonahs take refuge in the bellies of whales!

However, Conseil was still towing me. Sometimes he would raise his head, staring in front of him and uttering a cry, which would be answered by a voice that came nearer and nearer each time. But I could scarcely hear it. My strength was exhausted; my fingers were stiffening and parting and my hand was scarcely helping to hold me up; my mouth was opening convulsively and filling with salt water; I was chilled to the marrow. I raised my head one last time and began to sink. . . .

At that moment I bumped into something hard. I clung to it. Then I felt someone pulling me up to the surface, I felt my chest subsiding, and I fainted. . . .

I am certain that I came to soon after, thanks to the vigorous massage that I was getting. I half opened my eyes. . . .

"Conseil!" I murmured.

"Did Monsieur ring for me?" replied Conseil.

Then, by the final rays of the moon, which was sinking toward the horizon, I saw a figure that was not Conseil's, but that I immediately recognized.

"Ned!" I cried.

"Yes, it's Ned in person, monsieur, and I am still after my prize!" replied the Canadian.

"Were you thrown into the sea by the collision too?"

"Yes, Professor, but I was luckier than you, because almost immediately I found a floating island."

"An island?"

"Or, should I say, your gigantic narwhal."

"Do explain, Ned."

"I soon found out why my harpoon had not penetrated his skin and had slid off his hide."

"Why, Ned, why?"

"The reason is, Professor, that this monster is made of steel!"

Here I had to gather my wits, remember what had happened, and be sure of what I was saying.

For the Canadian's last words had produced a sudden reaction in my brain. I quickly hauled myself up to the highest point of the half-immersed creature or object that was providing us with a refuge. I felt it with my foot. Obviously it was a hard, impenetrable surface, and not that soft substance of which most of the great marine mammals are made.

But this hard body might be a bony shell, similar to that of antediluvian animals, in which case I could classify the monster among the amphibian reptiles, such as tortoises or alligators.

But it wasn't! The blackish back that supported me was smooth and shiny, without any overlapping scales. When one tapped it, it made a metallic sound, and however incredible it might seem, it appeared to be made of riveted plates.

There could be no doubts whatsoever! The animal, the monster, or the natural phenomenon that had intrigued experts all over the world, bewildered and confused the sailors of both hemispheres, was, it must be admitted, a still more astonishing phenomenon, a phenomenon created by the hand of man.

I could not have been more surprised had I discovered the existence of the most fabulous, the most mythological being. It is easy enough to believe that all things prodigious come from the Creator. But suddenly to find the impossible, mysteriously contrived by human hands, and set before one's very eyes—this was utterly confusing!

But there was no time to waste wondering. Here we were, stretched out on the back of a sort of marine craft, which, as far as I could judge, was the shape of an immense fish, made of steel. Ned Land had already made up his mind on that point, and Conseil and I could do nothing but agree.

"So," I said, "this thing must have a means of locomotion inside and a crew to work it?"

"It must have," replied the harpooner, "and yet, during the three hours I've been on this floating island, it has shown no sign of life."

"You mean this boat hasn't moved?"

"No, Monsieur Aronnax. It just floats on the waves, but it doesn't move."

"But we know, without any doubt, that it possesses great speed. And as an engine is needed for that, as well as a mechanic to work the engine, I conclude that we are saved."

"Hm!" said Ned, who evidently was not so sure.

At that moment, as though to show that I had been right, there was a bubbling sound at the rear end of that strange machine, which was obviously driven by a propeller, and it began to move. We just had time to cling to its superstructure, which protruded about a yard out of the water. Fortunately, it was not going very fast.

"As long as she moves only horizontally," muttered Ned,

"I've no objection. But if it takes it into its head to dive, then I wouldn't give two dollars for my hide!"

The Canadian might well have quoted an even lower price, because it was imperative that we communicate with whatever kind of beings were concealed inside the machine. I examined its surface to find some sort of opening, some panel, or a "manhole"—to use a technical expression; but the lines of rivets along the joints in the plates were quite firm, tight-fitting and uniform.

Furthermore, the moon had disappeared, leaving us in total darkness. We should have to wait for daybreak before we could find out how to get inside this underwater craft.

Our salvation therefore depended entirely on the caprices of the mysterious helmsmen who were steering this machine, for if they decided to dive, we were lost! Unless this happened, I did not doubt that it would be possible to get in touch with them. If they did not produce their own air, they would of necessity have to surface from time to time to take in fresh supplies of "breathable molecules." So there had to be some kind of opening to establish contact between the inside of the craft and the outer air.

As for our chances of being saved by Commander Farragut, there was no hope of that. We had drifted westward, and I estimated that our speed, which was fairly slow, was about twelve knots. The propeller was pounding the water with mathematical regularity, sometimes emerging above the surface and throwing up sheets of phosphorescent spray to a great height.

At about four o'clock in the morning, the craft began to move faster, and we found it difficult to hold on at this breakneck speed, with the propeller blades threshing furiously behind us. Fortunately, Ned found a large mooring ring, fixed to one of the plates, and we managed to hang on to that.

Eventually the long night came to an end. I can no longer remember all the impressions that I had during that time, but I do remember one detail: at times, when the sea and the wind were quiet, I thought I could hear vague sounds, strains of fleeting harmony, produced by far-off music. What was the mystery of this submarine craft, of which the whole world was vainly seeking an explanation? What sort of beings inhabited this strange vessel? What mechanical device enabled it to move from place to place with such prodigious speed?

Daylight came. The morning mists enveloped us, but they very soon dispersed. I was just going to make a careful examination of the top part of the hull, a sort of horizontal platform, when I felt her gradually sinking.

"A thousand devils!" exclaimed Ned Land, kicking furiously at the plates so that they gave forth a hollow echo. "Open up, you inhospitable——!"

It was difficult to make oneself heard above the deafening pounding of the screw. Fortunately, though, the craft stopped sinking.

Suddenly there was a loud noise of iron bolts sliding aside from within. A hatch opened, a man emerged from it, and then, uttering a strange cry, disappeared immediately.

A few moments later, eight hulking men with masked faces appeared, and without uttering a sound, dragged us down inside their formidable machine.

Chapter VIII

MOBILIS IN MOBILI

THIS ABDUCTION, so brutally executed, was accomplished with the speed of lightning. My companions and I scarcely had time to realize what had happened. I don't know what their feelings were as they were being dragged down into this floating prison, but I felt a cold shiver run through me. Whom did we have to contend with? Doubtless some new pirates who were exploiting the sea in their own way.

As soon as the narrow hatch closed behind me, I was in total darkness. My eyes, which had just become accustomed to the light outside, could see nothing. I felt my naked feet clinging to the rungs of an iron ladder. Ned Land and Conseil, manhandled in the same way, followed me. At the bottom of the ladder a door opened, and immediately closed behind us with a resounding noise.

We were alone. But where? I could neither tell nor imagine. All was black, but so pitch-black that even after a few minutes my eyes had not yet managed to see anything but those vague glimmers that one imagines he sees on the darkest of nights.

Nevertheless Ned Land, who was furious at what had happened, was giving full vent to his indignation.

"A thousand devils!" he cried. "These people must be descendants of the Scots for all the hospitality they offer you! I wouldn't be surprised if they were cannibals; but I can assure you they won't eat me without my having something to say about it!"

"Keep calm, Ned, keep calm," Conseil replied quietly. "You're getting angry before there is any need to. We're not in the pot yet!"

"Not in the pot," replied the Canadian, "but in the oven, without doubt! It's dark enough here and fortunately I still have my bowie knife, and I can always see well enough to use that. The first of those bandits to lay hands on me—"

"Do not get worked up, Ned," I told the harpooner, "and do not get us into trouble by being violent, because it is useless. How do you know they are not listening to us? Let us try and find out where we are!"

I groped my way forward. After five steps I came to an iron wall made of riveted plates. Then, turning around, I bumped into a wooden table, near which stood a number of stools. The floor of our prison was covered with a thick layer of matting, which deadened the sound of footsteps. We found no sign of either a door or a window in the walls. Conseil, walking around the room in the opposite direction, met me, and we came back into the middle of the cabin, which must have been 20 feet long by 10 feet wide. As regards its height, Ned Land, although he was very tall, could not touch the ceiling.

Half an hour had already passed without any change in the situation when the darkness surrounding us was suddenly changed into a violently bright light. Our prison was suddenly lit up by such a brilliant glare that at first my eyes could scarcely bear it. By its whiteness and its intensity I realized that it was the same dazzling light that had produced the magnificent phosphorescence around the submarine craft. Involuntarily I closed my eyes, but when I opened them I saw that the source of the light was a frosted half globe set in the ceiling.

"At last we can see!" cried Ned Land, who stood on the alert, knife in hand.

"Yes," I replied, venturing a play on words, "but the situation is nonetheless obscure."

"Monsieur must be patient," said the imperturbable Conseil.

The sudden deluge of light in the cabin now enabled me to study its smallest details. It contained nothing but the table and five stools. The invisible door must have been hermetically closed. We listened, but could catch no sound. Everything seemed dead inside this ship. Was it moving, was it floating on the surface, or was it diving down into the depths of the sea? I had no idea.

However, the luminous globe had not been turned on without reason, and I hoped that before long some members of the crew would appear. When one casts someone into a dungeon to forget about him, one doesn't bother to light his prison.

I was not mistaken. There was a noise of sliding bolts, a door opened, and two men appeared.

One of them was short, muscular, broad-shouldered, and strongly built, with a large head, thick black hair, a thick moustache, and quick, penetrating eyes; his whole person had that southern vivacity that is typical, in France, of the inhabitants of Provence. Diderot has rightly maintained that a man's gestures are metaphorical, and this little man was the

58

living proof of that assertion. One could sense that in his native language, his usual manner of speaking would be very colorful, replete with metaphors, dramatic gestures, and suggestive figures of speech. However, I could never verify this, because in my presence he spoke only in a strange and incomprehensible language.

The second stranger merits a more detailed description. A student of Gratiolet or of Engel could have read his features like an open book. Even I could easily determine his predominant characteristics: self-confidence, because his head was nobly set on the curve of his shoulders, and his black eyes surveyed the scene with cool self-assurance; serenity, because his complexion was pale rather than ruddy, indicating an unusual control of his emotions; energy, indicated by the rapid contraction of his eyebrows; courage, because his deep breathing was indicative of an expansive vitality. He was proud, and his firm and calm gaze reflected lofty thoughts. The harmony of his facial expression and the gestures of his body and countenance—to judge him from the standpoint of a physiognomist—gave an overall impression of indisputable frankness.

In spite of myself, I felt reassured by his presence and I had reason to believe that our interview would turn out well.

Whether he was thirty-five or fifty I could not tell. He was tall, had a broad forehead, a straight nose, a clearly defined mouth, magnificent teeth, fine tapered hands which, to use a term employed in palmistry, were eminently "psychical"—that is to say, worthy to serve a man of passionate sensitivity. He was, beyond the shadow of a doubt, the most remarkable man I had ever seen. There was something about his eyes that was most unusual. They were set rather far from each other and could encompass almost a quarter of the horizon at a glance. This faculty, which I verified later, was enhanced by a power of vision even greater than that of Ned Land. When this stranger fixed his eyes on an object, the line of his eyebrows contracted, his large eyelids closed around the pupils, so as to narrow the span of vision, and then he would gaze. What vision! How well did his vision magnify distant details! How well did he fathom the very depths of your soul! How well did he pierce through those layers of water, so opaque to our eyes! And how well he scrutinized the deepest secrets of the sea!

The two strangers wore caps made of sea-otter fur, boots of sealskin, and clothes made of a special kind of cloth that fitted loosely and allowed complete freedom of movement.

The taller of the two, evidently the Captain, scrutinized us with the closest possible attention, without uttering a word.

Then, turning toward his companion, he spoke to him in a language I could not recognize. It was a sonorous, flexible, harmonious tongue, whose vowels seemed to be accentuated in a great variety of ways.

The other man would reply with a nod of the head and add one or two utterly incomprehensible words. Then he would look at me as though to ask me a question.

I replied in good French that I could not understand his language; but he seemed not to understand, and the situation became somewhat embarrassing.

"If Monsieur would just tell our story," said Conseil, "perhaps these gentlemen could pick up a few words!"

So I began recounting our adventures, pronouncing all the syllables very clearly, and without omitting any details. I gave our names and occupations, then formally presented Professor Aronnax, his servant Conseil, and Master Ned Land, the harpooner.

The man with the soft, calm eyes listened to me quietly, even politely, and with remarkable attention. But nothing in his face indicated that he had understood my story. When I had finished, he said not a word.

The only thing left to do appeared to be to speak English. Perhaps we should be able to make ourselves understood in that language, which is more or less universal. I know it, much as I know German, well enough to read it fluently, but not well enough to speak it correctly—and the problem here was to make oneself understood.

"Come on," I said to the harpooner. "It's your turn, Master Land; roll out the best English ever spoken by an Anglo-Saxon, and try to do better than I."

Ned did not have to be asked a second time, and began our tale all over again. I understood him more or less; fundamentally, the content was the same, although the form differed. The Canadian, carried away by his temperament, made his narrative very animated. He complained vehemently at being imprisoned in violation of human rights, asked by virtue of what law he was being thus detained, invoked the principles of habeas corpus, threatened to prosecute anyone who held him without due cause, ranted, gesticulated, shouted, and finally, by means of expressive signs, made it clear that we were dying of hunger.

This, of course, was perfectly true, but we had almost forgotten about that.

Much to his amazement, the harpooner did not seem to have been much better understood than I had been. Our visitors did not bat an eye. Evidently, they understood neither the language of Arago nor that of Faraday.

Much perplexed after having vainly exhausted our philological resources, I did not know what to do. But then Conseil said:

"If Monsieur will permit, I will tell the story in German."

"What! You know German?" I exclaimed.

"Because I'm Flemish, you see, monsieur. I hope Monsieur doesn't mind."

"On the contrary, my boy, I am very pleased."

So Conseil, in his quiet voice, related for the third time the various stages of our journey. But in spite of his elegant turns of phrase and his clear, elegant pronunciation, no success was achieved with the German tongue.

At last, at my wits' end, I scratched together everything I could remember of my childhood studies, and tried to tell our story in Latin. True, Cicero would have stopped up his ears and would have sent me back to the kitchen, where I belonged. However, I managed to get to the end—but without any positive results.

After this final attempt failed, the two strangers exchanged a few words in their incomprehensible language, and withdrew without having made as much as a reassuring gesture in our direction, as they might have done in any country in the world . . . and closed the door behind them.

"This is infamous!" cried Ned, who burst into a rage for the twentieth time. "What! We speak French, English, German, and Latin to those impudent fellows, and neither of them has the civility to reply!"

"Calm down, Ned," I said to the seething harpooner, "being angry will not get you anywhere."

"But don't you realize, Professor," our irate companion continued, "that one might perfectly well die of hunger in this iron cage?"

"Nonsense," said Conseil philosophically, "we can hold out for a long time yet!"

"My friends," I said, "we must not give up hope. We have been in more difficult situations than this. Do me the favor of waiting awhile before you jump to any conclusions about the captain and crew of this boat."

"My mind is already made up," retorted Ned, "they're a lot of impudent knaves. . . ."

"All right, from what country?"

"From the Land of Knavery, of course!"

"My good Ned, that country has not yet been clearly marked on the map, and I must admit that the nationality of these two strangers is most difficult to determine! They are not English, or French, or German; that's about all I can say.

However, I should be tempted to guess that the Captain and his mate were born in southern latitudes. There is something southern about them. But whether they are Spaniards, Turks, Arabs, or Indians, I cannot tell from their appearance. And as for their language, it's quite incomprehensible."

"That's the misfortune of not knowing all languages," said Conseil, "or the disadvantage of not having one universal language!"

"And that wouldn't be any good," replied Ned Land. "Don't you see that those people have their own language, a language invented to reduce to despair good folk who are asking for their dinner! But in every country in the world, doesn't opening your mouth, working your jaws up and down, and snapping your teeth and lips make any other explanation superfluous? Doesn't that mean the same thing, whether you are in Quebec or the Pomotou Islands, in Paris or the Antipodes? Does one have to say: 'I'm hungry, give me something to eat'?"

"Oh, I don't know," said Conseil, "some people are so stupid!"

As he spoke these words the door opened, and a steward entered. He brought us clothes, coats and seamen's trousers, made of a material that I did not know. I hastened to put them on, and my companions followed suit.

Meanwhile the steward, who might well have been deaf and dumb, had laid the table for three.

"That's more like it," said Conseil, "that looks promising."

"Bah!" grumbled the harpooner, "What d'you imagine they eat here? Tortoise liver, filet of shark, or seadog steaks?"

"We shall see!" said Conseil.

The dishes, covered by silver lids, were placed symmetrically on the table, and we sat down. Obviously we were dealing with civilized people, and except for the flood of electric light in our room I could have imagined myself in a dining room at the Adelphi Hotel in Liverpool, or the Grand Hôtel in Paris. However, I must say that there was neither bread nor wine. The water was fresh and clear, but it was only water—which was not to the taste of Ned Land. Among the dishes that were served us, I recognized various fish, which had been delicately prepared; but with regard to some dishes, I was unable to express any opinion, and I could not have said to which kingdom, vegetable or animal, they belonged. The service at table, however, was elegant and in the best taste. Every implement, spoon, fork, knife, and plate bore a letter encircled by a motto, of which I reproduce here a facsimile:

Mobile within the mobile element! What an apt motto for this undersea craft,—as long as the preposition *"in"* is translated "within" and not "on." The letter *N* no doubt indicated the initial of the enigmatic personage who was in command in the depths of the sea.

Ned and Conseil, however, were not bothering to think about such things. They were wading into their food, and I didn't hesitate to follow their example. Besides, I was now reassured as to our fate, and it seemed obvious to me that our hosts had no intention of letting us die of starvation.

Nevertheless, everything on this earth comes to an end sometime, even the hunger of people who have had nothing to eat for fifteen hours. Thus, when our appetites were satisfied, we felt irresistibly sleepy. This was all too natural a reaction after the endless night we had spent fighting against death.

"I shall certainly sleep well," said Conseil.

"And I'm asleep already!" replied Ned Land.

My two companions stretched out on the cabin carpet, and before long were in the deepest slumber.

I gave in less easily to the need for sleep. Too many thoughts crowded into my mind, too many insoluble questions presented themselves, too many fantasies danced before my half-closed eyes! Where were we? What strange power swept us in that sea? I felt—or I thought I felt—the craft sinking down into the deepest depths of the ocean. I became obsessed by violent nightmares. In these mysterious regions I saw a whole world of strange animals, in which our underwater craft, like some living, moving, formidable creature, seemed, like them, to have been spawned. . . . Then my mind became calmer, my imagination dissolved into a vague somnolence, and very soon I fell into a gloomy slumber.

Chapter IX

NED LAND'S TANTRUMS

HOW LONG I SLEPT I DON'T REMEMBER; but it must have been quite a long time, for we emerged from our slumbers completely rested after our exertions. I was the first to wake up. My companions had not yet moved and were still stretched out in their corner—two motionless forms.

As soon as I had risen from my rather hard couch, I felt that my brain was working again and my mind was clear. I then began a careful inspection of our cell.

Nothing had changed. The prison was still a prison, and the prisoners, still prisoners. However, the steward, taking advantage of our somnolent state, had cleared the table. So there was nothing to suggest that the situation would change in any way, and I wondered, quite seriously, whether we were fated to live indefinitely in this cage.

The prospect was such an unpleasant one that even though my mind was cleared of its obsessions of the day before, I nevertheless felt my chest strangely heavy. I was finding difficulty in breathing. The heavy air was insufficient for my lungs. Although our cell was very large, we evidently had used up a great deal of the oxygen it contained. I recalled that a man consumes, in one hour, all the oxygen contained in one hundred liters, or 3½ cubic feet, of air, and that this air, when it has accumulated almost the same amount of carbon dioxide, becomes unbreathable.

So it was urgent that the air in our prison should be renewed, which would undoubtedly mean changing all the air in our submarine craft.

At this point a question occurred to me. What did the Captain of this floating habitation do about air? Did he obtain it by chemical means, using heat to generate oxygen from potassium chlorate, and absorbing the carbon dioxide with caustic potash? If this was so, he must have maintained contact of some kind with the shore, in order to procure the materials necessary for such a process. Or was he content to release air from time to time, under high pressure, from tanks, depending on the needs of the crew? Perhaps that was what he did.

Or else—and this method would be more convenient and economical, and was therefore more probable—he might find it sufficient to come up to the surface, like a cetacean, and take on a twenty-four hours' supply of air. Whatever the means he employed, it seemed to me wise to do it without delay.

Indeed, I was already reduced to gasping in order to extract from our cell what little oxygen was left in it when, all of a sudden, I was refreshed by a whiff of pure, salty air. There was no mistaking the sea breeze, invigorating and full of iodine! I opened my mouth wide and filled my lungs with fresh molecules. At the same time I felt the boat roll, not too violently yet quite discernibly, and realized that the iron-plated monster had surfaced to take a deep breath, like a whale. The ship's ventilation system was now self-evident.

When I had filled my lungs with this pure, fresh air, I looked for the "air pipe," so to speak, which conveyed to us this welcome current, and I soon found it. Above the door, there was a ventilator through which passed a stream of fresh air, replacing the polluted air in the cell.

I had just reached this point in my observations when Ned and Conseil woke up, almost at the same moment, awakened, no doubt, by the invigorating air. They rubbed their eyes, stretched their arms, and in a moment were on their feet.

"Has Monsieur slept well?" Conseil asked with his usual politeness.

"Very well, my boy," I replied. "What about you, Master Ned Land?"

"Like a log, Professor. But if I am not mistaken—it feels as if I'm breathing sea air?"

A seaman could not make a mistake about that, and I told the Canadian what had happened while he was asleep.

"Good!" he said. "That explains the roaring we heard when the narwhal was within sight of the *Abraham Lincoln*."

"Precisely, Master Land. It was taking a breather."

"But I've no idea what time it is, Monsieur Aronnax—unless it happens to be dinner time?"

"Dinner time, my worthy harpooner? You should at least say 'breakfast time,' because I am certain—"

"That we slept for twenty-four hours?" replied Conseil.

"I think so," I answered.

"I won't argue with you about that," Ned Land rejoined. "But, breakfast or dinner, the steward will be welcome, whichever he brings."

"Or both," said Conseil.

"I quite agree," replied the Canadian. "We have a right to two meals, and I am sure I could do justice to both."

"Well, Ned, let us wait and see," I said. "It is obvious that these strange people have no intention of letting us die of hunger, for if that were so, there wouldn't have been any point in giving us that last meal."

"Unless they want to fatten us up!" replied Ned.

"I protest," I answered. "I don't think we have fallen into the hands of cannibals!"

"One meal doesn't prove anything," the Canadian replied gravely. "How do you know these people haven't been missing their fresh meat for a long time, and that being the case, three healthy, well-fattened people like the Professor, his servant, and me—"

"Get those ideas out of your head, Master Land," I said to the harpooner, "and above all do not take that as an excuse to be angry with our hosts, because that might only make the situation worse."

"In any case," said the harpooner, "I'm hellishly hungry, and whether it's breakfast, lunch, or dinner, it hasn't come yet!"

"Master Land," I replied, "we have to conform to ship's regulations, and I can only suppose that our stomachs are ahead of the cook's clock."

"Well, we'll have to adjust to his clock," Conseil rejoined calmly.

"That is just like you, Conseil," retorted the impatient Canadian. "You never show your temper, do you? Always calm! You are fully capable of saying grace before receiving your blessings and you would rather starve than complain!"

"What is the use of complaining?" asked Conseil.

"Well, at least you'd be complaining, and that's something! And if these pirates—and I say 'pirates' out of respect for the Professor, who forbids me to call them cannibals—if these pirates think they're going to keep me suffocating in this cage without listening to the curses I use to spice my temper, they're very much mistaken! Do you think they're going to keep us locked up in this iron box much longer?"

"To tell the truth, friend Land, I have no more idea than you have."

"Well, but what do you *think*?"

"I think that a mere chance has let us into an important secret. So, if the crew of this underwater craft is interested in keeping it, and if their interest is of more consequence than the lives of three men, I should conclude that our existence is more than a little compromised. Should the opposite be the case, then the monster that has swallowed us up will land us back to our own people at the first opportunity."

"Unless they make us join the crew," said Conseil, "and keep us here—"

"Until," interjected Ned Land, "a faster or more skillful frigate than the *Abraham Lincoln* captures this gang of pirates and makes the whole lot—including ourselves—walk the plank."

"Well reasoned, Master Land," I replied. "But as far as I know, they haven't yet made us any proposal of that kind. So there is no point in discussing what course of action we should follow in such a case. As I said, let us wait and be counseled by circumstances; and let us not do anything, since there is nothing to be done."

"But that's not true, Professor!" replied the harpooner, who did not want to retreat. "We must do something."

"And what would you do, Master Land?"

"Escape!"

"To escape from a prison on land is often difficult enough, but when it comes to an underwater prison, it seems to me quite impossible."

"Come on, friend Ned," said Conseil, "what have you got to say to Monsieur's objection? I find it difficult to believe that an American has come to the end of his resources!"

The harpooner, obviously embarrassed, said nothing. To flee from the circumstances in which fortune had landed us was out of the question. But a Canadian is half a Frenchman, and this was clearly proved by Master Ned's reply.

"So, Monsieur Aronnax," he went on after a few seconds' thought, "you can't imagine what people do who cannot escape from prison?"

"No, my friend, I cannot."

"It's quite simple. They must arrange things so they can remain!"

"I'll say one thing," remarked Conseil, "I'd sooner be inside this monster than on top or underneath it!"

"Yes, but only after having kicked out the jailers, turnkeys and warders," added Ned Land.

"What was that, Ned? Do you mean you would seriously consider seizing the ship?"

"Very much so," answered the Canadian.

"But that is impossible."

"Why, monsieur? We might get a good chance sometime, and I don't see what could stop us from taking advantage of it. If there are only about twenty men on board, they certainly won't force two Frenchmen and a Canadian to retreat!"

It seemed wiser to accept the harpooner's suggestion than to argue about it. So I simply replied:

"Let us wait for things to happen, Master Land, and we

shall see. But until something does happen, please be patient. Our only chance is to think up some ruse, and you will not create any good opportunities by flying into a rage. So promise me that you will accept the situation without getting too worked up about it."

"I promise, Professor," Ned Land replied somewhat unconvincingly. "Not an angry word shall pass my lips, not a violent gesture shall betray me, even if the service at table leaves much to be desired."

"So I have your word, Ned," I said to the Canadian.

The conversation lapsed, and each of us devoted himself to his own thoughts. I will admit that despite the harpooner's assurances, I was under no illusion. I could not imagine that we should ever have those opportunities of which Ned Land had spoken. To be navigated with such a sure hand, the submarine needed a numerous crew, and consequently, if it came to a fight, we should be strongly outnumbered. Besides, we needed above all to be free, and we were not. I could not even see any way of escaping from this iron-plated cell, which had been so hermetically sealed. And assuming that the strange Captain of this ship had a secret to guard—which seemed at least probable—he would not let us move freely on board. Would he now get rid of us by violent means, or would he one day cast us off on some remote corner of land? This was the unknown factor. However, all these possibilities seemed to me entirely plausible and one had to be a harpooner to have any hope of regaining one's freedom.

I realized that the longer Ned Land thought the matter over, the more bitter he became. I could hear him gradually beginning to grumble and mutter curses to himself, and I saw his gestures becoming threatening. He would get up and prowl around like a wild beast in a cage, banging the walls with his feet and fists. Moreover, time was passing, we were becoming more and more famished, and the steward was nowhere to be seen; if they really had any good intentions toward us, considering that we were survivors of a shipwreck, they had neglected us much too long.

Ned Land, tormented by the aching void in his ample stomach, was becoming more and more worked up, and despite his promise, I really was beginning to fear an explosion, should any member of the crew appear.

For another two hours the Canadian's fury mounted. He called out, he shouted, but all in vain. The iron-plate walls were deaf to his cries. I could not even hear the slightest noise inside the ship, which seemed to be dead. It was not moving, or I should have felt the hull tremble beneath the movement of the propeller. She was probably deep down in the sea, far from land. The gloomy silence was frightening.

We were isolated, shut away in a cell to be sure, but I could not believe that it would last. The hope that I had felt after our interview with the Captain was gradually fading. The gentleness in that man's look, the kindhearted expression on his face, his noble bearing—I was beginning to forget all that. I was now seeing quite a different image of this enigmatic person, such as I imagined he must be—pitiless and cruel. I felt him to be outside humanity, inaccessible to any feelings of pity, and the implacable enemy of his fellowmen, against whom he must have sworn an undying hatred.

But did this man intend to leave us here to die of starvation, shut up in this confined space, and exposed to the horrible temptations induced by extreme hunger? This appalling thought grew and grew in intensity in my mind, and fired by imagination, I became filled with insensate horror. Conseil remained calm. But Ned Land kept roaring like a wild animal.

At that moment there was a noise outside: the sound of steps echoed on the iron floor. The bolts were withdrawn, the door opened, and the steward appeared.

Before I could make a move to stop him, the Canadian threw himself on the unfortunate man, hurled him to the ground, and caught him by the throat. The steward was choking in his powerful grasp.

Conseil was already trying to drag the harpooner's hands off his half-suffocated victim, and I was going to join my efforts to his, when suddenly I was rooted to the spot by the following words, spoken in French:

"Stop, Master Land! And you, Monsieur le Professeur, be good enough to listen to me."

Chapter X

THE MAN OF THE SEAS

IT WAS THE CAPTAIN WHO HAD SPOKEN.

Ned Land got up quickly, and the steward, who had almost been strangled, staggered out in obedience to a sign from his master. Such was the Captain's power on board that the man did not betray, by the smallest gesture, the resentment he must have felt against the Canadian. Conseil, who could not help taking an interest in the proceedings, and I, who was bewildered, waited in silence to see what would happen.

The Captain, leaning against a corner of the table, his arms crossed, studied us with rapt attention. Was he hesitating to speak? Was he sorry he had uttered those words in French? One could well believe it.

After a few moments' silence, which none of us dared break, he said, in a calm, penetrating voice:

"Gentlemen, I speak French, English, German, and Latin equally well. So I could have answered you at our first interview. But I wanted to make your acquaintance first, and then think the matter over. Your four separate accounts, which were basically consistent, confirmed for me your identities. I now know that chance has brought before me Monsieur Pierre Aronnax, Professor of Natural History at the Paris Museum, engaged in a scientific expedition abroad; Conseil, his servant; and Ned Land, a Canadian-born harpooner on board the frigate *Abraham Lincoln*, a ship of the United States Navy."

I bowed in agreement. The Captain was not asking me a question, so I did not have to answer. He expressed himself with perfect fluency, without a trace of an accent. His phrases were clear-cut, his words well-chosen, and his ease of speech remarkable. However, I did not feel he was a fellow countryman of mine.

He then continued, "You undoubtedly have thought, monsieur, that I have taken a long time to come back and pay you this second visit. The reason is that once having established your identity, I wanted to give mature consideration to the question of how I should treat you. I have had many doubts.

70

Due to the most annoying circumstances, you find yourself in the presence of a man who has broken with humanity. You have intruded on my existence—"

"Without meaning to," I said.

"Without meaning to?" the stranger replied, raising his voice a little. "Didn't the *Abraham Lincoln* mean to pursue me all over the ocean? Did you not mean to secure a passage on board the frigate? Was it by accident that your shells bounced off my hull? Was it unintentional that Ned Land struck it with his harpoon?"

I detected in these words an ill-contained irritation. But I had quite a natural reply to make to these remonstrations, and I made it.

"Monsieur," I said, "you are doubtless unaware of all the talk that has been going on about you in Europe and America. You do not realize the stir created in public opinion, on both these continents, by the various accidents caused by the collisions with your craft. I will not bother you with all the innumerable speculations with which people have sought to explain the inexplicable phenomenon of which you alone held the secret. But you should know that, in pursuing you across the high seas into the Pacific Ocean, the *Abraham Lincoln* imagined that it was giving chase to a powerful sea monster, of which the seas must be rid at all costs."

A half smile hovered on the Captain's lips; then he said in a calm voice:

"Monsieur Aronnax, would you venture to suggest that your frigate would not have pursued and bombarded a submarine vessel as readily as it did a monster?"

This question embarrassed me, for certainly Commander Farragut would not have hesitated. He would have considered it his duty to destroy the menace, be it narwhal or machine.

"You therefore realize, monsieur," the stranger continued, "that I have the right to treat you as enemies."

I said nothing. What good was it to argue about such a suggestion when superior force can demolish the best of arguments?

"For a long time," the Captain went on, "I hesitated. I was under no obligation to grant you hospitality. If I were to part company with you, I should have no interest in seeing you again. I should put you back on the platform of this ship where you previously took refuge. I should order the ship to dive, and I should forget that you had ever existed. Wouldn't that be within my rights?"

"It might be the right of a savage, perhaps," I replied, "but not of a civilized man."

"Monsieur le Professeur," the Captain was quick to reply, "I am not what you would call a civilized man! I have broken completely with society for reasons only I have the right to appraise. I do not therefore obey any of its rules, and I suggest that you never invoke them in my presence."

That was plain speaking. A flash of anger and disdain had lit up the stranger's eyes, and I had a glimpse of what must have been a terrible past in this man's life. Not only had he placed himself outside the sphere of human laws, but he had made himself independent, free in the strictest sense of the word, beyond reach! Who would dare to pursue him to the bottom of the sea, since he thwarted all efforts directed against him on the surface? What vessel could stand the shock of his submarine monitor? What armor, however thick it might be, could resist the blows of his lance? No man on earth could demand that he account for his actions. God, if he believed in Him, and his conscience, if he had one, were the only judges to whom he might look.

Such were the thoughts that quickly passed through my mind as this strange man remained silent, as though absorbed and withdrawn into his own shell. I thought of him with a mixture of fear and interest, just as Oedipus must have thought of the Sphinx.

After a fairly long silence, the Captain continued.

"I hesitated," he said, "but I reflected that my interest might well coincide with that natural pity to which all human beings do have a right. You shall stay on board my ship, since fate has brought you here. You shall be free, but in exchange for this freedom, which, be it said, is only relative, I will impose just one condition on you. It will be sufficient to give me your word that you will abide by it."

"But sir," I replied. "I suppose this condition is one that an honorable man can accept?"

"Yes, monsieur, it is. It is possible that certain unforeseen events may compel me to confine you to your cabins for a few hours or even days. Since it is my desire never to use violence, I shall expect you, in such a case, more than in any other that may arise, to show passive obedience. In doing this, I absolve you from all responsibility, taking everything upon myself, since I am making it impossible for you to see things that must not be seen. Do you accept this condition?"

So this meant things happened on board that were, to say the least, strange, and that should not be seen by people who had not placed themselves outside the bounds of society! Of all the surprises the future held for me, this would surely not be the least.

"We accept," I replied. "However, I would ask your permission, sir, to put one question to you, just one."

"Yes?"

"You have said that we should be free on board your ship?"

"Entirely."

"And I should like to ask you exactly what you mean by 'free.' "

"Well, the freedom to come and go, and see, and even watch everything that goes on here—except under certain rare circumstances—the freedom, that is, that we ourselves have, I and my companions."

Obviously, we did not understand each other.

"Forgive me, sir," I rejoined, "but this freedom is only the one that all prisoners have, of being able to walk about their cell! That cannot possibly be sufficient for us."

"But it must be sufficient for you!"

"What! give up all hope of ever seeing our country, our friends, and our relatives again!"

"Yes, monsieur, but to give up that intolerable yoke which men believe to be freedom is perhaps not so painful as you think!"

"Never," cried Ned Land. "Never will I give my word not to try to escape!"

"I do not ask you for your word, Master Land," the Captain replied coldly.

"Sir," I replied, carried away despite myself, "you are abusing your position to take advantage of us! This is cruelty!"

"No, monsieur, it is clemency. You are prisoners of war! I am keeping you here, although one simple order would suffice to have you thrown into the bottomless ocean! You attacked me! You have stumbled on a secret that no man on earth shall ever penetrate, the secret of my whole existence! And you imagine that I am going to send you back to that world that must never hear of me again? That is out of the question! In keeping you I am not guarding you, I am protecting myself!"

These words of the Captain's indicated he had adopted an attitude against which no argument could prevail.

"In other words, sir," I continued, "you are merely giving us the choice between life and death?"

"Exactly."

"My friends," I said, "there is only one answer to such a question. But nevertheless we are bound by no promise to the master of this ship."

"None at all, monsieur," the stranger replied. Then, in a milder voice, he went on:

"And now let me finish what I was going to say to you. I know you, Monsieur Aronnax. You, if not your companions, will not have so much reason to complain of the fate that has linked your life with mine. Among the books that I like best to study you will find the work you have published on the ocean depths. I have read it many times. In it, you go as far as land-based science could go. But you do not know everything, nor have you seen everything. Let me tell you, Professor, you will not regret the time you spend on board. You are going to travel through a wonderland. Astonishment and amazement will probably become your habitual state of mind. You are not likely to become bored with the endless spectacle offered for you to feast your eyes on. I plan to revisit, in another underwater journey around the world—perhaps it will be my last, who knows?—everything that I have so far been able to study on the bottom of the sea, where I have so often been, and you shall be my fellow student. From this day on, you will be entering a new world, you will be seeing what no man has yet seen—for I and my companions do not count anymore—and our planet, thanks to me, will deliver up to you its last secrets."

I cannot deny that these words had a powerful effect on me. He had caught me in my weak spot, and for a moment I forgot that contemplation of sublime things could not compensate me for loss of my freedom. Moreover, I was depending on the future to solve this grave problem. So I contented myself with replying:

"Sir, even if you have cut yourself off from humanity, I cannot believe you have rejected all human sentiments. We are the victims of a shipwreck, charitably picked up by you, and we shall not forget this. I must admit that if my interest in science could take the place of my need for freedom, the prospects of our association could offer me great compensations."

I thought that the Captain was going to hold out his hand for me to shake in conclusion of our agreement. But he did nothing, and I was disappointed in him for not doing so.

"One last question," I said, just as this extraordinary being seemed about to withdraw.

"Yes, Professor?"

"How should I address you?"

"To you," replied the Captain, "I am just Captain Nemo. To me, you and your companions are just passengers on board the *Nautilus*."

Captain Nemo called out, and a steward appeared. He then

gave him orders in that strange language that I could not identify, after which he turned toward the Canadian and Conseil and said:

"A meal is ready in your cabin. Please follow this man."

"I won't say no to that!" replied the harpooner.

So he and Conseil finally left the cell where they had been incarcerated.

"And now, Monsieur Aronnax, our lunch is ready. Permit me to lead the way."

"At your service, Captain."

I followed Captain Nemo, and as soon as I passed through the door I found myself in a sort of corridor, lit by electricity, resembling a passage in an ordinary ship. About ten yards farther on, a second door opened before me.

I came into a dining room decorated and furnished in somewhat severe taste. High oak dressers, inlaid with ebony, stood at either end of the room; the shelves, whose edges were scalloped, sparkled with china and earthenware and glass of inestimable value. Flat dishes glistened beneath lights set in the ceilings; fine paintings softened the glare.

In the center of the room stood a richly appointed table. Captain Nemo pointed to the place I was to take.

"Please sit down," he said to me. "Enjoy a good meal; you must be dying of hunger."

Lunch consisted of a number of dishes the materials for which could only have come from the sea, as well as some foods of whose nature and origin I knew nothing. I will admit that it was very good; the taste was quite peculiar, but I found it easy to get used to. These various delicacies seemed to me to be rich in phosphorus, and I assumed that they must have come from the sea.

Captain Nemo kept looking at me. I did not ask him anything, but he guessed my thoughts, and of his own accord, he answered the questions I was longing to put to him.

"Most of these dishes are unknown to you," he said. "However, you can eat them without fear. They are healthful and nourishing. I gave up land food a long time ago and am none the worse for it. My crew, who are fit and well, eat the same food."

"Then, all these foods are *really* products of the sea?"

"Yes, Professor; the sea supplies all my needs. Sometimes I put out my nets, and when I draw them in again they are full to bursting. Sometimes I go hunting in regions seemingly inaccessible to man, and I flush out the game that lies concealed in my underwater forests. My flocks, like those of old Father Neptune, graze without fear in the immense prairies of the ocean. Here I have a vast domain that I exploit myself, a domain sown and stocked by the hand of the Creator with all things imaginable."

I looked at Captain Nemo with some astonishment, and replied:

"I realize perfectly well, sir, that your nets provide excellent fish for your table; but I find it harder to understand how you can pursue aquatic game in your underwater forests. Even less do I understand how a piece of meat, however small it may be, can figure in your menu."

"Moreover, monsieur," the Captain rejoined, "I never make use of the flesh of land animals."

"Then what is this?" I said, pointing to a dish that still contained some slices of filleted meat.

"What you believe to be meat, Professor, is only fillet of turtle. And here is some dolphin's liver that you would take for a pork stew. My cook is very skillful, and he excels in processing these various products of the ocean. Taste them all. Here is a preserve of holothurian that a Malay would declare to be unmatched anywhere in the world; there is a cream supplied by the udders of cetaceans, and sugar by the great fucus plants that grow in the North Sea; finally, let me offer you some anemone jam, which is as good as that made from the most tasty fruits."

More as a curious man than as a gourmet, I tasted all these things, while Captain Nemo enchanted me with his incredible tales.

"But this sea, Monsieur Aronnax," he said, "this prodigious, inexhaustible provider, does more than just feed me; she dresses me too. These materials that clothe you have been woven from the fibers of certain shellfish; and they have been dyed with the purple of the ancients and shaded with violet tints that I extract from the Mediterranean sea hare. The scents that you will find on the dressing table in your cabin have been produced by the distillation of sea plants. Your bed is made of the softest sea grass. Your pen is made of whalebone, while the ink you use is juice secreted by the cuttlefish or the squid. I now receive everything from the sea, just as someday the sea will receive me!"

"You love the sea, Captain, don't you?"

"Yes, I love it! The sea is everything! It covers seventenths of the earth. Its breath is pure and wholesome. The sea is an immense desert where man is never alone, for he feels life pulsating all about him. The sea is nothing but the means which permits man to lead an almost supernatural existence; it is all movement and love. It is the living infinite, as one of your poets has said. And in fact, Monsieur le Professeur, nature manifests itself by its three kingdoms: the mineral, the vegetable, and the animal. The last is well represented here by the four groups of zoophytes, by three classes of articulates, by five classes of mollusks, by three classes of vertebrates, the mammals, the reptiles, and numberless legions of fish, representing an infinite order of animals embracing more than thirteen thousand species, of which only a tenth belong to fresh water. The sea is a vast reservoir of nature. It was through the sea that the earth, so to speak, began, and who knows but what it might not come to an end through the sea! Here we have perfect tranquillity, for the sea does not belong to despots.

"On the surface, they can still exercise their iniquitous laws, fight, devour each other, and indulge in all their earthly horrors. But thirty feet below its surface their power ceases, their influence fades, and their dominion vanishes! Ah, monsieur, to live in the bosom of the sea! Only there can independence be found! There I recognize no master! There I am free!"

Suddenly, amidst this burst of enthusiasm, Captain Nemo became silent. Had he allowed himself to be carried away beyond the bounds of his normal reserve? Had he been talking too much? For a few moments he walked up and down, obviously very agitated. Then his nerves grew calmer, his face again took on its usual serene reserve, and turning toward me, he said:

"And now, Professor, if you would like to inspect the *Nautilus,* I am at your service."

Chapter XI

THE NAUTILUS

CAPTAIN NEMO stood up and I rose to follow him. A double door at the back of the room opened, and I entered another compartment of the same size as the one I had just left.

It was a library. Tall pieces of furniture made of dark red rosewood streaked with black, inlaid with brass, contained on their deep shelves a great number of books, all bound in the same way. The bookcases extended all around the room, and where the lowest shelves ended, the walls were lined with spacious divans, upholstered in brown leather and most comfortably shaped. Light, moveable book rests, which could be brought closer or pushed away at will, provided a surface on which to place a book while reading. In the center, there was a large table covered with pamphlets, among which also lay some old newspapers. The whole harmonious apartment was lit by electric light from four frosted-glass globes, half sunk in the ceiling. I could not help admiring such an ingeniously arranged room, and indeed, could scarcely believe my eyes.

"Captain Nemo," I said to my host, who had just stretched himself out on one of the divans, "this is a library that would do honor to more than one palace on the Continent, and I'm really amazed when I think that it is always with you, no matter to what depths of the sea you may go."

"Where could one find more solitude, more tranquillity, Professor?" replied Captain Nemo. "Could you find such a completely restful atmosphere in your study at the museum?"

"No, sir, and I must admit it is a very poor place compared to yours. You must have six or seven thousand volumes here. . . ."

"Twelve thousand, Monsieur Aronnax. These are the only ties that still bind me to the earth. But the world came to an end for me on the day when my *Nautilus* dived beneath the waters for the first time. On that day, I bought my last books, my last pamphlets, and my last newspapers, and since that time I should like to think that humanity has neither thought any more thoughts nor written any more books. However, these books, Professor, are at your disposal, and you can make free use of them."

I thanked Captain Nemo, and I approached the shelves of the library. There were books on science, on ethics, and on literature, in large numbers and in every language, but I saw not a single work on political economy; such books seemed to be strictly proscribed on board. A curious detail was that these books were not clearly classified according to the languages in which they were written, and this confusion seemed to indicate that the Captain of the *Nautilus* must have no trouble reading any volume he might happen to lay his hands on.

Among these works I noticed masterpieces of both ancient and modern writers; that is to say, everything that humanity has produced that is most worthwhile in history, poetry, the novel, and science, from Homer up to Victor Hugo, from Xenophon to Michelet, from Rabelais to Georges Sand. But scientific books, particularly, were outstanding in this library; books on mechanics, ballistics, hydrography, meteorology, geography, geology, etc., held a place no less important than the works of natural history and I realized that these subjects were the Captain's main fields of study. I saw all of Humboldt, Arago, the works of Foucault, Henry Sainte-Claire Deville, Chasles, Milne-Edwards, Quatrefages, Tyndall, Faraday, Berthelot, the Abbé Secchi, Petermann, Commander Maury, Agassiz, etc., publications of the Academy of Sciences, bulletins of various geographical societies, and in a prominent place, the two volumes that had perhaps been the reason for my relatively charitable reception by Captain Nemo. Among the works of Joseph Bertrand, his book entitled *The Founders of Astronomy* even gave me an exact date; since I knew that it had appeared in the course of 1865, I was able to conclude that the *Nautilus* had not been launched before that. Therefore, Captain Nemo had begun his submarine existence no more than three years before. Moreover, I hoped that more recent works would enable me to pinpoint the time exactly; but I would have plenty of time to make my inquiries, and I did not want to put off our tour of inspection of the marvels of the *Nautilus*.

"Sir," I said to the Captain, "I thank you for putting this library at my disposal. There are some treasures of science here and I shall be happy to peruse them."

"This room is not only a library," said Captain Nemo, "it is also a smoking room."

"A smoking room!" I cried. "Do you mean to say one may smoke on board?"

"Surely."

"Well, sir, I am forced to believe you have kept up relations with Havana."

"None at all," replied the Captain. "Please accept this cigar, Monsieur Aronnax; although it does not come from Havana, you will certainly be pleased with it, if you are a connoisseur."

I took the cigar offered me, whose shape reminded me of a Havana cigar, but which seemed to be made of golden leaves. I lit it from a little brazier on an elegant bronze stand, and inhaled the first mouthfuls with all the delight of the enthusiastic smoker who has not had a puff for two days.

"It's excellent," I said, "but it's not tobacco."

"No," replied the Captain, "this tobacco comes from neither Havana nor the East. It's a sort of seaweed rich in nicotine, which the sea supplies us rather sparingly. Do you think you will miss your Havana cigars?"

"Captain, from this day on I shall despise them."

"Do smoke these at your pleasure, without worrying about their origin. No government department guarantees their quality, but I don't think they are any the worse for that."

"On the contrary."

At that moment Captain Nemo opened a door opposite that through which I had come into the library, and I entered an enormous, splendidly lit saloon.

In shape it was a vast, canted quadrilateral, thirty feet long, eighteen wide, and fifteen high. A luminous ceiling, decorated with light arabesques, shed a bright, soft light on all the marvels displayed in this museum—for this was indeed a museum, in which an intelligent and prodigal hand had brought together many treasures of nature and art, with that artistic improvisation found only in a painter's studio. The walls were draped with materials of austere pattern, and on them hung about thirty pictures by well-known masters, all framed in the same way, with glittering trophies in between. I saw canvases of the greatest value, most of which I had admired in private collections in Europe and at exhibitions. The various schools of the ancient masters were represented—a Madonna by Raphael, a Virgin by Leonardo da Vinci, a nymph by Correggio, a woman by Titian, an Adoration by Veronese, an Assumption by Murillo, a portrait by Holbein, a monk by Velásquez, a martyr by Ribera, a country fair by Rubens, two Flemish landscapes by Teniers, three little genre paintings by Gerard Dow, Mestu, and Paul Potter, two canvases by Géricault and Prud'hon, and a few seascapes by Backuysen and Vernet. The works of modern painting included pictures signed by Delacroix, Ingres, Decamp, Troyon, Meissonier, etc.; and some admirable small reproductions of statues in marble or bronze, copies from the most beautiful models of antiquity, stood on pedestals in the corners of this magnificent museum. That state of stupefaction that the Captain of the *Nautilus* had predicted was already beginning to possess me.

"I hope, Professor," my strange host said, "you will excuse the casual way in which I am receiving you, and the untidiness of this room."

"Sir," I replied, "without seeking to know who you are, may I be permitted to guess that you are an artist?"

"No more than an amateur, I'm afraid, monsieur. At one time I used to enjoy collecting these beautiful works, created by the hand of man. I was an avid collector; I used to ferret about tirelessly in search of new pieces, and I have been able to bring together a few things of great value. They are my last souvenirs of a world that is dead for me. In my eyes, your modern artists are already ancient; they are two or three thousand years old. I make no distinction between them. The great masters are ageless."

"And what about these composers?" I asked, pointing to scores by Weber, Rossini, Mozart, Beethoven, Haydn, Meyerbeer, Hérold, Wagner, Auber, Gounod, Massé, and a number of others, scattered about on top of a large organ, which filled one of the panels of the saloon.

"These musicians," Captain Nemo replied, "are contemporaries of Orpheus, for chronological differences are effaced in the memory of the dead—and I am dead, Professor; as dead as those friends of yours who lie six feet below the ground!"

Captain Nemo was silent, and appeared to be lost in deep reverie. I felt considerable emotion as I studied him, silently analyzing the peculiarities of his physiognomy. Leaning on the corner of a valuable mosaic table, he was no longer aware of my presence and seemed to have forgotten me.

I therefore respected his mood of meditation, and continued to examine the wealth of curiosities that filled this room.

Next to the works of art, a prominent place was occupied by natural rarities. These consisted mainly of plants, shells, and other products of the ocean, which must have been the personal finds of Captain Nemo. In the middle of the saloon a jet of water, electrically illuminated, fell into a large bowl made from the shell of a giant clam. This shell, which had come from the largest of acephalous mollusks, had a delicately scalloped rim about twenty feet in circumference; it was even larger than those beautiful clam shells given to François I by the Republic of Venice and made into two gigantic holy-water basins at the church of Saint-Sulpice in Paris.

Around this fountain, in elegant glass cases framed in copper, I found the most precious sea specimens that a naturalist was ever permitted to feast his eyes on, all classified and labeled. Imagine how delighted I was!

The cases containing the zoophytes included very curious specimens of the two groups of polyps and echinoderms. In the first group were tubipores, gorgonids arranged like a fan, soft sponges of Syria, isidae of the Moluccas, pennatules, an excellent virgularia from the Norwegian seas, variegated umbellales, alcyonariae, a whole series of madrepores, which my teacher, Milne-Edwards, has so expertly classified into sections, among which I saw some wonderful flabella, oculinae from the Island of Bourbon, the "Neptune's Chariot" of the Antilles, superb varieties of coral—in short, every species of those curious polyps of which entire islands are formed, islands that may someday become continents. Among the echinoderms, remarkable for their "spiny skins," there were starfish or sea stars, pentacrines, sea urchins, sea cucumbers, asterophons, feather stars—a complete collection of this division.

Now, a nervous conchologist would have fainted before other, more numerous cases, in which the mollusks were classified. In them I saw a collection of inestimable value which, for lack of time, I cannot describe here in its entirety. Of these specimens, however, I must mention in passing the elegant royal hammerfish of the Indian Ocean, whose even white spots stood out brightly on a red and brown background; an imperial spondyle, bright-colored, bristling with spines—a rare specimen in European museums, whose value I estimated at not less than twenty thousand francs; a common hammer shell from the seas of New Holland, which can be obtained only with difficulty; exotic cockles from Senegal with fragile white bivalve shells, which a breath could shatter like a soap bubble; several varieties of the aspergillus from Java, resembling calcareous tubes, edged with leafy pleats, highly prized by collectors; a whole series of trochi, some greenish yellow, caught in the American seas, others a reddish-brown, found in Australian waters, the former from the Gulf of Mexico, remarkable for their imbricated shell, the latter found in the southern waters and distinctly star-shaped; and the rarest of all, the magnificent spur shell of New Zealand.

Then there were remarkable sulfurized tellins, precious varieties of venus and cytherean shells, the trellised sundial from the Tranquebar coasts, the marble turban conch with its pearl gleam, the green parrot shell from the China Sea, the almost totally unknown conical shell of the genus Coenodulli, many varieties of the polished cowries that serve as money in India and Africa, the "sea-glory," the most precious East In-

dian shell, and finally, littorinidae, "delphiniums," turritelli-
dae, janthinidae, ovulidae, miter shells, helmet shells, purpurae,
whelks, harp shells, murexes, tritons or trumpet shells, cerithi-
dae, spindles, strombidae, wing-shells, limpets, hyalines, cleo-
dores, and many shells so delicate and so fragile that science
has baptized them with the most charming of names.

Apart, in special cases, there were displays of chaplets of
pearls of the greatest beauty, which, under the electric light,
sparkled like tiny jets of flame: pearls of a pale pink, torn
from the pinnate leaves of the Red Sea; green-colored pearls
of the haliotyde iris; yellow, blue, black pearls, curious products of various mollusks of every sea, and certain species of
mussels found in northern streams; finally, several specimens
of inestimable value, distilled by the rarest of pearl oysters.
Some of these pearls were larger than the egg of a pigeon
and were more valuable than the pearl sold to the Shah of
Persia for three million francs by the traveler Tavernier.
They even excelled that other pearl, now in the possession of
the Imam of Muscat, which I had always thought unrivaled
in the world.

It was impossible, of course, to estimate the value of that
collection. Captain Nemo must have spent millions in gathering these specimens, and I was wondering what the source of
his immense wealth might be when I was interrupted by the
Captain.

"I see you are examining my shells, Monsieur le Professeur. I am sure they must be of great interest to a naturalist.
They have a special charm for me, however, because I collected them all with my own hands. Not a single sea in this
world has escaped my search."

"I can understand, Captain, what a joy it must be to live in
the midst of such riches. You are among those who collect
their own treasures. If I were to express my total admiration
for these treasures, however, I would have none left for the
admirable craft that bears them! Please understand me. I
have no wish to pry into secrets which are purely your own,
but I must confess that the *Nautilus*, with its instruments and
its wonderful energy and power, arouses my greatest curiosity. I see some instruments on these walls that are unfamiliar
to me. May I presume . . . ?"

"Monsieur Aronnax," replied the Captain, "as I have already told you, you have complete freedom aboard my ship.
You are free to inspect its minutest details, if you wish. I
shall be delighted to act as your guide."

"I don't know how to thank you, sir, and I have no wish to
take advantage of your kindness. I should like it, however, if
you would explain to me the use of these instruments."

"There is a similar set in my room and that is where I shall have the pleasure of explaining them to you. But first, let me show you to your quarters. You should know what your accommodations are aboard the *Nautilus*."

I followed Captain Nemo who, leading the way through one of the doors provided in each section of the saloon, brought me into one of the passages of the ship. He led me forward, where I found not a cabin but an elegant room, with a bed, a dressing table, and various other pieces of furniture. I could not but thank my host.

"Your room adjoins mine," he said to me, opening a door, "and mine is next to the saloon we have just left."

I entered the Captain's room, which had a severe, almost monastic air. A small iron bedstead, a work table, some bedroom furniture, and very subdued lighting. There was no comfort, only the barest necessities.

Captain Nemo pointed to a chair.

"Do sit down," he said.

When I was seated, he began to tell me the story of the *Nautilus*.

Chapter XII

ALL BY ELECTRICITY

"MONSIEUR," said Captain Nemo, pointing to the instruments hanging on the walls of his room. "There are all the instruments required to navigate the *Nautilus*. There is a similar set of instruments in the saloon. Whether I am here or in the saloon, they are always before me, and I can tell at a glance the exact location and direction of my ship in the ocean. Some of these instruments are known to you, such as the thermometer, which registers the temperature inside the *Nautilus;* the barometer, which weighs the weight of the air and forecasts the changes in the weather; the hygrometer, which measures the degree of moisture in the atmosphere; the storm glass, whose mixture, if it decomposes, foretells the imminence of storms; the compass, which guides my course; the sextant, which measures the altitude of the sun, from which I determine my latitude; the chronometers, which enable me to calculate my longitude; and, finally telescopes for day and night use, which make it possible for me to scan every point of the horizon when the *Nautilus* is sailing on the surface of the waves."

"Those are all the usual instruments of the navigator," I answered, "and I know their use. But you have some here which must have been designed, without doubt, to meet the special needs of the *Nautilus*. That dial with a moving needle which I see over there is a manometer, isn't it?"

"Yes, it is a manometer. When in touch with the water outside of our ship, it not only measures the pressure against it but indicates also the depth in which we are moving."

"And is that a new type of sounding equipment?"

"Those are thermometric sounding lines which register the temperature in the different levels of the sea."

"And how about those other instruments whose use I can't even guess?"

"Well, Monsieur le Professeur, I will explain these to you," said Captain Nemo. "Please, follow me carefully."

He paused for a few moments, and then he continued:

"There is a powerful agent, responsive, quick, and easy to use, pliable enough to meet all our needs on board. It does everything. It supplies light and heat for the ship and is the very soul of our mechanical equipment. That agent is electricity."

"Electricity!" I exclaimed, surprised.

"Oui, monsieur."

"But Captain, you have a rapidity of movement which does not conform well with electric power, whose dynamic force has remained very limited and so far has been able to produce only small amounts of power!"

"Monsieur le Professeur," Captain Nemo replied, "my electricity is not the electricity known to the rest of the world. That is all I will say about it for the present."

"Very well, monsieur, I will not press the point. I am happy just to be astonished at the results you have achieved. But there is one question to which I should like an answer, if it isn't too indiscreet to ask. The material that you use to produce this marvelous agent is consumed very quickly. Zinc, for example; how do you replenish it, since you no longer have any contact with land?"

"Your question will be answered," replied Captain Nemo. "First, let me say that there are zinc mines at the bottom of the sea; there are also mines of iron, silver, and gold whose exploitation would certainly be practicable. But I have chosen not to use these land metals, preferring to go no further than the sea itself for the means to produce my electricity."

"The sea?"

"Yes, monsieur. Those means were not lacking. Indeed, by establishing a circuit between wires sunk at different depths, I could have obtained electricity by means of the reaction to the different temperatures 'felt' by those wires; but I preferred to use a more practical method."

"Which is?"

"You know the composition of seawater. Remember that seawater is ninety-six and one-half percent water and about two and two-thirds percent sodium chloride; furthermore, there are smaller amounts of chlorides of magnesium and potassium, bromide of magnesium, magnesium sulfate, and sulfate and carbonate of lime. But sodium chloride forms a large part of it. I extract that sodium from seawater and use it to produce electricity."

"Sodium?"

"Yes, monsieur. Mixed with mercury, it forms an amalgam which replaces zinc in Bunsen batteries. The mercury is never consumed. Only the sodium is consumed, and this is supplied by the sea. I can tell you, moreover, that sodium batteries are most powerful, since their motive force is double that of zinc batteries."

"I can well understand, Captain, how sodium, with its excellent substances, would function in conditions such as you have. There is plenty of it in the sea. But it has to be produced, it has to be extracted. How do you do that? Obviously, you could use your batteries to extract it, but if I am not mistaken, the amount of sodium needed by such electrical equipment would exceed the quantity extracted. So, in the process, you would consume more than you would produce!"

"But you see, Professor, I do not use batteries to extract it. I simply use heat generated by coal."

"Coal?" I said, pressing him for an answer.

"Well, let us say sea coal, if you like," replied Captain Nemo.

"Do you mean you get coal from mines under the sea?"

"You will eventually see the system in operation, Monsieur Aronnax. I am only asking you to be patient. Besides, you will have plenty of time to be patient. Just keep one thing in mind: I owe everything to the sea; the sea produces electricity, and the electricity gives the *Nautilus* heat, light, movement—in short, electricity is the very soul of our ship."

"How about the air you breathe?"

"I could manufacture air, but that isn't at all necessary, since I can float to the surface whenever I choose to. However, even if electricity does not provide me with breathable air, it does at least work the powerful pumps that store it in special tanks, so that I can, if I need to, remain submerged in the deep waters as long as I wish."

"Captain," I replied, "I am delighted and I admire your achievements. Obviously, you have discovered something that other men will undoubtedly discover someday: the real dynamic power of electricity."

"I do not know whether they will ever discover it," answered the Captain coldly. "However that may be, you at least have some knowledge of how I use this precious power. You will notice, also, that this same electric power gives us a continuous uniform light, which we could not obtain from the sun. Now, look at that clock; it is electric, and it works with a regularity that defies comparison with the very best chronometers. I have divided it into twenty-four hours, like the Italian clocks, since for me there is neither night, nor day, nor sun, nor moon, but only this artificial light that I take with me to the bottom of the sea. You see, at this moment, it is ten o'clock in the morning."

"Precisely."

"Here is another use of electricity. That dial, suspended in front of us, serves to indicate the speed of the *Nautilus*. An electric wire connects it to the log, and the needle shows the

87

actual speed of the engine. You see, at this moment we are moving at the moderate speed of fifteen miles an hour."

"Marvelous indeed!" I replied. "I can see, Captain, how right you are to make use of this power, which is destined to replace wind, water, and steam."

"But that isn't all, Monsieur Aronnax," said Captain Nemo, getting up. "If you will be kind enough to follow me, we will pay a visit to the stern of the *Nautilus*."

Indeed, I already knew the layout of the forward part of this submarine craft, which, going from amidships toward the bow, was as follows: a dining room about five meters long, separated from the library by a watertight bulkhead; the library, also about five meters long; the large saloon, ten meters long, separated from the Captain's cabin by another watertight bulkhead; the Captain's cabin, another five meters; my cabin, two and a half meters; and finally, an air tank, extending about seven and a half meters to the bow. Total length: about thirty-five meters, or 115 English feet. The watertight bulkheads had doors that were shut hermetically by rubber seals, thus guaranteeing the safety of the *Nautilus* in the event of a leak.

I followed Captain Nemo along the passages until we came to the center of the ship. There, there was a sort of well, situated between two bulkheads. An iron ladder, fastened to the wall with a hook, led upward. I asked the Captain what it was for.

"That takes you up to the dinghy," he replied.

"What, you have a dinghy?" I exclaimed in astonishment.

"We have, and it is an excellent craft, both light and unsinkable. We use it for fishing and excursions."

"But if you want to get in the boat, you have to rise to the surface?"

"Not at all. The dinghy is attached to the upper part of the ship's hull, and is housed in a special compartment. It is completely decked over, completely watertight, and held in place by strong bolts. This ladder leads to a manhole in the hull corresponding to a similar hole in the side of the dinghy. By means of this double aperture, I can get into the dinghy. The crew shuts the opening in the *Nautilus*, and I shut the other —that of the dinghy—by pressure. When I undo the bolts, the boat shoots to the surface at a prodigious speed. Then I open the deck hatch, carefully sealed until then, step my mast, hoist my sail, take out my oars, and I am on my way."

"How do you get back on board?"

"I do not come back, Monsieur Aronnax; the *Nautilus* comes for me."

"On your orders?"

"On my orders. I am connected to the ship by an electric wire. I send a telegram, so to speak, and that does it."

"Of course," I said, astonished at these marvels. "What could be simpler!"

After passing by the cage of the staircase leading to the platform, I saw a cabin about two meters or seven feet long, in which Conseil and Ned Land, delighted with their food, were devouring it with relish. Then a door opened into the kitchen, which was about three meters or ten feet long and located between two large storerooms.

Electricity, more powerful and more adaptable than gas, performed all the tasks of the kitchen. Wires, which were connected to the stoves, were also connected to platinum plates, which absorbed the heat and distributed it at a regular temperature. Electricity heated also the distillation plant, which produced excellent drinking water by a process of vaporization. Next to this kitchen was a bathroom, conveniently laid out, complete with hot and cold taps.

Behind the kitchen were the crew's quarters, about five meters or seventeen feet long. The door was closed, so I was unable to see the living arrangements, which might perhaps have given me some idea of the number of men needed to operate the *Nautilus*.

At the back there was a fourth watertight bulkhead, behind which was the engine room. A door opened, and I found myself in this compartment, where Captain Nemo—certainly a first-class engineer—had installed his machinery.

The engine room, brightly lit, measured not less than twenty meters, or about sixty-five feet, in length. Naturally, it was divided into two sections: the first consisted of the equipment that generated electricity, and the second, the mechanism that turned the propeller.

At first I was struck by a strange smell that filled this compartment. Captain Nemo noticed my reaction. "That is the residue of gas produced by sodium; its odor is of slight consequence. Besides, we ventilate the ship thoroughly every morning."

Of course, I examined the machinery of the *Nautilus* with the greatest interest.

"You see," Captain Nemo said to me, "we use Bunsen and not Ruhmkorff components, which are less powerful. Bunsen components are fewer in number, but they are large and powerful, and we have found them superior. The electricity that is generated is conducted aft. There, through large electromagnets, it sets in motion a system of rods and gears that transmit the power to the shaft of the propeller. This propeller, which has a diameter of nineteen feet and a pitch of twenty-three feet, can do up to one hundred and twenty revolutions per second."

"And what speed does that give you?"

"A speed of fifty knots."

There was something that was not very clear to me, but I refrained from asking. How could electricity possibly develop such power? What was the reason for this almost unlimited source of energy? Was it due to the excess voltage obtained by means of a new type of coil? Did the secret lie in the transmission, which, by means of a hitherto unknown system of levers, could increase the power immeasurably?* These were things I could not understand.

"Captain Nemo," I said, "I have noted the results you have achieved and I do not attempt to explain them. I saw the *Nautilus* maneuvering around the *Abraham Lincoln*, and so I have first-hand knowledge of her speed. But speed is not everything. You have to see where you are going! You have to be able to steer to the right, to the left, up or down! How do you attain great depths, where you run into increasing resistance amounting to hundreds of atmospheres? How do you return to the surface? How do you manage to stay at any depth you please? Am I indiscreet in asking these questions?"

"Not at all, Monsieur le Professeur," replied the Captain after a moment's hesitation. "Not at all—since you are never to leave this submarine. Come to the saloon. It is our real laboratory. You will learn all there is to know about the *Nautilus!*"

---

* There has recently been talk of a discovery of this kind, whereby a set of levers of a new type produces considerable power. Can it be that the inventor has met Captain Nemo?—J.V.

Chapter XIII

A FEW FIGURES

A MOMENT LATER, we were sitting on a divan in the saloon, smoking cigars. The Captain spread out before me a drawing that gave the plan, section, and elevation of the *Nautilus.* Then he began to elaborate.

"Here, Monsieur Aronnax, you have the various dimensions of the boat you are in. Its shape is that of an elongated cylinder with conical ends. It looks very much like a cigar, a design already adopted in London for constructions of the same nature. The length of the cylinder, from end to end, is exactly seventy meters, or 228.9 feet, and the maximum breadth of the beam is eight meters, or 26.16 feet. So you see it isn't quite built in the ratio of ten to one, like your fast steamers, but its lines are sufficiently long and its curves sufficiently gradual for it to cut the water smoothly and easily.

"These two measurements will enable you, by means of a simple calculation, to work out the surface area and volume of the *Nautilus.* Its area is 1,011.45 square meters; its volume 1,500.2 cubic meters; which means that when entirely submerged it displaces fifteen hundred cubic meters, or fifteen hundred metric tons.*

"When I drew up the plans of this ship, destined for underwater navigation, I intended that when floating on the surface she should be nine-tenths submerged; that is, that only one-tenth should be above the watermark. Therefore, under these conditions, she would only displace nine-tenths of her volume, or 1,356.48 cubic meters, and would only weigh the same number of tons. So, in building her in accordance with the above dimensions, I could not exceed this weight.

"The *Nautilus* has two hulls, one inside the other, joined by T-shaped irons, which gives the ship enormous strength. Indeed, because of this cellular arrangement, it resists like a block, as though it were solid. Its sides cannot give; they hold by virtue of their own structure, and not because they are

---

* English equivalents (see Conversion Table) would be: surface area, 10,885 square feet; volume, 52,980 cubic feet; displacement, 1,658 tons. Since Nemo works mainly with round figures, it is easier for the reader to keep in mind the metric figures—M.T.B.

kept in place by rivets. This homogeneous construction and the perfect combination of the materials used enable the ship to defy the roughest seas.

"The two hulls are made of steel plates, whose density is 7.8 times that of water. The first hull, which is not less than two inches thick, weighs 394.96 metric tons. The second hull, including the keel, which is twenty inches high and by itself weighs sixty-two metric tons; the machinery, the ballast, the various accessories and instruments; bulkheads, braces, and so on, add up to another 961.62 tons. This, added to 394.96, makes 1,356.58 metric tons, or just about the desired weight. You agree?"

"Yes."

"So," the Captain continued. "When the *Nautilus* is on the surface under these conditions, a tenth of her is above the water. I have therefore built tanks of a capacity equal to that tenth, that is, able to hold 150.72 tons, and if I fill them with water, the boat, which then displaces 1,507 tons, will be completely submerged—which is just what happens, Professor. These tanks are situated in the lower part of the *Nautilus*. I open the valves, they fill up, and the boat sinks until it is just below the surface."

"That is clear, Captain, but now we come to a serious problem. I understand perfectly well how you can submerge just below the surface. But in diving deeper, does your submarine not encounter a pressure, and therefore an upward thrust, at the rate of one atmosphere per thirty-two feet of water, or just about fifteen pounds per square inch?"

"Quite right, monsieur."

"So, unless you fill the *Nautilus* completely, I do not see how you can force her down into deep water."

"Monsieur le Professeur," replied Captain Nemo, "let us not confuse statics with dynamics, or we will make some very serious errors. Very little effort is involved in reaching the lower levels of the ocean, for all bodies, as you know, tend to sink. Let us go on with our reasoning."

"I am with you, Captain."

"When I wanted to determine the increase in weight necessary to submerge the *Nautilus*, I only had to determine the reduction in volume that seawater undergoes as we move down deeper and deeper."

"That is quite evident," I replied.

"Now, if water is not absolutely incompressible, it is, nevertheless, slightly compressible. According to recent calculations, this reduction is only .0000436 per atmosphere, or for each thirty-two feet of depth. If we have to dive thirty-two hundred feet, that is, under a pressure of one hundred atmospheres, this reduction would be, then, .00436. I should then have to increase the weight from 1,507.2 to 1,513.77 tons. The increase, consequently, would be only 6.57 tons."

"Is that all?"

"Yes, Monsieur Aronnax, that is all. The calculation is easy to verify. Now, I have auxiliary tanks that can hold a hundred tons, so you see I can go down to a considerable depth. When I want to rise to the surface, all I have to do is to empty all my tanks, and the *Nautilus* will emerge above the waterline by one-tenth of its total capacity."

This reasoning was sound, based as it was on figures.

"I accept your calculations, Captain," I replied. "I couldn't dispute them, since your daily experience proves them to be correct. But I still see one real difficulty."

"What is that, monsieur?"

"When you are about thirty-two hundred feet down, the hull of the *Nautilus* has to bear a pressure of a hundred atmospheres. If, therefore, at that moment, you wish to empty the auxiliary tanks in order to lighten your craft and rise to the surface, the pumps have to overcome that pressure of a hundred atmospheres, which is equivalent to about fifteen hundred pounds per square inch. This would necessitate a power—"

"That only electricity can give me," interjected Captain Nemo. "I repeat, monsieur, that the dynamic power of my engines is almost infinite. The pumps of the *Nautilus* have prodigious force, as you must have noticed when their jets of water burst like a torrent over the *Abraham Lincoln*. Besides, I use the reserve tanks only for reaching average depths of seven hundred and fifty to one thousand fathoms, with a view to saving my engines. When I want to visit the depths of the ocean, two or three leagues down, I use slower but no less infallible means."

"What means do you use, Captain?" I asked.

"We now come to the problem of how the *Nautilus* is steered."

"I am very impatient to know."

"In order to steer this ship to port or to starboard—to turn, that is, on a horizontal plane—I use an ordinary rudder with a large rake, fixed to the back of the sternpost, activated by a wheel and tackle. But I can also move the *Nautilus* upwards or downwards, along a vertical plane, by means of two sloping fins, attached to the sides, opposite the center of flotation; these fins can be shifted into any position from inside the ship by means of powerful levers. If they are kept parallel to the boat, the latter moves horizontally; if they are inclined, the *Nautilus*, depending on the angle and the thrust of

93

its propeller, either dives following a diagonal line of my choice, or else rises following that diagonal. And if I want to return to the surface more rapidly, I disengage the propeller, and the pressure of the water causes the *Nautilus* to rise vertically as fast as a balloon filled with hydrogen rises in the air."

"Excellent, Captain, excellent!" I cried. "But how can the steersman follow the course you have set underwater?"

"The steersman occupies a cage with glass windows that protrudes above the upper part of the hull; the panes are made of biconvex glass."

"Do you mean you have glass that can resist such pressure?"

"Certainly. This glass can be shattered by a sharp blow, but it can resist considerable pressure. During experiments carried out in 1864, in fishing by electric light in the northern seas, we saw plates of this material, less than a third of an inch thick, stand up to a pressure of sixteen atmospheres, at the same time letting through heat rays which split up unevenly on its surface. Now, the glass that I use is never less than nine inches thick at the center, that is to say about thirty times that thickness."

"I can understand that, Captain Nemo, but, in order to see properly, light must dispel darkness. This makes me wonder how, in dark waters—"

"Behind the steersman's cage there is a powerful electric reflector, whose rays can light up the sea for half a mile."

"Magnificent, Captain, magnificent! I understand now the cause of that phosphorescence attributed to a narwhal which so intrigued the scientists. By the way, would you be kind enough to tell me whether the collision of the *Nautilus* with the *Scotia,* which caused such a stir, was the result of an accident?"

"Just an accident, monsieur. I was sailing no more than one fathom below the surface when the collision occurred. I saw that no serious damage had been done."

"None whatever. But what about your collision with the *Abraham Lincoln?*"

"I am very sorry, Professor, that such a thing should have happened to one of the best ships in the American Navy. But I was being attacked, and I had to defend myself! However, I was happy just to put the frigate out of action, so as not to cause me any trouble. She will have no problem getting repairs at the nearest port."

"Ah, Captain," I exclaimed with enthusiasm. "What a truly marvelous ship your *Nautilus* is!"

"Yes, Professor," replied the Captain with feeling. "I love

her as though she were a part of me! On board ordinary ships, when they are faced with the perils of the ocean, men's first impression is that a bottomless abyss has opened underneath them, to quote the apt words of the Dutchman Jansen; on the other hand, on board the *Nautilus*, a man's heart never fails him. The double hull of this boat is as strong as iron; there are no defects to fear—no rigging to be overstrained by pitching and tossing; no sails to be carried away by the wind; no boilers to burst; no danger of fire, since this craft is made of iron plates and not of wood; no running out of coal, since she is powered by electricity; no collision to worry about, since this ship is the only one navigating in deep waters; no storm to brave, since we are a few meters down, where the waters are perfectly calm! There, monsieur! There you have a ship *par excellence!* And if it is true that the engineer has more confidence in a ship than the builder, and the builder more confidence in a ship than the captain himself, understand why I have complete confidence in the *Nautilus*, since I am her captain, her builder, *and* her engineer!"

Captain Nemo was quite carried away by his own eloquence. His blazing eyes and impassioned gestures made him appear like a different man! Yes, indeed, he loved his ship as a father loves his child!

However, there was just one question, indiscreet perhaps, that I couldn't resist asking.

"You are, then, an engineer by profession, Captain Nemo?"

"Yes, Monsieur le Professeur," he replied. "I studied in London, Paris, and New York, when I still lived on land."

"But how were you able to build the marvelous *Nautilus* in secret?"

"Each of its components, Monsieur Aronnax, was sent to me from a different part of the world, under various names. The keel was forged by Creusot, in France; the propeller shaft at Penn and Company, London; the iron plates for the hull at Lairds, in Liverpool; the propeller at Scott's, in Glasgow. The reservoirs were made by Cail and Company of Paris, the engines by Krupp, in Prussia, and the spur at the workshops of Motala, in Sweden. The precision instruments were made by Hart Brothers of New York—and so on. Each of these suppliers received my orders under a different name."

"But," I rejoined, "you had to assemble and adjust these various components."

"I set up my workshops on a small deserted island in mid-ocean, Professor. There, my workmen—that is, my worthy companions, whom I had instructed and trained—and I built our *Nautilus*. Then, when the work was completed, we destroyed by fire all trace of our activity. If I had been able, I would have blown up the island also."

"I presume the cost must have been prohibitive?"

"Monsieur Aronnax, an iron vessel costs about eleven hundred and twenty-five francs per ton. The *Nautilus* displaces fifteen hundred tons. This amounts to one million, six hundred and ninety-seven thousand francs—that is, two million francs, if we include the furnishings, or four to five millions if we include the works of art and the collections."

"One last question, Captain Nemo."

"Why not, Monsieur le Professeur."

"You must be very rich?"

"Very, very rich, monsieur, fabulously rich. I could pay off the national debt of France—twelve billion francs—without any financial embarrassment."

I stared in astonishment at this strange, unusual man as he spoke. Was he taking advantage of my credulity? Time would tell.

Chapter XIV

THE BLACK CURRENT

THAT PART OF THE EARTH'S SURFACE that lies underwater is estimated to total 148 million square miles. That is to say, water covers more than 94 billion acres of our globe. The total volume of this liquid mass is more than 2 billion cubic miles; it could form a sphere with a diameter of more than 2,000 miles; its total weight would be about 3 quintillion tons. To grasp the significance of that figure, we should note that a quintillion is to a billion what a billion is to one: there are as many billions in a quintillion as there are ones in a billion! And this mass—these 3 quintillion tons of fluid—is about equal to all the water discharged by all the rivers on the planet over a period of forty thousand years!

During the geological epochs, the igneous period was succeeded by the aqueous. The earth was completely immersed in water. Gradually, during the Silurian period, mountaintops began to appear, islands rose above the waters, disappeared in partial deluges, rose again, settled, formed continents, and, finally, the land became fixed geographically, such as it is today. Land, in its struggle with water, emerged victoriously and conquered about 38 million square miles—more than 24 billion acres.

The emergence of these continents divided the waters into five oceans: the Arctic, the Antarctic, the Indian, the Atlantic, and the Pacific.

The Pacific extends north to south between the two polar circles, and east to west between Asia and America, across 145 degrees of longitude. It is the most tranquil ocean of all. Its currents are wide and slow; it has moderate tides and an abundant rainfall. Such is the ocean I was first destined to travel in the most unusual circumstances.

"Monsieur le Professeur," Captain Nemo said, "if you do not mind, we will take our correct bearings and thus fix our point of departure for this voyage. It is almost noon—a quarter to twelve, to be exact. We are going to rise to the surface."

He pressed an electric bell three times. The pumps began to empty the tanks; the needle of the manometer indicated

97

the change in pressure as the *Nautilus* kept rising. Then the ship stopped.

"Here we are," said the Captain.

I went out to the central staircase that led up to the platform. I mounted the metal steps, passed through a number of open hatches, and reached the superstructure of the *Nautilus*.

The platform was only three feet out of the water. The bow and stern of the *Nautilus* were spindle-shaped, and the ship resembled a long cigar. I noticed that its iron plates, which slightly overlapped each other, resembled the shells that cover the bodies of large land reptiles. This was the reason why, despite telescopes of the best quality, the *Nautilus* had always been mistaken for an aquatic animal.

At about the middle of the platform, the dinghy, half sunk inside the ship's hull, protruded slightly. Both fore and aft, there were two cages of medium height with sloping walls, parts of which were paneled with thick lenticular glass; one case was for the steersman, the other held the powerful electric searchlight that lighted its course.

The sea was extremely beautiful, the sky crystal clear, and the long vessel rolled gently on the undulating crests of the waves. A light easterly breeze rippled the surface of the water. There was no mist on the horizon, nothing to obstruct our visibility.

There was nothing in sight—not a reef, not an island. The *Abraham Lincoln* was nowhere to be seen. There was nothing but a vast, deserted open sea.

Captain Nemo, sextant in hand, measured the altitude of the sun, which was to give him his latitude. He waited for a few minutes until the sun "touched" the horizon.* As he watched, not a muscle moved. The instrument could not have been more still in a hand of marble.

"Midday," he said. "Whenever you wish, Monsieur le Professeur. . . ."

I cast a final glance at the shores of Japan and at that sea, touched with yellow, and went down into the big saloon.

The Captain noted his bearings, calculated his longitude by the chronometer, and checked it against his previous bearings. "Monsieur Aronnax," he said, "we are at longitude one hundred and thirty-seven degrees, fifteen minutes west."

"From which meridian?" I asked quickly, hoping that the Captain's reply might give me a clue to his nationality.

"I have various chronometers, monsieur," he replied, "set

---

* The navigator focuses the image of the horizon on a fixed mirror and the sun's image on a movable mirror; then he moves the sun image until it "touches" his horizon image; the distance of the move measures the angle of the sun's altitude.—M.T.B.

by the meridians of Paris, of Greenwich, and of Washington. However, I shall do you the honor of using the Parisian."

His reply revealed nothing; I bowed, and the Captain continued:

"Longitude thirty-seven degrees fifteen minutes west of the Paris meridian, and latitude thirty degrees, seven minutes north—we are about three hundred miles off the coast of Japan. Today is the eighth of November, the time is midday, and we now begin our voyage of exploration under the sea."

"God preserve us!" I replied.

"And now, Professor," the Captain added, "I leave you to your studies. I have set our course at east-northeast, at a depth of twenty-seven fathoms. Here are large-scale maps by which you may follow the route. The saloon is at your disposal, and with your permission, I will retire."

Captain Nemo bowed. I was left alone, deep in thought. My mind was completely absorbed by the commander of the *Nautilus*. Would I ever know the nationality of this strange man who boasted that he belonged to no nation? Who or what had provoked his hatred against humanity? Was he contemplating and seeking vengeance against those who had provoked that hatred? Was he one of those frustrated scientists —one of those geniuses whose work had been spurned—as Conseil had remarked—a modern Galileo, or perhaps one of those scientists, like the American Maury, whose career was ruined by a political revolution? It was too early for me to say. Destiny had just cast me on board his ship; my life was in his hands. He had received me with coolness, but hospitably. He had never shaken the hand I held out to him, and he had never offered me his.

For a whole hour I remained lost in my reflections, endeavoring to get to the bottom of this mystery, which I found so fascinating. Then my eyes fell on the vast planisphere spread out on the table, and I put my finger on the very spot where our latitude and longitude crossed.

The sea, like the continents, has its large rivers. They are special currents, recognizable by their temperature and by their color, the most remarkable of which is known as the Gulf Stream. Science has discovered the direction of five principal currents that flow around the globe: one is in the North Atlantic, a second in the South Atlantic, a third in the North Pacific, a fourth in the South Pacific and a fifth in the South Indian Ocean. It is probable that there was a sixth current in the north of the Indian Ocean when the Caspian and Aral Seas were part of the great lakes of Asia forming only one expanse of water.

At this very point on the planisphere was indicated one of

these currents, the Japanese Kuroshio, or Black Current, which leaves the Gulf of Bengal, where it is warmed by the direct rays of the tropical sun, crosses the Strait of Malacca, flows along the Asian coast, curves into the North Pacific and reaches the Aleutian Islands, carrying with it trunks of camphor trees and other indigenous products, and blending the pure indigo of its warm water with the waves of the ocean. It was this current that the *Nautilus* was now to pass through. I followed it with my eyes, fascinated, until it disappeared—swallowed by the vast waters of the Pacific.

Just then Conseil and Ned appeared at the door of the saloon. They were dumbfounded at the display of marvels that met their eyes.

"Where are we! Where are we!" cried the Canadian. "Are we at the museum of Quebec?"

"If Monsieur will permit me," exclaimed Conseil, "it looks more like the Hôtel du Sommerard!" *

"My friends," I replied, motioning to them to come in, "you are not in Canada, nor in France; you are on board the *Nautilus,* more than one hundred and sixty feet below the surface of the sea."

"If Monsieur says so, it must be so," replied Conseil, "but frankly, this room is enough to astonish even a Fleming like me."

"You should be astonished, my friend. Take a good look. There is plenty of work to be done here for an expert classifier like you."

There was no need to encourage Conseil, for the worthy fellow was already bending over the showcases and murmuring words in the language of naturalists: "Class of Gastropods, family of buccinoids, genus of porcelains, species of Cyproea Madagascariensis," etc.

During that time Ned Land, who was not much of a conchologist, questioned me about my interview with Captain Nemo. Had I discovered who he was, where he came from, where he was going, to what depths he was dragging us? And a thousand and one questions I had no time to answer.

I told him everything I knew, or rather everything I didn't know, and asked him whether he had heard anything.

"I have seen nothing, I have heard nothing," replied the Canadian. "I haven't seen any sign of the crew. Do you suppose they, too, are run by electricity?"

"By electricity!"

*Alexander du Sommerard, a French archeologist (1779–1842), was a great lover of art objects. He traveled extensively in France and Italy, studying old monuments and buying all sorts of objects. His collections were finally assembled in the Hôtel de Cluny in Paris.—M.T.B.

"Really, Monsieur Aronnax, I wouldn't be surprised if they were. But seriously," continued Ned Land, who was obsessed by one idea, "could you tell me how many men there are on board: ten, twenty, fifty, a hundred?"

"I wouldn't know, Master Land. But, believe me, you had better give up any notion you may have of seizing the *Nautilus* or of escaping, for the time being. This ship is a masterpiece of modern technology, and I should be very sorry indeed not to have seen it. Many people would willingly accept a situation such as this, if it were only to gaze at all these wonders! Do not be disturbed, Ned, and let us try and see what is happening around us."

"See!" cried the harpooner. "We can't see anything! We will never see anything beyond this iron prison! We are moving, we are navigating, but all blindly!"

Ned Land had scarcely uttered these words when suddenly we were plunged into total darkness. The luminous ceiling was extinguished so suddenly that my eyes felt a painful sensation, such as one feels when one emerges from pitch-darkness into a dazzling light.

We had remained silent, we did not move, not knowing whether a pleasant or unpleasant surprise was in store for us. Suddenly there was a sliding sound as if panels, set in the side of the *Nautilus*, were moving.

"This is the end, once and for all!" cried Ned Land.

"Order of hydromedusas," murmured Conseil.

Suddenly a light appeared on both sides of the saloon, coming through two oblong panels. The watery mass outside was vividly illuminated by electric gleams. Only two plates of crystal separated us from the sea. At first I trembled at the thought that this fragile wall might crumble, but it was reinforced by strong bands of copper that gave it an almost infinite power of resistance.

The sea was distinctly visible over a radius of a mile around the *Nautilus*. What a spectacle! Who could possibly describe the effects of those beams of light flashing through that mass of translucent water! Who could possibly paint the soft tints of color that were reflected as those beams flashed from the upper stratum to the lowest level of the sea!

The clarity of seawater is well known and is greater than the transparency of land water. The mineral and organic substances that it holds in suspension intensify its transparency. In certain areas of the ocean—the Antilles, for example—the sandy bed, more than 75 fathoms down, can be seen with amazing clarity. The sun's rays can penetrate only to a depth of 150 fathoms. In the midst of this liquid mass, through which the *Nautilus* was traveling, the brilliancy of the searchlight seemed to create its own undulating waves. It was no longer illuminated water, but liquid light.

If we accept the hypothesis of Ehrenberg, who believes in the existence of phosphorescent illumination in the depths of the sea, then nature has certainly reserved for the inhabitants of the ocean one of its most magnificent sights, which I was now able to judge for myself from the thousands of different effects of that light. On each side I had an open window facing this unexplored abyss. The darkness of the saloon made the brilliancy outside particularly striking. We looked out as if that transparent crystal were the window of an immense aquarium.

The *Nautilus* seemed to be motionless. There was nothing close at hand against which to gauge movement. Occasionally, however, the waves created in the water by the ship's prow flashed past us at great speed.

Filled with amazement, we leaned against the windows, and none of us had yet broken that silence of astonishment when Conseil said:

"Well, Ned, you wanted to see; now you can see!"

"How strange! Strange, indeed!" Ned kept muttering. He found that spectacle fascinating and irresistible and forgot for the moment both his anger and his desire for freedom. A man would travel much farther than this to see such wonders!

"Ah," I exclaimed, "now I can understand better what inspires that man! He has created a world of his own, full of the most astonishing marvels!"

"What about the fish?" the Canadian remarked. "I don't see any fish."

"Why should you care, Ned," retorted Conseil. "You know nothing about fish."

"I know nothing about fish—I, a fisherman!" cried Ned Land.

An argument broke out between the two friends, for both knew a great deal about fish, each from a different point of view, however.

As everyone knows, fish form the fourth and last class of the subdivision of vertebrates. They are defined as "vertebrates with a double circulatory system, cold-blooded, breathing through permanent gills, and destined to live only in water." There are two distinct series: *bony fish*—that is, fish whose spinal column is made of bony vertebrae; and *cartilaginous fish*—those whose spine is composed of cartilaginous vertebrae.

The Canadian was perhaps aware of this distinction, but Conseil knew much more about this subject. Although they were good friends, Conseil was not prepared to admit that he was in any way less informed than Ned.

"Ned," he said, "you are a killer of fish and a very clever fisherman. You have caught a great number of these interesting animals. I would bet, though, that you don't know how to classify them."

"Oh yes I do," the harpooner replied in all seriousness. "They can be classified into fish that can be eaten and fish that can't!"

"That's the distinction of a glutton," rejoined Conseil. "Tell me if you know the difference between bony fish and cartilaginous fish."

"Of course I do, Conseil."

"And the subdivision of the two main classes?"

"Well, I think I know that too," replied the Canadian.

"Well, Ned, just listen to me and try to remember! Bony fish are divided into six orders. First, the acanthopterygians, whose upper jaw is complete and mobile, and whose gills are shaped like a comb. This order comprises fifteen families, three-fourths of all fish known to man. Type: the common perch."

"Good enough to eat," replied Ned.

"Second, the abdominals, whose ventral fins are underneath the abdomen and behind the pectorals, without being attached to the shoulder bone. This order is divided into five families, which include most of our freshwater fish. Types: carp and sea pike."

"Phew!" said the Canadian with some scorn, "freshwater fish!"

"Third, the subbrachians, whose ventral fins are beneath the pectorals and attached to the shoulder bone. This order comprises four families. Types: plaice, dab, brill, sole, etc."

"Excellent! Excellent!" exclaimed the harpooner, determined to consider fish only from the point of view of food.

"Fourth," continued Conseil, without allowing himself to be put off, "the apods, with elongated bodies, no ventral fins, covered with thick skin, often gluey. In this order there is only one family. Types: common eel and the electric eel."

"Mediocre, mediocre," answered Ned.

"Fifth," said Conseil, "the lophobranchiates, with jaws complete and mobile, and whose gills are formed with little tufts arranged in pairs. Only one family in this order. Type: sea horse, pipefish."

"Very bad! Horrible!" said the harpooner.

"Sixth and last," continued Conseil, "the plectognathians, whose upper jaw is attached and fixed onto the skull, making it immobile. A species having no true ventral fins. Two families. Types: Globefish, moonfish."

"Even a common pot would consider it a disgrace!" cried the Canadian.

"Well, did you understand everything, Ned?" Conseil, the savant, asked.

"Not a word, friend Conseil," replied the harpooner. "But keep going; I find you very, very interesting just the same."

"As regards cartilaginous fish," Conseil continued imperturbably, "they consist of only three orders."

"Good. So much the better."

"First, the cyclostomes, with round mouths and gills that consist of a large number of openings. This order has only one family. Type: the lamprey."

"We love that one," said Ned.

"Second, the selachians, with gills like the cyclostomes, but with mobile lower jaws. This order, which is the most important order in this class, includes two families. Types: the ray and the shark."

"What!" cried Ned, "rays and sharks are in the same order! All I can say, Conseil—on behalf of the rays—is this: don't put them in the same tank!"

"Third," rejoined Conseil, "the sturionians, whose gills are formed, normally, of one opening, with a gill cover. In this order there are four genera. Type: the sturgeon."

"Ah, friend Conseil, you've kept the best till the end—in my opinion, anyway. Is that all?"

"Yes, my worthy friend," replied Conseil, "and remember that when one has mastered all this, he still knows nothing, for the families are subdivided into genera, subgenera, species, and varieties."

"Well, Conseil," said the harpooner, leaning against the pane, "just take a look at those 'varieties' that are passing by!"

"Fish!" cried Conseil. "This is like being at an aquarium!"

"No," I replied, "because an aquarium is only a prison, and those fish are as free as the birds of the air."

"Well, Conseil, go ahead and name them," said Ned.

"I'm afraid I can't do that," replied Conseil. "It's up to my master now."

Indeed, the worthy lad, who had an obsession for classifying, was not a naturalist, and I do not know whether he could have distinguished a tunny from a bonito. In a word, he was the opposite of the Canadian, who could name all these fish without hesitation.

"A triggerfish," I said.

"A *Chinese* triggerfish," Ned Land added.

"Genus: balistes; family: sclerodermi; order: plectognathi," murmured Conseil.

Without a doubt, Ned and Conseil put together would have made one distinguished naturalist.

The Canadian was not mistaken. A school of triggerfish, with flat bodies, grainy skin, a pointed spur on their dorsal fins, gamboled all around the *Nautilus*, splashing the waters with their four rows of sharp, pricklish spurs on each side of their tails. Nothing is more fascinating than their bodies, with their gray dorsals and their white bellies, with touches of gold scintillating in the dark eddies of the waves. Among them rays swayed like sheets in the wind, and among these I noticed, to my great delight, a Chinese ray, with a yellowish dorsal, a soft pink belly, and with three sharp spurs behind its eye—a very rare species, whose existence was still questionable in the days of Lacépède. He had never seen one except in a collection of Japanese drawings.

For two hours a whole army of aquatic animals escorted the *Nautilus*. As they gamboled about, leaping and splashing, vying with each other in speed and beauty, I identified the green labre, or sea partridge; the banded mullet with its two black stripes; the round-tailed goby, white but with touches of violet on its back; the Japanese scombrus, an admirable mackerel of those waters, with a blue body and silvery head; the blue-gold azuros, whose name describes them adequately; striped giltheads, with fins tinged in blue and yellow; a second type of gilthead with a black band on its caudal fin; a third type with an elegant corset of six stripes; aulostomi, veritable woodcocks of the sea, some species of which attain three feet in length; Japanese salamanders; spiny sea eels, six feet in length, with small piercing eyes and huge mouths bristling with teeth.

There was no end to our cries of admiration and amazement. Ned called out the names of the fishes, Conseil classified them, and I was in ecstasy in the presence of such speed, graceful movements, and the beauty of their forms. Never before had I had the opportunity to see these vivacious animals, living and free, in their native setting.

I shall not mention all the varieties and species of fish that appeared before my dazzled eyes—a complete collection, it seemed, of all the fish that swarm the seas of Japan and China. They swam in schools, were more numerous than birds in the air, attracted, undoubtedly, by the beams of our searchlight.

Suddenly, however, the lights of the saloon were turned on, the panels closed, and that enchanting vision vanished. I remained deep in thought until my eyes fell on the instru-

105

ments hanging on the walls. The compass indicated our direction to be still east-northeast; the manometer indicated a pressure of five atmospheres, corresponding to a depth of 160 feet; and the electric log gave our speed at fifteen miles per hour.

I expected to see Captain Nemo, but he did not appear. The clock on the wall pointed at five.

Ned and Conseil returned to their cabin. I went back to my room. My dinner was ready. It consisted of turtle soup, made of the most delicate sea tortoise; a surmullet, whose flesh is white and somewhat flaky, and whose liver, served separately, made an exquisite dish; and fillets of holocanthus, whose taste seemed to me to be superior even to the salmon.

I spent the evening reading, writing, and meditating. Then, overcome by sleep, I stretched out on my couch of seaweed and fell into a deep slumber, while the *Nautilus* sailed smoothly through the Black Current.

Chapter XV

A WRITTEN INVITATION

THE NEXT DAY, the 9th of November, I awakened after having slept for twelve hours. Conseil came, in accordance with his wont, to ask "whether Monsieur had a good night," and to offer his services. He had left his Canadian friend sleeping so soundly that one would have thought he had never done anything else in his life.

I let Conseil babble on as he pleased, without bothering to answer him. I was preoccupied with the absence of Captain Nemo, who had not appeared during our session the day before, and whom I hoped to see that day.

I put on my garments made of byssus. This fabric had more than once aroused Conseil's curiosity. I explained to him that the fabric was made from the glossy, silky threads with which certain mollusklike animals, very plentiful on the coast of the Mediterranean, attached themselves to rocks. Formerly beautiful material had been made from these silky threads—a cloth which was both soft and warm—and used for making stockings and gloves. The crew of the Nautilus used this fabric to clothe themselves, and had no need for cotton plants, sheep, or silkworms.

When I had dressed, I went to the big saloon. It was deserted. I immersed myself immediately in the study of the treasures of conchology displayed in the glass cases. I began to probe into the great herbals filled with the rarest marine plants. Although pressed and dried, they still retained their lovely colors. Among these precious hydrophytes I found whorled cladostephae; peacock padinae; caulerpae, shaped like vine leaves; graniferous callithamnion; delicate ceramiacea, with scarlet tints; fan-shaped agars; acetabularia, resembling pressed mushrooms, formerly considered to be zoophytes—a complete series of algae.

The whole day went by without my being honored by a visit from Captain Nemo. The panels of the saloon remained closed. Perhaps they did not want us to be surfeited with these beautiful sights of the sea.

The direction of the Nautilus remained at east-northeast,

her speed at twelve miles, and her depth between 150 and 180 feet.

The next day, the 10th of November, I continued to be left alone in solitude. I saw no member of the crew. Ned and Conseil spent the greater part of the day with me. They, too, were surprised at the inexplicable absence of the Captain. Was that strange man ill? Was he thinking of changing his plans about us?

After all, as Conseil pointed out, we still enjoyed complete liberty and we were still well fed; our host was keeping his side of the bargain. We could not complain; on the contrary, the peculiar nature of our situation offered us such excellent compensations that we had no right as yet to criticize him.

This was the day when I began to keep a diary of our adventures, which subsequently enabled me to relate those events with the most scrupulous accuracy, and strangely enough, this diary was written on paper made from seaweed.

Early on the morning of the 11th of November, the fresh air wafting through the *Nautilus* told me we had surfaced to replenish our supply of oxygen. I went to the central staircase and up to the platform.

It was six o'clock. The sky was overcast and the sea gray but calm. There was scarcely a billow. I had hoped to find Captain Nemo, but he wasn't there. Would he come? The only person I saw was the steersman in his glass cage. I sat down on the hull of the dinghy and breathed with delight the fresh breeze of the sea.

Gradually the rays of the sun rising above the eastern horizon dispelled the mist. The sea glowed with a resplendent trail of light. The clouds, scattered in the sky, were permeated with beautiful shades and tints; and numerous *langues de chat*—little light clouds with indented edges*—forecast a windy day.

But what did the *Nautilus*, indifferent to storms and tempests, care about the wind!

I was admiring that beautiful sunrise, so invigorating, so exhilarating, when I heard someone coming up to the platform.

I prepared to greet Captain Nemo, but it was only his second-in-command who appeared. He stood on the platform, completely oblivious of my presence. With a powerful telescope at his eye, he scrutinized all points of the horizon with the greatest care. Then, having completed his observations, he approached the panel and uttered a phrase, which I have re-

* Sometimes called, in English, mare's tails.—M.T.B.

membered, since it was repeated every morning under identical circumstances.

"Nautron respoc lorni virch."

I hadn't the slightest idea what it meant.

Having uttered these words, the second-in-command returned below. Thinking that the *Nautilus* was going to submerge, I went down the hatch and returned to my room.

Five days went by without the slightest change in our situation. Every morning I went up on the platform and heard the same words spoken by the same person. There was no sign of Captain Nemo.

I had resigned myself to the idea that I should never see him again when, on the 16th of November, returning to my room with Ned and Conseil, I found a note on the table, addressed to me.

I couldn't wait to open it. It was penned in a clear, neat handwriting, somewhat Gothic in style, reminiscent of German script.

The note was addressed in the following terms:

Professor Aronnax
On board the *Nautilus*
November 16th, 1867

Captain Nemo invites Monsieur le Professeur Aronnax and his friends to a hunting party, to be held tomorrow morning in the forests of the Isle of Crespo. He hopes nothing will prevent Monsieur Aronnax and his friends from participating.

The Commander of the *Nautilus*,
Captain Nemo

"A hunt!" cried Ned.

"And, what's more, in the forests of the Isle of Crespo!" added Conseil.

"Does that mean this 'character' is going ashore?" asked Ned Land.

"Obviously it means just that," I said, rereading the letter.

"We must accept," said the Canadian. "Once on terra firma, we can decide what to do. Incidentally, I shouldn't mind having a few morsels of fresh venison."

Without attempting to reconcile the contradiction between Captain Nemo's obvious distaste for continents and islands and his invitation to go hunting in a forest, I replied:

"First of all, let us see what the Isle of Crespo is like."

I consulted the planisphere and found, at latitude 32° 40′ north and longitude 167° 50′ west, a small island visited in 1801 by Captain Crespo, marked on old Spanish maps as

"Roca de la Plata"—that is, "Silver Rock." We were therefore about eighteen hundred miles from our starting point, and the course of the *Nautilus*, which had been slightly changed, was bringing her back toward the southeast.

I showed my companions that little rock lost in the middle of the North Pacific.

"If Captain Nemo does go ashore occasionally," I said, "he at least chooses deserted islands!"

Ned Land nodded, but said nothing. He and Conseil then left me. After supper, served by the silent, impassive steward, I fell asleep, not without some anxiety, however.

The next day, the 17th of November, when I woke up, I realized the *Nautilus* was motionless. I got up hurriedly and walked into the big saloon.

Captain Nemo was there, waiting for me. He got up, greeted me, and asked if we were going to accompany him.

As he made no reference to his absence during the week, I refrained from mentioning it, and simply replied that my companions and I were ready to follow him.

"However, sir," I added, "I would like to ask you one question."

"By all means, Monsieur Aronnax. If I can answer it, I will."

"Captain, how is it that you, who have cut yourself off completely from land, own forests on the Isle of Crespo?"

"Professor," the Captain replied, "the forests that I possess require neither the light nor the heat of the sun. They are inhabited by neither tigers, nor panthers, nor any other quadruped. They are known only to me. They grow exclusively for my benefit. They are not terrestrial forests; they are forests that grow under the sea."

"Forests under the sea!" I exclaimed.

"Yes, Professor."

"And you are offering to take me there?"

"Precisely, Monsieur le Professeur."

"On foot?"

"Of course, and you will not even get your feet wet."

"And we will hunt at the same time?"

"Yes, we will hunt at the same time."

"With gun in hand?"

"With gun in hand, of course, monsieur."

I looked at the Captain of the *Nautilus* with an expression that was not at all flattering.

"He must have more than a touch of insanity," I kept thinking to myself. "He had an attack that lasted a week, and he isn't quite out of it yet. What a pity, though! I liked him better when I thought he was a strange 'character' than I do now—a madman!"

My face must have shown quite clearly what I was thinking, but Captain Nemo invited me to follow him. I did, completely resigned to any eventuality.

We went into the dining room, where our lunch was already on the table.

"Monsieur Aronnax," the Captain said, "I hope you don't mind sharing an informal lunch with me. We can talk while we eat. Although I promised to take you for a walk in the forest, I did not promise to take you to a restaurant there. I suggest that you have a very good lunch now, just in case we have a very late dinner."

I did justice to the meal, which consisted of various fishes and slices of holothurian, excellent zoophytes, seasoned with very appetizing algae, such as Porphygia laciniata and Laurentia primafetida. We drank pure water to which Captain Nemo added a few drops of a fermented liquor, extracted by the Kamschatcha process from a seaweed known as *Rhodomenia palmata.* Captain Nemo ate his lunch without uttering a word and then continued:

"Monsieur le Professeur, when I suggested that we go hunting in my forests of Crespo, you thought that I was contradicting myself. When I told you that these were submerged forests, you thought I was mad. Professor, one must never judge men too lightly."

"But Captain, believe me—"

"Be kind enough to listen to me and see whether you are justified in thinking me mad, or accusing me of contradicting myself."

"I am listening."

"You know as well as I do, Professor, that man can live underwater provided he can carry with him a sufficient supply of breathable air. While working underwater, a workman wears a waterproof garment, his head in a metal helmet, and he receives air from the outside by means of pumps equipped with proper controls."

"That is the equipment used by divers," I said.

"True. However, the diver, under these conditions, is not free to move. He is attached to a rubber pump that feeds him air, but which keeps him chained to the land. If we were so restricted, we of the *Nautilus* could not go far."

"And how do you manage to be free to move?"

"By using the Rouquayrol-Denayrouze apparatus, invented by two of your countrymen. I have perfected it for my own use. This improved machine permits you to function under these new physiological conditions without suffering any organic damage whatsoever. The tank consists of a reservoir made of thick iron plates, in which I can store compressed air under a pressure of fifty atmospheres. This tank is fastened to the back with straps, like a soldier's pack. Its upper section is in the form of a box from which air, held by a bellowslike mechanism, can escape only under normal pressure. In the original Rouquayrol, two rubber tubes emerge from the tank and converge in a mask which encloses the nose and the mouth of the operator; one tube takes in fresh air, the other expels foul air. The breather can close one or the other with his tongue, as he may require. But I encounter terrific pressures at the bottom of the sea, and so I have to enclose my head in a copper sphere, somewhat similar to that worn by divers. The two tubes, however—the intake and the output—are attached to this metal helmet."

"I quite agree, Captain Nemo. However, the supply of air you carry must soon be exhausted. As soon as it contains less than fifteen percent oxygen, it becomes unbreathable."

"True. But Monsieur Aronnax, the pumps of the *Nautilus*, as I told you, enable me to store air under considerable pressure, so that the tank of this apparatus can supply breathable air for nine or ten hours."

"If that is the case, I have no further objections to raise," I replied. "But I should like to ask you how you light up your way on the ocean bed?"

"With the Ruhmkorff apparatus, which I fasten to my waist. It is composed of a Bunsen pile, which works, not with potassium bichromate, which is not available, but with sodium. A coil collects the electricity that is produced, and conducts it to a special lantern. In this lantern there is a spiral glass which contains only a residue of carbonic gas. When the apparatus is turned on, this gas becomes luminous, giving out a continuous white light. With these tools, you see, I can breathe and I can see."

"Captain Nemo, your answers are so convincing that I no longer have any doubts. However, while I am forced to admit the excellence of the Rouquayrol and Ruhmkorff equipment, I have some reservations about the guns we are to carry."

"These guns are not guns that use powder," replied the Captain.

"Is it an air gun, then?"

"Of course. How could I manufacture gunpowder on board without having saltpeter, sulfur, or charcoal?"

"Furthermore," I said, "to fire effectively underwater, in an atmosphere fifty-five times denser than air, one would have to overcome considerable resistance."

"That would be no problem. Fulton invented—and Coles

and Burley of England, Furcy of France, Landi of Italy have perfected—a watertight gun that can fire under such conditions. But of course, not having gunpowder, my gun uses compressed air, which the pumps of the *Nautilus* supply in abundance."

"But isn't the air used up very quickly?"

"True, but haven't I my Rouquayrol reservoir, which can, if necessary, supply me with more air? A tap is all we need. But you will soon see for yourself, Monsieur Aronnax, that we use very little air and few bullets in these hunting expeditions."

"Still, it seems to me that in this semidarkness, immersed in a liquid that is very dense compared to the atmosphere, a shot cannot carry very far, nor can it be so deadly."

"Monsieur, with a gun such as mine, all hits are fatal; an animal has only to be touched, however slightly, and it drops stone-dead, as if struck by lightning."

"How can that be?"

"Because the bullets ejected by this gun are not ordinary bullets. They are little capsules invented by Leniebroeck, an Austrian chemist, and I have a considerable supply. These glass capsules are covered with steel and weighted with a pellet of lead. They are little Leyden jars, highly charged with electricity! On the slightest impact they are discharged. The animal, however powerful it may be, falls dead. Besides, they are so small that an ordinary gun can hold ten of them."

"I cannot think of any more objections," I replied, getting up from the table. "I will get my gun and follow you wherever you go."

The Captain led me to the stern of the *Nautilus*, and as we passed Ned and Conseil's cabin, I called out to my two companions to follow us.

We came to a compartment near the engine room, where we were to put on special suits for our excursion.

Chapter XVI

A STROLL ON THE OCEAN BED

THIS COMPARTMENT WAS, properly speaking, both the arsenal and the dressing room of the *Nautilus*. A dozen sets of diving suits were hanging on the wall, ready for use.

When he saw them, Ned Land showed an obvious repugnance to wearing one.

"But Ned," I said to him, "the forests of the Isle of Crespo are really underwater forests!"

"I see," muttered the disappointed harpooner, whose hopes of tasting fresh meat were fading. "What about you, Monsieur Aronnax, are you going to put on one of those things?"

"It is a must, Ned."

"Well, that's up to you, sir," replied the Canadian, shrugging his shoulders. "As far as I am concerned, I would never wear one unless forced to do so."

"Nobody is going to force you, Master Ned," said Captain Nemo.

"What about Conseil? Is he going to risk it?" asked Ned.

"I go wherever Monsieur goes," replied Conseil.

At a call from the Captain, two members of the crew came to help us put on those heavy waterproof garments, made of seamless rubber and designed to withstand considerable pressure. They resembled suits of armor, but were both strong and flexible, consisting of a pair of trousers and a tunic. The trousers ended in thick boots, with heavy leaden soles. The material of the tunic was stretched over bands of copper, which crossed the chest, protecting it from the pressure of the water, and leaving the lungs free to breathe. The sleeves ended in a supple pair of gloves, which did not interfere with the movements of the hand.

All this was a far cry from the bulky diving suits—the cork breastplates, waistcoats, water suits and boxes, etc.—which were invented and so highly praised in the eighteenth century.

Captain Nemo and one of his companions—a Herculean fellow who must have possessed enormous strength—and Conseil and I were soon wearing our diving attire. The only thing left to do was to encase our heads in our round metal helmets. But before proceeding to this operation, I asked the Captain permission to examine the guns that had been reserved for our use.

A member of the crew of the *Nautilus* gave me a gun of simple design, whose large butt was made of steel and which was hollow inside. This served to hold the supply of compressed air that a valve, worked by a spring, released into the chamber. A box of projectiles, in a groove in the butt end, contained about twenty electric bullets. They were forced into the chamber by means of another spring. After one shot was fired, the next would be made ready.

"Captain Nemo," I said, "this is a perfect weapon and easy to handle. I ask nothing better than to try it out. But how are we going to get to the bottom of the sea?"

"At this moment, Monsieur le Professeur, the *Nautilus* is lying in thirty feet of water. We are all set to leave."

"But how do we get out of here?"

"You will see."

Captain Nemo put his head inside his spherical helmet. Conseil and I did likewise, but not before we had heard an ironical "Have a good hunt!" from the Canadian. The top part of our garment ended in a threaded copper collar upon which the metal helmet was screwed. Three holes, protected by thick glass, made it possible for us to see in every direction by just turning our heads inside. As soon as the helmet was in place, the Rouquayrol apparatus, which had been placed on our backs, began to work, and I realized that I could breathe with ease.

With the Ruhmkorff lamp hanging from my belt and gun in hand, I was ready to go. But I had to admit that, imprisoned in this heavy clothing and weighed down by my soles of lead, I could not have moved.

However, this lasted for a moment only, and I found myself pushed into a small chamber adjoining the cloakroom. My companions, towed in the same manner, followed. I heard a watertight door close behind us, and we were in total darkness.

A few minutes later I heard a high-pitched hissing, and I felt a cold sensation rising up from my feet to my chest. Obviously a valve had been turned inside the ship, letting in the water from the outside. We were soon immersed, and when the chamber was full, a second door on the side of the *Nautilus* opened. Something like a twilight appeared, and a moment later, our feet were touching the bottom of the sea.

How can I possibly remember and describe that excursion under the waters of that ocean? Words are so inadequate to describe such marvels! If the brush of an artist is incapable of reproducing the extraordinary effects to be seen in the depths of a clear sea, how could a pen describe them?

Captain Nemo walked ahead, and his companion, a few paces behind, followed us. Conseil and I walked side by side as if it were possible to exchange words through our metal headgear. I no longer felt the weight of my clothes, of my shoes, of my air tank, nor the weight of the thick spherical helmet, inside which my head could toss about like an almond in its shell. The reason was that all these objects, being immersed in water, lost a weight equal to that of the liquid displaced. Thanks to this physical law, first discovered by Archimedes, I felt quite comfortable. I was no longer an inert mass, but I could move with considerable freedom.

The light that filtered through at a depth of thirty feet was astonishingly strong. The sun's rays easily penetrated the aqueous mass dispersing its color. I could clearly make out objects a hundred yards away. Beyond that, the sea bottom began to develop subtle shades of ultramarine, turning blue in the distance, and faded away into a vague obscurity. Indeed, the water that surrounded me was somewhat like air, denser than the atmosphere on the earth, but almost as clear. Above me, I could see the quiet surface of the sea.

We were walking on fine sand, with a smooth, even surface, not undulated like the sand on beaches that retains the imprint of the waves. This dazzling carpet reflected the rays of the sun with surprising intensity, and explained the powerful reflection that permeated all that liquid mass. Would I be believed if I were to say that at a depth of thirty feet I could see as well as in broad daylight?

For a quarter of an hour I trod this sparkling sand, strewn with the impalpable dust of millions of shells. The hull of the *Nautilus*, resembling a long shoal, disappeared by degrees, but later on, when darkness fell over the waters, a reflector with its clear rays would help us on our return journey to the ship. The effect is a difficult one to understand by those who have only seen misty beams that stand out in the dark on land. On land, the dust that saturates the air gives them the appearance of a luminous fog; but on the sea, and under the sea, these electric beams are transmitted with incomparable purity. We kept on walking; the vast sandy plain seemed boundless. My hands seemed to be pushing aside liquid curtains that closed quietly behind me, and my footprints disappeared quickly under the pressure of the water.

Soon I could discern the outline of forms in the distance, and I recognized them as magnificent rocks, carpeted with beautiful zoophytes, and I was greatly impressed by this strange sight.

116

It was then ten o'clock in the morning. The rays of the sun, which fell on the surface of the waves, were reflected as if passing through a prism, and tinted the fringes of flowers, rocks, shells, and polyps with all the colors of the solar spectrum. It was an enchanting spectacle, a feast for the eyes, a fairyland of interwoven colors, a veritable kaleidoscope of green, yellow, orange, violet, indigo, and blue—the canvas of an obsessed colorist using all the colors of his palette!

If only I could have communicated those vivid sensations I was feeling to Conseil! If only I could have vied with him in expressing our deep emotions and admiration! If only I had known how to communicate our thoughts by means of that sign language used by Captain Nemo and his companions! For want of anything better I kept talking to myself, I kept muttering into that copper helmet I was wearing, wasting words and air needed, perhaps, for our return. In the presence of that magnificent spectacle, Conseil had stopped also. Evidently that worthy lad, surrounded by such fine specimens of zoophytes and mollusks, was very busy classifying them—classifying! The soil was literally covered with polyps and echinoderms. Various species of isis; cornulaires living in isolated spots; clusters of virginal oculines, formerly known as white coral; prickly fungi resembling mushrooms; clinging anemones—all created a brilliant flower garden enameled with porphitae, with their collarettes of blue tentacles—sea stars that studded that sandy plain, warted asterophytons which resembled the fine lace embroidered by the hands of water nymphs, whose festoons were set in motion by the gentle eddies caused by our footsteps. I found it very painful to crush underfoot those brilliant specimens of mollusks, which covered the ground by the thousands—concentric combshells; hammer shells; donacidae, veritable jumping shells; top shells; red helmet shells; shells with angel wings; aphasmidia and many others—all the creations of this fecund and inexhaustible sea.

We had to keep moving, however. Above our heads were schools of physalia, Portuguese men-of-war with tentacles floating in their train; medusae, whose umbrellas of opal or rose-pink, touched with a tint of blue, sheltered us from the rays of the sun; fiery pelagiae, which, had it been dark, would have lighted our path with their phosphorescent light!

I saw all these marvels within a quarter of a mile, scarcely pausing to have a closer look and following Captain Nemo, who beckoned to me to come on. Soon the nature of the terrain changed. The sandy plain was succeeded by a layer of viscous mud, which Americans call "ooze," consisting entirely of siliceous and calcareous shells. Then we walked through a stretch of seaweed and pelagian vegetation that had not yet been uprooted by the waters, and which grew in profusion. It was like a closely knit lawn, so soft underfoot that it could have competed with the most luxurious carpets woven by human hands. But as we walked along with this green carpet under our feet, there was no lack of verdure overhead. A light network of marine plants, classified under that endless family of seaweed, of which more than two thousand species are known, grew crisscross just below the surface of the water. I could see long strips of fucus, some globular, some tuberous; Laurenciae and cladostephae of most delicate foliage, some *Rhodomenia palmata*, resembling the fan of a cactus. I noticed that the green plants stayed closer to the top and the red ones were deeper down, leaving to the black and brown hydrophytes the task of forming gardens and flower beds in the lower depths of the ocean.

Algae are truly a marvel of creation, one of the wonders of the world's flora. This family is responsible for producing both the smallest and the biggest vegetation in the world. Thousands of these almost imperceptible plants have been counted in a cubic inch of water, and seaweed has been found whose length exceeds 150 feet.

About an hour and a half had passed since we had left the *Nautilus;* it was about midday. I confirmed this by the sun's rays, which were no longer refracted. The magical colors gradually disappeared, and the emerald and sapphire tints vanished from our firmament. We walked with a regular step that resounded on the ground with surprising intensity. The slightest sounds were transmitted with a speed to which the ear is not accustomed on land. Indeed, water is a better conductor of sound than air, and it has four times the speed of air.

The ground began to slope rather sharply, and the light became uniform in color. We reached a depth of over three hundred feet and were thus subjected to a pressure of about ten atmospheres. My diving suit was designed so well that I was not affected by this pressure. I experienced some discomfort in moving my fingers, but even this disappeared. As for the fatigue that one would expect after walking two hours wearing such a strange diving suit, there was no sign of it. On the contrary, my movements, aided by the water, came quite easily.

When we reached the depth of three hundred feet, I could still see the rays of the sun, though feebly. Their brilliance had turned into a reddish twilight, halfway between day and night. However, we could still see where we were going, and we had no need yet to use our Ruhmkorff lamps.

Captain Nemo stopped. He waited for me to catch up with him, and with his finger he pointed to some dark masses, visible in the shadow not too far away.

"That must be the forest of the Isle of Crespo," I thought. And so it was.

Chapter XVII

A SUBMARINE FOREST

AT LAST WE REACHED THE EDGE OF THE FOREST, doubtless one of the most beautiful in Captain Nemo's immense domain. He considered it his own and maintained that he had the same rights to it that the first men, in the early days of creation, had to theirs. After all, who was there to question his possession of this underwater property? What other pioneer bolder than he could come, ax in hand, to chop down these gloomy brushwoods?

The forest consisted of large treelike plants, and as soon as we entered beneath its vast arcades, I was immediately struck by the strange manner in which the branches grew—something I had never seen before.

None of the plants that carpeted the soil—none of the branches of the trees—crept or bent, nor did any extend outward horizontally. All grew straight up toward the surface. Every filament, every strip of vegetation, stood up rigidly, like a stalk of iron. The fucus and the lianas grew in perpendicular lines, governed by the density of the element that produced them. Whenever I pushed the plants aside with my hand, they immediately resumed their former position. Here, indeed, was a kingdom of the vertical.

I soon got used to this strange phenomenon, and to the semidarkness that surrounded us. The soil in the forest was strewn with sharp rocks, difficult to avoid. The submarine flora seemed to me fairly complete and even richer than that found in the arctic or tropical zones, which are less prolific. However, for a few minutes I unconsciously confused the kingdoms, taking the zoophytes for hydrophytes and animals for plants. And who could have avoided that error? For the fauna and flora are barely distinguishable in this world of the deep!

I noticed that all the plants were attached to the soil by an almost imperceptible bond. Devoid of roots, they seemed not to require any nourishment from sand, soil, or pebble. All they required was a point of support—nothing else. These plants are self-propagated, and their existence depends entirely on the water that supports and nourishes them. Most of them do not sprout leaves, but sprout blades of various whimsical shapes, and their colors are limited to pink, carmine, green, olive, fawn, and brown. I had the opportunity to observe once more—not the dried specimens I had studied on the *Nautilus*—but the fresh, living specimens in their native setting. I observed the padinae spreading out like the tail of a peacock, ready to catch the lightest breeze; scarlet ceramiaceae; the laminaria with their long edible shoots; the nereocysti, fern-shaped and rose-colored, which, when in bloom, may reach a height of fifty feet; clusters of acetabula, whose stems grow bigger as they shoot upward, and many other plants of the deep sea—all without a flower! "A strange and eerie world," a witty naturalist has observed, "a world where the animals sprout flowers and the vegetables do not."

Among these various shrubs, tall as trees in temperate zones, there were in the damp shadows masses of real bushes of living flowers, hedges of zoophytes, on which blossomed meandrines, zebralike with tortuous grooves; some yellow caryophylliae; grassy tufts of zoanthariae; and to complete the illusion, fish flies flew from branch to branch like a swarm of hummingbirds, while yellow lepisachanthae, with bristling jaws and pointed scales, dactylopterae, and monocentridae rose up under our feet like a flock of snipe.

At about one o'clock, Captain Nemo gave the signal to halt. I was quite pleased; we stretched out under an arbor of alariae, whose long thin blades stood up like arrows.

I found this short rest delightful. The only thing that was lacking was the charm of conversation. But it was impossible to talk and impossible to answer. All I could do was to place my big copper headpiece near Conseil's head. I saw the good fellow's eyes shining with pleasure, and to show his satisfaction he kept shaking his head within his shell in the most comic manner imaginable.

Since we had been walking for about four hours, I was astonished by the fact that I did not feel particularly hungry. I do not know how to explain this condition of the stomach; but, on the other hand, I felt an almost irresistible desire to sleep, which is what happens to all divers. My eyes soon began to close behind the thick pane, and I fell into a deep slumber, which I had so far been able to ward off only because I was walking. Captain Nemo and his stalwart companion had already stretched out in the clear water and gone to sleep.

I was unable to tell how long I had remained in this state of oblivion, but when I woke up, it seemed to me that the sun was sinking toward the horizon. Captain Nemo had already gotten up, and I was beginning to stretch my limbs when an unexpected apparition caused me to rise to my feet quickly.

A few steps away a monstrous sea spider, three feet high, was peering at me with squinting eyes, ready to leap on me. Although my diver's suit was thick enough to protect me against the bites of this animal, I could not help recoiling in horror. At that moment, Conseil and the sailor from the *Nautilus* woke up. Captain Nemo pointed to the hideous crustacean, and his companion immediately slew it with the butt of his gun. I saw the grisly legs of the monster writhing in horrible convulsions.

This encounter made me think of even more fearsome animals that must haunt these dark depths, and it occurred to me that against them my diver's suit would be no protection. Up to then I had given no thought to this, but I resolved to be on my guard. I imagined, incidentally, that our halt marked the farthest point of our walk, but I was mistaken, for instead of returning to the *Nautilus*, Captain Nemo continued his daring excursion.

The ground continued to slope downward, leading us to still greater depths. It must have been about three o'clock when we came to a narrow valley, situated between sheer rocky walls, more than 450 feet down. Thanks to the perfection of our apparatus, we had exceeded by nearly 300 feet the limit that nature seemed to have imposed upon man's underwater excursions.

I said about 450 feet, although I had no instrument to determine this depth. But I knew that even in the clearest seas, the rays of the sun cannot penetrate farther down. The darkness, therefore, became total, as was to be expected. Even ten paces away no object was visible. I was thus groping my way forward, when I suddenly saw a brilliant white light. Captain Nemo had just switched on his electrical lamp, his companion did likewise, and Conseil and I followed their example. By turning a screw, I connected the coil with the spiral glass in my lantern, whereupon the sea, lit up by our four lamps, was illuminated for a hundred feet all around us.

Captain Nemo continued to plunge into the dark depths of the forest, in which trees were becoming rarer and rarer. I noticed that the vegetable life disappeared sooner than the animal life. The pelagian plants were already abandoning the soil, which had become arid and which a prodigious number of animals—zoophytes, articulata, mollusks, and fish—continued to populate densely.

As I walked along, it occurred to me that the light from our Ruhmkorff lamp was bound to attract some of the inhabitants of these murky regions. However, if they approached

122

us at all, they certainly kept too far away to be shot. Several times I saw Captain Nemo stop and raise his gun to his shoulder; then, after watching for a few moments, he would move on.

Finally, at about four o'clock, the fascinating expedition came to an end. A massive wall of superb, impressive rocks rose up before us; it was a heap of gigantic blocks, an enormous cliff of granite dotted with dark grottos and no practicable means of ascent.

It was the shore of the Isle of Crespo; we had struck land!

Captain Nemo suddenly stopped. A signal from him made us halt, and although I was anxious to climb that wall, I had to stop. This was the spot where Captain Nemo's domains ended. He did not want to go any farther. Beyond that was that portion of the globe on which he must never more set foot.

So we began our return. Captain Nemo resumed the leadership of his little troop, and strode forward without hesitation. It seemed to me that we were not following the same route on our return to the *Nautilus*. The new path, which was very steep and very arduous, brought us much closer to the surface. However, this reentry into the upper levels of the sea was not so sudden as to cause decompression to take place too rapidly. If this had happened, we might have suffered those internal injuries so fatal to divers. Soon, daylight returned and became stronger, and since the sun was already low on the horizon, its refracted rays again tinted various objects with a spectral halo.

Thirty feet down, we were walking amid a shoal of little fish of all kinds, more numerous and more agile than the birds of the air, but no aquatic game worth shooting had yet appeared.

At that moment, I saw the Captain swiftly raise his weapon to his shoulder and aim at a moving object in the bushes. When he fired, I heard a slight hissing sound, and an animal fell stone-dead a few steps away.

It was a magnificent sea otter, an enhydrus, the only exclusively marine quadruped. It was five feet long and must have been very valuable. Its skin, chestnut-brown above and silver underneath, would have made one of those beautiful furs so sought after on the Russian and Chinese markets. The fineness and luster of its coat were such that it could easily fetch a minimum price of two thousand francs. I admired this curious mammal, with its round head, short ears, round eyes, white whiskers like those of a cat, webbed feet and nails, and a tufted tail. This valuable carnivore, hunted and tracked by fishermen, is becoming extremely rare and has taken refuge in the North Pacific, where it will probably soon become extinct.

Captain Nemo's companion came and picked up the animal and slung it over his shoulder, and we went on our way.

For an hour we walked across a sandy plain, which sometimes rose to within six feet of the surface. I could see our reflections, upside down, right above our heads, where we were accompanied by a group of people identical to ourselves in their motions and gestures—except that they were walking along with their feet in the air and their heads on the ground.

There was another effect to be noted. This was the passage of thick clouds, which formed and vanished rapidly; however, when I observed them closely, I realized that these "clouds" were due to the varying depth of the water over a ground swell; I could even see the billows with their foamy white crests breaking and spreading above us. The shadows of large birds appeared overhead, skimming the surface of the sea.

In this connection, I witnessed one of the finest shots ever to thrill the heart of a hunter. A massive bird, which was very clearly visible, came gliding toward us, and Captain Nemo's companion took aim at it and fired when it was only a few feet above the surface. The bird dropped like a stone, and it fell within the reach of the hunter, who picked it up. It was an albatross of the most beautiful kind, an admirable specimen of a pelagian bird.

This incident had not delayed our march, which continued for another two hours, first across sandy plains and then through fields of algae, where walking was rather slow. To tell the truth, I was about to collapse when I saw a light glimmer in the murky distance half a mile away. It was the searchlight of the *Nautilus*. In twenty minutes' time we ought to be on board, and then I should be able to breathe comfortably, for it seemed to me that my tank was now supplying me only with air poor in oxygen. But I was making my calculations without taking into account a meeting that was to delay us a bit.

I was lagging about twenty paces behind when I suddenly saw Captain Nemo turn around and come toward me. With a violent push he flung me to the ground, while his companion did the same to Conseil. At first I could not make out the reason for this unexpected attack, but felt reassured by the fact that the Captain was lying flat beside me and not moving.

I was stretched out on the ground, sheltered by a bush of algae, when, raising my head slightly, I saw two huge forms pass by noisily, emitting phosphorescent gleams.

My blood froze in my veins! I realized that these creatures

124

were formidable sharks, two tintoreas, terrible creatures with enormous tails and a dull, glassy stare. They eject phosphorescent matter from holes situated around their muzzles. These are like monster fireflies, capable of picking up a man and crushing him whole in their iron jaws! I don't know whether Conseil had been busy classifying them, but I observed their silvery bellies and their fearsome jaws, bristling with teeth, from a very unscientific point of view, more as a potential victim than as a naturalist.

Fortunately, however, these voracious beasts do not see well, and they passed by without noticing us, barely touching us with their brownish fins. We had escaped, by a miracle, a danger that was certainly greater than an encounter with a tiger in the jungle.

Half an hour later, guided by the beam of light, we reached the *Nautilus*. The outer hatch had been left open, and Captain Nemo closed it as soon as we had entered the first chamber. Then he pressed a button, and I heard the pumps start up inside the ship; the water began to flow all round us, and in a few moments the chamber had been completely emptied. Then the inner door opened, and we stepped into the dressing room.

There, we were stripped of our diving suits, not without some difficulty, and exhausted by fatigue and lack of sleep, I retired to my room, full of wonder after our amazing excursion into the depths of the sea.

Chapter XVIII

FOUR THOUSAND LEAGUES
UNDER THE PACIFIC

THE NEXT DAY, the 18th of November, I had completely recovered from my exertions of the day before, and went up to the platform at the very moment when the second-in-command of the *Nautilus* was uttering his daily phrase. It suddenly struck me that the expression either referred to the state of the sea or meant "nothing in sight."

The ocean was deserted. Not a ship on the horizon. The crests on the Isle of Crespo had disappeared during the night. The sea, absorbing all the colors of the spectrum except the blue, reflected them in every direction and covered the water with an admirable shade of indigo. A broad, wavy pattern played on the silken surface of the sea.

While I stood there admiring the splendor of the ocean, Captain Nemo appeared. He did not seem to be aware of my presence and proceeded to make a series of astronomical observations. Then, leaning on the cage of the searchlight, he appeared lost as he gazed at that vast expanse of the sea.

Meanwhile, some twenty sailors of the *Nautilus*, all well-built, energetic men, had come up on the platform. They had come to haul in the fishing nets that had been cast during the night. Evidently, these sailors belonged to different nationalities, although they all appeared to be European. I was sure that I recognized some Irishmen, Frenchmen, Slavs, and a Greek or Cretan. These were men of few words. They spoke to each other only in that weird language whose origin I could not even guess, and I could not, therefore, question them.

The nets were hauled on board. They were drag nets, similar to those used on the coast of Normandy—large pockets, held partly open by a floating rod and a chain threaded through the lower meshes. These pouches, as they were dragged along, swept the ocean bottom with their iron meshes, picking up every sort and kind of fish in their path. That day they brought up some curious specimens from those waters teeming with life: anglerfish, whose clownish antics qualify them for the stage; black commersons, equipped with antennae; triggerfish, encircled with red stripes; poisonous globefish, whose venom is very subtle; olive-colored lampreys;

macrorhynchi, with silvery scales; trichiuri, whose electric shock is as effective as that of the electric eel or the numb-fish; scaly notopteri, with brown transverse bands; green cod; several varieties of freckled gobies, etc. Also some larger fish: a caranx with a big head and a body three feet long; several handsome bonitos, blue and silver striped; and three splendid tuna, whose great speed had not helped them elude the net.

I estimated that this catch brought in more than a thousand pounds of fish, which was good but nothing unusual. These nets are left to drift for several hours, trapping within their folds a whole aquatic world. Hence, we never lacked food of excellent quality. The speed of the *Nautilus* and its electric light always attracted fresh supplies, whenever needed.

This catch was immediately lowered through the hatch to the galley, some to be eaten fresh, the rest to be preserved.

This operation over and the supply of fresh air replenished, I thought the *Nautilus* would resume her underwater voyage. I was about to return to my room when Captain Nemo unexpectedly turned toward me and said:

"Look at that ocean, Professor. Doesn't it have an individuality of its own? Doesn't it have its moods of anger and its fits of compassion? Yesterday it slept just as we slept, and now, here it is awaking after spending a peaceful night."

He had not said, "Good day" or "Good evening." It was just as though this strange man were continuing a conversation that we had begun earlier.

"Look," he continued. "It is awakening under the caresses of the sun and is ready to renew its daily existence! It is a fascinating study to follow the workings of its organism. It has a pulse, arteries, and its spasms, too; I agree with the learned Maury, who maintained that it has a circulation as real as the circulation of the blood in animals."

Obviously, Captain Nemo did not expect me to reply, and it seemed to me pointless to punctuate his speech with "of course," "certainly," or "how right you are." He seemed to be talking to himself, pausing after each phrase. He was meditating aloud.

"Yes," he said, "the ocean has a real circulation, and to keep it going, the Creator of all things has only to change its temperature or its salinity, or to multiply its animalcules. The change in temperature varies the density, causing currents and countercurrents. Evaporation, which is nil in the extreme north, but very high in equatorial regions, brings about a permanent exchange of the tropical and polar waters. Moreover, I have actually come across currents flowing from north to south and south to north, which form the ocean's respira-

127

tory system. I have seen a molecule of seawater, heated at the surface, dropped down into the depths, attain its maximum density at two degrees below zero, then, cooling further, become lighter and rise again. At the Pole you will see the results of this phenomenon, and you will understand why, through this law of a provident Nature, water can only freeze at the surface."

As Captain Nemo was finishing his sentence, I asked myself: "The Pole! Is this intrepid character actually going to take us there!"

The Captain was silent for a moment, surveying the sea that was the subject of such a thorough and unceasing study for him. Then he went on:

"Salts are present in considerable quantity in the sea, Professor. If you were to extract all the salts it contains, you would obtain a mass equal to four and a half million cubic leagues, which, spread out over the globe, would form a layer more than thirty feet high. Do not imagine that the presence of these salts is due only to a caprice of Nature! Far from it. It is they that make the waters less evaporable, so that the winds cannot pick up too much vapor, which, when condensed, would submerge the temperate zones. Salts play an immense role—the role of stabilizing the overall ecology of the earth!"

Captain Nemo stopped, got up, walked a few steps along the platform, and came back to me.

"And the microscopic organisms," he continued, "those billions of animalcules, of which there are millions in a drop of water and eight hundred thousand of which are required to make one milligram—their role is no less important. They absorb marine salt, assimilate the solid elements in the water, and, by making corals and madrepores, they build calcareous continents. Then the drop of water, deprived of its mineral element, becomes lighter, comes up to the surface again, absorbs the salts left by evaporation, becomes heavier, descends again, and brings to the animalcules new elements to absorb. We have, then, a double current, ascending and descending—a continuous movement and continuous life! The life of the sea is more intense than life on land, more exuberant, more infinite, spreading throughout the parts of this ocean. They say it is the element of death for man, but it is the element of life for myriads of animals—and for me!"

Whenever Captain Nemo spoke like this, he was a transformed man, and he aroused an extraordinary emotion within me.

"That," he added, "that is living! That is the true existence! I visualize the existence of nautical towns, clusters of submarine dwellings which, like the *Nautilus*, would rise to the surface every morning to breathe—free towns, independent cities, if ever there were! But still, who knows whether or not some despot—"

Captain Nemo ended his sentence with a violent gesture. Then, addressing me directly, as if to drive away some depressing thought, he said:

"Monsieur Aronnax, do you know how deep the ocean is?"

"I only know, Captain, what the principal soundings have indicated."

"Could you give me those figures, so that I may check them if the occasion arises?"

"Here are some that I recall," I replied. "If I'm not mistaken, an average depth of twenty-seven thousand feet has been found in the North Atlantic, and eight thousand feet in the Mediterranean. The most remarkable soundings have been made in the South Atlantic, near the thirty-fifth parallel, and they gave forty thousand to forty-nine thousand feet. It is calculated that if the bottom of the sea were leveled, its average depth would be about four miles or so."

"Well, Professor," replied Captain Nemo, "we shall show you something better than that. Incidentally, the average depth in this part of the Pacific, I assure you, is only thirteen thousand feet."

Having said this, Captain Nemo walked to the hatch, and disappeared down the ladder. I followed him down and went into the big saloon. Immediately the propeller began to turn, and soon the log indicated a speed of twenty miles.

During the days and weeks that followed, I seldom saw Captain Nemo. His appearances were rare. His second-in-command would regularly mark the ship's course on the chart, so that I could always tell the exact route of the *Nautilus*.

Conseil and Land spent long hours with me. Conseil had described the wonders of our expedition to our friend, and the Canadian was sorry he had not gone with us. However, I hoped that another opportunity would present itself to visit the forests on the bottom of the ocean.

Almost every day, for some hours, the panels in the saloon were kept open, and we never tired of exploring the mysteries of the underwater world.

The general direction of the *Nautilus* was southeast, and her depth between 300 and 450 feet. One day, however, for some strange reason, she was diverted diagonally by means of her inclined planes and reached a depth of 6,500 feet. Here the thermometer showed a temperature of 39.65° F., a temperature which, at that depth, seemed common to all latitudes.

On the 26th of November, at three o'clock in the morning, the *Nautilus* crossed the Tropic of Cancer at longitude 172°. On the 27th, we passed within sight of the Sandwich Islands, where the famous Captain Cook died on the 14th of February, 1779. We had then traveled 4,860 leagues from our point of departure. When I came up on the platform that morning, I saw, two miles away to leeward, Hawaii, the biggest of the seven islands forming that archipelago. I could clearly see its cultivated coastline, the various chains of mountains that run parallel to the coast, and the volcanoes dominated by Mauna Kea, rising 15,000 feet above sea level. Our catch in this area included several peacock flabella, a graceful polyp, peculiar to this part of the ocean.

The *Nautilus* continued to head southeast. On the 1st of December, we crossed the equator at longitude 142°, and on the 4th of the same month, after a speedy, uneventful passage, we sighted the Marquesas. At latitude 8° 57' south and longitude 139° 32' west. I could see, three miles away, Martin's Peak in Nouka-Hiva, the main island in the group, which belongs to France. I saw only the wooded mountains against the horizon, because Captain Nemo did not like to hug the coast too closely. Here, our fishing nets caught some fine specimens; cooryphenae, with their azure fins and golden tails, whose flesh is unsurpassed; hologymnosae, with hardly any scales, but which have an exquisite flavor; ostorhincae, with bony jaws; and yellow-tinged thasards, as good as bonitos—all worthy morsels for our table!

After leaving these charming islands, which are under the protection of the French flag, the *Nautilus,* from the 4th to the 11th of December, traveled about two thousand miles. The only incident worthy of note during these two thousand miles was the sight of a vast shoal of calamaries, a strange species of mollusk, closely related to the cuttle. French fishermen called them *encornets,* and they belong to the class of cephalapod, order of the dibranchiate, which includes cuttles and argonauts. These aquatic animals were studied with considerable interest by the naturalists of antiquity, and provided orators of the agora with numerous metaphors. According to Athenaeus,* a Greek doctor who lived before the time of Galen, they were considered an excellent dish for the tables of the rich.

* A great Greek scholar (170–230 A.D.) who wrote the *Banquet of the Learned,* a volume of immense learning, in which he quotes from fifteen hundred works and seven hundred writers, dealing with customs, manners, art, science, etc.—M.T.B.

It was during the night of the 9th-10th of December that the *Nautilus* ran into this shoal of mollusks, which are very active during the night. There were millions of them. They were migrating from the temperate to the warmer zones, following the same route as the herrings and sardines. We watched them through the thick crystal panes, swimming backward at great speed, propelled by means of their locomotive tube, chasing fish and other mollusks, eating the smaller ones, in turn devoured by the bigger ones, and waving, in an indescribable confusion, the ten arms that nature has placed on their heads like the tresses of pneumatic serpents. In spite of our great speed, it took us several hours to sail through this shoal. Our nets captured a vast number of these creatures, among which I recognized the nine species that d'Orbigny has classified for the Pacific Ocean.

The ocean, during this cruise, offered us an incessant and infinite display of its most marvelous treasures. There was a continuous change of decor and scenery, as if staged to please our vision, and we were called upon not only to contemplate the works of the Creator in this vast expanse of liquid world, but also to delve into the most redoubtable mysteries of the sea.

During the day of the 11th of December, I was busy reading in the large saloon, while Ned Land and Conseil were watching the luminous waters through the half-open panels. The *Nautilus* was not moving; her tanks had been filled. She was at a depth of three thousand feet, a region rarely inhabited by living creatures, and where large fish seldom appear.

At that moment I was reading a charming book by Jean Macé, called *The Slaves of the Stomach,* and was enjoying some of its ingenious ideas, when Conseil interrupted me.

"Would Monsieur like to come here a moment?" he said to me in a strange voice.

"What is the matter, Conseil?"

"Would Monsieur come and have a look?"

I got up, leaned in front of the glass pane, and looked.

There, in the full glare of the searchlight, an enormous, motionless, blackish mass was suspended in the water. I examined it carefully, trying to determine the nature of that gigantic cetacean. But suddenly a thought occurred to me.

"A ship!" I cried.

"Yes," replied the Canadian, "a disabled ship that has sunk perpendicularly."

Ned Land was right. We had before us a vessel whose tattered shrouds still hung from their chains. The hull seemed to be intact, and the wreck must have occurred only a few hours before. Three stumps of masts, broken off about two

131

feet above the deck, showed that the ship must have sacrificed them; lying over on its side, it had filled up, and was listing. What a sad spectacle was this broken hulk, lost beneath the waves! But sadder still was the sight of its deck, on which a number of bodies, bound with ropes, were still lying! I counted four men, one of whom was standing, clasping the wheel, and also a woman, who had half emerged from the poop, holding a child in her arms. She was young, and in the bright lights of the *Nautilus*, I could clearly see her features, which had not yet been decomposed by the water. With a supreme effort she had raised her infant above her head, and the poor child still had his arms around his mother's neck! The postures of the four sailors were frightful, distorted as they were by their convulsive movements; they had died making a supreme effort to free themselves from the ropes that bound them to the ship. Only the helmsman, with a calm and grave expression on his face, his gray hair drooping over his forehead, his hand clutching the wheel, stood erect, as if he were still steering his ship through the deep waters of that sea!

What a spectacle! We stood silent, with palpitating hearts, in the presence of that spectral tragedy, photographed, as it were, in the last moments of a dying agony! In the distance enormous sharks, their eyes afire with hunger, were already speeding toward that sunken ship, lured by the prospect of human flesh!

As the *Nautilus* maneuvered around that submerged vessel, I caught a glimpse of her name on the stern:

Florida, Sunderland.

Chapter XIX

VANIKORO

THIS TERRIBLE SIGHT was only the first of a series of disasters that the *Nautilus* was destined to encounter on her travels. Since we were now navigating through more-frequented waters, we often saw hulls of ships in the last stages of decomposition, while deep down, on the bed of the ocean, we saw guns, cannonballs, anchors, chains, and a thousand other iron objects rusting away in the water.

Meanwhile the *Nautilus,* in which we lived in complete isolation, continued on her way. On the 11th of December, we sighted the Tuamotu Islands which Bougainville had called the "Dangerous Group," which extend 500 leagues from east-southeast to west-northwest, between latitudes 13° 30' and 23° 50' south, and longitudes 125° 30' and 151° 30' east, from the Ducie Isle to the Lazareff Island. This archipelago covers an area of 370 square leagues, and is formed by about sixty groups of islands, among which the Gambier group, which is under the protectorate of France. These are all coral islands. The slow but continuous growth of these islands, due to the work of polyps, may someday link them together. At a later epoch, this new island will link up with neighboring archipelagos, and a fifth continent will extend from New Zealand and New Caledonia all the way to the Marquesas Islands.

One day, when I explained my theory to Captain Nemo, he replied with reserve:

"There is no need for new continents, but there is need for new men."

The course of the *Nautilus* took her in the direction of the island of Clermont-Tonnerre, one of the strangest in the group, discovered in 1822 by Captain Bell of the *Minerva.* This gave me an opportunity to study the madreporal system that has created the islands in these waters.

Madrepores, which one must be careful not to confuse with corals, have a tissue lined with a calcareous or limestone crust. Variations in their structure led my famous teacher, Mr. Milne-Edwards, to classify them in five sections. The tiny animalcules that secrete this polypary live by the millions inside their cells. It is their calcareous deposit that forms rocks, reefs, and islands, both large and small. Sometimes, they may form a ring, surrounding a lagoon or a small inland lake, which is connected with the sea through gaps in their structure; elsewhere, they may form barrier reefs similar to those off the coast of New Caledonia and the various Pomotou Islands. Sometimes, as at Réunion and Mauritius, they create fringed reefs and high, straight walls, near which the depth of the water is considerable.

A few cables' lengths off the coast of the island of Clermont-Tonnerre, I admired the gigantic work accomplished by these microscopic builders. These limestone walls are the special work of madrepores known as millepores, porites, astraea, and maeandra. These polyps flourish especially in beds agitated by rough waters near the surface, and so they begin their work at the top and work down. Thus, these constructions gradually grow downward with the accumulation of their secretions. At least, that is the theory put forward by Mr. Darwin to explain the formation of atolls. In my opinion, this theory is more logical than the theory that the madreporal structures are superimposed on the summits of mountains or volcanoes, which then submerge a few feet below the surface.

I could observe these curious walls very closely. The sounding we took showed them to be more than nine hundred feet deep, and the beams of our searchlight made the limestone scintillate.

When Conseil asked me how long it took to build these colossal barriers, he was astonished to hear that experts estimated the rate of growth at one-eighth of an inch per century.

"Which means that building these walls took . . . ?"

"A hundred and ninety-two thousand years, my lad, which makes those 'days' referred to in the Bible a good bit longer. Furthermore, the formation of coal—that is to say, the mineralization of forests submerged by floods, and the cooling of basalt rocks—took a much longer time. However, I must add that the 'days' of the Bible represent epochs, and not an interval between sunrise to sunrise, for according to the Bible itself, the sun does not date from the first day of Creation."

When the *Nautilus* surfaced again, I could visualize the complete development of this island of Clermont-Tonnerre, which was low and covered with forests. Its madreporal rocks had evidently been fertilized by whirlwinds and storms. One day a seed, borne aloft and carried away by some hurricane from the neighboring land, fell on these calcareous deposits, mixed with the decomposed refuse of fish and sea vegetation,

134

and formed a vegetable humus. Perhaps a coconut, driven ashore by the waves, was washed up on this new coast, where it germinated. The tree, in growing, caught the water mists, and a stream was born. Gradually vegetation grew. Some animalcules, worms, and insects, living in tree trunks on other islands, were swept onto these shores by the wind. Turtles came here to lay their eggs. Birds nested in the young trees, and in this way animal life developed. Then, attracted by green vegetation and the fertility of the land, man made his appearance. This is how these islands came into being, through the immense achievement of microscopic animals.

Toward evening, Clermont-Tonnerre faded away into the distance, and the *Nautilus* changed her course somewhat. After touching the Tropic of Capricorn at longitude 135°, we sailed west-northwest, following the whole of the intertropical zone. Although the summer sun was consistently hot, we did not suffer at all from the heat, for at fifteen or twenty fathoms' depth, the temperature did not rise above 50°-55° F.

On the 15th of December, we left the charming archipelago of the Society Islands, and graceful Tahiti, queen of the Pacific, to the east. In the morning, I saw a few miles to leeward the high summits of that island. Its waters supplied our kitchen with excellent fish, including mackerel, bonitos, albacores, and some varieties of sea serpent known as the moray eel.

The *Nautilus* had traveled 8,000 miles. The log read 9,720 miles when we sailed through the Tonga Islands, where the crews of the *Argo*, the *Port-au-Prince*, and the *Duke of Portland* perished, and the archipelago of Navigators, where Captain Langle, the friend of La Pérouse, was killed. Then we sighted the archipelago of Viti, where savages massacred both the crew of the *Union* and Captain Bureau of Nantes, who commanded the *Aimable-Joséphine*.

This archipelago, which extends over a distance of a hundred leagues from north to south and ninety leagues from east to west, is situated between latitude 6° and 2° south, and between longitude 174° and 179° west. It consists of a number of islands, islets, and reefs, among which are the islands of Viti-Levu, Vanoua-Levu, and Kandubon.

Tasman discovered this group in 1643, the very year in which Torricelli invented the barometer and Louis XIV ascended the throne. I leave it to the reader to decide which of these three men benefited humanity most. Then came Cook in 1714, d'Entrecasteaux in 1793, and, lastly, Dumont-d'Urville in 1827, who disentangled the geographical chaos of this archipelago. The *Nautilus* sailed close to the Bay of Wailea, the scene of the terrible adventures of Captain Dillon, who was the first to throw light on the mystery of the wreck in which La Pérouse had met his end.

We dragged our nets across this bay several times, and collected a large quantity of excellent oysters. We opened them at the table, following the advice of Seneca, and gorged ourselves. These mollusks belonged to a species, known by the name of ostrea lamellosa, which is very common in Corsica. The oyster bed at Wailea must have been immense, and if it had not been kept under control by various means, the accumulation of these shellfish would have filled the bays, since each oyster can produce as many as two million eggs.

If Master Ned Land had no reason to repent of his gluttony on this occasion, it was because the oyster is the only food that never causes indigestion. Indeed, a man must eat no less than sixteen dozen of these acephalous mollusks to provide himself with the 315 grams of nitrogen necessary for his daily diet.

On the 25th of December, the *Nautilus* sailed into the midst of the archipelago of the New Hebrides, discovered by Quiros in 1606, explored by Bougainville in 1768, and given their present name by Cook in 1773. This group consists mainly of nine large islands that form a strip measuring 120 leagues from north-northwest to south-southeast, between latitudes 15° and 2° south, longitudes 164° and 168°. We passed near the island of Aurou, which, when we saw it at midday, looked like a mass of green woods, dominated by a very high peak.

That day Ned Land seemed to resent the lack of a Christmas celebration, a family occasion that Protestants observe with great fervor.

I had not seen Captain Nemo for a week when, on the morning of the 27th, he came into the big saloon, looking, as usual, like someone who had been absent five minutes.

I was busy following the route of the *Nautilus* on the planisphere when the Captain came up and put his finger on a point on the map and uttered just one word:

"Vanikoro."

This was the name of the islands where the ships of La Pérouse had sunk. I jumped to my feet immediately.

"Are we going to Vanikoro?" I asked.

"Yes, Monsieur le Professeur," replied the Captain.

"And shall we visit those famous islands on which the *Boussole* and the *Astrolabe* were wrecked?"

"If you wish, Professor."

"When will we be in Vanikoro?"

"We are there now, Professor."

136

Followed by Captain Nemo, I went up to the platform, and from there I scanned the horizon with great interest.

To the northeast, two volcanic islands of different size emerged, surrounded by a coral reef whose perimeter measured forty miles. This was the island of Vanikoro, which Dumont d'Urville named the Isle de la Recherche. We were facing the little haven of Vanou, situated at latitude 16° 4′ south by longitude 164° 32′ east. The land seemed to be covered with greenery from the shore right up to the peaks inland, dominated by Mount Kapogo, 2,856 feet high.

After penetrating the outer ring of rocks through a narrow strait, the *Nautilus* found itself inside the reef, in thirty to forty fathoms of water. In the green shade of the mangroves I saw savages, a dozen or so, who showed great surprise at our approach. Did they think, perhaps, that the long black body coming toward them on the surface of the water was some kind of formidable cetacean, against which they should be on their guard?

Just then Captain Nemo asked me what I knew about the shipwreck of La Pérouse.

"Only what everybody else knows, Captain," I replied.

"Would you mind telling me what everybody else knows?" he said in a somewhat ironical tone.

"No trouble at all."

I told him what the last works of Dumont d'Urville had made known. Here is a brief summary of them.

La Pérouse and his second-in-command, Captain de Langle, were sent by Louis XVI, in 1785, to sail around the world. They set forth in the corvettes *La Boussole* and *l'Astrolabe*, which were never seen again.

In 1791 the French Government, understandably worried about the fate of the two corvettes, manned and equipped two big supply ships, the *Recherche* and the *Espérance*, which set sail from Brest on the 28th of September, under the orders of Bruni d'Entrecasteaux. Two months later, it was learned through the report of a certain Captain Bowen of the *Albemarle* that the wreckage of ships had been seen on the coast of New Georgia. D'Entrecasteaux, however, paid no attention to this report—which, be it said, seemed somewhat dubious—and made for the Admiralty Islands, mentioned in a report of Captain Hunter as the place where La Pérouse's ship had been wrecked.

But his search was in vain. The *Espérance* and the *Recherche* sailed past Vanikoro without stopping, and, in short, this voyage was disastrous, because D'Entrecasteaux, two of his lieutenants, and several members of the crew lost their lives.

137

The first person to find indisputable traces of the wrecks was an experienced old sailor of the Pacific, Captain Dillon. On the 15th of May, 1824, his ship, the *St. Patrick,* was off the island of Tikopia, one of the New Hebrides group, when a Lascar came alongside in a canoe and sold him a silver sword handle with engraved characters on the hilt. The Lascar maintained moreover that six years earlier, during a visit to Vanikoro, he had seen two Europeans belonging to ships that had been wrecked many years before on the reefs of the island.

Dillon guessed that they must be the ships of La Pérouse, whose disappearance had caused a stir throughout the world. So he decided to go to Vanikoro, where, according to the Lascar, there was a lot of wreckage to be seen; however, adverse winds and currents prevented him from doing so.

Dillon, therefore, returned to Calcutta, where he succeeded in arousing the interest of the Asiatic Society and the East India Company. A ship, which was given the name of *Recherche,* was placed at his disposal, and he set sail on the 23rd of January, 1827, accompanied by a French deputy.

The *Recherche,* after calling at several points in the Pacific, dropped anchor off Vanikoro on the 7th of July, 1827, in the very harbor of Vanou where the *Nautilus* was anchored at this moment.

There, Dillon collected numerous remains of the wreck: iron utensils, anchors, parts of pulley blocks, swivel guns, an eighteen-pound cannonball, pieces of navigation instruments, a section of taffrail, and a bronze bell bearing the inscription *"Bazin m'a fait"* ("Bazin made me"), the foundry mark of the arsenal of Brest about the year 1785. There were no longer any possible doubts.

Dillon, completing his investigation, remained at this sinister location until October. Then he left Vanikoro, sailed toward New Zealand, putting into Calcutta on the 7th of April, 1828, and returned to France, where he was given a warm welcome by King Charles X.

At the same time, Dumont d'Urville, knowing nothing of Dillon's search, had already gone elsewhere to look for the wreck. A whaler had reported that medals and a cross of Saint-Louis had been seen in the possession of savages in Louisiade and New Caledonia.

D'Urville, commanding the *Astrolabe,* had therefore set sail and reached the port of Hobart Town two months after Dillon had left Vanikoro. There, he learned the results achieved by Dillon, and was told, in addition, that a certain James Hobbs, second-in-command of the *Union* of Calcutta, having landed on an island situated at latitude 8° 18′ south and longitude 156° 30′ east, had noticed that the natives of these regions were using iron bars and red cloth.

Dumont d'Urville was perplexed; he was undecided whether he should believe these reports published by newspapers of questionable integrity. Nevertheless, he decided to follow Dillon's trail.

On the 10th of February, 1828, the *Astrolabe* called at Tikopia, where she took on, as a guide and interpreter, a deserter who had been living on that island, and made for Vanikoro. She sighted the latter island on the 12th of February, sailed along its reefs until the 14th, and, on the 20th, finally anchored within the barrier, in the harbor of Vanou.

Several officers made a tour of the island on the 23rd, and brought back some unimportant trifles. The natives, resorting to evasions and other subterfuges, refused to lead them to the scene of the wreck. This shifty behavior made the Frenchmen think they had ill-treated the shipwrecked sailors, and indeed, the natives did seem to fear that Dumont d'Urville had come to avenge La Pérouse and his unfortunate companions.

On the 26th, however, realizing that there were to be no reprisals and persuaded by gifts, they conducted Jacquinot, the second-in-command, to the wreck.

There, in two or three fathoms of water, between the reefs of Pacou and Vanou, lay anchors, guns, and pigs of lead and iron, all caked with limy secretions. The sloop and the whaler of the *Astrolabe* were sent to the spot, and after much effort, their crews succeeded in hauling up an eighteen-hundred-pound anchor, a cast-iron cannonball, a lead pig, and two copper swivel guns.

Questioning the natives, Dumont d'Urville learned also that La Pérouse, after having lost his two ships on the reefs of the island, had built a smaller ship, only to go down a second time—where? No one knew.

The captain of the *Astrolabe* then had a memorial built in honor of the famous navigator and his crew. This was a simple quadrangular pyramid, set on a coral base, with no metal fittings that might have tempted the covetousness of the natives. Dumont d'Urville was ready to leave, but the health of his crew had been seriously undermined by fever caused by the unhealthful climate, and, very ill himself, he could not set sail until the 17th of March.

In the meantime the French Government, fearing that Dumont d'Urville had not been informed of Dillon's researches, had sent the corvette *La Bayonnaise* to Vanikoro. The corvette had been stationed on the west coast of America, and was commanded by Legoarant de Tromelin. The *Bayonnaise* reached Vanikoro a few months after the *Astrolabe* had left, obtained no new information, but noted that the savages had respected the memorial put up to La Pérouse.

Such was the gist of the story I told Captain Nemo.

"So," he said to me, "no one knows what happened to the third ship built by those shipwrecked sailors on the island of Vanikoro?"

"No, no one knows."

Captain Nemo did not say anything, but motioned to me to follow him into the big saloon. The *Nautilus* submerged a few yards below the waves, and the panels opened.

I rushed to the window, and there, under a thick coat of coral, covered with fungi, siphonules, aleyonarians, madrepores, through myriads of very attractive fish—girelles, glyphisidons, pompheridae diacopae, holocentri—I recognized debris that d'Urville had not been able to dredge up: iron stirrups, anchors, cannon, gunshot, capstan fittings, the stem of a boat—all objects clearly showing the wreck of some vessel, now carpeted with living flowers.

As I surveyed this scene of desolation, Captain Nemo said to me in a serious voice:

"Captain La Pérouse set sail on the 7th of December, 1785, with his ships *La Boussole* and *l'Astrolabe*. First he dropped anchor in Botany Bay, visited the Friendly Isles and New Caledonia, then made for Santa Cruz and put into Namouka, one of the islands of the Hapai group. Then his ships struck the unknown reefs of Vanikoro. The *Boussole*, which was leading, ran aground on the south coast. The *Astrolabe* came to her aid and suffered the same fate. The first ship went down almost immediately, the second, stranded to leeward, lasted a few days. The natives gave the shipwrecked sailors a friendly reception. They settled on the island and built a smaller vessel with the debris of the two large ships. Some of the sailors actually decided of their own free will to stay in Vanikoro. The rest, weak and ill, left with La Pérouse. They sailed in the direction of the Solomon Islands and they perished, to a man, on the west coast of the principal island of that group, between Cape Deception and Cape Satisfaction."

"But how do you know all this?" I exclaimed.

"Here is something I found on the very scene of the last wreck."

Captain Nemo showed me a tin box, stamped with the French coat-of-arms and corroded by the salt water. He opened it and I saw a sheaf of papers, yellow and discolored, but still legible.

They were the orders issued by the Minister of the Navy

himself to Captain La Pérouse, with notations in the margin in the hand of Louis XVI himself!

"A fine death for a sailor!" said Captain Nemo. "A coral tomb is a peaceful tomb—and may heaven bless me and my companions with no other!"

Chapter XX

THE TORRES STRAIT

DURING THE NIGHT of the 27th and the 28th of December, the *Nautilus* left Vanikoro at great speed. Her direction was southwest, and in three days she had covered the 750 leagues that separate La Pérouse's group from the southeast point of Papua.

Early in the morning, on the 1st of January, 1868, Conseil joined me on the platform.

"Will Monsieur permit me to wish him a Happy New Year?"

"Well, well, Conseil! It's just as if I were in Paris, in my study, at the Jardin des Plantes. I accept your good wishes with pleasure and thank you. But I should like to know what you mean by 'A Happy New Year,' under the present circumstances. Will this year see the end of our imprisonment, or will it see the continuation of this strange voyage?"

"Really I am at a loss to answer Monsieur," replied Conseil. "We are seeing some very strange things, and for the past two months we haven't had time to be bored. It is strange indeed! Every new marvel we see is more astonishing than the preceding one, and if this continues, who knows what the end will be. Nevertheless, we will certainly never have another opportunity like this."

"Never, Conseil."

"Besides, Monsieur Nemo, who more than justifies his Latin name, couldn't trouble us less, even if he didn't exist." *

"I am inclined to agree, Conseil."

"I should say, then, if Monsieur doesn't mind my saying so, that a good year would be a year that would enable us to see everything. . . ."

"See everything, Conseil? That might take a long time. What does Ned Land think of all this?"

"Ned Land disagrees with me in everything," replied Con-

* *Nemo* means, in Latin, "nobody," "no man," "no one."—M.T.B.

142

seil. "He's a positive thinker with an imperious stomach. For any Anglo-Saxon worthy of the name the lack of bread and meat, especially beefsteaks, the lack of brandy or gin, drunk in moderation, is unthinkable."

"As far as I am concerned, Conseil, nothing like that disturbs me. I have no difficulty whatsoever in adjusting to the diet on board."

"Neither have I," replied Conseil. "And I am as anxious to remain here as Master Land is to escape. If the year which is just beginning isn't a good one for me, it will be for him, and vice-versa. No matter what happens, someone will always be pleased. But for Monsieur, I wish him everything that may give him pleasure."

"Thank you, Conseil. However, a New Year's gift is out of the question now. A good handshake will have to do for the moment. It is all I have to give."

"Monsieur has never been more generous," replied Conseil, whereupon the good lad left me.

On the 2nd of January, we had traveled 11,340 miles, or 5,250 leagues, since we had left the waters of Japan. Before the *Nautilus* stretched the dangerous waters of the Coral Sea, on the northeast of Australia. Our ship was cruising along not far from that dangerous bank on which Cook's ships had almost been lost on the 10th of June, 1770. Cook's ship struck a rock and did not sink only because a piece of coral, detached by the collision, remained lodged in the hole in the hull.

I should have been delighted to visit that reef, which is 360 leagues long and against which the sea, always turbulent, breaks with tremendous power and makes a noise like the rumble of thunder. But at that moment the fins of the *Nautilus* were steering us down to a great depth, and I could see nothing of the high coral walls. I had to be satisfied to study the fish that had been brought up in our nets. I found some albacore, a species of mackerel as large as a tunny, with bluish sides and transverse stripes that actually disappear when the animal dies! These fish followed us in schools, and provided us with very delicate fare. We also took a large number of giltheads, about two inches long, which taste like dories, and flying pyrapedes, real underwater swallows, which, on a dark night, light first the air and then the water with their phosphorescent glow. Among mollusks and zoophytes we caught several species of alcyonarians, echinids, hammer shells, spur shells, sundials, cerithidea, and hyalleae. The flora gave us some beautiful floating seaweeds, laminariae, and macrocystes, impregnated with that mucilage that seeps through their pores. I found also an admirable Nemastoma geliniaroida, which we classified among the natural curiosities of the museum.

Two days after crossing the Coral Sea, on the 4th of January, we came to the Papuan coast, and Captain Nemo took the opportunity to inform me that he intended to reach the Indian Ocean through the Torres Strait. That was all he said. Ned was pleased, for this route would bring him closer to the waters of Europe.

The Torres Strait is considered dangerous not only because of the reefs with which it bristles, but also because of the savages that inhabit its coasts. It separates New Holland from the large island of Papua, also known as New Guinea. Papua is 400 leagues long by 130 leagues wide, and has a surface of 40,000 geographical leagues. The position is between latitudes 0° 19′ and 10° 2′ south, and longitudes 128° 23′ and 146° 15′. At midday, as the second-in-command measured the height of the sun, I noticed the peaks of the Arfalx Mountains, which are very pointed and stand out, one behind the other, at different levels.

This country, discovered in 1511 by the Portuguese Francisco Serrano, was visited successively by Don José de Meneses in 1526, by Grijalva in 1527, by the Spanish General Alvar de Saavedra in 1528, by Juigo Ortez in 1545, by the Dutchman Shouten in 1616, by Nicolas Sruic in 1753, by Tasman, Dampier, Fumel, Carteret, Edwards, Bougainville, Cook, Forrest, MacClure, and by d'Entrecasteaux in 1792, by Duperrey in 1823, and by Dumont d'Urville in 1827. "This is the very heart of the territory occupied by the 'Blacks' * of the Malayan Archipelago," Monsieur de Rienzi has said. I had few doubts that the hazards of this passage would bring me face to face with the redoubtable Andamans.

The *Nautilus* was ready to enter the most dangerous strait in the world, one that even the most courageous navigators scarcely dare attempt—a strait that Luis Paz de Torres braved on his return to Melanesia from the South Seas and that, in 1840, nearly brought total disaster to the battered corvettes of Dumont d'Urville. The *Nautilus*, although superior in facing all the dangers of the sea, was going to face those coral reefs also.

The Torres Strait is about thirty-four leagues wide, obstructed by countless islands, islets, breakers, and rocks that make it almost impossible to navigate. Consequently, Captain

* Verne is not referring to the Melanesian inhabitants of the Andaman Islands but rather to the small tribes of aborigines who lived in the more inaccessible regions of the island and who were still practicing head-hunting and cannibalism.—M.T.B.

Nemo took all the necessary precautions to effect passage. The *Nautilus*, just touching the surface, moved forward at a moderate speed, while her propeller, like a cetacean's tail, beat the waves slowly.

Taking advantage of this situation, my two companions and I had taken our places on the platform, which was deserted. In front of us protruded the steersman's cage, and unless I was very much mistaken, Captain Nemo himself must have been there, directing the movements of the *Nautilus*.

I had before me some excellent charts of the Torres Strait, surveyed and drawn by the hydrographical engineer Vincendon Dumoulin and Ensign Coupvent-Desbois, now an admiral, both of whom served on the staff of Dumont d'Urville on his last voyage of circumnavigation. These maps, together with those made by Captain King, are the best ones to untangle the complications of this narrow passage, and I examined them with close attention.

The waters around the *Nautilus* surged and seethed furiously. The current, running southeast to northwest at a speed of 2½ miles, broke on the coral visible here and there.

"That's a nasty sea indeed!" said Ned Land.

"Quite detestable," I agreed, "and it is not at all suited to a ship such as the *Nautilus*."

"This damned captain," said the Canadian, "must be certain of his course, 'cause I can see some patches of coral that would smash his hull to a thousand pieces if he even touched them!"

The situation was indeed perilous, but the *Nautilus* seemed to slip through the menacing reefs as if by magic. She was not following exactly the same route as the *Astrolabe* and the *Zélée*, which proved fatal to Dumont d'Urville; instead, she navigated further north, coasted along Murray Island and came back southwest toward Cumberland Passage. I thought we were going to sail right through it when, turning back to the northwest, we sailed through a series of little-known islets toward Tound Island and Mauvais Channel: the Evil Channel.

I wondered whether Captain Nemo, foolhardy as he was, would commit his ship to this passage where Dumont d'Urville's two corvettes had run aground, when, changing his course for a second time and cutting straight through to the west, he made for the island of Gueboroar.

It was then three o'clock in the afternoon. The sea was covered with breakers and it was nearly high tide. The *Nautilus* approached the island, which I can always recall because of its unusual fringe of pandanus, or screw pines. We were skirting it at a distance of less than two miles.

Suddenly I was thrown on the deck. The *Nautilus* had just struck a reef, and was lying motionless with a slight list to port.

When I got up, I saw Captain Nemo and his second-in-command on the platform. They examined the ship's position and discussed it in their incomprehensible idiom.

This was the situation: two miles to starboard lay the island of Gueboroar, whose coast curved from north to west like a huge arm. Toward the south and east we could see crests of coral, bared by the ebbtide. We had run aground in one of those seas where the tides are moderate—a difficult situation for refloating the *Nautilus*. However, so solidly was she built that she had suffered no damage. But if she could neither float nor move, she ran the risk of being stuck on these rocks forever. If such were the case, Captain Nemo's submarine would be done for.

I was thinking about all this when the Captain, cool, calm, and in complete control of himself—he seemed neither excited nor vexed—came up to me.

"An accident?" I asked him.

"No," he replied, "an incident."

"Nevertheless, an incident," I rejoined, "that may force you to become once more an inhabitant of the land you abhor."

Captain Nemo gave me a curious look and shook his head, by which he clearly meant that nothing would ever compel him to set foot on land again. Then he said:

"Monsieur Aronnax, the *Nautilus* is not incapacitated. She will continue to carry you through the marvels of the ocean. Our voyage has only just begun, and I have no wish to deprive myself of the honor of your company so soon."

"But Captain Nemo," I went on, pretending not to notice the ironical tone of his words, "the *Nautilus* has run aground at high tide. As you know, the tides are not very strong in the Pacific, and if you cannot lighten the *Nautilus*—which seems impossible to me—I do not see how you can refloat her."

"You are right, Professor," replied Captain Nemo, "the tides are not very strong in the Pacific, but, in the Torres Strait, there is a difference in some places of four to five feet between high tide and low tide. Today is the fourth of January; within five days we shall have a full moon. Now, I should be very much surprised if that obliging satellite were not to raise the water sufficiently to render me a service—a service for which I shall be indebted to her alone."

146

Without another word, Captain Nemo, followed by his lieutenant, went back down into the *Nautilus*. The ship remained motionless, as if the coral polyps had already cemented her in their construction.

"Well, monsieur?" said Ned Land, coming up to me when the Captain had gone below.

"Well, Ned, we will have to wait until the high tide on the ninth; apparently the moon will be thoughtful enough to refloat us on that date."

"As easy as all that?"

"As easy as all that."

"Why doesn't the Captain cast his anchors into the deep, set his engines to pull on the chains, and do everything to set himself free?"

"Why do that if the tide will do it?" Conseil replied simply.

The Canadian looked at Conseil and shrugged his shoulders. It was the sailor in him speaking.

"Let me tell you, Professor," he said. "You can believe me when I tell you that this piece of scrap iron will never sail again, either on or under the water. She's only good now to be sold as scrap iron. I think the moment has now come to part company with Captain Nemo."

"Ned," I replied, "I do not believe the *Nautilus'* situation is as bad as all that; in four days we shall know how far we can rely on these Pacific tides. Incidentally, it might be advisable to escape if we were off the coast of England or of Provence, but we are off the coast of Papua, which is quite different. There will be time enough to think seriously about that if the *Nautilus* cannot be refloated. That, I think, would leave us in a very deplorable situation."

"But don't you think we should at least see what the land is like?" Ned Land continued. "Look, there is an island. On that island there are trees; under those trees there are animals, purveyors of chops and steaks, which I wouldn't mind getting my teeth into."

"Ned is right about that," said Conseil. "I agree with him. Could not Monsieur obtain permission from his friend Captain Nemo to have us taken ashore, just so we don't lose the feel of terra firma?"

"I can ask him," I replied. "But I know he will refuse."

"Let Monsieur risk it," said Conseil. "We will at least know how much we can depend on the Captain's good nature."

Much to my surprise, Captain Nemo granted me the permission I asked. He did so very graciously and willingly, without so much as asking me to promise to return on board.

But a flight through the wilds of New Guinea would be a very perilous undertaking, and I should not have advised Ned Land to attempt it. Better to be a prisoner aboard the *Nautilus* than to fall into the hands of the Papuan natives.

The dinghy was placed at our disposal for the following morning, and I did not try to find out whether Captain Nemo would be accompanying us. I did not even imagine that any member of the crew would row the boat, but that Ned Land would be given that task. The land was only two miles away at the most, and it was only child's play for the Canadian to steer the light dinghy between the reefs so fatal to big ships.

The next day, the 5th of January, the dinghy was uncovered, removed from its compartment, and launched into the sea from the top of the platform. Two men were sufficient for this operation. The oars were already in the boat, and all we had to do was take our seats.

At eight o'clock, armed with electric rifles and hatchets, we cast off from the *Nautilus*. The sea was fairly calm, and there was a slight breeze offshore. Conseil and I took the oars and rowed briskly, while Ned steered us through the narrow channels between the breakers. The dinghy was easy to handle, and cut through the waters at a good rate.

Ned Land could not contain his joy. He was like a prisoner just escaped from jail, and the thought that he would have to return never entered his mind.

"Meat!" he kept repeating. "We're going to have meat! Real meat and real game! What if there isn't any bread! Mind you, I don't say that fish isn't good, but it's not good to overdo it! A piece of fresh venison, grilled on the hot coals, will be a nice change from our usual diet."

"Gourmand!" retorted Conseil. "You're making my mouth water."

"It remains to be seen," I said, "whether or not there is any game in these forests, and if so, whether the game is of the kind and size that is more likely to hunt than be hunted."

"Perhaps so, Monsieur Aronnax," replied the Canadian, whose teeth seemed to have been whetted like the blade of an ax, "but I would eat a tiger if there's no other quadruped on this island—a nice loin of tiger would be just the thing!"

"Ned worries me," said Conseil.

"Well, whatever you say," continued Ned Land, "any animal that has four legs and no feathers, or two legs and feathers, will be my first target!"

"I see!" I replied. "Master Land's indiscretions are about to start all over again!"

"No fear of that, Monsieur Aronnax," rejoined the Canadian. "Just keep rowing! In less than half an hour, I promise you one of my tasty dishes."

At half past eight the dinghy landed gently on a patch of sand, having successfully crossed the coral reef encircling the island of Gueboroar.

Chapter XXI

A FEW DAYS ON LAND

IT WAS EXCITING to be setting foot on land again! Ned felt the ground with his foot, as if he were taking formal possession of it. Two months had passed since we had become, to quote Captain Nemo, "passengers on board the *Nautilus*"— but, in reality, prisoners of her Captain.

A few minutes later, we were about a gunshot away from the shore. The soil was almost entirely madreporal, but some dried-up beds of streams, strewn with granite debris, showed that the island was of primordial formation. The horizon was hidden behind a curtain of magnificent forest. Gigantic trees, sometimes as much as two hundred feet high, were joined to each other by garlands of trumpet vines, which formed natural hammocks that a light breeze could rock to and fro. There were mimosas, rubber trees, casuarinas, teaks, hibiscus, pandanus, and palm trees, mingling in great profusion; and in the shadow of their green vault, at the foot of their huge trunks, grew orchids, leguminous plants, and ferns. The Canadian, however, did not notice all these magnificent examples of Papuan flora, rejecting the pleasant in favor of the useful. Soon he spied a coconut palm, knocked down some of its fruit and opened them, and we drank the milk and ate the meat with a relish that was a protest against the regular fare on board the *Nautilus*.

"Excellent!" Ned Land said.

"Exquisite!" answered Conseil.

"Do you suppose," asked the Canadian, "your Captain Nemo would object to our bringing a load of coconuts on board?"

"I do not think so," I replied, "but he will not want to taste any!"

"So much the worse for him!" said Conseil.

"And so much the better for us!" retorted Ned Land. "There'll be more for us to eat."

"I should just like to say one thing, Master Land," I said to the harpooner, as he was getting ready to ravage another coconut palm. "The coconut is a good thing, but before filling the boat with them, don't you think it would be better to find

150

out whether this island produces something else equally useful? Fresh vegetables, for instance, would be well received on board the *Nautilus*."

"Monsieur is right," replied Conseil, "and I propose that we reserve three spaces in our boat: one for fruit, another for vegetables, and the third for venison, of which I haven't yet seen the slightest sign."

"You must not give up hope, Conseil," replied the Canadian.

"So let us move on," I interjected, "and keep our eyes open. Although the island appears to be uninhabited, it may well harbor some natives who are less fussy than we are about the nature of the game!"

"Ha, ha!" said Ned Land, moving his jaws up and down very significantly.

"Ned, how can you!" exclaimed Conseil.

"Yes," replied the Canadian, "I'm beginning to understand the charms of cannibalism!"

"What are you saying, Ned!" cried Conseil. "You a cannibal! I won't feel safe sharing my cabin with you if you talk like that! Do you think I want to wake up some morning and find myself half devoured?"

"Friend Conseil, I'm very fond of you, but not enough to want to eat you, unless I have to!"

"I'm not sure I trust you," replied Conseil. "Come on, let's start hunting! We've simply got to shoot some game to satisfy this cannibal, or else, one of these mornings, Monsieur will find only a few bits of his servant left over to wait on him."

While this banter was going on, we were passing beneath the somber arches of the jungle. For two hours we wandered about in all directions.

We were fortunate in our search for edible vegetables, for one of the most useful plants of the tropics provided us with a valuable food that had been lacking on board ship.

This was the breadfruit tree, very plentiful on the island of Gueboroar, and the type I noticed was the seedless one, known to the Malays as *rima*.

This tree was different from the others, since it had a tall straight trunk about forty feet high. Its top was gracefully rounded and made up of large, multilobed leaves, which made it easily identifiable to a naturalist as the artocarpus, successfully grown in the Mascarene Islands in the Indian Ocean. Great globe-shaped fruits hung down from the heavy foliage; they measured about four inches across, and were marked on their outside rind with hexagonal furrows. This useful vegetable has been a blessing in areas lacking wheat,

151

for without having to be cultivated or cared for, it produces fruit for eight months of the year.

Ned Land was well acquainted with this fruit, having already eaten it on numerous voyages, and he knew how to prepare the edible part. Moreover, the sight of it aroused in him an irrepressible desire.

"Professor," he said to me, "I'll die if I don't have some of that breadfruit!"

"Then by all means have some, Ned. Have as much as you want. We are here to gain experience, so let us gain it."

"It won't take long," replied the Canadian, and with the aid of a magnifying glass, he lit a fire of dead wood, which was soon crackling merrily. While he was doing this, Conseil and I were selecting the best fruit of the artocarpus. Some of them had not yet reached a sufficient degree of ripeness, and their thick rind concealed a white pulp that had not yet become fibrous. On the other hand, there were a great many others that were yellowish and glutinous in consistency, just waiting to be picked.

This fruit had no kernel. Conseil brought a dozen of them to Ned Land, who placed them, cut into thick slices on the charcoal fire, repeating as he did so:

"You'll see how good this bread is, monsieur!"

"Especially when one has had to go without for so long," said Conseil.

"It's more than just bread," added the Canadian. "It's a delicate pastry. Haven't you ever had any, sir?"

"No, Ned."

"Well, get ready to have something really tasty. If you don't come back for more, I'm no longer the king of harpooners!"

After a few minutes, the part of the fruit nearest the flames was completely charred. Inside there was a sort of white paste, like soft bread crumbs, whose taste was reminiscent of artichoke.

I found the bread excellent and ate it with great gusto.

"Unfortunately," I said, "this stuff cannot be kept, and there doesn't seem to be much point in collecting a supply to take back to the ship."

"What do you mean!" cried Ned Land. "You're talking like a naturalist, but I'm going to act like a baker. Conseil, go and collect some of this fruit, and we'll pick them up on the way back."

"How do you prepare them?" I asked the Canadian.

"By making a fermented paste with the pulp that will keep indefinitely and not go bad. When I want to have some, I'll have it cooked by the galley, and you'll see, it'll taste good even if it is a bit acid."

"So this kind of bread doesn't need anything to go with it, Ned?"

"Oh yes it does, Professor," replied the Canadian. "You need some fruit, or at any rate some vegetables."

"So let us look for fruit and vegetables."

When we had finished collecting the breadfruit, we set out to complete our "onshore" provisions.

Our search was not in vain, for by midday we had collected an ample supply of bananas. This delicious product of torrid zones ripens throughout the year, and the Malays, who call them *pisang,* eat them without cooking them. Together with these bananas we picked some enormous jackfruit, which have a very pronounced taste, some juicy mangoes, and some incredibly big pineapples. Our harvesting took up quite a lot of time, but we didn't mind.

Conseil kept watching Ned. The harpooner walked ahead through the jungle, pausing now and again to pick, with an expert hand, the excellent fruits needed to complete his supplies.

"Well," asked Conseil, "do we need anything else now, Ned?"

"Hum!" was all the Canadian said.

"What! Aren't you satisfied?"

"All these vegetables don't make a meal," replied Ned. "They're only the trimmings, or the dessert. What about the soup and the roast?"

"Come to think of it, you are right," I said. "Ned promised us some cutlets, but I do not think we will get them."

"Monsieur," said the Canadian, "the hunt isn't over yet; it hasn't even begun. Patience, my friends! We will certainly come across some flesh or fowl, here or elsewhere."

"And if it isn't today, it will be tomorrow," added Conseil. "We shouldn't go too far, though. I suggest we return to the boat."

"What! Already!" cried Ned.

"We will have to get back before nightfall," I said.

"What time is it?" asked the Canadian.

"It must be at least two o'clock," replied Conseil.

"How time flies on dry land!" exclaimed Ned Land with a sigh of regret.

"Let's go back," replied Conseil.

We walked back through the forest, completing our harvest by raiding the cabbage palms, which had to be picked by climbing trees, some small beans, which I recognized as the *abrou* of the Malays, and some yams of superior quality.

When we reached the boat, we were weighted down with provisions. Even so, Ned Land found we hadn't enough. Luck was with him, for just as we were about to climb in, he noticed some trees, twenty-five or thirty feet high, belonging to the palm family. These trees, which are as valuable as the breadfruit, are justly considered one of the most useful in the Malay Archipelago.

They were sago palms, plants that grow wild and, like blackberry bushes, multiply by means of their sprouts and berries.

Ned Land certainly knew how to work with trees. Taking his ax and wielding it with great vigor, he soon felled two or three sago palms, whose maturity could be determined by the white dust on their leaves.

More as a naturalist than as a hungry man, I watched him work. He began by stripping a piece of bark off each trunk; this bark was about an inch thick, and was covered with a network of long fibers, which formed inextricable knots held together with a sort of glutinous flour. This flour was the sago, an edible substance used mainly for food by the Malayans.

For the time being, Ned was content to cut the trunks into chunks, as though he were collecting firewood; later on, he would extract the flour and sift it through a piece of cloth to separate it from its fibrous ligaments, before drying it in the sun and letting it harden into little balls.

At last, at five o'clock in the evening, loaded with all our treasures, we left the island, and half an hour later reached the *Nautilus*. No one came out to receive us. The enormous steel cylinder seemed deserted. So, after taking the provisions on board, I went to my room. My supper was ready, and after supper I went to bed.

The next day, the 6th of January, there was no new development on board—not a sound inside the ship, not a sign of life. The dinghy had remained alongside the *Nautilus* just where we had left it. We decided to return to the island of Gueboroar. Ned Land hoped to have better luck than the day before and wanted to hunt in another part of the forest.

At sunrise we were already on our way. The boat sailed easily with the waves that carried us straight toward the shore, and reached the island in a few minutes.

We disembarked, and deciding that the best plan was to rely on Ned Land's instinct, we followed the Canadian, whose long legs threatened to outdistance us.

Ned went westward along the coast, and then, fording some streams, came to the plateau, which was fringed with magnificent forests. There were some kingfishers flitting along the water's edge, but we couldn't get near them. Their caution proved to me that these birds knew what to do when dealing with bipeds like us, and I realized that if the island were not inhabited, it was, at least, frequented by human beings.

After crossing a fairly wide expanse of grassland, we came to the edge of a little forest, animated with the song and flutter of numerous birds.

"Only birds here," said Conseil.

"Yes, but some are good to eat!" replied the harpooner.

"Not at all, Ned," replied Conseil. "I see only parrots here."

"Conseil," said Ned seriously, "the parrot is a pheasant to those who have nothing better to eat."

"And let me add," I interposed, "that, properly prepared, it is by no means to be despised."

Indeed, beneath the dense foliage of this wood, a world of parrots flitted from branch to branch, just waiting for a better education to learn how to speak a human language. At that time, however, they kept chattering with multicolored parakeets and solemn-looking cockatoos, who seemed to be meditating on some philosophical problem, while bright red lories flashed to and fro, like streaks of bunting blown in by the wind, amidst the noisy flight of kalaos and Papuans of the finest shades of blue. All in all they formed a delightful collection of birds, though none too edible.

One bird, however, was missing in this collection—a bird peculiar to this part of the world and never seen outside the Aru and Papuan Islands. But I was destined to admire it before long.

Having passed through a fairly dense thicket, we came on a plain covered with bushes. It was then that I saw rising in the sky some magnificent birds, whose long feathers compelled them to fly against the wind. Their undulating flight, the grace with which they swept through the air, and the beauty of their colors were truly enchanting to the eyes. I had no difficulty in recognizing them.

"Birds of paradise!" I cried.

"Of the order of sparrows, section of clystomores," added Conseil.

"And belonging to the partridge family?" suggested Ned Land.

"I do not think so, Master Land. However, I am counting on your skill to capture one of these charming products of tropical nature!"

"I'll do my best, Professor, although I'm more accustomed to handling a harpoon than a gun."

The Malays, who sell many of these birds to the Chinese, use various means to catch them, none of which we could use. Sometimes they use snares, placed at the tops of tall trees where birds of paradise like to perch. Sometimes they catch them with a strong glue that renders them incapable of movement. They even go so far as to poison the waters where the birds are in the habit of drinking. All we could do was to shoot them on the wing, which meant that we had a very slim chance of hitting them. Indeed, we wasted a lot of ammunition.

At about eleven o'clock in the morning, we had crossed the first ridge of mountains in the center of the island without shooting anything. We were tantalized by hunger. The hunters had decided to rely for their food on the proceeds of the hunt, and had made an error in so doing! Fortunately, however, Conseil, much to his own surprise, brought down two birds with one stone, and provided lunch. He shot both a white pigeon and a ring dove, which were plucked, hung on a spit, and roasted over a glowing wood fire. While these delectable creatures were cooking, Ned prepared the breadfruit. The two birds were then devoured to the bone and declared excellent. Nutmeg, with which they stuff themselves, flavors their meat and makes it delicious.

"As good as if they had been stuffed with truffles," remarked Conseil.

"Well, Ned, what more do you want?" I asked the Canadian.

"Some four-footed game, Monsieur Aronnax," replied Ned Land. "Those birds were no more than an appetizer, something for the mouth to practice on. I will not be happy until I've killed an animal that has some good chops."

"Nor will I, Ned, until I've caught a bird of paradise."

"Well, let's get on with the hunt," said Conseil, "but let's work back towards the sea. We've gotten to the first mountain slopes, and I think it would be best to return to the forest."

Since this seemed to be a sensible piece of advice, we followed it. After walking for an hour, we came to a veritable forest of sago palms. Now and again some harmless snake darted away from under our feet. The birds of paradise fled as we approached, and I was giving up all hope of getting one when Conseil, who was walking in front, suddenly bent down with a cry of triumph and came to me with a magnificent bird of paradise.

"Bravo, Conseil!" I exclaimed.

"Monsieur is very kind," replied Conseil.

"Not at all, my lad. That was a masterstroke! To actually catch one of these birds alive, catch it with your hands!"

"If Monsieur will examine it with care, he will see that it wasn't such a difficult feat."

"Why, Conseil?"

"This bird is as drunk as a lord."

"Drunk?"

"Yes, monsieur. Drunk from all the nutmeg it was eating under the tree where I found it. Look, Ned, take a look at the disastrous effects of intemperance!"

"Hell," retorted the Canadian. "Considering all the gin I've drunk in the last two months, you can't throw *intemperance* in my teeth!"

In the meantime, I examined the strange bird. Conseil was right. The bird of paradise, inebriated by the heady nutmeg juice, was reduced to impotence. It couldn't fly; it could scarcely walk. I was little concerned about that; I decided to let it sleep it off.

The bird belonged to the most beautiful of the eight species found in Papua and the neighboring islands. He was a "great emerald," one of the rarest. He was about a foot long, his head was fairly small, and his little eyes were situated near the opening of the beak. But what a marvelous combination of colors he was: a yellow beak, brown feet and claws, nut-colored wings with purple tips, a pale yellow head and neck, an emerald throat, and a chestnut-colored breast and stomach! Two cornet-shaped, downy feathers rose above his tail, which consisted mainly of very fine, long, light feathers. This plumage added to and completed the beauty of this marvelous bird, which the natives have poetically named "the Sun Bird."

How I wished I could take this superb specimen back to Paris, as a gift to the Jardin des Plantes, which hasn't a single live specimen.

"Are they very rare?" asked the Canadian, speaking as a hunter who rarely considers game from an aesthetic point of view.

"Very rare, my friend, and especially difficult to catch alive. Even when they are dead, they still bring a big price on the market. The natives often make fake ones, just as pearls or diamonds are faked."

"What!" cried Conseil. "They fake these birds of paradise?"

"Yes, Conseil."

"Does Monsieur know how they do it?"

"I do. During the monsoon season, the birds of paradise lose the magnificent feathers around their tails, known to nat-

157

uralists as the subalary feathers. These feathers are collected by fakers, who are very skilled in the art of faking birds, using, for example, a partridge killed for that purpose. They dye the suture, varnish the bird, and send the product of their skill to European museums and collectors."

"Well," said Ned Land, "if they don't have the bird itself, they have its feathers, and unless they eat it, I don't see much harm in that!"

If my desires were satisfied by possession of a bird of paradise, the desires of the Canadian hunter were still far from quenched. Fortunately, at about two o'clock, Ned Land shot a magnificent wild pig, of the kind the natives call *bari-outang*. This animal was just what we needed to satisfy our hunger for quadruped meat, and we were happy to have it. Ned Land was very proud of his shot. Hit by an electric bullet, the pig had fallen stone-dead.

The Canadian stripped and drew the animal cleanly and cut half a dozen chops for our evening grill. We then resumed a hunt that was to be memorable for further exploits by Ned and Conseil.

Our two friends were beating the bushes when they suddenly flushed out a number of kangaroos, which made off in leaps and bounds on their springy legs. But the animals were not quick enough for our electric bullets, and they were stopped in their tracks.

"Well, Monsieur le Professeur," exclaimed Ned Land, intoxicated by the excitement of the chase, "what excellent game! Just the thing for a stew! What a wonderful supply for the *Nautilus!* Two . . . three . . . we got five of them! We'll eat all that meat ourselves, and those imbeciles in the crew will not have a single bite!"

I really believe the Canadian, carried away by his enthusiasm, would have slaughtered every one of those animals if he had not been talking so much! Instead, he had to be satisfied with a mere dozen of those marsupials, "which," said Conseil, "constitute the first order of aplacental mammals." These particular specimens were of a smaller type, a sort of "rabbit kangaroo" that lives inside tree trunks and whose speed is extraordinary. They are not very big, but their flesh is of excellent quality.

We were quite pleased with the results of our hunt. The jubilant Ned proposed that we return the next day to this enchanted island, which he wanted to depopulate of all edible quadrupeds. But he did not know that circumstances would ordain otherwise.

At six o'clock in the evening we were back on the beach. Our dinghy was in its usual place. The *Nautilus*, emerged above the water, looked like a long reef, some two miles from shore.

Without delay, Ned Land set to work preparing dinner. He was very knowledgeable about that type of cooking. Very soon the *bari-outang* chops, grilled over the embers, filled the surrounding air with a delightful, fragrant odor.

Was I beginning to be carried away by the enthusiasm of this Canadian? Was I actually intoxicated at the sight of a piece of fresh-grilled pork? May I be forgiven, just as I forgave Master Land—and for the same motives!

The dinner, it must be admitted, was excellent. The magnificent menu included two ring doves, sago paste, breadfruit, a few mangoes, a half a dozen pineapples. The fermented juice of coconuts added to our pleasure. And I remember that my worthy companions were not expressing themselves with their usual clarity!

"What do you say we don't go back to the *Nautilus* this evening?" suggested Conseil.

"What do you say we never go back!" added Ned Land.

Just then a stone fell in our midst, punctuating the harpooner's suggestion.

Chapter XXII

LIGHTNING ACTION BY
CAPTAIN NEMO

WITHOUT GETTING UP, we looked in the direction of the forest. My hand stopped halfway to my mouth, while Ned's, of course, was at his lips.

"A stone doesn't fall from the sky," said Conseil. "When it does, it's called a meteorite."

Just then a second stone, carefully aimed, knocked a juicy pigeon leg out of Conseil's hand, giving added weight to his remark.

We sprang to our feet, raised our rifles, and prepared to face any attack that might be forthcoming.

"Could they be monkeys?" exclaimed Ned Land.

"Or something on that order," replied Conseil. "Savages!"

"Back to the boat!" I cried, backing toward the sea.

Indeed, the time had come to beat a retreat, for a score of natives, armed with bows and slings, had appeared on the edge of a thicket, scarcely a hundred paces to our right.

Our boat was beached about twenty yards away. The savages were advancing with caution, but there was no doubt about their hostility. Stones and arrows rained about us.

Ned Land had no intention of abandoning his provisions, and despite the imminence of danger, did not retreat until he had slung his pig over one shoulder and the kangaroos over the other.

In two minutes we were at the shore. To load the boat with provisions and arms, push it out to sea, and pick up the two oars, was the work of a moment. We were scarcely more than two cables' lengths away when a hundred savages, screaming and gesticulating, waded into the water up to their waists. I glanced at the *Nautilus* to see whether the appearance of these natives had brought out any of the crew onto the platform. Not a sign. The huge craft lay motionless and silent, without a sign of life.

Twenty minutes later we were climbing on board. The panels were open. After mooring the dinghy, we went down into the interior of the *Nautilus*.

The sound of music greeted my ears when I entered

the saloon. Captain Nemo was at his organ in a mood of musical reverie.

"Captain!" I exclaimed.

He did not hear me.

"Captain!" I repeated, nudging him gently out of his reverie.

Startled, he turned around.

"Ah, it is you, Professor," he said. "Did you have a successful hunt? Did you find any botanical specimens?"

"Yes, we did, Captain," I replied. "But unfortunately, we also brought back a crowd of bipeds who seem to be getting uncomfortably close."

"Bipeds! What do you mean?"

"Savages, Captain."

"Savages!" replied Captain Nemo, not without a touch of irony. "Are you astonished, Monsieur le Professeur, that having set foot on land, you discovered savages? Is there a land that isn't infested with them? But, Monsieur le Professeur, are these people, whom you call savages, worse than those on any land?"

"But Captain—"

"All I can say, monsieur, is that they are to be found everywhere."

"Well," I replied, "unless you want to entertain them on board the *Nautilus*, you would do well to take some precautions."

"Be reassured, Professor, there is nothing to be concerned about."

"But there are many of them."

"How many did you count?"

"A hundred, at least."

"Monsieur Aronnax," replied Captain Nemo, whose fingers had wandered back to the organ keys. "If all the natives of Papua were gathered on the beach ready to attack, the *Nautilus* would still have nothing to fear."

As the Captain's fingers ran nimbly over the keyboard, I noticed he was touching only the black keys, which gave his music an essentially Scottish flavor. Soon, lost in musical reverie, he had forgotten my presence, and I made no attempt to disturb him.

I went back on the platform. Night had fallen. In this low latitude the sun sets suddenly. There is no twilight. The island of Gueboroar was scarcely visible. Numerous fires ablaze on the beach indicated that the natives had no intention of leaving.

I remained on the platform a few hours all alone. At times I thought of those natives—without any fear, however, for the Captain's unshakable confidence was contagious—and at times, forgetting the natives, I was charmed by the splendor of the tropical night. My thoughts brought back memories of France, where those same stars would be shining in a few hours. The rays of the moon shone brilliantly in the midst of the constellations of the zenith. Then the thought struck me that the day after the morrow this obliging satellite would reappear, raise these waves, and extricate the *Nautilus* from her bed of coral. Toward midnight everything was calm beneath the trees on the shore and on the dusky surface of the water. I returned to my cabin and fell into a peaceful slumber.

The night passed without incident. Probably the Papuans were frightened at the sight of that monster, aground in the bay, for the hatches had been left open, and they could easily have entered the *Nautilus*.

At six o'clock in the morning—on the 8th of January—I returned to the platform. The shadows of morning were disappearing, and as the mist lifted, the shores and the peaks of the island became visible.

The natives were still there, more numerous than the day before—five or six hundred, perhaps. Some of them, taking advantage of the low tide, appeared on the crests of the coral reefs, less than two cables' lengths from the *Nautilus*. I could see them clearly. They were a fine breed of Papuans, built like athletes, with high broad foreheads, noses large but not flat, and white teeth. Their woolly hair, tinted red, stood out in sharp contrast against their black bodies, which glistened like those of the Nubians. From the lobes of their ears, pierced and distended, hung strings of beads made of bone. Most were naked. I saw women among them, wearing crinolines of grass from their hips to their knees, held by belts made of vegetable plants. Some chiefs were wearing crescents and collars around their necks, made of red and white beads. Nearly all were armed with bows, arrows, and shields, and carried over their shoulders something resembling a net, filled with round stones which they shoot from their slings with great skill.

One of the chiefs had come close enough to the *Nautilus* to examine it with care. He must have been a *mado* of high rank, for he was draped with a mat of banana leaves, indented around the edges and painted in bright colors.

I could easily have shot that native, who was only a short distance away, but I thought it better to wait until their actions became really hostile. There is a tacit agreement between Europeans and savages: Europeans may retaliate but do not attack.

162

During the period of low tide, the natives prowled about the *Nautilus*, but they were not troublesome. I could hear the word *"assai"* repeated at frequent intervals, and by their gestures I understood that they were inviting me to come ashore. However, I thought it best to decline their invitation.

The dinghy made no trip that day, much to the displeasure of Master Land, who was anxious to complete his supply of provisions. Instead, the skillful Canadian spent his time preparing the meats and the various flours he had brought back from the island of Gueboroar. At about eleven o'clock in the morning, when the coral reefs began to disappear beneath the rising tide, the natives returned to land. I noticed that their numbers had increased considerably on the beach. Probably they were coming from neighboring islands, or from the mainland of Papua. However, I had not yet seen a single native canoe.

Having nothing better to do, I thought it might be a good idea to drag a net through those beautiful clear waters, in which shells, zoophytes, and pelagian plants were clearly visible. This was the last day that the *Nautilus* would spend in the area—provided she was refloated at high tide the following day, as Captain Nemo had predicted.

I summoned Conseil, who brought me a light fishing net, similar to those used for oysters.

"What about those savages?" Conseil asked me. "If Monsieur doesn't mind my saying so, they look rather harmless to me!"

"Nevertheless, my lad, they are cannibals."

"One can be a cannibal and be respectable," replied Conseil, "just as one can be greedy about food and yet be a good man. One does not exclude the other."

"Quite right, Conseil, I agree with you. There are respectable cannibals who devour their prisoners with decency. However, since I don't particularly want to be devoured, even with decency, I intend to be on my guard, especially since the Captain of the *Nautilus* is not taking any precautions. And now to work."

For two hours we concentrated on fishing, but without bringing up anything unusual. The net was filled with Midas' ears, melanians, harps, and the most beautiful hammer shells I had ever seen. We also brought up holothurians, pearl oysters, and a dozen little turtles, which we saved for the ship's galley.

But at a moment when I least expected it, I laid my hands on something most unusual, a malformation of nature, something extremely rare. Conseil had just drawn his net, filled with a variety of ordinary shells, when suddenly he saw my hand plunge, pull out a shell, and he heard a conchiferous sound—that is, the most piercing sound that a human throat can emit.

"Well, well, what has Monsieur got there?" asked Conseil in amazement. "Has Monsieur been bitten?"

"No, no, my lad. But I would have willingly given a finger for this find."

"What find?"

"This shell," I said, holding up the object of my triumph.

"But that's only an olive porphyry, genus oliva, order of pectinibranchia, class of gastropods, division of mollusks."

"Yes, of course, Conseil; but instead of being curled from right to left, this olive shell is curled from left to right!"

"Is that possible?" exclaimed Conseil.

"Yes, my lad, this is a left-handed shell!"

"A left-handed shell!" repeated Conseil, full of excitement.

"Just look at the spiral."

"Ah, Monsieur should believe me," said Conseil, taking the precious shell with a trembling hand, "I have never felt so thrilled!"

Indeed, this was something to be thrilled about! It is a well-known fact, as naturalists will tell you, that right-handedness is a law of nature. The stars and their satellites, as they move and rotate about the heavens, revolve from right to left. Usually man uses his right hand rather than his left, and consequently the things he creates, such as staircases, locks, watch springs, etc., are so contrived as to function from right to left. Nature has generally followed the same law in rolling up her shells. All of them, with rare exceptions, form right-handed spirals, and when, by chance, one turns out to be left-handed, collectors will pay its weight in gold to possess it.

Conseil and I were deep in thought, fascinated by our find. I was thrilled at the thought of adding this precious object to the museum's exhibits. Conseil was holding the rare specimen in his open hand when a stone, from the sling of a native, struck and shattered it!

I uttered a cry of anguish! Conseil snatched at my gun and drew a bead on a savage, who was aiming his sling about ten yards away. I wanted to stop Conseil, but he fired, and the shot broke the bracelet of amulets on the native's arm.

"Conseil," I cried, "Conseil!"

"Doesn't Monsieur realize that the cannibal attacked us?"

"A shell is not worth the life of a man!" I told him.

"The knave!" cried Conseil. "I'd rather he had broken my shoulder than that shell!"

Conseil meant what he said, but I did not agree with him.

The situation had changed during the last few minutes without our being aware of it. There were now about twenty canoes surrounding the *Nautilus*. These canoes, made of hollow tree trunks, long, narrow, moved quickly and smoothly, and were balanced by means of long bamboo pontoons which floated on the water. They were adroitly steered by half-naked paddlers, and with some anxiety, I saw these canoes coming toward us.

Obviously, these Papuans had already had encounters with Europeans and were acquainted with their vessels. But this long iron cylinder lying in the bay, without masts or funnels, was evidently perplexing to them. Clearly, they were somewhat afraid, for up to now they had kept at a respectful distance. However, seeing it motionless, they began to gain confidence, and were now trying to find out more about it. This was exactly what we had to prevent them from doing. Our weapons, which were noiseless, were not likely to have any great effect on these natives, who only respect noisy firearms. If there were no thunder, men would have little fear of lightning—although the danger is in the lightning, not in the thunder.

As the canoes came closer to the *Nautilus,* a shower of arrows struck the hull.

"Heavens! It's hailing!" exclaimed Conseil. "Perhaps the hailstones are poisonous!"

"We must inform Captain Nemo," I cried, slipping down through the hatch.

I made my way to the saloon, but found no one there. I ventured to knock at the door that opened into the Captain's room.

I was answered by a "Come in." I entered. Captain Nemo was poring over what looked like an algebraic problem, in which x and other algebraic signs abounded.

"Am I disturbing you?" I asked politely.

"I am afraid you are, Monsieur Aronnax," the Captain replied, "but I imagine you have a good reason for wanting to see me?"

"Very serious indeed! We are surrounded by native canoes, and in a few minutes we shall certainly be attacked by several hundred savages."

"I see," said Captain Nemo calmly, "so they have come with their canoes, have they?"

"Yes, sir."

"Well, monsieur, all we have to do is close the hatches."

"Quite so, and I was just coming to tell you—"

"Nothing simpler, I assure you," said Captain Nemo, and

pressing a button, he proceeded to issue an order to the control post.

"Well, that is that," he said, after a moment's pause. "The dinghy is back in place and the hatches are closed. You don't think for one moment that these gentlemen can pierce a hull that your cannonballs could not pierce, do you?"

"No, Captain. But there is one other danger."

"What is that?"

"Tomorrow, when we have to open the hatches to take in a fresh supply of air. . . ."

"Quite right, monsieur. Our ship does breathe like the cetaceans."

"Well, if at that moment the platform is occupied by the natives, I do not see how you will prevent them from getting in."

"Do you mean, Professor, that you expect these Papuans to board the *Nautilus?*"

"I am sure of it."

"Well, monsieur, let them try. I see no reason to try and stop them. After all, these Papuans are poor little devils. I do not want my visit to the island of Gueboroar to cost the life of any one of those unfortunate people."

I decided to withdraw, but Captain Nemo bade me stay and invited me to sit down and chat with him. He questioned me with interest about our excursions ashore and our hunt. He found it difficult to understand the need for meat that obsessed the Canadian. The conversation touched on other subjects, and Captain Nemo, although not particularly communicative, was extremely amiable.

Among other things, we talked about the position of the *Nautilus,* which had run aground in the strait where Dumont d'Urville had almost perished. On this subject, the Captain said:

"He was one of your really great sailors and one of your most intelligent navigators! He was the Captain Cook of the French. An unlucky scientist! Imagine an expert and experienced navigator like him, who had braved the icebergs of the South Pole, the coral reefs of Oceania, and the cannibals of the Pacific, perishing miserably in a railway accident! Imagine what this dynamic man must have thought, if indeed he was able to think at all during the last moments of his life; imagine what his final thoughts must have been!"

When he spoke like this, Captain Nemo seemed strangely moved, and I considered this much to his credit.

Then, chart in hand, he returned to the subject of the French navigator, his voyages around the globe, his two attempts to reach the South Pole, which led to the discovery of

Adélie Land and Louis-Philippe Land, and his hydrographic surveys of the main islands in Oceania.

"What your d'Urville did on the surface of the water," Captain Nemo told me, "I have done in the ocean depths, more easily and more completely than he. The *Astrolabe* and the *Zélée* were continually buffeted by hurricanes, while the *Nautilus* has the advantage of being a peaceful laboratory, situated motionless in calm waters!"

"However, Captain," I said, "there is one point of resemblance between the corvettes of Dumont d'Urville and the *Nautilus.*"

"And what is that, monsieur?"

"The *Nautilus* has also run aground!"

"The *Nautilus*, Monsieur le Professeur," replied Captain Nemo coldly, "has not run aground. The *Nautilus* is built to lie on the seabed, and the backbreaking work and difficult maneuvers imposed on d'Urville in refloating his corvettes do not concern me at all. The *Astrolabe* and the *Zélée* almost sank, but my *Nautilus* is in no such danger. Tomorrow, on the day and at the appointed hour, the tide will gently raise her, and she will resume her voyage through the seas."

"Captain," I said, "I do not doubt—"

"Tomorrow," Captain Nemo continued, getting up, "at two forty in the afternoon, the *Nautilus* will be afloat and will leave the Torres Strait without mishap."

These words were spoken very curtly, and Captain Nemo bowed slightly as he finished. I was obviously being dismissed, and I returned to my room.

Conseil was there. He wanted to know what had happened in my interview with the Captain.

"My lad," I said, "when I told him that his *Nautilus* was threatened by Papuans, all I got from the Captain was sarcasm. All I can say is: Have confidence in him and have a good peaceful sleep."

"Monsieur has no need of my services?"

"No, thank you, my friend. Tell me, what is Ned Land doing?"

"I hope Monsieur won't mind my saying so," replied Conseil, "but our friend Ned is preparing a kangaroo pie that is going to be delicious!"

Left alone, I decided to go to bed, but I slept badly. I could hear deafening cries and the footsteps of the savages walking up and down on the platform above. The night went by. The crew did not stir from their habitual calm. They were as worried by the presence of the cannibals as soldiers in a fort would be by ants crawling all over their fortifications.

At six o'clock in the morning I got up. The hatches had not yet been opened, nor had the supply of air been renewed, but the tanks, which had been filled in case of emergency, were discharging oxygen into the stale atmosphere on board.

I worked in my room until midday without seeing Captain Nemo even for a moment. The crew did not seem to be making any preparations to move off.

I waited a little longer, and then went to the saloon. The clock said half past two. In ten minutes the tide would be at its highest, and unless Captain Nemo had miscalculated, the *Nautilus* would be freed from her predicament. Otherwise, months would go by before she could leave her coral bed.

However, I soon began to feel significant vibrations, and heard the hull scraping the coral bed.

At 2:35, Captain Nemo came into the saloon.

"We are ready to leave," he said.

"Ah!" was all I could say.

"I have given orders to open the hatches."

"What about the Papuans?"

"The Papuans?" replied Captain Nemo, with a slight shrug of his shoulders.

"Will they not invade the *Nautilus?*"

"How?"

"By coming in through the open hatches."

"Monsieur Aronnax," Captain Nemo replied calmly, "it is not so simple to enter through the hatches of the *Nautilus*, even when they are open."

I stared at the Captain.

"You do not understand me?" he asked.

"I am afraid I do not."

"Well, come with me and you will see."

I went out to the central staircase. There, Ned Land and Conseil, who were very intrigued, stood watching some members of the crew opening the hatches, while furious yells and fearful cries were heard from the outside.

The panels opened outward, and immediately we saw a score of terrible-looking faces peeping in. But the first savage to put his hand on the rail of the staircase was thrown backward by some strange, invisible force, and ran away with awful screams and weird contortions.

Ten of his companions followed him, and all met the same fate.

Conseil was beside himself with pleasure, while Ned Land, carried away by his impulsive nature, leaped to the stairs. But as soon as he grasped the railing with his two hands, he, too, was thrown back!

"A thousand devils!" he exclaimed. "I've been struck by lightning!"

That cleared up the mystery for me. The railing, connected with the ship's electric power, could be electrified up to the platform. Anyone touching it received an electric shock, which could be fatal if Captain Nemo wished it to be so. He had an electric barrier between him and any assailant—a barrier no one could cross with impunity.

Meanwhile, the Papuans had beaten a retreat, frightened out of their wits, while we, who couldn't help seeing the funny side, consoled and massaged the unfortunate Ned Land, who was cursing as one possessed.

At that moment the *Nautilus*, lifted up by the last undulating waves of the rising tide, left her coral bed on the fortieth minute of the hour, at the exact time fixed by the Captain. Her propeller threshed the waters slowly and majestically. Then she gradually picked up speed, and sailing smoothly on the surface of the ocean, left the dangerous Torres Strait, safe and sound.

Chapter XXIII

AEGRI SOMNIA—BITTER DREAMS

ON THE FOLLOWING DAY, the 10th of January, the *Nautilus* continued her course underwater, at a speed which I estimated at not less than thirty-five miles an hour. Her propeller turned so fast I could neither follow nor count its revolutions.

When I considered how this powerful electrical energy propelled her, provided the *Nautilus* with heat and light, defended her from outside attacks, and transformed her into a forbidden object, which no profane hand might touch without being electrocuted, my admiration knew no bounds—an admiration that was easily transferred from the craft to the engineer who had conceived it.

We headed directly west, and on the 11th of January we doubled Cape Wessel, situated at longitude 135° and latitude 10° north, which forms the eastern point of the Gulf of Carpentaria. The reefs were still numerous, but more sparsely scattered, and were indicated on the map with perfect precision. The *Nautilus* easily avoided the Money Shoals to port, and the Victoria Reefs to starboard, situated at longitude 130°, on the 10th parallel, which we were following faithfully.

On the 13th of January, Captain Nemo, reaching the Sea of Timor, came upon the island of that name at longitude 122°. This island, whose area covers 1,625 square leagues, is governed by rajahs. These princes claim to be sons of the crocodiles—that·is to say, the most noble descent to which a human being can lay claim. Moreover, their scaly ancestors swarm in all the rivers of the island, and are the objects of great veneration. They are protected, pampered, adulated, and fed. Young maidens are offered to them for food, and woe to the stranger who lifts a hand against these sacred lizards.

But the *Nautilus* had no reason to quarrel with these animals. The Island of Timor was visible only for a moment, at noon, when the second-in-command charted her position. Hence I could only catch a glimpse of the little isle of Rotti, part of the same archipelago, where women enjoy a very well-established reputation for their beauty on the Malayan markets.

From this point the *Nautilus* veered to the southwest, in the direction of the Indian Ocean. Where would Captain Nemo's fancies take us next? Would he return toward the coasts of Asia or approach the shores of Europe? Either alternative was improbable for a man who was a fugitive from inhabited continents. Would he sail toward the south? Would he double the Cape of Good Hope, then Cape Horn, and go as far as the South Pole? Would he return again to the seas of the Pacific, where his *Nautilus* could roam with ease and independence? Only the future could tell.

After skirting the reefs of Cartier, Hibernia, Seringapatam, and Scott, final symbols of the struggle between land and sea, we lost sight of the land altogether on the 14th of January. The *Nautilus* slowed down noticeably, and changing her direction as she saw fit, sometimes cruised in the depths of the water and sometimes floated on the surface.

During this stage of the voyage, Captain Nemo conducted some interesting experiments on the varying temperatures of the sea at different levels. Under normal conditions, such information is obtained by using rather complicated instruments, which must be lowered from the surface, and whose results are, at best, questionable. If thermometric soundings are used, the glass often shatters under the pressure of the water; if an apparatus is used that functions on the principle of resistance of metals to electrical currents, the results cannot be accurately controlled. Captain Nemo, on the other hand, was able to go down in person to take the temperatures in different levels of the sea, and his thermometers, in direct contact with these different levels, provided him immediately and reliably with the data sought.

Thus, either by filling her tanks, or by descending obliquely using her inclining fins, the *Nautilus* could submerge to depths of three, four, five, seven, nine, and ten thousand meters. The final result of these experiments was that the sea maintained, at a depth of one thousand meters in any latitude, a permanent temperature of 4½° Centigrade or 40° Fahrenheit.

I followed these experiments with intense interest. Captain Nemo threw himself passionately into his work. I often asked myself what his purpose was in collecting this information. Was it for the benefit of his fellow beings? That was unlikely, because sooner or later his labors were destined to perish with him in some unknown sea! Unless he intended to bequeath the results of his experiments to me. But that, of course, would presuppose an end to this strange voyage—an end that was not foreseeable as yet.

Whatever the case, the Captain, nevertheless, informed me of the different figures he had obtained and which established the relative densities of the water in the principal seas of the globe. From the information he gave me, I drew a personal lesson that had nothing to do with science.

It was during the morning of the 15th of January. The Captain, with whom I was strolling on the platform, asked me whether I knew the different densities of the sea waters. I answered in the negative, and added that scientific research had not provided reliable information in this field.

"I have obtained this information," he said to me, "and I can assure you of its accuracy."

"Fine," I replied, "but the *Nautilus* is a world of its own and the secrets of its scientists are not shared by others."

"You are right, Professor," he said, after a short silence. "It is a world apart. It is as foreign to the earth as are the planets which accompany this globe around the sun. One will never know the work the scientists on Saturn or on Jupiter are doing. However, since chance has joined our destinies, I can tell you the results of my observations."

"I am listening, Captain."

"You know, Professor, that seawater is denser than fresh water, but this density is not uniform. In fact, if I represent the density of fresh water as one, I find a density of one and twenty-six thousandths in the waters of the Pacific, one and twenty-eight thousandths in the waters of the Atlantic, and one and thirty thousandths in the waters of the Mediterranean. . . ."

Ah! I thought, he does venture in the Mediterranean?

"One and eighteen thousandths in the waters of the Ionian Sea, and one and twenty-nine thousandths in the waters of the Adriatic."

Decidedly, the *Nautilus* did not shun the frequented seas of Europe, and I concluded that he would take us—before long, perhaps—toward more civilized continents. I thought Ned Land would learn of this with understandable satisfaction.

For several days, our time was spent studying the salinity of the water at different depths, its electric qualities, its coloring, and its transparency. At all times, Captain Nemo displayed an ingenuity that was equaled only by his gracious conduct toward me. Then, for a few days, he would disappear and I would live once more in isolation.

On the 16th of January, the *Nautilus* appeared to lie dormant just a few meters beneath the surface of the waves. Her electrical equipment was switched off, and her motionless propeller left her to drift at the mercy of the current. I imagined that the members of the crew were busy making repairs, necessitated, perhaps, by the strain caused by the continuous working of the ship's mechanisms.

My companions and I were then witnesses to a strange spectacle. The saloon hatches were open, and since the searchlight of the *Nautilus* was not in use, a vague darkness reigned in the midst of the water. The stormy sky, covered with dense clouds, gave only a murky light to the upper level of the ocean.

I was observing that with the sea in these conditions, even the largest fish appeared as scarcely definable shadows. Suddenly, however, the *Nautilus* was immersed in a bright light. I thought, at first, that the searchlight had been turned on and that it was projecting its electric beams into that liquid mass. I was wrong; after a quick look, I realized my error.

The *Nautilus* was floating in a phosphorescent aura, which was dazzling in the darkness. It was caused by myriads of luminous animalcules, whose brilliance was intensified as they glided over the metal hull of the submarine. Then I caught sight of flashes of light in the midst of these luminous swarms, resembling molten lead poured into white-hot furnaces, or metallic masses brought to red-white heat. Such was the brightness that, by contrast, certain luminous areas actually cast shadows amidst this blaze where all shadow should have vanished! No! It was no longer the soft radiancy of our usual light! This light possessed an unprecedented vitality and intensity! This was a living light!

This was, indeed, an infinite agglomeration of pelagic infusoria, globules of diaphanous jelly provided with threadlike tentacles; as many as twenty-five thousand of them have been counted in thirty cubic centimeters of water. Their light was further intensified by the phosphorescence peculiar to the medusa, starfish, aurelia, piddocks, and other luminous zoophytes, impregnated with the tissue of organic matter decomposed by the sea, and perhaps with the mucus secreted by the fish.

For several hours the *Nautilus* floated in these glittering waves, and our wonder grew as we watched the great marine animals playing in their midst like salamanders. In the midst of this fire that did not burn, I saw those swift, elegant porpoises, tireless clowns of the ocean; swordfish up to three meters long, intelligent prophets of the storm whose formidable blades sometimes struck the panels of the saloon. Then some smaller fish appeared on the scene: the triggerfish, the leaping mackerel, the wolf fish, and hundreds of others which streaked darkly through the luminous water.

This dazzling spectacle held us spellbound! Perhaps certain atmospheric conditions increased the intensity of this phenomenon, or perhaps a storm was churning the waves above the surface of the sea. But at a depth of a few meters, the *Nautilus* lay undisturbed by its fury. She rocked gently in those quiet waters.

As we proceeded on our journey, we were always enchanted by new wonders. Conseil observed and classified his zoophytes, his articulata, his mollusks, and fish. The days sped by, and I no longer counted them. Ned, naturally, tried to vary the ship's menu. Like snails, we were indeed becoming attached to our shells, and I declare, it is easy enough to become a perfect snail.

We seemed to have become so accustomed to this natural manner of living that we no longer thought any other existed in this world. However, an incident occurred that soon reminded us of our strange situation.

On the 18th of January, the *Nautilus* was at longitude 105°, latitude 15° south. The weather was threatening, the sea was rough and turbulent. The wind blew violently from the east. The barometer, which had been dropping for days, indicated a coming storm.

I climbed up on the platform just as the second-in-command was taking our position. I waited as usual for him to pronounce his daily phrase. But on that day he substituted another, no less incomprehensible. Almost immediately I saw Captain Nemo appear. He studied the horizon with the aid of a spyglass.

For a few minutes the Captain stood motionless, without taking his eyes off the point he was observing with his spyglass. Then he lowered his spyglass and exchanged a few words with his second-in-command. The latter appeared to be in the throes of an emotion that he was trying vainly to control. Captain Nemo, more in command of himself, remained cool. He appeared to raise certain objections to which the second-in-command replied with formal assurances. At least, that is what I inferred from the differences of their tones and gestures.

I also looked intently in the direction indicated, but saw nothing. Sky and water blended in a perfect, clean line on the horizon.

Meanwhile, Captain Nemo kept pacing from one end of the platform to the other without looking at me, perhaps without even seeing me. His gait was firm, but less regular than usual. Sometimes he stopped, and with his arms folded across his chest, he gazed at the sea. What could he be looking for on that vast expanse? The *Nautilus* was hundreds of miles from the nearest shore!

The second-in-command had again taken up his spyglass and was obstinately peering at the horizon. He paced to and fro, and stamped his feet; his agitated state was in sharp contrast to that of his Captain.

The mystery was soon to be revealed; and before long, on Captain Nemo's orders, the vessel increased her speed.

Once more, the second-in-command called for the Captain's attention. Nemo pointed his spyglass in the direction indicated. He observed for a long time. Very much intrigued, I went down to the saloon and brought up an excellent telescope that I normally used; then, leaning on the searchlight cage, which jutted out at the fore of the platform, I began to scan the horizon.

But no sooner had I put the telescope to my eye when it was violently snatched from my hands. I turned around. Captain Nemo stood before me, but I no longer recognized him. His features were transformed. His eyes, lighting up menacingly, sank back beneath his furrowed brows; his teeth were set, his body stiff, his fists clenched, and his head hunched between his shoulders, he betrayed a hatred that pervaded his whole person. He did not stir. My telescope, which had fallen from his hand, rolled to his feet.

Had I, without wishing to do so, provoked this anger? Did this unfathomable person think that I had discovered some secret that was forbidden to the guests of the *Nautilus*?

No! I was not the object of his hatred, for he was not looking at me. His eyes remained obstinately fixed upon that mysterious point on the horizon.

At last Captain Nemo recovered his habitual calm. He addressed a few words to his lieutenant in that language foreign to me, then he turned toward me.

"Monsieur Aronnax," he said in a somewhat commanding tone, "I am asking you to observe one of the conditions of our bargain."

"What is that, Captain?"

"You must be confined, you and your companions, until I decide to grant you your freedom again."

"You are the master," I replied, looking him in the eye. "But may I ask you one question?"

"None, monsieur."

I had no choice but to obey, since any resistance would have been impossible.

I went down to the cabin occupied by Ned Land and Conseil, and I informed them of the Captain's decision. You can imagine how this news was received by the Canadian! There was, besides, no time for explanations. Four men of the crew were waiting at the door, and they conducted us to the cell where we had spent our first night aboard the *Nautilus*.

Ned Land ventured to complain; there was no answer. The door was closed behind him.

"Can Monsieur tell me what this is all about?" Conseil asked me.

I told my companions what had happened. They were as astonished as I, but equally puzzled.

Meanwhile, I was deep in thought. I could not rid my mind of the strange fear that had possessed Captain Nemo. I found it impossible to connect two logical ideas, and I was soon involved in the most absurd suppositions. I was aroused from my engrossing thoughts by Ned Land:

"Well! Lunch is served!"

Indeed, the table had been set. It was evident that Captain Nemo had given this order at the same time that he had ordered the speed of the *Nautilus* to be increased.

"Will Monsieur allow me to make a suggestion?" Conseil asked me.

"Yes, my lad," I replied.

"Well, sir, I suggest that Monsieur eat his repast. It would be wise because we never know what may happen!"

"You are right, Conseil."

"Unfortunately," said Ned Land, "they've only given us the usual fare."

"Ned, my friend," retorted Conseil, "what would you have said had there been no meal at all?"

This reasoning cut short any further complaints from the harpooner.

We sat down. The meal passed in relative silence. I ate little. Conseil "forced himself," in the interests of prudence, and Ned Land, in spite of himself, did not miss a bite. When the repast was over, each withdrew into a corner.

Just then, the luminous sphere that lit the cell went out, and we were left in total darkness. Ned Land lost no time in falling asleep, and to my surprise, Conseil also allowed himself to sink into a deep slumber. I wondered what could have been the reason for this irresistible need to sleep, when I also felt my brain overcome by an intense drowsiness. I tried to keep my eyes open, but they kept closing, despite my efforts. A painful suspicion crossed my mind. Evidently, some sedative had been put in the food that we had just eaten. The prison alone then was not enough to conceal the plans of Captain Nemo; he had felt the need of putting us to sleep also!

176

I heard the hatches closing. The motion of the waves, which had caused the ship to roll slightly, ceased. Had the *Nautilus* left the surface of the ocean? Had she submerged again into the quiet depths of the waters?

I tried to fight off my drowsiness. It was impossible; my breathing grew weaker. I felt a mortal chill freeze my heavy, almost paralyzed, limbs. My eyelids, like leaden seals, fell over my eyes. Now I could not raise them. A morbid sleep, full of delusions, overwhelmed my whole being. Then the visions disappeared and left me in a state of oblivion.

Chapter XXIV

THE CORAL KINGDOM

THE NEXT MORNING I woke up, surprisingly enough, with a clear head. Much to my amazement I was in my own room. My companions, I assumed, had been returned to theirs, also. Neither they nor I knew what had happened during the night. Only the future could possibly unravel that mystery.

Then it occurred to me to leave my room. Was I free once more, or was I still a prisoner? I was perfectly free. I opened the door, went along the passages and up the central staircase. The hatches, which had been closed the day before, were now open. I went out on the platform.

Ned Land and Conseil were there waiting for me; I asked them what had happened to them. They knew nothing. They had fallen into a heavy sleep and had no recollection whatsoever. They also had been astonished to awaken in their cabin.

And the *Nautilus?* She seemed as quiet and mysterious as ever, moving along the surface at a leisurely speed. Nothing on board seemed to have changed.

Ned Land with his sharp vision scanned the sea. It was deserted. Nothing was visible on the horizon, no sail and no land. There was a brisk westerly breeze blowing, and long billows, whipped up by the wind, made the ship roll.

The *Nautilus*, after taking on a fresh supply of air, kept at an average depth of fifty feet, so she could surface quickly— something that was done several times during that day of the 19th of January, contrary to the usual routine. When this occurred, the second-in-command would go up on the platform and repeat the usual phrase, which could be heard down below.

Captain Nemo kept out of sight. Of the crew, I saw only the impassive steward, who served me with his usual silence and efficiency.

At about two o'clock I was in the saloon, busy classifying my notes, when the door opened and the Captain came in. I greeted him, and he returned my greeting almost imperceptibly, without saying a word. I returned to my work, hoping that he might say something that would throw some light on the events of the night before. He said nothing. I looked at him: his face was tired and his eyes were red from lack of sleep; I thought his expression was one of profound sadness, of genuine grief. He paced to and fro, sat down, got up again, picked up a book, put it down again the next minute, and consulted his instruments without taking the usual notes —he was restless and could not keep still for a moment.

Finally, he came over to me and said:

"Are you a physician, Monsieur Aronnax?"

I was so taken aback by this question that for a few seconds I looked at him without answering.

"Are you a doctor?" he repeated. "A number of your colleagues have studied medicine: Gratiolet, Moquin-Tandon, and others."

"Yes," I said. "I am a doctor, and medical resident at several hospitals. I practiced for several years before joining the museum."

"Good."

Obviously my reply had satisfied Captain Nemo, but not knowing what he was driving at, I waited for the next question before uttering another word.

"Monsieur Aronnax," said the Captain, "would you be kind enough to attend to one of my men?"

"Have you a sick man on board?"

"Yes, monsieur."

"I am at your disposal."

"Come, then."

I will admit my heart was beating fast. I cannot say why, but I felt there must be some connection between the illness of a member of the crew and the events of the previous day, and that mystery preoccupied me at least as much as the sick man.

Captain Nemo led me aft into a cabin near the crew's quarters.

There, on a bed, lay a man of about forty with energetic features—a real Anglo-Saxon type.

I bent over him. He was not just ill, he was wounded. His head was propped up on two pillows and swathed in bandages that were soaked in blood. I undid the bandages; the wounded man stared with wide open eyes, without a word of complaint.

It was a ghastly wound. The skull had been smashed by a blunt instrument, exposing the brain, which had suffered a deep internal lesion. Clots of blood had formed in the bruised and broken mass, whose color resembled the dregs of wine. He had suffered both contusion and concussion, and his breathing was slow. Now and then his face twitched spasmodically. The paralysis of his brain was massive, affecting both feelings and movement.

I felt the patient's pulse. It was intermittent. The extremities of his body were already getting cold. It was evident that death was approaching; there was nothing I could do. After having dressed his wounds, I rebandaged his head. I turned to Captain Nemo.

"Where did he get this wound?" I asked.

"What does that matter!" the Captain replied evasively. "A collision broke one of the levers in the engine room and it hit this man on the head. The second-in-command was in danger. He threw himself forward to receive the blow—a brother gives his life for a brother—a friend dies for a friend—what could be simpler! That is the law aboard the *Nautilus!* But what do you think of his condition?"

I hesitated.

"You may speak," said the Captain. "This man doesn't understand French."

I took one last look at the wounded man and said:

"This man will die within two hours."

"Can nothing save him?"

"Nothing."

The Captain clenched his fist. Tears appeared in those eyes I had thought incapable of displaying any emotion.

For a few moments I watched the dying man, whose life was gradually ebbing away. He grew paler and paler beneath the glare of the electric light that fell on his deathbed. I looked at his intelligent face, furrowed with premature wrinkles, caused, perhaps, by misfortune or misery many years before. Would some last words escape his lips and tell me something of the secret of his life?

"You may leave now, Monsieur Aronnax," said Captain Nemo.

I left the Captain with the dying man and went back to my room, deeply moved by what I had seen. All day long I was uneasy, disturbed by sinister forebodings. I did not sleep well that night. During my waking moments, between strange dreams, I thought I heard deep sighs in the distance—like the chants of a funeral psalm. Could this be a prayer for the dead, murmured in a language I could not understand?

Next morning, I went up on the bridge; Captain Nemo was there. When he saw me, he came over to me.

"Professor," he said to me, "would you like to go on an excursion today under the sea?"

"With my friends?" I asked.

"If they wish."

"We are at your command, Captain."

180

"Be good enough to put on your diving suits, then."

There was no mention of the dead or dying man. I joined Ned Land and Conseil and told them of Captain Nemo's invitation. Conseil accepted immediately, and for once the Canadian, too, seemed quite willing to come.

It was eight o'clock in the morning. By half past eight, we were dressed for our new adventure and outfitted with our breathing and lighting equipment. The double doors were opened, and accompanied by Captain Nemo, who was followed by a dozen members of the crew, we set foot on the bottom of the sea, where the *Nautilus* lay at a depth of about thirty feet.

There was a gentle slope leading down to an uneven stretch of land, at a depth of about fifteen fathoms. This surface was completely different from the one I had encountered during my first excursion beneath the waters of the Pacific. Here there was no fine sand, no prairie, no pelagian forest. I immediately recognized this marvelous region into which Captain Nemo was leading us. It was the Coral Kingdom!

In the branch of zoophytes, class of alcyonaries, we find the order of gorgonaries, which comprises three groups: the gorgonians, the isidians, and the coralians. Coral belongs to the last group; it is a curious substance that was formerly classified, in turn, as belonging to the mineral, vegetable, and animal kingdoms. This substance was medicine to the ancients, but it is jewelry to the modern world. It was not definitely classified within the animal kingdom until 1694, by the naturalist Peysonnel, from Marseilles.

Coral is a colony of individual animalcules, assembled on a brittle, rocklike polypary. These polyps have an unusual type of generator that reproduces them by a continuous process of budding growth; while each creature has its separate existence, all participate in the life of the community—a sort of natural socialism, as it were. I knew about the most recent research on this curious zoophyte, which ramifies and becomes mineralized at the same time, as the naturalists have pointed out, and nothing could have been more interesting to me than to visit one of these petrified forests, planted by nature at the bottom of the sea.

Switching on our lights, we followed a bank of coral in the slow process of formation, which, with the passing of time, will one day shut off this part of the Indian Ocean. Our path was edged with tangled bushes, due to the intertwining of undersea shrubbery, covered with little starlike flowers studded with white lines. However, unlike plants growing on land, these, rooted in the rocks, grew downward.

Our lights created a thousand charming effects, as they

181

played among the vividly colored branches. These membranous cylindrical tubes seemed to undulate with the movement of the water. I was tempted to pick the fresh petals, ornamented with delicate tentacles, some in full bloom, others scarcely in bud, while small fish, resembling the flight of birds, darted rapidly among them and touched them gently as they swam. But if my hand reached out to pluck these living flowers, their sensitive organisms were alerted, and the whole colony was alarmed. The white petals would then recede into their red sheaths, flowers faded away under my very gaze, and whole bushes would be transformed into a mass of stony nipples.

Chance had brought me into the presence of the most precious specimens of this zoophyte.

This coral was just as good and just as valuable as the coral found off the shores of Italy, France, and the coastal regions of North Africa. Its brilliant delicate tints more than justify the poetic names given to it by the trade—*"fleur de sang"* and *"écume de sang"*—the flowers or foam of blood. It sells for as much as five hundred francs a kilo and in these beds there is enough to enrich a whole world of coral traders. The precious substance, often combined with other types of polypary, had formed compact, tangled masses called "macciota," among which I noticed some magnificent specimens of pink coral.

As we advanced the bushes grew thicker, the treelike formations taller. These were veritable petrified thickets, and long stretches of fantastic shapes opened up before us.

Captain Nemo led us through a dark gallery, whose gentle slope brought us down to a depth of about three hundred feet. Our lights at times produced magical effects as they played on the rugged contours of the natural arches and hanging formations, which resembled chaplets tipped with fiery dots. Among the coraline branches, I saw other polyps that were no less strange: melites; iris with very visible feelers; tufts of coraline, a species of seaweed hardened into a crust by their calcareous salts. Some of these were green, others red. Naturalists, after many long discussions, have finally and definitely relegated them to the vegetable kingdom. A scientist and thinker once said, "This may well be the veritable point at which life emerges mysteriously from the world of matter, without, however, completely severing the bonds that bind it to the inert source from which it springs."

After walking for two hours, we had finally reached a depth of approximately nine hundred feet, that is to say, the extreme limit at which coral begins to form. No isolated shrubbery here, no brushwood—nothing but an immense forest of large mineral vegetations, huge petrified trees, bound by garlands of plumarias, tropical creepers, all tinged with hues and reflected light. We walked under high branches, almost invisible in the shade of the waves, while at our feet tubipores, meandrines, stars, fungi, and cariophytes formed a flowery carpet strewn with dazzling gems.

What an indescribable spectacle! If we had only been able to communicate our feelings! Why were we imprisoned behind masks of metal and glass! Why were we prevented from talking to each other! If only we could have shared the life of all those fish that swarm in these crystal waters! Or better still, share the life of those amphibians which, for hours at a stretch, romp at will in sea and on land!

Captain Nemo had stopped. My friends and I stopped also, and turning, I saw the crew form a semicircle around their chief. Then I noticed that four of them were carrying an oblong object on their shoulders.

We were at the center of a vast clearing, surrounded by the lofty branches of a submerged forest. The rays of our lights created something resembling a twilight, which lengthened immeasurably the shadows on the bed of the sea. On the edges of the glade complete darkness reigned, except for an occasional spark emitted by the living skeletons of the coral.

Ned Land and Conseil were standing near me. As we watched, it occurred to me that I was going to be present at some strange ceremony. Looking closer at the ground, I saw the surface broken here and there by slight mounds, encrusted with calcareous deposits, but arranged in a regular pattern that betrayed the hand of man. In the middle of the clearing, on a pedestal of rocks thrown on top of each other, stood a cross of coral, whose long arms, one would have thought, were made of petrified blood.

At a sign from Captain Nemo, one of the men came forward to within a few feet from the cross and began to dig a hole with a pickax, which he detached from his belt.

Then it dawned on me! This clearing was a cemetery; the hole, a grave; the oblong object, the body of the man who had died during the night! Captain Nemo and his men had come to bury their comrade in this communal resting ground at the bottom of this inaccessible sea!

Never had I been moved more deeply nor felt a deeper impression; I could scarcely believe that this was not a dream!

Meanwhile, the grave was slowly being dug, while the fish, disturbed, fled here and there. I could hear the echo of the pickax striking on the hard ground; an occasional spark appeared as the ax struck a piece of flint lost at the bottom of the ocean. The grave became longer and deeper, and soon was deep enough to receive the body.

Then the bearers stepped forward. The body, wrapped in tissue of white byssus, was lowered into its watery grave. Captain Nemo, arms crossed over his chest, and all those who had been loved by the dead, knelt in prayer. We, too, stood, heads bowed, silent and respectful.

The grave was then filled in, creating a slight mound.

When this had been done, Captain Nemo and his men stood up, approached the tomb, knelt once more for a second, and held out their arms as a gesture of final farewell.

The funeral procession started on its way back to the *Nautilus,* passed once more beneath the arches of the forest, through the thickets, along the coral bushes—ascending all the way.

At last the lights of the ship came in sight, and their luminous trail guided us to the *Nautilus.* At one o'clock we were back.

As soon as I had changed my clothes, I went up to the platform and sat down by the searchlight, a prey of deep, conflicting thoughts.

Captain Nemo joined me. I stood and said:

"The man died during the night, as I had predicted?"

"Yes, Monsieur Aronnax."

"He is resting now beside his companions in the coral cemetery."

"Yes. Forgotten by all, but not by us! We dig the grave, and the polyps can be trusted to seal our tombs for eternity!"

Suddenly covering his face with clenched hands, the Captain made a vain attempt to suppress a sob. Then he added:

"That is our peaceful cemetery, hundreds of feet below the surface of the waves."

"Your dead sleep quietly there, Captain, well beyond the reach of sharks!"

"Yes, monsieur," Captain Nemo replied gravely. "Beyond the reach of sharks—and—of men!"

PART TWO

Chapter I

THE INDIAN OCEAN

WE NOW BEGIN the second stage of our journey under the sea. The first had ended with that moving scene in the coral graveyard, which had made such a deep impression in my mind. It was now evident that the life of Captain Nemo was destined to be spent in the bosom of those immense oceans and that he had even prepared his grave in the most inaccessible depths of the sea. No sea monster would ever trouble his last sleep there, nor the sleep of his crew—friends bound to each other in death as well as in life—nor would they ever be disturbed by men, he had added.

Always that same fierce, implacable defiance of human society!

I was no longer satisfied with Conseil's theory. That worthy lad still felt that the commander of the *Nautilus* was one of those unrecognized scientists, spurned by a society whose indifference they repaid with contempt and hatred. For Conseil, the Captain was still the misunderstood genius who, weary of this world's deceptions, had sought refuge in those inaccessible regions where his nature could have free play. In my opinion, this theory explained only one aspect in the life of Captain Nemo.

The mysterious incidents of that night, when we had been drugged and imprisoned, the violence with which he had snatched that telescope from my eyes to prevent me from scanning the horizon, the mortal wound inflicted upon a member of the crew by an unexplained collision of the *Nautilus*—all this led me to reexamine my thoughts. No, Captain

Nemo was not satisfied merely to flee humanity! His formidable craft served to satisfy not only his yearning for freedom but also, perhaps, an intense desire for vengeance!

At that moment nothing was very clear in my mind. Only faint glimmers of light stood out from the mysterious background of that strange man, and I could describe my thoughts only as they were shaped by the events themselves. Nothing bound us to Captain Nemo. He knew it was impossible for us to escape from the *Nautilus*. We were not honor-bound to remain on board. We were merely captives, only prisoners disguised as guests through a pretense of courtesy. However, Ned Land had not given up hope of regaining his freedom. There was no question that he would take advantage of the first opportunity to escape. Undoubtedly I would do the same. Nevertheless, I would not have escaped without a pang of regret, for the Captain, in his generosity, had permitted us to share the mysteries of the *Nautilus*. Should we hate or admire this man? Was he a victim of circumstances, or an executioner? To be perfectly frank, I did want to finish this underwater journey around the world, which we had begun so magnificently, before leaving him forever. I did want to see all those marvels accumulated beneath the waters of the world. I did want to see what no man had ever seen before, even if I might pay for my insatiable thirst for knowledge with my life! What had I learned so far? Nothing, or almost nothing, since we had traveled, so far, only six thousand leagues across the Pacific!

I realized, moreover, that the *Nautilus* was approaching inhabited lands, and that if an opportunity to escape were to arise, it would be cruel to sacrifice my companions because of my passion for the unknown. I would have to follow them, perhaps even guide them. But would such an opportunity ever present itself? I, as an individual deprived of his free will, longed for such an occasion, of course, but the scientist in me, curious for knowledge, dreaded it.

On that day, January 21st, at noon, the second-in-command came up on the platform to take our position. I went up also. I lit a cigar and I watched him as he carried out his work. It was obvious that he knew no French because on several occasions I passed remarks loud enough to evoke a reaction. If he understood them, he remained silent and impassive.

While he was looking through his sextant, one of the sailors—the powerful-looking man who had accompanied us on our first excursion, to the Isle of Crespo—came to clean the glass panes of the searchlight. I took the opportunity to examine the setup of this instrument, whose power was increased a hundredfold by the use of ringed lenses, arranged, like those of a lighthouse, to throw its intensive light in any direction. The electric device was so designed as to give the maximum amount of light. In fact, it worked like a vacuum, which ensured both intensity and stability. That vacuum gave a longer life to the graphite points at either extremity of the electric arc, something important for Captain Nemo, who could not have replaced them too easily. However, under these conditions, the wear and tear was almost negligible.

When the *Nautilus* was ready to submerge again, I went back to the saloon. The hatches were closed and our course was set due west.

We were then sailing through the waters of the Indian Ocean, that vast expanse of liquid with an area of 1,200,000,000 acres, whose waters are so clear that anyone peering down into their depths feels giddy. The *Nautilus* cruised at a depth of somewhere between three and six hundred feet, and went along like this for several days. To anyone who did not have any love for the sea, the hours would have seemed endless and boring. My daily walks on the platform, breathing the invigorating air of the sea, the sight of those teeming waters seen through the panels of the saloon, the wealth of books in the library, and the writing of my notes took all my time and left me not a moment of lassitude and boredom.

We all managed to keep in excellent health. The food on board agreed with us, and as far as I was concerned, we could have easily dispensed with those "variations" Ned Land ingeniously and in a spirit of protest managed to procure. Moreover, in such a constant temperature, we didn't even run the risk of catching colds. Besides, the madreporaria Dendrophyllia, known in Provence as sea fennel, of which there was a good supply on board, would have given us an effective cough remedy when mixed with the juicy flesh of its polyps.

For several days we saw great numbers of aquatic birds—palmipeds, sea mews, or gulls. Some were shot down with great skill, and when prepared in a certain manner, furnished us with a very pleasant dish. Among the large-winged birds, far from land, which rest on the crest of the waves when tired, I saw some magnificent albatrosses, birds belonging to the family of longipennates, whose harsh cries resemble the braying of an ass. The family of totipalmates was represented by the swift-flying frigate birds, which snatched fish swimming near the surface, and by numerous phaetons or tropic birds, including the red-striped phaeton, the size of a pigeon, whose plumage, shaded in pink, contrasts vividly with its black wings.

The nets cast by the *Nautilus* brought up several kinds of sea turtles, mainly the hawkbill variety, with their domelike back and very valuable shell. These reptiles, which dive easily, can remain underwater for a long time merely by closing a fleshy valve located in the external orifice of their nasal passage. Some of them were still asleep in their shells when caught. Their shells protect them from the ravages of other animals. The flesh of these animals was generally mediocre, but their eggs provided us with a regal dish.

As for the fish, they always filled us with the greatest admiration when we, standing at the open panels, pried into the secrets of their aquatic life. I noticed several species that I had never observed before.

I shall mention principally the ostracious or trunkfish peculiar to the Red Sea, the Indian Ocean, and the waters that bathe the coasts of South America. These fish, like the turtle, the armadillo, the sea urchin, and the shellfish, are protected by a hard shell that is neither chalky nor stony, but made of real bone, sometimes in the shape of a triangle, sometimes in the shape of a square. Among the triangle variety I observed some that were about two inches long, with a brown tail and yellow fins, whose flesh is both healthy and exquisite. I suggest that these be acclimatized to fresh water, a change that some sea fish can easily undergo. I shall cite also some quadrangular trunkfish with four large tubercles on their back; trunkfish with white flecks on their bellies, which can be trained like birds; trigoniae, armed with spines formed by an external growth of bony shell and whose peculiar grunts have given them the name "sea pigs"; dromedaries, with large conical humps, whose flesh is hard and leathery.

From the daily notes of Conseil, I would also add certain fish of the genus tetraodon peculiar to these waters: spenglerians, red-backed and white-chested, with three rows of longitudinal filaments; and electric tetraodons, seven inches long and very brightly colored. Then, among specimens of other genera, ovoids that resemble a brown-black egg and have white stripes and no tail; diodons, porcupines of the sea, armed with spikes, capable of inflating themselves until they look like a ball covered with spikes; sea horses, common to all seas; the long-snouted pegasus, whose pectoral fins are wing-shaped, enabling it—if not to fly—at least to leap into the air; pigeon spatulae whose tails are covered with shelly rings; macrognathae, bright-colored fish with jaws ten inches long; livid calliomores, with rough-shaped heads; myriads of jumping blennies, black-striped, with long pectoral fins, gliding along the surface at fantastic speed; delicious velifera, who can lift their fins like sails to catch favorable currents; splendid kurtidae, arrayed in yellow, sky-blue, silver, and gold; trichoptera, whose wings are formed of filaments; bullheads with lemon-colored spots, making hissing noises; gurnards, whose liver is supposed to be dangerous to eat; greenlings, with flaps over their eyes; and finally, bellows fish, with long tubular muzzles, true flycatchers of the sea, armed with a gun, undreamed of by the Chassepots or the Remingtons, which can kill an insect by hitting it with a drop of water!

Of the eighty-ninth genus of fishes, as classified by Lacépède, belonging to the second subclass of bony fish, characterized by the opercula and bronchial membranes, I noticed the scorpion fish, having a spiked head and one dorsal fin; these creatures may or may not be covered with small scales, depending on their subgenus. The second subgenus includes specimens of didactyla, thirteen or fifteen inches long, with yellow-striped, fantastic-looking heads. The first subgenus provides specimens of that bizarre fish justly called toadfish, with a large head, sometimes swollen with protuberances, bristling with spikes, and covered with nodules. Its hideous horns, its callous hide, and its poisonous sting make it both a dangerous and a most repulsive creature.

From the 21st to the 23rd of January, the *Nautilus* sailed at the rate of 250 leagues every twenty-four hours, or 540 miles a day, averaging about 22 nautical miles per hour. We were able to identify various kinds of fish because they were attracted by the electric light and sought to accompany us. Most of them, however, could not keep up with our speed and were left behind. Some of them, on the other hand, managed to swim side by side with the *Nautilus* for some time.

On the morning of the 24th, in latitude 12° 5′ south by longitude 94° 33′, we sighted Keeling Island, a madreporal formation covered with magnificent coconut palms, which had been visited by Charles Darwin and Captain Fitzroy. The *Nautilus* sailed past this desert island only a short distance from its shores, while our nets dragged up numerous specimens of polyps and echinoderms, as well as curious mollusks. Captain Nemo's store of precious exhibits was further enhanced by various types of miniature dolphin, to which I added a spiny starfish, a kind of polyp parasite often attached to a shell.

Very soon Keeling Island disappeared below the horizon, and our course was set northwest toward the tip of the Indian peninsula.

"These are civilized countries," Ned Land remarked to me that day. "Better than those Papuan islands, where you meet more savages than deer! In India, Professor, there are roads, railways, and English, French, and Hindu towns. You couldn't go five miles without meeting a fellow countryman. Don't you think the time has come to bid Captain Nemo a courteous farewell?"

"No, Ned, no," I replied in a very decisive tone of voice. "Let things ride, as you sailors say. The *Nautilus* is approaching populated countries. She is heading towards Europe. Just let her take us there. Once we reach home waters, we shall see what is the wisest thing to do. However, I don't imagine that Captain Nemo will permit us to go hunting on the coasts of Malabar or Coromandel as he did in the jungle of New Guinea."

"But don't you think, monsieur, that we might act on our own, without his permission?"

I did not answer the Canadian, because I preferred to avoid an argument. At heart, I really wished to follow to their very end the adventures that destiny held in store for us aboard the *Nautilus*.

After leaving Keeling Island, we slowed down and traveled at random but often diving down to great depths. On several occasions, using those side fins that could be set at an angle, we reached depths of two or three miles. However, we never plumbed the lowest depths of the Indian Ocean, which even soundings of over forty thousand feet have so far failed to do. The temperature at these lower strata is constant, and the thermometer generally registered 4° above zero C. or 39° F. I observed also that the upper strata were always colder in shallow waters than in the open sea.

On the 25th of January, the ocean was completely deserted, and the *Nautilus* spent all day on the surface, threshing the waves with her powerful propeller and splashing water up to a great height. Who would not have taken her for a gigantic cetacean under these conditions? I spent three-quarters of that day on the platform, gazing at the sea. Nothing appeared on the horizon until about four o'clock in the evening, when a long steamer, ploughing its way westward in the opposite direction, appeared on the horizon. I caught a glimpse of her masts for an instant, but she could not have seen the *Nautilus*, which did not rise too much above the water. I imagined this boat belonged to the P. and O. Line, which plies between Ceylon and Sydney, calling at King George's Point and at Melbourne.

At five o'clock in the evening, not long before that very brief twilight that occurs between day and night in the tropics, Conseil and I were astonished by a strange sight.

There is a charming creature which, according to the an-

190

cients, brings good fortune if it crosses one's path. Aristotle, Athenaeus, Pliny, and Oppianus had studied its habits and had written poetically about it in Greek and in Latin. They called it the *Nautilus* or the *Pompylius*. But to modern science this mollusk is now known as the argonaut.

If anyone interested in the subject had consulted Conseil, that worthy lad would have informed him that the division of mollusks comprises five classes; the first class, that of the cephalopods, which are sometimes naked and sometimes covered with a shell, consists of two families: the dibranchiata and the tetrabranchiata, which are distinguished by the number of their gills; the family of the dibranchiata comprises three species: the argonaut, the squid, and the cuttlefish; and the family of the tetrabranchiata consists of but one species: the nautilus. It would be inexcusable if, after being treated to all this terminology, an obdurate listener insisted on confusing the argonaut, which is equipped with suckers or siphons, with the nautilus, which has tentacles.

And indeed, what we now saw was a school of argonauts, traveling along the surface of the ocean. We counted several hundred of them. They belonged to the tubercle species peculiar to the Indian seas.

These graceful mollusks moved backward by sucking in water and expelling it again through their propulsory tubes. Of their eight tentacles, six were long and thin and floated on the surface, while the other two were rounded like palm leaves and held up to the wind like light sails.* I could clearly see their spiraled and fluted shells, which Cuvier had justly compared to elegant skiffs. And indeed, the shell is a boat, for the creature whom it carries has created it, but is not attached to it!

"The argonaut is free to leave its shell if it wants to," I told Conseil, "but it never does."

"That's just like Captain Nemo," Conseil remarked wisely. "He would have done better perhaps to have called his ship the *Argonaut*."

For about an hour, the *Nautilus* was surrounded by this school of mollusks. Then, suddenly, I do not know what fear possessed them; as if at a signal, they suddenly furled their sails, withdrew their arms, their bodies contracted, and their shells turned over, shifting their centers of gravity, and the whole flotilla disappeared beneath the water. It all happened

* Verne was reflecting here the view of his time, now known to be incorrect. The two arms that he says are held up like light sails actually clasp the shell. Only the female inhabits a shell, where she lays her eggs, and is free to come and go.—M.T.B.

191

in a flash, and no naval squadron has ever executed such a precise maneuver.

Just then night fell suddenly, and the waves, scarcely touched by the light breeze, lay quietly around the *Nautilus*.

The next day, the 26th of January, we crossed the equator at the 82nd meridian and reentered the Northern Hemisphere.

All that day we were escorted by a formidable school of sharks, fearful creatures that abound in these waters and render them extremely perilous. They were Philipps sharks, with brown backs and whitish bellies, armed with eleven rows of teeth; "eyed" sharks, whose necks are marked with a big black spot, encircled with white, resembling an eye; and Isabella sharks, with rounded snouts and dotted with dark spots. These powerful animals often hurled themselves against the glass panes of the saloon so violently that we felt quite unsafe. Ned Land could no longer contain his anger. He wanted to surface and harpoon these monsters. He was especially excited by the dogfish sharks, whose mouths were studded with teeth resembling a mosaic, and the big tiger sharks, which were about fifteen feet long. But soon the *Nautilus* increased her speed and left the swiftest of them behind with no difficulty.

On the 27th of January, at the entrance to the vast Bay of Bengal, we occasionally saw corpses floating on the surface. These were the dead of Indian towns, carried out to the sea by the Ganges. The vultures, the only undertakers in that country, had not been able to devour them completely. However, the sharks could be relied upon to finish that grisly task.

At about seven o'clock in the evening the *Nautilus* was half submerged, and seemed to be sailing through a milk-colored sea. As far as the eye could see, the ocean appeared to be lactified. Could it be the effect of the moonlight? It could not be. The moon, barely two days old, was still invisible below the horizon and immersed in the rays of the sun. The whole sky, although bright and sunny, seemed dark by contrast to the milky whiteness of the water.

Conseil could scarcely believe his eyes, and asked me to explain this strange phenomenon. Fortunately, I could give him an answer.

"This is what is known as the milky sea," I told him, "a vast stretch of white water, often seen off the coast of Amboyna and in this area."

"But," asked Conseil, "could Monsieur explain to me what produces this effect? I don't suppose this water has actually been changed into milk!"

"No, Conseil. This whiteness that you find so strange is

due to the presence of myriads of infusoria, a sort of tiny luminous worm; this creature is gelatinous and colorless to look at, no thicker than a hair, and no more than one-hundredth of an inch long. Some of them attach themselves to one another and form a white layer over a distance of several leagues."

"Several leagues!" exclaimed Conseil.

"Yes, my lad, and don't try to guess the number of all those infusoria. It's impossible to do so. If I'm not mistaken, ships have sometimes sailed through these milky seas for more than forty miles."

I don't know whether Conseil heeded my advice, but he appeared to be plunged in deep meditation, doubtless trying to work out how many hundredths of an inch could be packed into an area forty miles square. I continued observing this phenomenon. For several hours the *Nautilus* cruised through these milky-white waters, and I noticed that it glided through those foamy waves silently, as if it were floating in one of those frothy eddies that can be seen when two currents, flowing in opposite directions, converge.

Toward midnight the sea suddenly resumed its normal color. But behind us, as far as the eye could see, the sky continued to reflect the white color of the waves, and for a long time it seemed to be illuminated by the delicate glimmers of the aurora borealis.

Chapter II

ANOTHER EXCURSION WITH CAPTAIN NEMO

AT MIDDAY on the 28th of January, when the *Nautilus* came up to the surface at latitude 9° 4' north, I could see land about eight miles to the west. First of all, I noticed a group of mountains about two thousand feet high, very peculiarly shaped. Then I went below, and when our bearings had been marked on the chart, I saw that the land in question was Ceylon, that pearl that hangs from the lower lobe of the Indian peninsula.

I went into the library to look for a book about this island which is one of the most fertile in the world, and found a volume by H. C. Sirr, *Ceylon and the Singhalese*. Returning to the saloon, I noted a few basic facts about Ceylon, which has been given so many different names throughout the ages. Its position, I learned, was between latitudes 5° 55' and 9° 49' north and longitudes 79° 42' and 82° 4' east; its length 275 miles, and its maximum width, 150 miles; its circumference, 900 miles; and its surface area, 24,448 square miles, or somewhat less than that of Ireland.

At that moment, Captain Nemo and his second-in-command appeared. The Captain glanced at the chart, and turning to me, said:

"Ceylon is famous for its pearl fisheries. Would you like to visit them, Monsieur Aronnax?"

"I certainly would, Captain."

"Very good. No problem about that. We can visit the fisheries, but we will not see the fishers. The annual harvest hasn't yet begun. But it doesn't matter. I will give orders to head for the Gulf of Manaar. We should get there sometime tonight."

The Captain then spoke a few words to his second-in-command, who immediately left the room. A few minutes later the *Nautilus* returned to the deep, and the manometer showed a depth of thirty feet.

Studying the chart, I looked for the Gulf of Manaar, and found it at the 9th parallel, on the northwest coast of Ceylon. It was formed by a continuation of the waters off the little island of Manaar, and in order to reach the spot, we had to sail up the west coast of Ceylon.

"Professor," Captain Nemo said, "there are pearl fisheries in the Bay of Bengal, in the Indian Ocean, in the seas of China and Japan, in South American waters, in the Gulf of Panama, and in the Gulf of California; but the best pearls of all are obtained in Ceylon. It's a bit early to go there, of course, because the fishermen do not arrive in the Gulf of Manaar until March. With their three hundred boats, they spend about thirty days in lucrative exploitation of the sea's treasure. Each boat is manned by ten oarsmen and ten fishermen. The latter, divided into two groups, take turns diving, down to a depth of about forty feet, by means of a heavy stone which they hold between their feet and which is tied to the boat by means of a long rope."

"You mean," I said, "they still use these primitive means?"

"Yes, they still do," replied Captain Nemo, "although these fisheries belong to the most industrialized people in the world, the English, who took possession in 1802 by the Treaty of Amiens."

"But I should have thought that diving equipment like that used by you would prove extremely useful in this work."

"Indeed it would, because these poor fishermen cannot stay underwater very long. The Englishman Percival, in his description of his journey to Ceylon, mentions a Kaffir who stayed down for five minutes without coming up for a breath, but that seems pretty incredible to me. However, I do know that some divers can last as long as fifty-seven seconds, and the most skillful up to eighty-seven. But such cases are rare, and when these unfortunate men come back on board, bloody water pours from their ears and noses. I believe that the average time that pearl fishers can stay underwater is thirty seconds, during which they hasten to fill a small net with all the pearl-bearing oysters they can gather. In general, the fishermen do not live to be very old; their sight grows weak, ulcers form on their eyes, sores on their bodies, and often they are seized with apoplexy and die in the water."

"Yes," I said, "it's a melancholy task and one that serves only to satisfy the caprices of fashion! But tell me, Captain, how many oysters can a boat fish up in a day?"

"About forty or fifty thousand. It is even said that in 1814, when the British Government sent out some of its own divers, they collected seventy-six million oysters in twenty days."

"But are these fishermen at least adequately paid?" I asked.

"Not really, Professor. At Panama, they only make a dollar a week. More often, they get a penny for each oyster containing a pearl; but how many oysters contain no pearl at all!"

"A penny for those poor people, so their masters can get rich? How appalling!"

"So, Professor," Captain Nemo said to me, "your companions and yourself shall visit the Manaar oyster bed, and if by chance some early fisherman is already working there, we shall see how he does it."

"Good, Captain."

"By the way, Monsieur Aronnax, I suppose you are not afraid of sharks?"

"Sharks!" I exclaimed. That struck me as being a gratuitous question, to say the least.

"Well?" Captain Nemo repeated.

"I must admit, Captain, that I am not very well acquainted with that type of fish."

"We are used to them," rejoined Captain Nemo, "and in time you will be used to them. We will be armed, and on the way we might perhaps hunt a few. It's an excellent sport. I will see you early tomorrow, Professor."

After saying this in his noncommittal tone of voice, Captain Nemo left the saloon.

If one were invited to go bear hunting in the Swiss mountains, one would probably say: "Good! Tomorrow we will be hunting bears"; if one were invited to go lion hunting in the plains of Atlas, or tiger hunting in the Indian jungle, one's reaction would probably be: "Ah, I see. So we are going to hunt for tigers or lions!" But when one is invited to hunt sharks in their home grounds, one may well ask permission to think the matter over before accepting.

Indeed, when I passed my hand across my forehead, I detected a few drops of cold sweat.

"Yes, let us think this matter over," I said to myself, "and take our time. Hunting otter in underwater forests, as we did in the forests of the Isle of Crespo, that is all well and good. But to walk about the bottom of the sea where one is fairly certain to run into sharks, that is quite another matter! I know that in some countries, particularly in the Andaman Islands, the natives do not hesitate to attack sharks with a dagger in one hand and a noose in the other, but I know too that many who confront these formidable creatures do not come back alive. What is more, I am not a native, and even if I were, I do not think a little hesitation on my part would be out of place."

And so there I was, dreaming of sharks, of those huge jaws, bristling with row upon row of teeth capable of cutting a man in two. I could already feel a pain in my back in anticipation. Moreover, I couldn't get over the nonchalant way in which the Captain had issued his deplorable invitation. It had been said as if we were going to track down some harmless fox!

"All right," I thought, "we shall see. Conseil certainly will not want to come, and that will give me an excuse to get out of this predicament."

As for Ned Land, I was not so confident about him. The greater the danger, the more he was attracted to it.

I went back to Sirr's book, but found I was turning the pages over mechanically without reading. All I could see on those pages were the open jaws of sharks!

Just then Conseil and the Canadian came in. They looked calm, even happy. They didn't realize what was in store for them.

"Believe it or not, monsieur," said Ned Land, "Captain Nemo, may the Devil take him, has just made us a very pleasant proposal."

"Ah," I said, "you know!"

"If Monsieur does not mind," replied Conseil, "the Captain of the *Nautilus* has invited us—and Monsieur—to visit the magnificent pearl fisheries of Ceylon. His invitation was most gracious, and he acted very much like a gentleman."

"Did he give you any details about . . . ?"

"No details, monsieur," replied the Canadian, "except to say that he had already spoken to you about this little excursion."

"That is quite true. He did," I said. "But didn't he give you any details about, er . . . ?"

"None at all, monsieur. But you'll be coming with us, won't you?"

"I? Oh yes, of course! I can see you are looking forward to this, Master Land."

"Oh yes! It sounds very interesting indeed."

"It might even be dangerous!" I insinuated.

"Dangerous! A simple visit to an oyster bed!" replied Ned Land scornfully.

Obviously Captain Nemo had deemed it pointless to put the idea of sharks into the heads of my companions. I looked at them with a somewhat worried eye, as if they had already lost a limb. Should I warn them? Of course, but I didn't quite know how to go about it.

"Would Monsieur please give us some details about pearl fishing?" Conseil asked.

"Do you mean about the fishing itself," I asked, "or about the . . . attending circumstances?"

"About the fishing," replied the Canadian. "It's always best to know the lay of the land before setting out."

"Well, my friends, sit down, and I will tell you all I have just learned from the English author, H. C. Sirr."

Ned and Conseil sat down on a divan, and the Canadian said:

"Now, monsieur, just what is a pearl?"

"Well, Ned," I replied. "It depends. For the poet, the pearl is a tear shed by the sea; for Orientals, it's a bead of solidified dew; for women, it is an oblong-shaped jewel of enamel-like substance and glassy brilliance which they wear on their fingers, around their necks, or on their ears; for the chemist, it is a mixture of phosphate and carbonate of lime, with a little gelatin; and for the naturalist, it is an abnormal growth emanating from the organ that produces mother-of-pearl in certain mollusks."

"Division: mollusca," said Conseil, "class: acephali; order: testacea."

"Precisely, my learned Conseil. Now among these testacea, the abalone, the earshell, the tridacnae, the pinnae marinae—in short, all those that secrete mother-of-pearl—that blue, violet, or white substance that lines the inside of their shells—are also capable of producing pearls."

"Mussels too?" asked the Canadian.

"Yes, mussels in certain rivers in Scotland, Wales, Ireland, Saxony, Bohemia, and France."

"Good! I'll bear that in mind in the future," replied the Canadian.

"But," I continued, "the mollusk *par excellence* that secretes the pearl is the pearl oyster, that precious pintadine. The pearl is nothing but a nacreous concretion, deposited in globular form, either attached to the shell or buried in the folds of the oyster. On the shell it sticks fast; in the flesh it is loose. But it always has for its kernel a small hard substance, maybe a barren egg, or a sand grain, around which the pearly matter is deposited year after year, in thin concentric layers."

"Does one ever find more than one pearl in the same oyster?" asked Conseil.

"Yes indeed. Some oysters are veritable jewel boxes. I have even heard of an oyster—though I have some doubts on the matter—that contained no fewer than one hundred and fifty sharks."

"One hundred and fifty *sharks!*" cried Ned Land.

"Did I say sharks?" I exclaimed. "Of course, I meant one hundred and fifty pearls. Sharks wouldn't make sense."

"Indeed not," said Conseil. "But would Monsieur now tell me how these pearls are extracted?"

"They do it in various ways. When the pearls adhere to the shell, the fishermen may pull them off with pliers. But the most common way is to lay the pintadines out on mats made from a certain seaweed that covers the banks. They die in the open air, and after ten days or so they are in an advanced stage of decomposition. Then they are dipped into tanks of seawater, opened, and washed. Now the extractors begin their work. First they remove the layers of pearls, known in commerce as genuine silvers, bastard whites, and bastard blacks which are packed in cases of two hundred and fifty to three hundred pounds each. Then they take the parenchyma—or the flesh—of the oyster, boil it, and pull it through a sieve in order to catch the smallest pearls."

"And does the price of pearls vary according to size?" asked Conseil.

"Not only according to size, but also according to shape, their 'water'—that is to say, their color—and their luster—that is, that bright, dappled sparkle that makes them so attractive to the eye. The most beautiful are called virgin pearls or paragons. They are formed in the tissue of the mollusk. They are white, often opaque, but often they have the transparency of the opal. They are usually round or oval. The round make good bracelets, the ovals are made into pendants; being more precious, they can be sold singly. Pearls that adhere to the shell are irregular in shape, and they are sold by weight. Finally, we come to those small pearls known as seed pearls. They are sold by measure, usually to be used in embroidery for church ornaments and the like."

"But surely the task of separating pearls according to their size must be long and difficult?" suggested the Canadian.

"No, my friend, not at all. It is done by means of eleven sieves or strainers, pierced with varying numbers of holes. Pearls that do not pass through a sieve whose holes vary from twenty to eighty in number are of the first quality. Those that do not drop through a sieve having a hundred to eight hundred holes are second-class pearls. Finally, the pearls for which they must use a sieve having from nine hundred to a thousand holes are known as seed pearls."

"Very clever," said Conseil. "So separation and classification of pearls is done mechanically. And could Monsieur tell us how much money is made with these oyster beds?"

"According to Sirr's book," I replied, "the Ceylon pearl fisheries yield the annual sum of three million sharks."

"Francs. Monsieur means francs!" Conseil corrected me.

"Yes, yes, of course, francs," I agreed. "Three million francs! But I believe that these fisheries no longer bring in as much as they used to; and the same can be said for the

American fisheries which, during the reign of Charles V, yielded four million francs, an income now reduced to two-thirds that amount. The overall proceeds from pearl fishing can at present be taken as nine million francs."

"But," asked Conseil, "aren't there some famous pearls that have been valued at a very high price?"

"Yes, my lad, there are. It is said that Caesar offered Servilia* a pearl valued at one hundred and twenty thousand francs in today's currency."

"I've even heard it said," the Canadian remarked, "that there was a lady in ancient times who drank pearls in vinegar."

"Cleopatra," replied Conseil.

"It must have tasted awful," interjected Ned Land.

"Yes, horrible, Ned," replied Conseil, "but a little glass of vinegar worth a million and a half francs is not to be despised."

"Ah, I'm still sorry I didn't marry that woman," the Canadian murmured absentmindedly.

"Ned Land as the husband of Cleopatra!" joked Conseil.

"I was all set to get married, Conseil," replied the Canadian seriously. "It wasn't my fault if the affair didn't turn out well. I had even bought a pearl necklace for my fiancée, Kate Tender, but she went off and married another man. Believe it or not, the pearls in that necklace would not have passed through the largest sieve, and yet I didn't pay more than one dollar fifty for it!"

"But my good Ned"—I laughed—"those were just artificial pearls, hollow glass beads filled with a mother-of-pearl-like substance."

"And is that stuff expensive?" asked Ned.

"It is very, very cheap. It is nothing but the silvery substance found on the scales of a fish called the bleak, preserved in ammonia. It has no value."

"Perhaps that's why Kate Tender married someone else." Ned Land remarked philosophically.

"However," I said, "to get back to the subject of valuable pearls, I doubt if any king ever possessed a pearl superior to Captain Nemo's."

"You mean this one," said Conseil, pointing to a magnificent jewel in a glass case.

"I am sure I shouldn't be wrong in valuing it at two million—"

* Daughter of Q. Servilius Caepio. She was married to M. Innius Brutus, by whom she became the mother of Brutus, who killed Caesar. —M.T.B.

"Francs!" Conseil interposed quickly.

"Yes," I said. "Two million francs—and I am sure that all it cost the Captain was the trouble of bending down to pick it up."

"Ah!" cried Ned Land. "Who knows whether on our excursion tomorrow we may not come across another one like it?"

"Pooh!" said Conseil.

"And why not?"

"What good would millions of francs be to us on board the *Nautilus?*"

"I don't mean on board," said Ned Land. "I mean . . . elsewhere."

"Oh! Elsewhere!" said Conseil, nodding.

"Of course," I said, "Master Land is right. If ever we could bring back to Europe or America a pearl worth a few millions, it would at least lend great authenticity to—and, at the same time, set a high price on—the story of our adventures."

"I can believe that," remarked the Canadian.

"But," said Conseil, who always reverted to the practical, "is this pearl fishing dangerous?"

"Oh, not at all," I replied immediately, "especially if one takes certain precautions."

"And just what might the danger be?" asked Ned Land. "Swallowing a few mouthfuls of salt water?"

"That is quite true, Ned. But by the way," I said, trying to sound as matter-of-fact as Captain Nemo, "are you afraid of sharks, Ned?"

"Me!" replied the Canadian. "A professional harpooner! Why, it's part of my job to laugh at them!"

"It is not a question," I said, "of fishing for them with a hook and swivel, hoisting them up on deck, hacking off their tails, slitting open their bellies, ripping out their guts and throwing them into the sea."

"You mean, it's a question of . . . ?"

"Precisely."

"What, in the water?"

"In the water."

"Well, you know, with a good harpoon . . . You see, monsieur, these sharks are pretty clumsily built. They have to turn over on their bellies to catch you, and in the meantime . . ."

Ned Land had a way of saying that word "catch" that sent cold shivers down one's spine.

"What about you, Conseil? What do you think of sharks?"

"Well," said Conseil, "I'll be quite frank with Monsieur."

"This sounds more like it," I thought to myself.

"If Monsieur is prepared to face the sharks," said Conseil, "I see no reason why his faithful servant should not be at his side."

Chapter III

A PRICELESS PEARL

WHEN NIGHT FELL, I went to bed. I slept very badly. Sharks played an important part in my nightmares. I found that it was both just and unjust that the French word *requin* ("shark") should be so close, etymologically speaking, to the word *requiem*.*

On the following day, at four A.M., I was awakened by the steward that Captain Nemo had assigned to me. I rose quickly, dressed, and went along to the saloon.

Captain Nemo was waiting.

"Monsieur Aronnax," he said, "are you ready?"

"I am ready."

"Will you follow me."

"And my friends, Captain?"

"They are waiting for us."

"Aren't we going to put on our diving suits?" I asked.

"Not yet. I haven't taken the *Nautilus* too close to the coast, and we are still some distance from the Manaar reef. But the dinghy is ready. It will take us to the exact spot and save us a long walk. Our diving suits are in the dinghy, and we shall put them on before beginning our excursion under the water."

Captain Nemo led me to the center staircase leading to the platform. Ned and Conseil were waiting there, delighted at the prospect of a "pleasure trip." Five sailors of the *Nautilus*, their oars in place, were ready in the dinghy, which had been made fast alongside.

The night was still dark. Layers of cloud covered the sky and allowed only an occasional glimpse of the stars. I cast my eyes in the direction of land, but I saw only a dim line running along the three-quarters of the horizon from the southwest to the northwest. The *Nautilus*, which during the night had sailed up the west coast of Ceylon, was now to the west of the bay, or rather gulf, formed by this stretch of land and the Isle of Manaar. There, beneath the dark waters, lay

* In English, the man-eater shark is called a *requin* and some tropical sharks are known as *requiem sharks*.—M.T.B.

the pintadine reef, an inexhaustible pearl field that stretched out for more than twenty miles.

Captain Nemo, Conseil, Ned Land, and I took up our places at the stern of the dinghy. The mate held the helm; his four companions were at their oars; the rope was cast off and we set out.

The dinghy headed south. The oarsmen did not hurry. I noticed that their strokes, although pulled vigorously through the water, followed each other at intervals of ten seconds. This was the usual timing adopted by most navies. When the boat was sliding through the water under its own momentum, oars up, liquid drops splashed crisply onto the dark surface of the waves, like spatters of molten lead. A slight swell, from out to sea, caused the dinghy to roll gently, and little crests of water flapped against the bow.

We remained silent. What was Captain Nemo thinking about? Perhaps of that land we were approaching, which he found too near, unlike Ned, who doubtless found it too far. As for Conseil, he had come merely out of curiosity.

Toward half past five, the first tints of the horizon began to give definite shape to the upper line of the coast. Fairly flat to the east, it broadened out toward the south. We were still five miles off, and the shoreline mingled with the misty waters. Between us and the shore, the sea was deserted. Not a boat, not a diver. A profound silence reigned over this meeting place of the pearl fishers. As Captain Nemo had said to me, we had arrived in these parts a month too soon.

At six o'clock, day broke with that suddenness that is characteristic of tropical regions, where there is no real dawn or twilight. The sun's rays pierced the banks of clouds on the eastern horizon, and the radiant sun rose quickly into the sky.

I could see the land distinctly, with trees scattered here and there.

The dinghy approached the Isle of Manaar, which appeared to the south. Captain Nemo stood up and inspected the sea.

At a signal from him the anchor was dropped, but the chain was not allowed to run far, for the sea here was not more than three or four feet deep; this was one of the shallowest points of the pintadine sea bank. The dinghy swung around in the outgoing tide.

"Here we are, Monsieur Aronnax," said Captain Nemo. "Do you see that narrow bay? In a month it will be crowded with boats of the exploiters and these waters will be a veritable hunting ground for bold divers who will rummage the very bottom of these waters. The bay is well situated for this sort of fishing. It is sheltered from the strong winds, and the sea is generally calm, all of which is very helpful to divers. Let us put on our diving suits and begin our excursion."

I remained silent, but I could not help looking at those waters with apprehension. I began to don my diving suit with the help of the sailors on board. Captain Nemo and my two companions did likewise. None of the men of the *Nautilus* was to accompany us on this new excursion.

In a short while we were imprisoned up to our necks in our rubber clothing, with our air tanks strapped to our backs. There was no sign of the Ruhmkorff lights. Before placing my head in the copper helmet, I mentioned this to the Captain.

"Lights would be useless," replied the Captain. "We shall not be going very deep, and the rays of the sun will be sufficient to light up our path. Besides, it is not wise to carry an electric lantern here. Its brilliancy might well attract some dangerous denizens of these waters."

As Captain Nemo said that I turned to Ned and Conseil, but my two friends had already put on their metal helmets and could neither hear nor answer me.

I had one more question to put to the Captain.

"And our weapons," I asked him, "our guns?"

"Guns! What for? Mountain folk face the bear with a knife alone, and isn't steel surer than lead? Here is a strong knife. Put it in your belt and let us go."

I looked at my friends. They were armed like us, but Ned was also brandishing an enormous harpoon, which he had put in the dinghy before we left the *Nautilus*.

Then, following the Captain's example, I allowed the heavy copper sphere to be placed over my head, and our air tanks were immediately turned on.

A moment later, the sailors put us over the side one after the other, and we found ourselves standing on even sand, in four or five feet of water. Captain Nemo gestured with his hand. We followed him down a gentle incline and disappeared under the waves.

Once in the water, my fears and apprehension vanished. I became surprisingly calm again. The ease with which I could move increased my confidence, and the strange surroundings captivated my imagination.

The sunrays were already penetrating the waters, and their light was enough for us to distinguish even the smallest objects. After walking for ten minutes, we were in a depth of about fifteen feet, and the bottom leveled off.

Schools of strange fish of the genus of the monopteridae, resembling snipe in a marsh, rose at our feet. These fish have no fins except their tail. I recognized the Javanese, a real serpent, about a yard long, with its livid belly. It might easily be confused with a conger eel but for the gold stripes along its sides. Of the stromateid genus, whose bodies are very flat and oval, I noticed some with the most brilliant hues, carrying their dorsal fin like a scythe. These edible fish, dried and pickled, made an excellent dish known as *karawade*. I saw tranquebars, belonging to the apsiphoroidal genus, whose bodies are covered with a scaly armor made up of eight longitudinal sections.

In the meanwhile, the rising sun lit the depths more and more intensively. The sea bottom changed slowly as we went. From a fine sand, we came to an embankment of round-edged rocks, which was covered by a carpet of mollusks and zoophytes. Amidst the sparkling of these two species, I noticed placenae with flimsy and irregular shells—a sort of oyster peculiar to the Red Sea and the Indian Ocean; some orange lucinae with rounded shells; the awl-like terebellum; some fishy purpura which provided the *Nautilus* with an admirable dye; horned murices, up to six inches long, which stood up under the waves like hands ready to seize you; cornigerous turbinellae, bristling with spikes; lingulae hyantes; anatinae, mollusks sold for food on the Hindustan markets; panopyeres, which were slightly luminous; and finally, oculines, like magnificent fans, which form one of the richest treelike growths of these seas.

In the midst of these living plants, and beneath the arbors of hydrophytes, swam legions of clumsy articulates, especially the toothed raninae, whose shell was like a slightly rounded triangle; the birgi, peculiar to these waters; and the loathsome parthenopes, very repugnant to the eye. Another animal, no less hideous, which I met on several occasions, was the giant crab mentioned by Darwin. Nature has given this creature the instinct and the strength to feed on coconuts. It climbs trees that grow on the shore, knocks down coconuts, which break open when they fall, and opens them with its powerful claws. Here, beneath the clear waves, it could be seen moving with incredible speed, while errant turtles of a species frequently found along the coasts of Malabar clambered slowly among the scattered rocks.

Toward seven o'clock, we finally reached the banks where pearl oysters reproduce by the million.

These precious mollusks were clinging to the rocks, attached to them by a brown-colored byssus which prevents them from moving; for this reason these oysters are inferior to mussels, which have some freedom of movement, however limited.

The meleagrina pearl oyster, whose valves are much the

same size, has a round thick shell and a corrugated exterior. Some of these shells were flecked and streaked with greenish grooves, radiating from the top down. These were the young oysters. The others, ten years or older, had a rugged black shell and measured as much as six inches in diameter.

Captain Nemo pointed to that enormous mass of pearl oysters, and I realized that this was, indeed, an inexhaustible mine, for nature's creative powers, it seemed, were greater than the power of man to destroy. Ned Land, faithful to this destructive instinct in man, was quickly filling a mesh net with the finest specimens.

But we could not stop. We had to follow the Captain, who appeared to be proceeding along paths known only to him. The bottom rose noticeably, and sometimes I could raise my arm above the surface of the sea. Then the level of the bank would drop suddenly again. We often walked around high rocks tapered like pyramids. In the dark recesses of those rocks, there lurked giant crustaceans, poised on their claws like war machines, staring at us with glaring eyes, and around our feet crawled myrianidae, ariciae, and annelidae, extending their very long antennae and tentacles outward.

Just then a vast grotto appeared before us, hollowed out in a picturesque mass of rocks, covered with all the flora of the sea. At first it seemed to be in total darkness. The rays of the sun appeared to be dimmed by degrees, and the light, absorbed by the sea, disappeared beneath the waters.

Captain Nemo went in. We followed. My eyes soon became accustomed to that vague darkness inside. I could make out the contorted and whimsical curves of the vaults, supported by natural pillars resting on a granite foundation, which reminded me of the heavy columns seen in Tuscan architecture. Why was our inscrutable guide taking us into this crypt in the depths of the sea? I was soon to know.

After descending a fairly steep slope, our feet touched the bottom of a sort of circular pit. There, Captain Nemo stopped, and with a gesture of his hand, pointed to an object that I had not noticed.

It was an oyster of extraordinary size, a gigantic clam that could have been made into a holy-water basin, large enough to hold a little lake of holy water, a basin whose diameter was more than seven feet and larger than the one in the saloon of the *Nautilus*.

I approached this phenomenal mollusk. It was attached by its byssus to a block of granite, and it was growing and living alone in the quiet waters of that grotto. I guessed its weight to be around 650 pounds. Such an oyster would have some

30 pounds of meat, and only a Gargantuan stomach could digest a dozen or so.

Obviously Captain Nemo had already known of the existence of this bivalve. It wasn't the first time that he had paid it a visit, and I imagined that he had taken us there just to show us a curious marvel of nature. But I was mistaken. Captain Nemo had a special reason for wanting to see how this creature was coming along.

The two halves of the mollusk were partly open, and the Captain went up to it and inserted his dagger between the valves to prevent them from closing. Then, with his hand, he lifted the covering membrane, which formed a protective layer for the animal.

There, between the foliagelike folds, I saw a loose pearl the size of coconut. Its globular shape, its perfect clarity, its magnificent luster, made it a jewel of inestimable value. Overwhelmed by my curiosity, I stretched out my hand to grasp it, to weigh it, to feel it! But the Captain stopped me, indicated he did not want it touched, and withdrawing his dagger, allowed the two halves to close quickly.

Now I realized what he had in mind. By leaving this pearl inside the creature, he was permitting it to grow slowly but indefinitely. Each year the secretion of the mollusk would add additional concentric layers. Only he knew the grotto where the most admirable "fruit" of nature was maturing! Only he was cultivating this fruit, so to speak, so that someday he could display it in his precious collection! Perhaps, following the example of the Chinese and the Persians, he had been "breeding" that pearl by placing pieces of glass or metal under the fleshy fold of that creature. In any case, comparing this pearl with those which were already in the Captain's collection, I estimated its value at ten million francs, at least. But this, however, was only a marvel of nature, not a piece of jewelry to be worn by feminine ears. It was just a bit too heavy for that, I thought.

Our visit to the opulent tridacne was over. Captain Nemo left the grotto, and we climbed back to the oyster bank, where the clear waters were still undisturbed by the work of the divers.

We made our way, each strolling, stopping, or wandering off in somewhat various directions. I was no longer troubled by those fears that my imagination had so ridiculously exaggerated. The bottom of the sea kept rising toward the surface of the water and I was soon walking in three or four feet of water with my head out of the water. Conseil walked up to me, and putting his helmet beside mine, raised his eyes in a friendly greeting. But this high plateau lasted for only a very short distance, and we were soon back in the deep waters.

Ten minutes later, Captain Nemo stopped suddenly. I thought he had stopped in order that we might retrace our steps. Not at all. With a gesture, he ordered us to squat down beside him at the bottom of a deep crevasse. He pointed with his hand in a certain direction, and I looked very carefully to see what he saw.

Fifteen feet from me a shadow appeared, which dropped to the bottom of the sea. The disturbing thought of sharks flashed through my mind, but I soon realized I was mistaken. We were not being troubled by sea monsters. It was a man, an Indian diver, a poor devil, no doubt, who had come to gather "fruit" before the harvest. I could see the bottom of his boat anchored a few feet above his head. He dived and rose again and again. A stone, held between his feet, was tied with a rope and connected to the boat. This helped him to get to the bottom more rapidly. This was his only implement. Once down to the bottom, in about fifteen feet of water, he dropped to his knees and filled his bag with oysters picked at random. Then he would rise, empty his sack, pull up the stone, and start over again. Every trip took no longer than thirty seconds.

The diver did not see us. The shadow of a rock hid us. Besides, how could that poor Indian imagine that men, beings like him, were there beneath the water, watching him and observing every detail of his labors?

Several times he went up and down, but he could not bring up more than ten oysters at a time because he had to rip them from the rocks to which they were firmly attached. And how many of those oysters, for which he was risking his life, contained no pearls!

I kept watching him very closely. He worked with speed and precision. For half an hour, no danger seemed to threaten him. I was somewhat taken by the spectacle of that interesting manner of pearl fishing when suddenly, while the Indian was on his knees, I saw him make a gesture of terror, get up quickly, ready to spring to the surface.

I understood that terror! A gigantic shadow appeared above that unfortunate diver. It was a shark of huge dimensions, moving speedily toward him with his jaws wide open and fire in his eyes!

I was mute with horror, completely paralyzed. With a vigorous blow of his fin, the voracious monster shot toward the Indian, who jumped to one side and avoided the shark's bite. But he could not avoid the monster's tail, which struck him on the chest and threw him flat on the ocean floor. This scene had scarcely lasted more than a few seconds. Then the animal, turning over, came back, ready to cut the poor man in two, when I saw Captain Nemo, who was next to me, suddenly get up and, dagger in hand, make straight for the monster, ready to fight it hand-to-hand.

Just as the shark was ready to snap the unhappy diver in two, he saw his new adversary, and turning over, made straight for him.

I can still see the posture of Captain Nemo. Bracing himself, and with admirable sangfroid, he waited for the formidable enemy, and when the monster lunged at him, he sidestepped with incredible speed, avoided the jaws of the animal, and plunged his dagger into the belly of the monster. The battle was not over, however. A terrible struggle followed.

The shark had roared, as it were. Blood poured from its wounds. The waters turned red, and through those darkened waters I no longer saw anything.

Nothing, until a clear spot appeared in the water, when I saw the intrepid Captain holding fast to one of the fins, still struggling hand-to-hand with the monster, riddling, with blows of his dagger, the belly of the enemy, but unable to reach his heart. The shark churned the water so furiously that the rocking almost upset me. I would have liked to help the Captain, but paralyzed with horror, I was unable to move.

I looked on with dread. I saw the battle take a new turn. The Captain fell on the ground, brought down by the enormous weight of the creature. The shark's jaws opened wide, like a shearing machine, and it would have been all over with the Captain if Ned Land, with the speed of lightning, had not rushed forward and struck it with his harpoon. The waves were a mass of blood. The shark beat them with an indescribable fury. Ned Land, however, had not missed. This was the monster's death battle. Struck to the heart, it struggled with frightful convulsions, whose shocks knocked Conseil down.

In the meanwhile, Ned Land had extricated the Captain, who, apparently unhurt, went over to the Indian, cut the rope tying him to the rock, took him in his arms, and with one vigorous kick of the heel, brought him to the surface. Saved by a miracle, the three of us followed suit, and in a moment we reached the diver's boat.

The Captain's first care was to bring that poor fellow back to life. I did not know whether he would succeed. I had hopes, however, since the man had not been down very long, but he might have been killed by the monster's tail.

Fortunately, with both Conseil and the Captain working vigorously to revive him, he slowly regained his consciousness and opened his eyes. What must have been his surprise or his fear to see four large copper helmets bending over him? But, above all, what must he have thought when Captain Nemo pulled a bag of pearls from a pocket of his diving suit and put them in his hand? With a trembling hand the poor Indian accepted these alms from the man of the sea, but his startled eyes indicated that he did not know to what supermen he owed both his life and his fortune.

At a sign from the Captain, we returned to the oyster bed and, following the path already traversed, arrived, in about half an hour, at the anchor which held the dinghy. Once in the boat, with the aid of the sailors we took off our heavy helmets. Captain Nemo's first words were addressed to the Canadian.

"Thank you, Master Land."

"I was repaying a debt, that's all," answered Ned Land. A smile appeared on the Captain's face. That was all.

"Back to the *Nautilus*," he said.

The boat sped over the waves. A few minutes later we came across the floating body of the shark. By the black coloring on the tips of its fins, I could classify it as belonging to the terrible melanopteron of the Indian Ocean. It was more than twenty-five feet long, and its enormous mouth occupied more than a third of its body. It was an adult, as could be determined by its six rows of teeth arranged in the form of an isosceles triangle in the upper jaw. Conseil looked at it from a scientific point of view, and I am certain that he classified it correctly as belonging to a species of cartilaginous fish, class chondrichthyes, with fixed gills, order selachii, in the genus Squali.

While I was looking at that inert mass, a dozen of those voracious melanopterons suddenly appeared around the boat. But without paying attention to us, they fell upon that floating carcass and fought for every shred.

At eight thirty we were back on the *Nautilus*. Once there I took time thinking about that excursion to the Manaar beds. Two observations came clearly to mind. One was about the incomparable courage of Captain Nemo; the other, his devotion to a human being, a representative of that race from which he was fleeing beneath the sea. Whatever one might say, that strange man had not yet succeeded in completely killing his own heart.

When I called his attention to this, he answered, somewhat moved:

"That Indian, Monsieur le Professeur, lives in the land of the oppressed, and I belong, and—to my last breath—will always belong, to that land!"

Chapter IV

THE RED SEA

DURING THE DAY of the 29th of January, the island of Ceylon disappeared over the horizon, and the *Nautilus*, at a speed of twenty knots, entered into that labyrinth of channels that separates the Maldives from the Laccadives. We even cruised past the island of Kiltan, coral in origin, and which was discovered by Vasco da Gama in 1499, one of the nineteen main islands of the Laccadive Archipelago, situated between latitudes 10° and 14° 30′ degrees north, and longitudes 69° and 50° 72′ degrees east.

We had traveled 16,220 miles, or 7,500 leagues, from our point of departure in the Sea of Japan.

On the following day—the 30th of January—when the *Nautilus* rose once more to the surface of the ocean, there was no land in sight. Our course was north-northwest, and we were heading toward the Gulf of Oman, lying between the Arabian mainland and the Indian peninsula, and providing an entrance to the Persian Gulf.

It was evidently a dead end, without any possible outlet. Where was Captain Nemo taking us? I could not say. But that did not satisfy the Canadian, who had asked me where we were going.

"We are going, Master Ned, where the Captain's whims will take us."

"Those whims," replied the Canadian, "cannot take us very far. The Persian Gulf has no outlet, and if we enter it, it will not be long before we come back out again."

"Then we shall simply come back out again, Master Ned, and if, after the Persian Gulf, the *Nautilus* takes a notion to visit the Red Sea, the Strait of Bab el Mandeb will always be there to let us through."

"I don't have to tell you, sir," replied Ned Land, "that the Red Sea, like the Persian Gulf, has no outlet. The Isthmus of Suez has not yet been completed, and even if it were, a mysterious boat such as ours couldn't take any chances in a canal equipped with locks! So the Red Sea is not, for the moment, the way that will bring us to Europe."

"I did not say that we were returning to Europe."

"Well, what do *you* think is going to happen?"

"I think that after visiting the exotic coasts of Arabia and Egypt, the *Nautilus* will return to the Indian Ocean, perhaps through the Mozambique Channel, or perhaps around the Mascarene Islands, and then head straight for the Cape of Good Hope."

"And once at the Cape of Good Hope? What then?" asked the Canadian in his insistent manner.

"Well, it is possible that we may sail into the Atlantic, which we have not yet explored. It is evident, Ned, that you are getting tired of this voyage under the sea. These endless visions of the marvels of the sea bore you. As far as I am concerned, Ned, I should regret the end of a journey which few men will ever have the opportunity to take."

"But do you realize, Monsieur Aronnax," the Canadian answered, "that we have been prisoners aboard the *Nautilus* for almost three months?"

"No, Ned. I did not realize it, and I do not wish to. I am counting neither the days nor the hours."

"But when will it all end?"

"The end will come in good time. Besides, we can do nothing about it, and it is useless to argue. If you ever come to me, my good Ned, and say: 'We have a chance to escape,' I will discuss that with you. But such is not the case now, and, to be frank with you, I do not think Captain Nemo will ever venture into European waters."

It can be readily seen from this conversation that having become a fanatic on the subject of the *Nautilus*, I was beginning to identify myself with its commander.

Ned Land ended the conversation, muttering words as if talking to himself: "That's all very well, but in my opinion, one cannot be happy unless one is free."

For four days, until the 3rd of February, the *Nautilus* roamed the Gulf of Oman, at various speeds and depths. It seemed to be cruising at random, as if uncertain which route to take, but it never crossed the Tropic of Cancer.

On leaving this sea we caught a glimpse of Muscat, the most important town in the country of Oman. I admired its exotic appearance, built as it was amidst the black cliffs that surrounded it, on which its white houses and forests stood out in bold relief. I saw the rounded domes of its mosques, the elegant spires of its minarets, its fresh green terraces. But it was no more than a passing vision, for soon the *Nautilus* plunged once more beneath the waves of the dark coastal waters.

Then—at a distance of six miles—we skirted the Arabian coast of Mahrah and Hadramaut, its undulating ridge of mountains relieved only by an occasional ancient ruin. On the 5th of February, we finally entered the Gulf of Aden, a veritable funnel that led into the neck of Bab el Mandeb, through which the waters of the Indian Ocean pour into the Red Sea.

On the 6th of February, the *Nautilus* came within sight of Aden, perched on a promontory and connected to the mainland by a narrow isthmus—an inaccessible Gibraltar, whose fortifications were restored by the English after its capture in 1839. I caught a glimpse of the octagonal minarets of that town, which—according to the historian Edrisi—had once been the richest commercial center along the coast.

I was certain that Captain Nemo, having reached this point, would now turn back. To my great surprise he did no such thing.

The next day, on the 7th of February, we entered the Strait of Bab el Mandeb, whose name in Arabic means "The Gate of Tears." This strait is about thirty miles long and twenty miles wide, and for the *Nautilus,* traveling at top speed, sailing through it was just a matter of an hour. I saw nothing on the way, not even the Perim Island, fortified by the British for the defense of Aden. There were, in this strait, too many English and French steamers plying the routes between Suez and Bombay, Calcutta and Melbourne, Bourbon and Mauritius, for the *Nautilus* to cruise in the open sea. So she moved at a prudent depth beneath the waves.

Finally, at noon, we entered the Red Sea.

The Red Sea, that famous lake of Biblical tradition, is rarely refreshed by rains and never replenished by any important stream. Its evaporation is incessant and excessive, so that the water level drops by about five feet a year! A strange lake indeed! If it were closed off all around, it would, perhaps, have dried up completely. Its level is lower than that of its neighbors, the Caspian and the Dead Sea, whose levels remain constant, since their evaporation is equal to the waters that flow into their basins.

The Red Sea is 1,600 miles long and has an average width of about 150 miles. In the days of the Ptolemies and the Roman emperors, it was the great commercial artery of the world; with the building of the Suez Canal, the region will regain much of its prestige, a prestige that the Suez railways have already partly recovered.

I did not even try to understand the whim that had led Captain Nemo to bring us into this gulf, but I approved wholeheartedly of the *Nautilus'* having entered it. We traveled at a moderate speed, sometimes on the surface, sometimes diving to avoid a ship. I was therefore able to observe both the upper and lower strata of this very strange sea.

On the 8th of February, in the early hours of the morning, we came in sight of Moka, a town now in ruins, whose walls would crumble at the mere sound of a cannon. An occasional date tree grows here and there. At one time it was a city of considerable importance, with six public markets and twenty-six mosques. Its walls, defended by fourteen forts, were about two miles in circumference.

Then the *Nautilus* approached the shores of Africa, where the sea is considerably deeper. Through the open panels, in waters clear and crystal, we were fascinated at the sight of marvelous shrubs of dazzling corals, at huge masses of rock covered with a resplendent tapestry of green algae and fuci. What indescribable and ever-changing spectacles appeared along the coast of Libya! What colorful landscapes, whose beauty was enhanced by steep reefs and small volcanic islands! And how beautiful were the shrublike forms that appeared on the eastern shores as the *Nautilus* cruised slowly on the surface of the sea! Along the coast of Tehama the zoophytes not only flourished beneath the sea, but formed an intricate and picturesque lacework that rose sixty feet above the water! The latter were more whimsical in shape, but less colorful than the former, whose freshness is kept vivid by the water.

How many delightful hours I spent looking through those panels of the saloon! How many new specimens of underwater flora and fauna I admired beneath the gleams of our searchlight! Agaric fungoids; slate-colored sea anemones; the thalassianthus aster, among others; tubular pores, shaped like flutes, waiting only for the breath of the god Pan to produce music; conchs peculiar to these waters, spiral-shaped at the base, inhabiting the hollows in madreporic formations; finally, thousands of specimens of a polypary which I had not yet seen—the common sponge.

The common sponge, first in the order of polyps, is a strange and curious product whose usefulness is indisputable. The sponge is not a plant, as some naturalists still maintain, but an animal of the lowest species, a polyp inferior to that of coral. Its animal nature is not in question, and we can't possibly accept the opinion of the ancients, who regarded it as an intermediary species between the plant and the animal. I must say, however, that naturalists do not agree about the structure of the sponge. For some, it is a polyp; for others, like M. Milne-Edwards, it is in a category all its own.

The class of the sponges contains about three hundred species. They are found in most seas and, some of them, in certain rivers, in which they have been given the name of "fluviatiles." But their favorite waters are those of the Mediterranean, the Greek archipelagos, the coasts of Syria, and the Red Sea. There we find sponges of the best quality, whose price can go up to a hundred and fifty francs: the blond Syrian sponge, the hard Barbary sponge, etc. But since I could not hope to study these zoophytes in the seaports of the Levant, because we were separated by the insuperable Isthmus of Suez, I was happy to observe them in the waters of the Red Sea.

I called Conseil to my side while the *Nautilus*, at an average depth of twenty-five to thirty feet, sailed slowly past those beautiful rocks on the eastern coast.

Sponges of all kinds and shape grow here—pediculated, foliated, globular, and digital. They well deserve the names given them by fishermen, such as baskets, chalices, distaffs, elk's horn, lion's foot, peacock's tail, Neptune's glove. Fishermen, it seems, are better poets than scientists. From their fibrous tissue, infused with a semifluid, gelatinous substance, there trickles a tiny stream of water, which is expelled by a contracting movement after giving life to each cell. This gelatinous substance disappears at the death of the polyp, but releases ammonia as it decomposes. Nothing is then left except the horny and gelatinous fibers that constitute the domestic sponge. They are put to various uses, according to their degrees of elasticity, permeability, and resistance to wear and tear.

Those polyps we saw were clinging to rocks, to the shells of mollusks, and even to the stems of hydrophytes. They decorate every nook and turn of the rocks, some spreading out, others standing upright, and still others hanging like growths of coral. I explained to Conseil that these sponges were gathered in two ways—dredging or by hand. The latter, of course, requires the use of divers. This was preferable because it did not damage the fibers of the polypary, and therefore brought better prices.

Other zoophytes that swarmed around the sponges consisted primarily of a very elegant kind of medusa. The mollusks were represented by varieties of squid, which, according to Orbigny, are peculiar to the Red Sea, and the reptiles were represented by the *virgata* turtles, belonging to the genus chelonia, which supplied our table with wholesome and delicate dishes.

As for fish, they were abundant and often unusual. Here are some that the nets of the *Nautilus* most frequently hauled aboard: brick-red oval-shaped rays marked with blue spots and recognizable by their double set of stingers; silver-backed arnacks; whiptail stingrays; bockats, about six feet long, flapping through the waves like empty overcoats; aodons, without a single tooth in their mouths, although related to the sharks; dromedary-ostracions, whose hump ends in a curled needle a foot and a half long; ophidians, veritable marine eels, with silvery tails, bluish dorsals, brown pectoral fins tinted with gray; fiatolae, a species of stromateidae, striped with narrow gold and decked with the three colors of the French flag; blennies, fifteen inches long; superb specimens of caranxes, decorated with seven transverse black stripes, with blue and yellow fins and gold and silver scales; centropodes, flame-gold mullets with yellow heads; gobies, parrot fish, rockfish, etc., and a thousand other fish common to the oceans we had already explored.

On the 9th of February, the *Nautilus* was sailing in the widest part of the Red Sea, lying between Suakin on the west coast and Koonfidah on the east, 190 miles apart.

That day, at noon, after taking our bearings, Captain Nemo came up to the platform where I was standing. I promised myself not to let him leave without at least asking him about his future plans. When he saw me, he came to me and graciously offered me a cigar.

"Well, Monsieur le Professeur," he said. "How do you like the Red Sea? Have you observed all the wonders it offers? Have you studied its fish, its zoophytes, its sponge beds, and its coral forests? Have you noticed all the towns nestling along its shore?"

"Yes, Captain Nemo," I replied. "And the *Nautilus* has lent itself magnificently to all my studies. What a remarkable craft!"

"Yes, monsieur, intelligent, bold, and invulnerable! It fears neither the terrible storms of the Red Sea, nor its currents, nor its reefs."

"As a matter of fact," I said, "this sea has always been considered among the worst and—unless I'm mistaken—it was absolutely detested by the ancients."

"Yes, it was certainly detested, Monsieur Aronnax. The Greek and Latin historians have little good to say about it, and Strabo* maintained that it is particularly dangerous during the period of the Etesian winds and the rainy season. The Arabian Edrisi, who refers to it as the Gulf of Colzoum, tells us how ships perished in great numbers on its sandbanks, and that no one dared navigate it by night. It is, he claims, a sea

---

* Greek geographer and historian (c. 63 B.C.–A.D. 21). His works are a rich source of ancient knowledge of the world.

subject to terrible hurricanes, strewn with unfriendly isles, and with not much to offer either beneath or above the surface. In fact, the same opinion is shared by Arrian, Agatharcides, Artemidorus."

"One can readily see," I answered, "that these writers had never sailed on the *Nautilus*."

"I am afraid not," replied the Captain. "When it comes to that, I do not see that the moderns are much more advanced than the ancients. It took several centuries to discover steam. It may take another century before we may see another *Nautilus!* Progress is so slow, Monsieur le Professeur."

"Certainly," I replied, "your ship is a century ahead of its time, perhaps even more. What a shame such a secret should have to die with its inventor!"

Captain Nemo did not answer. After a few moments, however, he continued.

"You were speaking of ancient historians and what they thought of the dangers of sailing in the Red Sea, were you not?"

"Yes, indeed. But do you not think their fears were somewhat exaggerated?"

"Yes and no, Monsieur Aronnax," said Captain Nemo, with an assurance that indicated a vast knowledge concerning the Red Sea. "What is no longer a danger to modern ships, which are well rigged, solidly built, and in perfect control, thanks to the invention of steam, presented all sorts of dangers to the vessels of the ancients. Just imagine venturing on this sea in boats built with planks held together with palm ropes, smeared with powdered resin, and covered with the fat of dogfish! They had no instruments to chart their course, and they navigated by guesswork, driven only by their own resources, in waters they barely knew! Under such conditions, shipwrecks were inevitable. But in our day, steamers plying between Suez and the South Seas have nothing to fear from the furies of this gulf, in spite of the prevailing monsoons. Their captains and their passengers no longer need to offer propitiatory sacrifices before their departure, nor is there need to wear garlands and golden wreaths on their return, to appease their gods."

"I agree," I said, "and steam seems to have killed all gratitude in the heart of the seamen. But, Captain, since you appear to have studied this sea with particular care, can you tell me the origin of its name?"

"There are, Monsieur Aronnax, many theories about that. Would you care to know the opinion of a chronicler of the fourteenth century?"

"Yes, indeed."

"This imaginative person claims that its name was given to the Red Sea after the passage of the Israelites, when Pharaoh perished in the waters that closed about him at Moses' command:

> *En signe de cette merveille,*
> *Devint la mer rouge et vermeille.*
> *Non puis ne surent la nommer*
> *Autrement que la rouge mer.*

"To commemorate that marvel,
The sea turned red and vermilion;
What else could one call it then,
Except the Red Sea!"

"A poet's explanation, Captain Nemo," I replied, "but I do not find it altogether satisfactory. Tell me, what is your personal opinion?"

"My opinion, Monsieur Aronnax, is that the name 'Red Sea' is a translation of the Hebrew word 'Edom' and, if the ancients gave it this name, it was because of the special color of these waters."

"Until now, however, I have seen only clear water without any particular color."

"No doubt, but as we get closer to the end of the gulf, you will observe this strange phenomenon. I remember having seen the Bay of Tor completely red, like a lake of blood."

"Do you attribute this color to the presence of microscopic algae?"

"Yes, it is a sticky purple substance produced by little tiny plants known as *trichodesmia*. It takes millions of them to occupy one square inch! Perhaps you will see this phenomenon when we reach Tor."

"So, Captain Nemo, this is not the first time you have sailed the Red Sea aboard the *Nautilus*?"

"No, monsieur."

"A little while ago you spoke about the passage of the Israelites and the catastrophe that befell the Egyptians. May I ask you whether you have found evidence of that great historical event beneath the surface of the waters?"

"No, Professor, and for a very good reason."

"Which is . . . ?"

"The spot where Moses crossed with his people is now so sand-bound that camels can hardly bathe their legs. I need not tell you the *Nautilus* would not have enough water in which to navigate."

"And where is that spot?" I asked.

"A little above Suez, in the sound that once formed a deep

estuary when the Red Sea extended as far as the salt lakes. Now, whether that passage was miraculous or not, the Israelites did cross that plain to reach the Promised Land, and Pharaoh's army did perish at that point. I think that if excavations were undertaken under those sands, a great quantity of arms and tools of Egyptian origin would be discovered."

"That is obvious," I replied. "Let us hope that one of these days, archeologists who are ambitious enough to make a reputation for themselves will undertake these excavations, especially after the Suez Canal is completed and new towns are built on this isthmus. However, the canal is not of much use to a ship such as the *Nautilus*."

"True, of course, but very useful for the rest of the world," added the Captain. "The ancients understood only too well the importance, for commercial reasons, of connecting the Red Sea and the Mediterranean, but they did not dream of building a direct canal; they chose the way of the Nile. Very probably the canal which joined the Nile to the Red Sea was first begun by Sesostris, if tradition may be believed. What is certain is that in 615 B.C., Necos undertook the construction of a canal—fed by the waters of the Nile—across the Egyptian plain facing Arabia. This canal could be traveled in four days, and its width was such that two triremes could pass each other. It was continued by Darius, son of Hystaspes, and probably finished by Ptolemy II. Strabo saw it used for navigation, but because it sloped down gently from its source, near Bubastis, to the Red Sea, it was navigable only for a few months of the year. This canal served commerce until the time of the Antonines; it was abandoned because it filled up with sand. It was then restored on orders of Caliph Omar; it was finally filled up in 761 or 762 by Caliph Al-Mansor, who wished to prevent provisions reaching Mohammed ben Abdallah, who had rebelled against him. During the Egyptian campaign, your General Bonaparte found traces of these works in the desert of Suez. Surprised by the tide, he almost perished a few hours before reaching Hadjaroth, in the same place where Moses had camped three thousand three hundred years before him."

"At any rate, Captain, what the ancients did not dare to undertake—the junction between two seas which would shorten the route from Cadiz to the Indies by fifty-six hundred miles—de Lesseps has undertaken, and before long he will have transformed Africa into a huge island."

"Yes, Monsieur Aronnax. You have every reason to be proud of your countryman. He is a man who bestows a greater honor to a nation than the greatest captains! Like many others, he had to face only hardships and frustration, but he has triumphed, for he possesses the will of a genius. But it is deplorable to think that this great work of his, which should have been an international undertaking, and which could have brought glory to any one nation, will owe its success to the energies of one single *man*. All honor then, to Monsieur de Lesseps!"

"Yes, all honor to that great citizen," I replied, much surprised by the feeling with which Captain Nemo had just spoken.

"Unfortunately," he continued, "I will not be able to take you through the Suez Canal, but you will be able to gaze at the long promontories of Port Said the day after tomorrow, when we shall be sailing in the Mediterranean."

"In the Mediterranean!" I cried.

"Yes, Monsieur le Professeur, in the Mediterranean. Does that surprise you?"

"What astonishes me is that we will be there the day after tomorrow."

"Really?"

"Yes, Captain. Although I should no longer be surprised at anything, in view of what has happened since you took me aboard."

"But why should you be so surprised?"

"I am thinking of the fantastic speed at which you must travel to sail around Africa, double the Cape of Good Hope, and be in the Mediterranean the day after tomorrow!"

"And what makes you think that the *Nautilus* is going around Africa, Professor? Who has said anything of doubling the Cape of Good Hope?"

"How else, Captain, unless the *Nautilus* can sail on dry land or pass over the isthmus. . . ."

"Or sail under it, my dear Professor?"

"Under it!"

"Why not?" replied the Captain calmly. "A long time ago, nature created under this strip of land what man is now creating on its surface."

"What! You mean there is a—passage—underground?"

"Yes, an underground passage which I have named the Arabian Tunnel. It runs under the Suez and flows to the Gulf of Pelusium."

"But isn't this isthmus formed of shifting sands?"

"Down to a certain depth, yes. But about one hundred and seventy-five feet down, there is nothing but solid rock."

"Did you discover this passage by chance?" I asked, absolutely astonished.

"By chance and by reasoning, Monsieur le Professeur, but more by reasoning than by chance."

"As I listen to you, Captain, I find that my ears can scarcely believe what they hear."

"Ah, monsieur, '*Aures habent et non audient*'—'They have ears but hear not'—is an eternal truth. Not only does this underground passage exist, but I have used it several times. Without it, I should never have ventured into this dead end, the Red Sea."

"Would it be presumptuous to ask how you discovered this tunnel?"

"Monsieur," replied the Captain, "there can be no secrets between people who will never separate."

I pretended not to get the point and simply waited for the Captain's story.

"Monsieur le Professeur," he began, "it is the simple reasoning of a naturalist that led me to the discovery of this passage. Only I know of its existence. I had noticed that in the Red Sea and in the Mediterranean there were many fishes that were identical—ophidia, fiatoles, girelles, exocoeti, persegae, and joels. Having assured myself of this fact, I asked myself whether any communication existed between the two seas. If so, the underground current had obviously to flow from the Red Sea to the Mediterranean, simply because of the difference in their levels. I therefore fished a great number of specimens in the Suez waters. I passed a copper ring through their tails, and threw them back into the sea. A few months later, off the coasts of Syria, I caught some of them again, identified by their copper rings. I had therefore proved that there was some passage between the two seas. I looked for it in my *Nautilus,* discovered it, sailed through it, and before long, Professor, you, too, will have traveled through my Arabian Tunnel!"

Chapter V

THE ARABIAN TUNNEL

ON THAT SAME DAY I reported to Conseil and Ned that part of the conversation that I knew was of special interest to them. When I told them that within two days we would be sailing in the Mediterranean, Conseil clapped his hands with glee, but the Canadian shrugged his shoulders.

"An underground passage!" he cried. "A passage between the two seas! Who ever heard of such a thing!"

"Listen, Ned," replied Conseil. "You had never heard of the *Nautilus*, had you? No! But it does exist! You shouldn't shrug your shoulders so readily, and don't reject the existence of something just because you have never heard of it."

"Well, we will know soon enough," replied Ned, shaking his head. "After all, nothing would please me more than to believe in the existence of this tunnel, and I hope to God that we will soon be sailing in the Mediterranean."

That same evening, in latitude 21° 30′ north, the *Nautilus*, floating on the surface of the sea, approached the Arabian coast.

Djeddah, the important trading center of Egypt, Syria, Turkey, and India, came into view. I could see clearly the cluster of buildings, ships moored at the quays, and other ships anchored offshore. The sun, low on the horizon, made the white buildings of the town stand out in bold relief. On the outskirts of the town, the Bedouin quarter, built of wood or rushes, was clearly visible.

Soon, in the shadow of the evening, Djeddah disappeared from our view and the *Nautilus* dived beneath the waves, which were tinged with phosphorescent lights.

Next day, February 10th, several ships appeared, sailing in the opposite direction. The *Nautilus* once more had to submerge in the depths of the sea. But at midday, when we took our bearings, the sea was deserted, and we sailed again on the surface of the water.

Accompanied by Ned and Conseil, I went up on the platform. The coast to the east was barely visible through the mist.

223

Leaning against the dinghy, we were chatting of this and that, when Ned, pointing in the distance, said:

"Look, Professor. Can you see anything over there?"

"No, Ned," I replied, "but my eyesight is not as sharp as yours, as you know."

"Look carefully," he continued, "over there, on the starboard beam, roughly at the level of the searchlight! Don't you see a mass which appears to be moving?"

"Oh yes!" I said, "I see it now—something that looks like a black body, floating on the water."

"Another *Nautilus?*" remarked Conseil.

"No," replied the Canadian. "I may be wrong, but it looks like a sea animal."

"Are there whales in the Red Sea?" Conseil asked.

"Yes, my lad. Occasionally, they are seen in these waters."

"It isn't a whale," commented Ned, who kept his eyes fixed on the black object. "The whales and I are old friends. I could not be mistaken by their looks."

"Let us be patient," said Conseil. "The *Nautilus* is heading in that direction, and we will know what it is shortly."

Soon that blackish object could not be more than a mile away. It resembled a black reef stranded in the middle of the open sea. "What could it be?" I wondered.

"Ah! It's moving! It's diving!" shouted Ned. "Great heavens! What can it be? It doesn't have the forked tail of a whale or of a cachalot! And its fins resemble the stumps of limbs!"

"But what could it be, then?" I cried.

"Well!" said the Canadian. "There she is on her back with her teats up in the air!"

"It's a siren!" cried Conseil, "a real siren, if I may be permitted to say so."

That word "siren" cleared up the matter for me. I realized that this animal belonged to that order of sea animals that had inspired the ancients to create the fables of the mermaid —half woman, half fish.

"No," I said to Conseil, "it is not a siren, but a strange creature, nevertheless. Only a few specimens remain in the Red Sea. It is a dugong."

"Order of Sirenia, division of Pisciformae, subclass of monodelphians, class of mammals, branch of vertebrates," answered Conseil. And after this, there was nothing more to be said.

Ned kept his eyes fixed on that object. His eyes were ablaze with excitement; his hand seemed ready to launch his harpoon. He looked as if he were waiting for the right moment to plunge into the sea and come to grips with that animal in its native haunts.

"Ah! monsieur," he said, trembling with excitement. "I have never struggled with an animal like that!" All of his being was concentrated in the utterance of the word "that."

At that moment Captain Nemo appeared on the platform. He spotted the dugong, looked at Ned, understood, and addressed himself directly to Ned.

"If you had a harpoon in your hands, wouldn't it be burning your fingers now?"

"Most assuredly, sir."

"And wouldn't you like to take up your old trade again, just for one day, and add this cetacean to the list of your trophies?"

"I should like to do that very much, sir!"

"Very well, then. Go ahead, by all means."

"Thank you, sir," answered Ned, whose eyes were ablaze.

"However," continued the Captain, "for your own good, I would advise you not to miss."

"Is it dangerous to attack these animals?" I asked, in spite of the Canadian's shrug of the shoulders.

"Yes, they are dangerous sometimes," answered the Captain. "They have a way of turning on their assailants and overturning their boats. However, Master Land need not fear this danger. His arm is strong and his aim is certain. I am merely suggesting that he not miss because the dugong is regarded as an exquisite dish and I know that Master Land does not scorn a tasty morsel."

"Ah," retorted the Canadian. "I am delighted to hear that!"

"Yes, Master Land. Its excellent flesh is very highly esteemed, and in Malaya it is reserved for the tables of princes. For this reason a relentless hunt goes on for this excellent animal that, like the manatee, its close relative, is becoming more and more rare."

"If that is the case," said Conseil, in a serious vein, "this dugong may well be the last of its race, and perhaps it would be better to spare it, in the interest of science."

"Perhaps," answered the Canadian, "it will be better to hunt it, in the interest of the kitchen."

"Go ahead, Master Land," said the Captain.

Just then seven men of the crew, silent and impassive as always, appeared on the platform. One carried a harpoon and a line such as is used by the whalers. The dinghy was removed from its socket and lowered to the water. Six oarsmen took their places and the mate moved to the tiller. Ned, Conseil, and I sat in the stern.

225

"Aren't you coming, Captain?" I asked.

"No, monsieur, but I wish you all good luck."

The dinghy set off, thrust forward by its six oarsmen. It headed rapidly toward the dugong, which was now floating about two miles from the *Nautilus*.

When we were a few cables' lengths from the cetacean, the boat slowed down and the oars paddled noiselessly through the quiet waters. Ned Land, harpoon in hand, stood upright at the front of the dinghy. The harpoon used to strike a whale is usually attached to a long rope, which unwinds rapidly when the wounded animal pulls it with him. But in this case the rope measured only about ten fathoms, or sixty feet, and its end was attached to a small barrel which, floating on the surface, would indicate the movement of the animal under the water.

I stood up and observed closely the Canadian's adversary. The dugong, which is also called the halicore, resembles the manatee. Its oblong body ends in a very long tail, and its lateral fins are like real fingers. It differs from the manatee in that its upper jaw is armed with two long sharp teeth that stick out on either side for its defense.

This dugong that Ned was preparing to attack was of colossal dimensions and it was, at least, more than twenty feet long. It lay motionless and seemed to be sleeping on the surface of the waves. This made the task of capturing it easier.

The dinghy moved cautiously to within fifteen or twenty feet of the animal. The oars were resting in their locks. I crouched. Ned Land, his body bent slightly backward, brandished his harpoon with his experienced hand.

Suddenly we heard a hissing sound, and the dugong vanished. The harpoon, hurled with powerful strength, seemed to have struck only water.

"A thousand devils!" cried the Canadian in anger. "I missed!"

"No," I shouted, "the animal is wounded. Look at that blood! But your harpoon did not stick in his body."

"My harpoon! My harpoon!" shouted Ned.

The sailors plied their oars and the mate steered the boat toward the floating barrel. The harpoon was recovered and the dinghy set off in pursuit of the animal.

The dugong rose to the surface to breathe from time to time. It could not have been hurt much, for it swam with remarkable speed. The boat, maneuvered by strong arms, surged in its wake. On several occasions the animal came within a few yards of us, and the Canadian made ready to strike, but the dugong would suddenly dive and disappear. It was impossible to touch it. The anger of the impatient Canadian knew no bounds. He hurled the most energetic curses in the English language at the poor creature. As for me, I was thoroughly irritated to see that dugong manage to elude all our efforts.

We pursued it relentlessly for an hour, and I was beginning to despair of ever capturing it, when the animal, seized with the idea of vengeance, for which it was to repent, turned toward the dinghy and attacked it. This maneuver did not, however, escape the watchful eye of the Canadian.

"Be on your guard now!" he shouted.

The mate uttered a few words in their strange language, without doubt warning them of the danger.

Having come within twenty feet of the dinghy, the dugong stopped, took a deep breath with its enormous nostrils located in the upper part of its muzzle, and, gathering speed, hurled itself upon us.

The dinghy could not avoid that blow. It almost overturned, and was flooded by one or more tons of water which we had to bail out. Thanks to the skill of the mate, however, who had maneuvered to take the blow at an angle and not full on, we did not sink. Ned Land, crouched at the bow, kept belaboring the massive creature with blow after blow of his harpoon.

The dugong had fastened its teeth on our gunwale and was lifting our boat out of the water, as a lion would lift a deer. We fell over each other, and I don't quite know how this struggle would have ended if the Canadian had not succeeded, finally, in piercing the heart of that massive beast.

I heard the grinding of its teeth on the iron gunwale, and suddenly the dugong disappeared, dragging the harpoon with it. But soon the barrel reappeared on the surface of the water, and a few seconds later the body of the animal, floating on its back, appeared also.

It took pulleys of enormous power to haul the animal up onto the platform. It must have weighed around eleven thousand pounds. It was quartered under the watchful eyes of the Canadian, who followed every detail of the operation. That evening for dinner the steward served me with some choice cuts, which had been skillfully prepared by the chef. I found it excellent, even superior to veal, if not to beef.

On the following day, the 11th of February, the larder of the *Nautilus* was further enriched with more delicious game. A flight of sea swallows came to rest on the *Nautilus*. They were of the species known as *Sterna nilotica*, peculiar to Egypt. They had black beaks, gray spotted heads, white spots around their eyes, grayish backs, wings, and tails, white bellies and throats, and their feet were red.

We also caught a few dozen Nile ducks, whose tails and the

tops of their heads were white with black spots. Their flavor was excellent.

The *Nautilus* was now sailing at moderate speed. It was sauntering, so to speak. I noticed that the water of the Red Sea was becoming less and less salty as we approached the Suez.

Toward five P.M., we sighted the Cape of Ras-Mohammed to the north. It is this cape that forms the extremity of Arabia Petraea, situated between the Gulf of Suez and the Gulf of Akaba.

The *Nautilus* entered the Strait of Jubal, which leads into the Gulf of Suez. I saw clearly a high mountain towering over Ras-Mohammed, between the two gulfs. It was Mount Horeb, or Sinai, at whose summit Moses met God face-to-face, and which the mind of the people imagines to be continuously crowned with lightning.

At six o'clock, the *Nautilus*, now on the surface and now underwater, sailed past Tor, nestling at the end of the bay, whose water appeared tinted with red, as Captain Nemo had already predicted.

Then night fell, and the deep silence was broken occasionally by the cry of a pelican and some night birds, or the sounds of waves beating against the rocks, or the distant wail of a steamer beating the waters of the gulf with its propeller.

Between eight and nine o'clock the *Nautilus* sailed a few yards below the surface. According to my reckoning, we should be very near Suez. Through the panels of the saloon I could see formations of rocks, brilliantly lighted by our searchlight. The strait seemed to be getting narrower and narrower.

At nine fifteen the ship had come to the surface, and I went up on the platform. Very impatient to pass through Captain Nemo's tunnel, I could not stand still, and I sought to breathe the fresh air of the night.

Soon, in the shadow, I spied a pale light, veiled by the mist, shining about a mile away.

"A floating lighthouse," someone said at my side.

I turned and recognized the Captain.

"It is the floating lighthouse of Suez," he continued. "We will not be long now in reaching the entrance to the tunnel."

"It cannot be easy to enter?"

"No, it isn't, monsieur. In fact, I always remain in the helmsman's cabin to direct the maneuver myself. And now, if you will be good enough to go below, Monsieur Aronnax, the *Nautilus* is about to submerge, and will not return to the surface until we have passed through the Arabian Tunnel."

I followed Captain Nemo. The hatch closed behind us, the

tanks were filled with water, and the *Nautilus* submerged about thirty feet.

As I was leaving him to return to my room, the Captain stopped me.

"Professor," he said. "Would you like to accompany me to the pilot's cage?"

"Yes, indeed! I didn't dare ask you," I replied.

"Come then. You will then be able to see everything that is to be seen in this trip through an underground, as well as an underwater, channel."

He led me toward the central staircase. Halfway down he opened a door, crossed an upper gangway, and we entered the pilot's cage, which, as we know, stood at the far end of the platform.

It was a cabin about six feet square, somewhat similar to the pilots' cabins on boats sailing the Mississippi and the Hudson Rivers. In the center was a wheel, placed vertically and connected to the rudder chains, which ran to the stern of the *Nautilus*. Four portholes with lenticular glass, grooved into the walls of the cabin, permitted the pilot to look in all directions.

The cabin was in darkness, but as soon as my eyes became adjusted to that darkness I saw the helmsman, a vigorous man, whose hands were resting on the spokes of the wheel. Outside the sea was vividly illuminated by our searchlight, located at the end of the platform.

"Now," said the Captain, "let us look for our tunnel." Electric wires connected the helmsman's cabin to the engine room, permitting the Captain to control both the speed and the course of the *Nautilus*. He pressed a metal button, and immediately the propeller slowed down.

I watched in silence the sheer high rock wall that we were skirting at that moment, and which formed the solid base of the coastal sandbanks. We followed it for an hour, gliding along only a few feet from it. Captain Nemo did not take his eyes off the compass and its two concentric circles, installed in the cabin. Repeatedly, at a signal from the Captain, the helmsman would change the course of the *Nautilus*.

Standing at the port window, I saw some magnificent substructures of coral, zoophytes, algae, and some crustaceans lying in the crevices of rocks, waving their enormous and elongated claws.

At 10:15 P.M., Captain Nemo himself took the wheel. A wide, deep black channel opened before us. The *Nautilus* plunged boldly into it. A strange rustling sound could be heard along its sides. It was the water of the Red Sea, roaring through the sloping tunnel, flowing toward the Mediterranean. The *Nautilus* moved along with the current, swift as an arrow, although the propellers were put in reverse to cut down our speed.

On the narrow walls of the tunnel I could only see the brilliant rays, the straight furrows of fire, traced by the electric beams of our searchlight. I placed my hand to my chest and felt my heart beating fast.

At 10:35, Captain Nemo left the wheel and turned to me. "The Mediterranean!" he said.

In less than twenty minutes the *Nautilus*, swept along by the current, had passed under the Isthmus of Suez.

Chapter VI

THE GREEK ARCHIPELAGO

THE NEXT DAY, February 12th, the *Nautilus* emerged to the surface. I rushed up to the platform. Three miles to the south I could see the vague outline of Pelusium. An underground torrent had carried us from one sea to another, but while it was possible to negotiate the tunnel downstream, it would have been impossible to do so upstream.

At about seven o'clock, Ned and Conseil joined me. These two inseparable companions had slept quite soundly, unconcerned with the great accomplishment of the *Nautilus*.

"Well, Monsieur le Naturaliste," asked the Canadian, in a slightly bantering tone, "where is that Mediterranean you were talking about?"

"We are cruising on it right now, my friend."

"What!" exclaimed Conseil. "You mean this happened during the night?"

"Yes, during the night. In a matter of minutes we passed through that impassable isthmus."

"I don't believe a word of it," replied the Canadian.

"You are quite wrong, Ned," I continued. "That low coastline which curves towards the south is the coast of Egypt."

"I am not as gullible as all that, Professor," answered the stubborn Canadian.

"If Monsieur says it is so, then it is," Conseil said to him.

"Moreover, Ned, Captain Nemo did me the honor of permitting me to remain at his side, in the helmsman's cabin, while he himself steered the *Nautilus* through that narrow passage."

"Do you hear that, Ned?" said Conseil.

"You have such good eyes," I asked. "Can't you make out the jetties of Port Said stretching out into the sea?"

The Canadian looked at them carefully.

"It's true," he said. "You're quite right, Professor, and your Captain is a masterful man. We are indeed in the Mediterranean. Good! Let's have a little chat, if you please, about our private little matter—but someplace where no one can hear us."

I realized, of course, what the Canadian was coming to. In

231

any case, I thought it best to discuss this matter, since he was taking it so seriously. The three of us went and sat down near the searchlight, where we were less exposed to the spray of the waves.

"All right, Ned, go ahead. We are listening," I said. "What do you have on your mind?"

"What I have to tell you is very simple," replied the Canadian. "We are in Europe, and before the whims of Captain Nemo drag us to the depths of the polar seas or take us back to Oceania, I suggest that we leave the *Nautilus*."

I must confess that these discussions with the Canadian always troubled me. I hadn't the least desire to deprive my companions of their freedom, but I personally hadn't the least desire to abandon Captain Nemo. Thanks to him and his craft, I was daily adding knowledge to my studies of the sea, and I was completely revising my book about the marine world in the very depths of the sea and doing it in the most natural environment. Would I ever have another opportunity to study the wonders of the sea? No, never! I could never consider the idea of abandoning the *Nautilus* before our explorations were completed.

"Tell me frankly, my friend," I said. "Is this life aboard the *Nautilus* really boring you? Are you really sorry that fate has thrown you in the hands of Captain Nemo?"

The Canadian hesitated a few moments before replying. Then, crossing his arms, he said:

"Frankly, I am not sorry to have taken this voyage under the seas. I'll be happy to have done it, but in order to have done it, it must end. That's how I feel about it."

"It will end, Ned."

"Where and when?"

"Where? I do not know. When? I cannot say or, rather, I think it will come to an end when the seas have nothing more to teach us. Everything that has a beginning must have an end in this world."

"I'm of the same opinion as Monsieur," replied Conseil, "and it is more than likely that having explored all the seas on this earth, Captain Nemo will give us the boot."

"The boot!" cried the Canadian. "A thrashing, you mean?"

"Let us not exaggerate, Master Land," I continued. "We have nothing to fear from the Captain, but I do not agree with Conseil's ideas, either. We know all the secrets of the *Nautilus*, and I do not think that its commander, in order to give us our freedom, will resign himself to having them revealed to the whole world."

"But just what do you think will happen?" asked the Canadian.

232

"There is always the chance that during the next six months we will have another opportunity that we can take advantage of."

"Oh, that's fine!" exclaimed Ned Land. "And where are we likely to be six months from now, if you please, Monsieur le Naturaliste?"

"Here or perhaps in China. The *Nautilus* moves fast, as you know. It speeds across the oceans as swallows fly through the air, or as an express train runs across continents. It does not fear sailing the well-traveled sea lanes. Who knows? It may well cruise along the shores of France, England, or even America, where an escape may be as feasible as it is here."

"Monsieur Aronnax," replied the Canadian, "your arguments are fundamentally wrong and devoid of sense. You always talk about the future: 'We will be there! We will be here!' Let us talk about the present: 'We are here and let us take advantage of it now.'"

I realized, of course, that Ned's arguments were sounder than mine. He was on solid ground, and I could not think of any new arguments to bolster my opinion.

"Monsieur," continued Ned. "Let us assume the impossible. Suppose the Captain were to offer you your freedom now —this very day—would you accept?"

"I do not know," I replied.

"And if he were to add that the offer he is making to you today would never be renewed? Would you accept?"

I did not answer.

"And what does my friend Conseil have to say about all this?" asked Ned Land.

"Your friend Conseil," replied the worthy lad calmly, "has nothing to say. He is absolutely unconcerned in this matter. Conseil is a bachelor just like his master and just like his companion. He has no wife, he has no parents, he has no children, waiting for his return home. Conseil is in the service of Monsieur, and he thinks like Monsieur, he talks like Monsieur, and to his great regret, he cannot be counted upon to decide this issue. Only two persons are facing each other here: on one hand we have Monsieur, on the other Ned Land. Conseil is here to listen, and he is ready to keep score."

I couldn't help smiling to see Conseil effacing his personality so completely. The Canadian must have been delighted, without doubt, not to have him as an opponent.

"Well then, monsieur," said Ned Land. "Since Conseil doesn't exist, this discussion is between you and me. I have spoken; you have listened. What is your answer?"

Evasions were no longer possible, and I faced the issue with the utmost frankness.

"Here is my answer, Ned," I said. "You are quite right, and my arguments are not as sound as yours. We cannot depend on Captain Nemo's goodwill. Plain common sense will prevent him from setting us free. On the other hand, plain common sense tells us to take advantage of the first opportunity to escape."

"Good, Monsieur Aronnax. You have spoken well and wisely."

"But," I said, "I must emphasize one important point. The opportunity must be a good one. Our first attempt to escape must succeed, for, if it fails, we shall never have another opportunity, and Captain Nemo will never forgive us."

"That's right," replied the Canadian. "But what you have said applies to all our attempts to escape, whether it takes place in two years or in two days. Therefore, the question remains the same: if the occasion arises, we must seize it."

"I agree. Now, tell me, Ned, what is your idea of a favorable opportunity?"

"Well! Suppose that on some dark night the *Nautilus* is not far from a European coast."

"In that case, you would try to swim to safety?"

"We would certainly do so if we were close enough to the shore, and if the ship were floating on the surface. We wouldn't, of course, if we were too far off, or if the ship were underwater."

"In that case, what would you do?"

"Try to put my hands on the dinghy. I know how to maneuver it. Once freed from its bolts, we would get inside and rise to the surface. The pilot stationed afore would not even see us escape."

"Very well, Ned. Keep your eyes open for such an occasion. But remember, if your plan fails, we are lost."

"I will keep that in mind."

"Now, Ned, would you like to know what I really think about your plan?"

"Of course, Monsieur Aronnax."

"I think—I am not saying I hope—I think that a favorable opportunity will never present itself."

"Why not?"

"Because Captain Nemo must be aware that we still hope to regain our freedom someday. He will be constantly on his guard, especially when sailing close to European shores."

"I agree completely with Monsieur," said Conseil.

"We'll see soon enough," replied Ned Land, who shook his head with an air of confidence.

"And now, Ned," I added, "let us leave it there. Not another word on this subject. When you are ready, let us know and we shall follow you. I rely entirely on you."

This conversation, which was to have such serious consequences later on, came to an end. I should add, however, that events seemed to confirm my prediction, to the great distress of the Canadian. Whether Captain Nemo distrusted us in these well-traveled sea lanes, or whether he wished to keep out of sight of the numerous ships sailing the Mediterranean, I do not know. Whatever it was, the *Nautilus* remained submerged most of the time, or kept far from the shores. When it did emerge, only the pilot's cage rose above the surface. When submerged, it dived to great depths, because in sailing between the Greek archipelago and Asia Minor, we did not even touch bottom at over six thousand feet.

For this reason I did not realize that we were near the island of Carpathos, one of the Sporades, until Captain Nemo, pointing to a spot on the map, recited the following verses of Virgil:

> *Est in Carpathia Neptuni gurgite vates*
> *Coeruleus Proteus. . . .*
>
> "In the sea of Carpathia lives Proteus,
> Sinister prophet of Neptune. . . ."

It was, in fact, the ancient abode of Proteus, the old shepherd of Neptune's flocks, now the island of Scarpanto, situated between Rhodes and Crete. I saw only its granite base through the panels of the saloon.

The next day, February 14th, I decided to spend a few hours studying the fish of the archipelago, but, for some unknown reason, the panels remained hermetically sealed. On taking our bearings, I gathered that the *Nautilus* was heading toward Candia, the ancient isle of Crete. When I had boarded the *Abraham Lincoln,* this entire island had just revolted against the despotism of the Turks. I did not know what had since happened to this insurrection, and I took it for granted that Captain Nemo did not know either, since he had no means of communicating with land. Hence I did not even mention this when he and I were in the saloon that evening. Moreover, he was silent and seemed preoccupied. Contrary to his usual custom, however, he had both panels opened and kept pacing from one to the other, keeping a close watch on the expanse of those waters. What was on his mind? I could

235

not imagine, and I spent my time studying the fish that swam before my eyes.

Among many, I noticed some gobies, mentioned by Aristotle, known as rocklings or sea loaches, frequently found in the salt waters near the delta of the Nile. Near them were semiphosphorescent snappers, a species of sparoid fish, which the Egyptians included among their sacred animals, and whose arrival in the Nile announced the coming of the fertile floods, and was welcomed with religious ceremonies. I also noticed some cheilinae about ten inches long, bony fish with transparent scales, livid in color and dotted with red. They eat enormous quantities of marine plants, which give them an exquisite flavor. They were highly prized by the gourmets of ancient Rome, and their entrails, cooked with lamprey eggs, peacock brains, and flamingo tongues, created an exquisite dish, which delighted the emperor Vitellius. Another inhabitant of these waters that attracted my attention and reminded me of the ancient world was the remora,* related to the sucking fish. The remora often travels attached to the belly of sharks. According to ancient legends, this little fish, by adhering to the keel of a ship, could bring it to a dead stop. One of them, they said, had actually held back Anthony's ship during the battle of Actium and had facilitated the victory of Augustus. How little it takes to change the destiny of a nation!

I also observed some magnificent anthias, which belong to the order of Lutianidae—a sacred fish to the Greeks, who attributed to them a power strong enough to drive sea monsters out of their waters. Their name means "flower"—a very appropriate name, due to their glimmering colors—with shades ranging from a deep red, through a white pale pink, to the most striking brilliancy of ruby—as well as to the fleeting soft reflections of their dorsal fins. I could not take my eyes from those marvels of the sea. But suddenly my vision was struck by an unexpected sight!

A man had suddenly appeared in the midst of those waters, a diver, with a leather purse attached to his belt. It was not a body floating in the water. It was a living man, swimming with vigorous strokes, rising from time to time to the surface to catch his breath, and diving down again.

Deeply moved, I turned to the Captain and cried out:

"A man! a shipwrecked man! We must save him, whatever the price!"

---

* There are a dozen species found in the tropical and temperate seas. They have large oval sucking discs and are hard to dislodge when attached to whales, sharks, porpoises, or even ships. In some parts of the tropics, fishermen use them to catch sea turtles. The professor describes how this is done on page 339.—M.T.B.

The Captain did not reply. He came to the window and leaned against the panel.

The man had approached and he was now looking at us, with his face pressed against the glass.

To my great astonishment, Captain Nemo signaled to him. The diver answered with a wave of his hand, rose immediately to the surface of the sea, and did not appear again.

"Do not be disturbed," the Captain said to me. "It's Nicolas, of Cape Matapan, nicknamed 'the Fish.' He is well known throughout the Cyclades. A tough and bold diver. He is thoroughly at home in water and he lives in it more than he does on land. He swims constantly from one island to another, and at times he goes as far as Crete."

"You know him, Captain?"

"Of course, Monsieur Aronnax!"

Then Captain Nemo went to a bureau standing by the left panel of the saloon. Next to the bureau I noticed a chest, bound with iron strips, having a plaque on the lid that bore the name *Nautilus* and its emblem: *MOBILIS IN MOBILE*.

The Captain, ignoring my presence, opened the bureau, which turned out to be a safe filled with ingots.

They were ingots of gold! Where did this precious metal, worth more than a fortune, come from? Where was the Captain getting this gold, and what was he going to do with it?

I looked on without saying a word. The Captain took out those ingots one by one and arranged them neatly in the chest, until it was filled to the top. I estimated that gold at more than two thousand kilograms—worth more than five million francs.

The chest was securely fastened, and the Captain wrote an address on the lid in what must have been modern Greek.

Then the Captain pressed a button, communicating with the control room. Four men appeared, and not without difficulty, they shoved the chest out of the room. I soon heard them working with pulleys to lift that chest on the iron stairway.

Then Captain Nemo turned to me and said, "Now, Monsieur le Professeur, what were you saying?"

"I wasn't saying a thing, Captain."

"Then, monsieur, you will permit me to bid you good night." And without another word, he left the room.

I went back to my room very perplexed. I tried to sleep, but in vain. What possible relationship could there be between the diver and that chest filled with gold? Soon I felt the ship rolling and pitching, and realized that the *Nautilus* was leaving the depths of the sea and rising to the surface. I heard the sound of footsteps on the platform. I realized that

237

the dinghy was being detached and put out to sea. I heard it strike the side of the ship, and then all noises ceased. However, two hours later, I heard the same noises, the same comings and goings. The dinghy was hauled on board, refastened in its sockets, and the *Nautilus* dived once more into the sea.

So, then, those millions had been delivered to their destination! Just where had they been delivered? Who was Captain Nemo's correspondent?

On the following day, I related the events of the previous night to Conseil and the Canadian—events that aroused my curiosity to the highest pitch. My companions were no less surprised than I.

"But where does he get these millions?" asked Ned Land.

I could not answer that question. After lunch, I went to the saloon and sat down to my work. Until five in the afternoon I organized my notes. Then I felt so hot that I had to take off my byssus coat. Was there something the matter with me? This was strange indeed, since we were not in the tropics. The *Nautilus* was in deep waters and there should have been no rise in temperature. I looked at the manometer. We were at a depth of sixty feet beyond the reach of earthly heat.

I continued with my work, but the temperature kept rising and was becoming intolerable.

"Could there be a fire on board?" I asked myself.

I was about to leave the saloon when Captain Nemo came in. He went over to the thermometer, consulted it, and came over to me.

"One hundred and eight degrees Fahrenheit!" he said.

"So I have noticed, Captain," I replied, "and if it gets any hotter, we will not be able to bear it."

"Oh! Monsieur le Professeur, this temperature will not go higher unless we want it to."

"You mean you can regulate it?"

"No, but I can move away from the furnace that is producing it."

"Is it coming from the outside?"

"Undoubtedly. We are cruising in a current of boiling water."

"How is that possible?" I cried.

"Look."

The panels opened, and I saw that the sea was entirely white around the *Nautilus*. Volumes of sulphurous vapors were bubbling in the midst of the waves, which were boiling like water in a cauldron. I touched one of the windows with my hand, but it was so hot that I had to withdraw it.

"Where are we?" I asked.

"We are near the island of Santorin, Professor," answered the Captain. "To be more precise, we are right in the channel that separates Nea Kaumene from Palea Kaumene. I wanted to offer you the spectacle of a submerged volcano."

"I thought the formation of these islands was completed."

"Nothing is ever completed in these volcanic zones," replied Captain Nemo, "and the earth is constantly altered by these infernal fires. As early as the year 19 A.D., according to Cassiodorus and Pliny, a new island, Theia the Divine, appeared in this very place where islands were recently formed. Later this island sank beneath the waves, but it reappeared in 69 A.D., only to disappear once more. From that time until recently, Pluto seemed to have been resting from his labors and these infernal regions were calm. But on February third, 1866, a new island, named George Island, emerged in the midst of sulphurous vapors, in the vicinity of Nea Kaumene, and settled down on the sixth of the same month. Seven days later, on the thirteenth of February, the island of Aphroessa appeared, leaving a channel over thirty feet wide between it and Nea Kaumene. I was in these waters when the phenomenon took place. I was in a position to observe all its phases. The island of Aphroessa, round in shape, measured three hundred feet in diameter and was thirty feet high. It was composed of black and vitreous lava, mixed with fragments of feldspar. Finally, on the tenth of March, a smaller island, called Reka, appeared near Nea Kaumene, and since then these three islands were fused together, forming one big island."

"In what channel are we now?" I asked.

"In this one," replied Captain Nemo, showing me a map of the archipelago. "You will notice that I have drawn in the new islands also."

"Will this channel be filled in one of these days?"

"It is very probable, Monsieur Aronnax, for since 1866, eight small islands have emerged near Port St. Nicholas of Palea Kaumene. It is evident that Nea and Palea will become one sometime in the future. If, in the middle of the Pacific, we have microscopic organisms creating continents, here we have volcanic eruptions. Look, monsieur, look at the work that is going on under those waves."

I returned to the window. The *Nautilus* had stopped. The heat was becoming unbearable. The sea, which had been white, was now turning red because of the presence of iron salt. Although the saloon was hermetically sealed, a very offensive odor of sulphur filled the room, and outside, scarlet flames cast such a brilliant light that our own light appeared dim.

239

I was immersed in perspiration, I was suffocating. I felt as if I were being cooked—yes, really cooked alive!

"We cannot remain for much longer in these boiling waters," I said to the Captain.

"No, it would not be wise," replied Captain Nemo calmly.

He gave an order. The *Nautilus* veered and moved away from that fiery furnace, which it could not face with impunity. A quarter of an hour later, we were breathing once more the fresh air of the sea.

The thought then struck me that if Ned Land had chosen to escape in these waters, we would never have come out of that sea of fire alive.

On the following day, February 16th, we left that basin lying between Rhodes and Alexandria which, it is said, has a depth of over nine thousand feet, and the *Nautilus*, passing wide of Cerigo, left the Greek archipelago after doubling Cape Matapan.

Chapter VII

ACROSS THE MEDITERRANEAN IN FORTY-EIGHT HOURS

THE MEDITERRANEAN, that incomparable blue sea, known to the Hebrews as "The Great Sea," to the Greeks as "The Sea," and to the Romans as *"Mare Nostrum"*—"Our Sea"—adorned with orange groves, aloes, and sea pine, scented with the fragrance of the myrtle, studded with rugged mountains, immersed in a pure, crystal-clear atmosphere, incessantly stirred by volcanic eruptions—this sea is a veritable battlefield in which Neptune and Pluto are perpetually struggling for the conquest of the world. On its shores and on its waters, says Michelet, man is continuously rejuvenated in one of the most invigorating climates of the globe.

Beautiful as it was, I could barely catch a glimpse of this basin, which covers an area of more than 800,000 square miles. Captain Nemo's special knowledge of these regions would have been immensely helpful, but that mysterious man did not appear once during that speedy crossing. I estimated that the *Nautilus* covered a distance of about 1,500 miles in forty-eight hours, cruising always beneath the waves. Having sailed from the waters of Greece on the 16th of February, by dawn on the 18th we had crossed the Straits of Gibraltar.

It was evident that Captain Nemo had no love for the Mediterranean, surrounded as it was by countries from which he was fleeing. Its waters and its breezes brought back too many memories, too many regrets, perhaps. Furthermore, he did not have that freedom of movement and independence that the wide and open seas offered him, and his *Nautilus* felt confined by those close shores of Africa and Europe. Our speed was now twenty-five miles an hour and it goes without saying that Ned Land, to his great disappointment, had to give up his plans to escape. He could not have launched the dinghy while we were traveling at a speed exceeding thirty or forty feet per second. To escape from the *Nautilus* under those conditions would have been as hazardous as jumping from a train traveling at the same speed—a rash move if ever there was one. Moreover, our craft surfaced only at night and only to replenish our supply of air. It navigated solely by its compass and log.

Under the circumstances, I saw as much of the Mediterranean as a passenger in a fast-moving train sees of the landscapes that sweep before his eyes. He can distinguish distant objects appearing on the horizon, but sees only a dim blur of the objects in the foreground as they flash by with the speed of lightning.

Nevertheless, Conseil and I were able to observe some species of those Mediterreanean fish, especially those whose fins were powerful enough to enable them to keep up with the *Nautilus*, if only for a very short time. We studied them carefully through the panels, and our notes will permit me to describe, however briefly, the animal life of that sea.

Among the numerous fish that swarm in these waters, I saw some clearly, I caught a passing glimpse of others, and some, because of the speed of the *Nautilus*, escaped me completely. My classification of those animals will, therefore, be whimsical rather than scientific, but this method will more than suffice to describe my fleeting impressions.

In the midst of those waters, brilliantly illuminated by our searchlight, I saw meandering lampreys, more than three feet long, of the kind found in almost every sea; oxyrrhyncha, a species of ray, whose flat bodies measure five feet across, with white bellies and ash-gray speckled backs, resembling large shawls carried away by the currents; other rays passed so swiftly that I was unable to determine whether they deserved to be called eagles, a name given them by the ancient Greeks, or whether they deserved to be called rats, toads, or bats—names given them by modern fishermen; milander sharks, twelve feet in length, especially feared by divers, vying with each other in speed; sea foxes, eight feet in length, gifted with a keen sense of smell, swam by, looking like large blue shadows; dorados, a species of sparoid, some of which measured four feet, appeared all dressed up in silver and blue, speckled with stripes that contrasted sharply with the dark color of their fins. This specimen, once sacred to Venus, has golden eyebrows. It is a very precious animal, denizen of all waters, whether fresh or salt, rivers, lakes, or oceans, and adaptable to any climate or temperature. Its forebears go back to geological times, and they have retained all their pristine beauty. Magnificent sturgeons, measuring twenty or thirty feet, possessing great speed, beat against our panels with their powerful tails, displaying their bluish backs speckled with brown spots. They resemble sharks, but lack the strength of that animal. They are found in all the seas. In the spring, they like to swim up large streams, struggling against the currents of the Volga, the Po, the Rhine, the Loire, and the Oder, feeding on herrings, mackerel, salmon, and cod.

Although they belong to the class of cartilaginous fish, their flesh is excellent. They may be eaten fresh, dried, pickled, or salted. In former days their flesh was considered more than worthy for the table of Lucullus.

But among the denizens of the Mediterranean that I observed with care when the *Nautilus* cruised near the surface, one belonged to the sixty-third genus of bony fish. They were tuna, with dark-bluish backs, silvery bellies, and dorsal stripes that glittered like gold. They are known to follow the course of ships, seeking the cool shade as protection from the tropical sun. They did not belie their reputation, because they followed the *Nautilus* just as they had followed the ships of La Pérouse. For hours they struggled to keep up with us. I never tired of admiring those animals, so beautifully fashioned for speed, with their small heads, their sleek and spindle-shaped bodies, and their forked tails. They attain a length of ten feet, and their dorsal fins are endowed with extraordinary power. They swam in a triangular formation, resembling the flight of certain birds, and with equal speed. The ancients used to say that they must have had a knowledge both of strategy and geometry. However, they cannot elude the snares of the fishermen of Provence, who prize them as much as did the natives of Propontis* and of Italy, and they hurl themselves, blindly and heedlessly, into the nets of the fishermen of Marseilles.

I shall mention in passing those Mediterranean fish of which Conseil and I could only catch a glimpse. There were whitish gymnotes, which swept by like clouds of intangible mists; conger eels, ten or thirteen feet in length, vividly colored with green, blue, and yellow; codfish, three feet long, whose liver makes a tasty morsel; coepolae-teniae, floating like thin delicate seaweed; gurnards, called lyre-fish by the poets, but which the sailors call the whistling fish, whose snouts are supplied with two triangular plates that resemble Homer's instrument; flying swallows or flying gurnards, which can swim with the speed of birds, which accounts for their name; a species of perch, redheaded, whose dorsal fins are speckled with filaments; aloe, a species of shad, which is extremely sensitive to the silvery sound of little bells, whose body is flecked with black, gray, brown, blue, yellow, and green; splendid turbots, pheasants of the sea, with yellowish fins, whose diamond-shaped body is spotted with brown and yellow; finally, a school of beautiful red mullets, real seabirds of paradise. Romans paid as much as ten thousand sesterces apiece just for the pleasure of seeing them die slowly, and with cruel eyes

* An old name for the Sea of Marmora (or Marmara).—M.T.B.

watched them change from a deep vermilion to a pale white.

Because of the vertiginous speed of the *Nautilus* as it moved through those fertile and prolific waters, we were unable to observe the miralets, the triggerfish, the tetrodons, the sea horses, the juans, the bellows fish, the blennies, the surmullets, the rainbow fish, the smelts, the flying fish, the anchovies, the sea breams, the boöps, the orphes, or any representatives of the order Pleuronectides, such as the dabs, flounders, plaice, or sole, all common both in the Atlantic and the Mediterranean.

As for marine mammals, I thought I saw, as we sailed into the Adriatic, two or three cachalots, with one dorsal fin, belonging to the genus of sperm whale; a few dolphins of the genus globicephala, rarely found elsewhere, the front part of whose heads are streaked with small zebralike lines. We saw also about a dozen or so white-bellied seals with black fur—known by the name of "monks" because they truly resemble Dominican friars—ten feet in length. Conseil believed he had seen a sea turtle six feet wide, with three jutting ridges running down its back. I was sorry not to have seen this tortoise, for according to Conseil's description, it must have been a luth, or leatherback, a very rare specimen. The only reptiles I saw were a few cacuans with elongated shells.

As for zoophytes, I did gaze with delight, but only for a few seconds, at a magnificent orange-colored galeolaria that clung to the port panel. It was a long, tenuous filament which spread into an infinite number of branches, ending in the most delicate filigree lacework ever spun by the rivals of Arachne. Unfortunately, I was not able to catch this wonderful specimen. Many other Mediterranean zoophytes would undoubtedly have escaped my notice if the *Nautilus*, during the evening of the 26th, had not slowed down considerably.

We were then sailing between Sicily and the coast of Tunis. In this narrow channel between Cape Bon and the Messina Strait, the seabed rises abruptly. At this point the seabed rises up to within sixty feet below the surface, whereas on each side of this ridge the depth goes down well over two hundred feet. The *Nautilus* had to maneuver very carefully in order to avoid crashing against that underwater barrier.

I showed Conseil the exact position of this long reef on a map of the Mediterranean.

"If Monsieur doesn't mind my saying so," said Conseil, "it looks like a real isthmus, connecting Europe to Africa."

"Yes, my lad, it cuts right across the entire strait of Libya, and the soundings made by Smith prove that the continents

244

were formerly connected between Cape Bon and Cape Furina."

"I can well believe it," said Conseil.

"I may well add," I replied, "that a similar barrier exists between Gibraltar and Ceuta, which in geological times connected them and closed off the Mediterranean completely."

"Well!" said Conseil, "what would happen if a volcanic convulsion were to raise these barriers above the water again?"

"It isn't very likely, Conseil."

"Will Monsieur permit me to continue? If this phenomenon were to occur, it would be very unfortunate for Monsieur de Lesseps, who is going to so much trouble to build the Suez Canal."

"Of course. But as I have just said, it isn't likely that it will ever occur. The violence of subterranean convulsions is constantly diminishing. Volcanoes, which were so numerous in the early days of this earth, are slowly becoming extinct. The heat in the inner bowels of the globe is cooling, and the temperature of its various strata is decreasing appreciably every century. This will eventually be a calamity to the earth, for this heat is the very life of our planet."

"But there is always the sun. . . ."

"The sun isn't hot enough, Conseil. The sun cannot breathe life into a corpse, can it?"

"No, I suppose not."

"Well, my friend, one of these days our earth will become a cold, lifeless body, and like the moon, which lost its vital heat a long, long time ago, will become uninhabitable and uninhabited."

"And how many centuries will that take?" asked Conseil.

"Perhaps many millions of years, my lad."

"Well," replied Conseil, "if that is the case, we will have more than enough time to complete our journey, unless, of course, Ned Land messes things up."

Conseil, reassured, went back to study the high barrier which the *Nautilus* was skirting at close range and at moderate speed.

There, on that rocky, volcanic soil, spread a whole world of living flora: sponges; holothurians, or sea slugs; translucent cydippiae, with reddish tendrils, emitting a faint phosphorescent glow; beroës, commonly known as sea cucumbers, immersed in a glistening rainbow of the solar spectrum; ambulatory or feather stars, a yard across, whose purple color cast a red glow around them; treelike euryales, of spectacular beauty; pavonaceae, with long stalks; countless numbers of edible sea urchins of various species; and green sea anemones

245

with grayish trunks and brown disks, almost invisible within their olive-hued tentacles.

Conseil had kept busy observing, above all, the mollusks and the articulata, and although a list of what he noted may be somewhat barren, I do not wish to do him an injustice by omitting his personal observations.

In the subkingdom of mollusks he mentions the numerous scallops, genus pectinidae; spondyli, spiny oysters, piled on top of each other; triangular wedge shells; trident-shaped hyalines, with yellow fins and transparent shells; orange-colored pleurobranchia, resembling eggs speckled with green dots; aplysia, known also as sea hare; dolabellae; fleshy acerae; parasol shells, peculiar to the Mediterranean; sea-ears or ear shells, which produce a very valuable mother-of-pearl; red-flamed scallops; corrugated cockles, which the natives of Languedoc prefer to oysters; clovis, preferred by the natives of Marseilles; a species of clam, abundant on the coast of North America, so popular in New York; gill-covered comb shells of various colors; lithodes, crouching inside their holes, whose peppery taste delights me; furrowed venericardiae, whose shells bulge with ridges; cynthiae, bristling with scarlet humps; carniaria, which resemble gondolas; crowned feroles; atlantes with spiral shells; gray thetys, with white speckles and covered with fringed mantillas; aeolides, resembling tiny slugs; cavoliniae, crawling on their backs; and among others, the auricula myosotis, oval-shaped; fawn-colored scalaria; littoral periwinkles; ianthine; cinerariae; petricolae; lamellaria; cabochons; pandoras; etc.

As for the articulata, they are properly divided, in Conseil's notes, into six classes, three of which belong to the marine world. These are the classes of the crustaceans, the cirrhopoda, and the annelids. The crustaceans are divided into nine orders and the first of these orders comprises the decapods, that is to say, animals whose head and thorax are generally joined together and whose mouths are formed by several pairs of jaws and having four, five, or six pairs of legs on their thorax. Conseil followed the classification of our teacher, Milne-Edwards, who divided them into three sections of decapod: the brachyura, the macrura, and the anomura.

These names are not strictly scientific, but they are correct and precise. Among the brachyura, Conseil mentions amathiae, whose forehead is armed with two big horns, one on each side; the inachidae scorpion, which, I do not know why, the Greeks used as a symbol of wisdom; some spider crabs, one species of which had apparently strayed into these shallow waters, because ordinarily they live in deep waters; xanthi, pilumnae, rhomboides, granular calappae—very easy to digest, Conseil notes; toothless corystes; ebaliae; cymobolides; woolly dorripi, etc. Among the macrura, subdivided into five families, we have the ceriaceae; the burrowers; the astaci; the palaemonidae, and the ochyzopodes. He mentions the rock lobsters, the female of which is highly esteemed as food; scyllari, or squills, and all kinds of edible species. Conseil does not cite, however, the subdivision of astaci, which includes the lobster proper, because the spiny lobster is the only denizen of the Mediterranean. Finally, among the anomura, he noticed the drocinae, who feel at home inside whatever abandoned shells they find; the homolae, with their spiny forehead; hermit crabs; porcelain crabs; etc.

Here the work of Conseil ended. He did not have enough time to complete the class of crustaceans by examining the stomatopods, the amphipods, the homopods, the isopods, the trilobites, the branchiapods, the ostrocodes, and the entomostracae. And in order to have completed his notes on the marine articulata he would have had to mention the class of cirrhopoda, which includes the cyclopes, the arguli, followed by the class of annelids, which he would not have forgotten to divide into the tubicoles and the dorsibranches. But once having passed the shallow waters of the straits of Libya, the *Nautilus* began to sail in deep waters and at its usual speed. From then on there were no more mollusks, articulata, or zoophytes. Only an occasional large fish swam by like a shadow.

During the night of February the 16th and 17th, we entered the second basin of the Mediterranean, whose greatest depth reaches nearly ten thousand feet. Using its inclined fins and driven by its propellers, the *Nautilus* submerged into the lowest depths of the sea.

In the absence of natural marvels, that mass of waters offered the most moving and terrifying scenes. We were then crossing that part of the Mediterranean that is so prolific with tragedies. From the coast of Algeria to the shores of Provence, how many ships had sunk beneath the waves! The Mediterranean is only a lake compared to the vast watery plains of the Pacific, but it is a capricious lake, with changing moods, which one day favors and caresses the frail vessels that seem to float between the deep blue of its waters and the azure sky, and on the morrow, lashed by the winds, it is raging and convulsive, smashing the strongest ships with the sharp and powerful blows of its billows.

During the swift journey across its depths, what tragedies I saw, scattered everywhere at the bottom of that sea! Some already encrusted with coral, others covered only with a layer of rust—anchors, cannons and cannonballs, chains, iron fittings, propellers, broken cylinders, boilers—and hulls, hanging in the water, some upright and others floating upside down.

Of those wrecked ships, some had perished in collisions, and others had struck against granite reefs. Some had sunk to the bottom perpendicularly, their masts still in place and their rigging tautened by the water. They appeared as if anchored in an immense, eerie dock, waiting for the moment to cast off. When the *Nautilus* moved among them and cast its brilliant light upon them, it seemed as if they were going to salute us with a dip of their flag. No, there was nothing but silence and death in this field of catastrophes!

I noticed that the number of wrecks at the bottom of the Mediterranean increased as we approached the Straits of Gibraltar. The shores of Africa and Europe come closer together there, and collisions, of course, occur more frequently in that narrow space. I saw numerous iron hulls, weird, fantastic wrecks of steamers, some lying flat, others standing upright, resembling formidable animals. One of these boats, ripped on one side, funnel bent, paddle wheels gone except for the framework, rudder separated from the stern but still held by a chain, and with its rear name plate corroded by the salty water, was a terrifying sight! How many lives had been destroyed in that shipwreck! How many victims had been swept beneath the waves! Had a sailor ever survived to tell the story of that terrible disaster, or did the waves still hold the secret of that tragedy? I do not know why, but it occurred to me that this ship, buried in the sea, could be the *Atlas,* which had disappeared with all on board twenty years before, and of which nothing more had been heard. Ah! What a grim story could be written about the depths of the Mediterranean, that vast burial ground where so much wealth has been lost, where so many victims have perished!

Swift and indifferent, the *Nautilus* moved at full speed among those ruins. On February 18th, at about three o'clock in the morning, we reached the entrance of the Strait of Gibraltar.

There are two currents in this strait: an upper current, which carries the water of the Atlantic Ocean into the basin of the Mediterranean. This was identified many years ago. Then there is a lower countercurrent, whose existence had to be proved by simple logic. The volume of water in the Mediterranean, incessantly increased by the waves of the Atlantic and by the rivers that flow into it, should raise the level of that sea year after year, because its evaporation is not sufficient to restore a balance. But this, as we know, is not the case. Hence, we had to assume the existence of an undercurrent, which carries the overflow of the Mediterranean through the Strait of Gibraltar into the Atlantic. It was precisely in this undercurrent that the *Nautilus* was sailing, and it soon sped through the narrow channel.

For just a moment, I caught a fleeting glimpse of the memorable Temple of Hercules, submerged, as we are told by Pliny and Avianus, together with the low island on which it stood. A few minutes later, we were cruising on the surface of the Atlantic.

Chapter VIII

VIGO BAY

THE ATLANTIC! A vast expanse of water whose surface covers 25 million square miles, 9,000 miles long, with an average width of 2,700. An important sea practically unknown to the ancients, except perhaps to the Carthaginians, those ancient Hollanders who, in their commercial wanderings, sailed the west coasts of Europe and Africa. An ocean whose parallel winding shores embrace an immense perimeter, and which is fed by the largest rivers in the world: the St. Lawrence, the Mississippi, the Amazon, the Plata, the Orinoco, the Niger, the Senegal, the Elbe, the Loire, and the Rhine—all pouring their waters into it from the most civilized as well as the most primitive countries. A magnificent plain, incessantly ploughed by ships of every nation, protected by all the flags in the world, ending in those two dangerous capes dreaded by seafarers, Cape Horn and the Cape of Tempests.

The *Nautilus* cut through its waters with its prow, after having sailed almost ten thousand leagues in three and a half months, a distance greater than the great circle of the earth. Where were we going now, and what had the future in store for us?

On leaving the Strait of Gibraltar, the *Nautilus* had headed for the open sea. It now emerged on the surface again, and so, once more, we were able to enjoy our daily strolls on the platform.

I went up immediately, accompanied by Ned Land and Conseil. At a distance of twelve miles, the vague outline of Cape St. Vincent appeared. This cape forms the southwestern tip of the Spanish peninsula. A strong wind was blowing from the south. The sea was high and surging. It beat against the *Nautilus,* which rocked violently, and it was practically impossible to stand on the platform, since enormous waves kept crashing against the ship. We went below after having taken a few breaths of fresh air.

I went back to my room, and Conseil returned to his cabin. The Canadian, however, looking somewhat preoccupied, followed me. Our rapid passage across the Mediterranean had not permitted him to carry out his plans, and he was unable to disguise his keen disappointment.

When the door of my room closed behind us, he sat down and looked at me in silence.

"I understand how you feel, Ned," I said, "but you are not to blame. Under the circumstances, even the thought of escaping would have been an act of folly."

Ned Land did not answer. His pursed lips and the frown on his brow indicated clearly that he was obsessed by a single thought.

"Look," I continued. "Let us not give up hope yet. We are now sailing along the coast of Portugal. France and England are not far off, where we could easily find refuge. Now, if the *Nautilus,* on leaving the Strait of Gibraltar, had headed south, and if it had sailed in regions where there are no continents, I would share your fears. But we know now that Captain Nemo does not shun well-traveled seas, and within a few days, I think you will be able to act with more security."

Ned Land fixed his gaze on me, stared, opened his pursed lips, and said:

"It's all set for this evening."

I sat up, startled. I was, I must confess, totally unprepared for this. I wanted to answer the Canadian, but I could not utter a word.

"We agreed to wait for a suitable opportunity," continued Ned Land. "That opportunity has come. This evening we will be only a few miles off the Spanish coast. The night is dark. The wind is blowing in from the sea. You have given me your word, Monsieur Aronnax, and I am counting on you."

I continued to remain silent. The Canadian rose, came over to me, and said:

"Tonight, at nine o'clock. I have alerted Conseil. At that time Captain Nemo will be in his room, probably asleep. Neither the mechanics nor the crew will be able to see us. Conseil and I will go to the central stairway. You, Monsieur Aronnax, will remain in the library close by, waiting for my signal. The oars, the mast, and the sail are in the dinghy. I have even stored some provisions in it. I have a wrench to unscrew the bolts which hold the dinghy to the hull of the *Nautilus.* Everything is ready for this evening."

"The sea is rough," I said.

"I agree," replied the Canadian, "but we must risk that. Our freedom is worth that risk. The dinghy, as you know, is sturdy, and a few miles, with a wind behind us, should offer no serious problem. Who knows? Tomorrow the *Nautilus* may be a hundred leagues away in the open sea. If everything works out well, within two or three hours we should be somewhere on dry land—or we'll be dead! May God be with us! This evening at nine o'clock, monsieur."

The Canadian withdrew, leaving me dumbfounded. I had imagined that I should have had time to reflect and to discuss the matter when the occasion arose. My stubborn companion gave me no time for this. But after all, what could I have said to him? Ned Land was right a hundred times over. It was just a chance, and he was taking advantage of it. Could I go back on my word and be responsible for the future of my companions for personal and selfish reasons? Couldn't Captain Nemo easily take us beyond the reach of all land on the very next day?

Just then a loud hissing sound made me realize that the tanks were being filled, and the *Nautilus* dove beneath the waves of the Atlantic.

I remained in my room. I avoided the Captain for fear that my deep emotions might betray me. It was a very depressing day for me. I was torn between the desire to regain my freedom and the reluctance to abandon that admirable *Nautilus*, leaving, besides, my studies of the seas unfinished. How could I leave that ocean—my Atlantic—as I was fond of calling it, without having explored its deepest waters, without having discovered all those detailed mysteries that the Indian Ocean and the Pacific had revealed to me? How could I end abruptly my "romance" in the middle of my story and interrupt my dream at the most exciting moment! During the unhappy hours that followed, I sometimes imagined myself and my companions safe on land, sometimes, hoping in spite of my reason, that something would happen to prevent Ned Land from carrying out his plans.

I went into the saloon on two occasions. I wanted to consult the compass. I wanted to see whether the direction of the *Nautilus* was bringing us nearer or farther away from the coast. No. The *Nautilus* continued to remain in Portuguese waters. She was heading north, sailing along the shores of the ocean.

There was no choice but to resign myself to the inevitable and make ready to escape. My luggage was not heavy, neither were my notes.

As for Captain Nemo, I wondered what he would think of our escape, what anxieties and what harm it might perhaps cause him, and what he would do in case we succeeded, and what if we failed. Certainly, I had no reason to complain about his conduct. On the contrary, never had hospitality been more open than his. He could not accuse me of being ungrateful for leaving him. We were not bound to him by an oath or even a promise. He was depending on the force of circumstances to keep us on board and not on any words of ours. His frank admission that he intended to keep us on board justified any attempt we might make in order to escape.

I had not seen the Captain since our visit to the isle of Santorin. Would fate bring us face-to-face before our escape? I both desired and feared it. I listened to see whether I could hear his footsteps in the room next to mine. Not a sound. The room must have been deserted.

I kept asking myself whether this strange person was really on board his ship. Since that night when the dinghy had left the *Nautilus* and had gone on that mysterious mission, my ideas about him had changed somewhat. I thought that Captain Nemo had maintained relations of some kind or other with those on land, regardless of what he said. Did he ever leave the *Nautilus?* He had often disappeared for weeks without my ever meeting him. What did he do on these occasions? Could it be that he was carrying out some secret missions, the nature of which escaped me? Had I been mistaken in thinking that he roamed the sea because of his hatred for mankind?

All these ideas, and a thousand others, assailed me at once. The field of conjecture had no limits in the strange situation in which we found ourselves. I felt an unbearable uneasiness. That day of waiting seemed an eternity, and in my impatience, the hours struck very slowly.

As always, my dinner was served in my room. I ate very little, for I was too disturbed. I rose from the table at seven o'clock. One hundred and twenty minutes—I counted them —still remained before I was to join Ned Land. My restlessness became more intense. My pulse beat violently, and I could not remain still. I paced up and down, hoping that moving to and fro would calm my disturbed mind. The prospect of failing or dying in our daring enterprise was the least of my worries. But at the thought of having our plans discovered before we got away, when I thought of being brought back in the presence of Captain Nemo, angry or, what was worse, grieved by my desertion, my heart beat faster.

I wanted to see the saloon for the last time. I went down and entered that museum where I had passed so many useful and pleasant hours. I gazed at all those riches and all those treasures like a man who, exiled for life, is leaving, never to return. Those marvels of nature, those artistic masterpieces, among which I had devoted so much of my life lately, I was now about to abandon forever. I should have liked to gaze once more at the waters of the Atlantic through the windows, but the panels were sealed, and a steel mantle separated me from that ocean that I still did not know.

As I wandered about the room, I drew near the door that opened into the Captain's room. To my astonishment the door was ajar. I drew back. If Captain Nemo were in his room, he could see me. However, hearing no noise, I drew near. The room was empty. I pushed the door open and stepped in. It had that same severe, monastic look.

Just then some etchings hanging on the wall, which I had not noticed on my first visit, drew my attention. They were portraits, portraits of great men of history, whose lives had been entirely dedicated to a great human ideal: Kosciusko, the hero whose dying words were *Finis Poloniae;* Botzaris, the Leonidas of modern Greece; O'Connell, the defender of Ireland; Washington, the founder of the American Union; Manin, the Italian patriot; Lincoln, shot by a defender of slavery; and finally, that martyr to the emancipation of the Negro race, John Brown, hanging on the gallows, so realistically drawn by Victor Hugo.

What bond existed between these heroic souls and the soul of Captain Nemo? Could I finally unravel the mystery of his life from this group of portraits? Was he a champion of oppressed peoples, the liberator of enslaved races? Had he played a role in political or social uprisings of our century? Had he been one of the heroes of the American Civil War—a tragic war, but forever glorious!

The clock struck eight. The first stroke of the bell hammer startled me and shook me from my dream. I trembled as if an invisible eye had penetrated the innermost secrets of my thoughts, and rushed out of the room.

My glance fell on the compass. We were still heading in a northerly direction. The log indicated a moderate speed; the manometer, a depth of about sixty feet. Events were certainly propitious to the plans of the Canadian.

I went back to my room and put on warm clothes: sea-boots, otter-fur cap, byssus overcoat lined with sealskin. I was ready. I waited. Only the vibrations of the propeller interrupted the deep silence that reigned on board. I listened carefully. Would not a sudden cry inform me that Ned Land had been caught in his attempt to escape? I was seized by a mortal dread. I tried in vain to regain my calm.

A few minutes before nine o'clock, I pressed my ear to the Captain's door. No sound. I left my room and went back to the saloon. It was dimly lit, but empty.

I opened the door that communicated with the library. The same dim light, the same solitude. I went and stood by the door that led to the central stairway, and waited for the signal.

At that moment, the vibrations of the propeller diminished noticeably and then stopped altogether. Why had the *Nautilus* stopped completely? Would this thwart Ned Land's plans? I could not say.

The silence now was broken only by the beating of my heart.

Suddenly I felt a slight shock, and I realized that the *Nautilus* had come to rest on the ocean bed. My uneasiness increased. The Canadian's signal did not come. I desperately wanted to join Ned Land in order to persuade him to postpone his attempt. I felt that we were no longer sailing under normal conditions.

Just then the door of the large saloon opened, and Captain Nemo appeared. He saw me and, without preliminaries:

"Ah! Monsieur le Professeur," he said in a friendly tone, "I have been looking for you. Do you know the history of Spain?"

A person could know the history of his country thoroughly and still not remember a single event if he were placed in the same circumstances I was. My mind was so troubled I could not think clearly and could not utter a word.

"Well," Captain Nemo insisted, "did you hear my question? Do you know the history of Spain?"

"Very sketchily," I replied.

"Indeed, even the learned," said the Captain, "do not know. So pray be seated," he added. "I am going to tell you a strange episode of that history."

The Captain stretched out on a divan and, mechanically, I sat down next to him in the dim light.

"Monsieur le Professeur," he said, "listen to me carefully. This story will interest you in one respect, for it will answer a question that you have undoubtedly been unable to solve."

"I am listening, Captain," I said, not knowing quite what he had in mind, and wondering whether this incident had any bearing on our plans to escape.

"Monsieur le Professeur," continued Captain Nemo, "with your permission, let us go back to 1701. You will certainly remember that at that time your king, Louis XIV, believing that a mere gesture of his could bury the Pyrenees, had imposed his grandson, the Duke of Anjou, on the Spanish. This prince, who reigned rather badly under the name of Philip V, had to face considerable opposition in his foreign policy.

"In fact, the previous year, the royal houses of Holland, Austria, and England had concluded an alliance at the Hague, with the object of forcibly depriving Philip V of the crown of Spain in order to place it upon the head of an arch-duke, to whom they prematurely gave the name of Charles III.

"Spain was forced to resist this coalition, but she was almost without an army or a navy. However, Spain was not without money, provided, of course, that her galleons loaded with gold and silver from America could reach her ports. Towards the end of the year 1702, Spain was waiting for a rich convoy which France was escorting with a fleet of twenty-three vessels, commanded by Admiral de Château-Renaud. This convoy was to be protected from the ships of the coalition, sailing the high seas of the Atlantic.

"This convoy was supposed to dock at Cadiz, but the admiral, hearing that the English fleet was cruising in this area, decided to head for a French port.

"The Spanish commanders of the convoy protested against this decision. They insisted on being taken to a Spanish port, and if not to Cadiz, then to the Bay of Vigo, located on the northwest coast of Spain, which was not then blockaded.

"Admiral de Château-Renaud was weak enough to yield to their demands, and the galleons entered Vigo Bay.

"Unfortunately, this bay has an open harbor which cannot be defended. It was necessary to unload the galleons quickly before the arrival of the combined fleets of the coalition. They would have had sufficient time to accomplish this, if a miserable question of rivalry had not arisen. Are you following the chain of events, Professor?"

"Yes, of course," I said, still not knowing why I was being given this history lesson.

"Permit me to continue. This is what happened. The merchants of Cadiz had the sole privilege of receiving all merchandise that came from the West Indies. Unloading ingots at Vigo Bay was, therefore, a violation of their rights. They complained to Madrid, and they obtained an order from the weak Philip V, requesting that the convoy cease unloading and that the fleet remain sequestered at Vigo Bay until the enemy fleet had sailed away.

"Just as this decision was being enforced, on the twenty-second of October, 1702, the English vessels arrived in Vigo Bay. Admiral de Château-Renaud, despite his inferior forces, fought bravely, but when he saw that the riches of the convoy were going to fall into the hands of the enemy, he set fire to the galleons, scuttled them, and they sank with all their immense treasures."

Captain Nemo paused. I must confess that I still could not see why this story should be of any interest to me.

"Well?" I asked him.

"Well, Monsieur Aronnax," Captain Nemo answered. "We are in Vigo Bay, and it is entirely up to you to unravel this mystery, if you are interested."

The Captain stood up and motioned to me to follow. I had now had time to recover. I obeyed. The saloon was in darkness, but through the transparent panels the waters of the sea were glittering. I looked out.

For a half mile around the *Nautilus* the waters glittered under the gleams of our searchlight. The bottom of the sea was clear, clean, and sandy. Members of the crew, in their diving suits, were busy clearing the blackened debris of rotted casks and chests out of wrecks. The ground was covered with bars of gold, silver, piles of coins and jewels, taken out of casks and chests. Loaded with that precious booty, the men returned to the *Nautilus,* deposited their burdens, and went back to that inexhaustible mine to fish for more gold and silver.

I was beginning to understand. This was the scene of the battle of the 22nd of October, 1702. In this very spot the galleons, laden with treasures for the Spanish Government, had sunk to the bottom. It was here that Captain Nemo came to fill his own coffers with the millions that he carried aboard his *Nautilus* to take care of his needs. It was for him and for him alone that America had delivered her precious metals. He was the only heir, and there were no sharers to these treasures—snatched from the Incas as well as from the people conquered by Hernán Cortés.

"Did you know, Monsieur le Professeur," he said, smiling, "that these seas contained such treasures?"

"I knew," I replied, "that someone calculated that there were two million tons' worth of silver lying around these waters."

"That is quite true. However, it would cost more than that to bring these treasures to the surface. But all I have to do is to harvest what other men have lost, and this is true not only of this bay, but of thousands of other places, which I have recorded on my map. Do you understand now why I am a billionaire?"

"I do indeed, Captain. I should tell you, however, that by doing what you are doing here at Vigo Bay, you are merely forestalling the works of a rival company."

"What company, may I ask?"

"A company that has obtained the privilege to search for these sunken galleons from the Spanish Government. The shareholders are lured by the possibility of acquiring enormous profits, for the value of these riches is estimated to be about five hundred million francs."

"Five hundred million!" Captain Nemo exclaimed. "There was that much, yes, but not any longer."

"In that case," I said, "a warning to the shareholders would be an act of charity. Although who can tell whether such a warning would be well received? What gamblers regret most is not the loss of their money, but the loss of their foolish hopes. But, nevertheless, I pity them less than the thousands of needy people who might have benefited from a fair distribution of this wealth. Now, however, these riches will never benefit them."

I had no sooner uttered this regret than I realized that it must have offended Captain Nemo.

"Never benefit them?" he replied animatedly. "Do you think, monsieur, that these riches are lost to them because I gather them? Do you for one moment think that I go to the trouble of collecting all these treasures just for my own benefit? What makes you think that I do not make good use of them? Do you think that I am unaware that there are human beings who are suffering, people who are oppressed in this world, wretches who need to be comforted, victims to be avenged? Don't you understand—"

Captain Nemo stopped suddenly, sorry, perhaps, for having talked too much. Whatever the reasons may have been that had driven him to seek his independence under the seas, he had remained a man, in spite of all! His heart was still beating for suffering humanity, and his immense charity was given not only to oppressed races, but to the unfortunate individual as well!

And I finally realized that those millions that I had seen while we were cruising around the waters of Crete had been delivered to the insurgents of that unhappy island.

Chapter IX

THE LOST CONTINENT

THE NEXT MORNING, February 19th, the Canadian came into my room. I was expecting his visit, and he looked very disappointed.

"Well, monsieur?" he said.

"Well, Ned, I am afraid luck was against us yesterday."

"Yes, it certainly was! That damned Captain had to stop just at the very moment we were ready to escape."

"You see, Ned, he had to transact some business with his banker."

"His banker?"

"Or, should I say, his bank. I mean this ocean, where his wealth is safer than it could ever be in a state treasury."

I then told the Canadian what had happened the day before, with the secret hope of bringing him around to the idea of not deserting the Captain, but the only effect this had on him was to fill him with regret that he himself had not been able to take a stroll through the battlefield of Vigo—for his own personal benefit!

"After all," he said, "we're not done yet! Our harpoon missed its target, that's all! Next time we shall score a bull's-eye, and—this evening, perhaps. . . ."

"What is our course now?" I asked.

"I don't know," replied Ned.

"Well, at midday we shall have our bearings."

The Canadian returned to Conseil. When I was dressed, I went into the saloon. The compass was far from reassuring, for the *Nautilus* was heading south-southwest, so that we were turning our backs on Europe.

I waited impatiently for our bearings to be marked on the chart. At about half past eleven, the tanks were emptied and we came up to the surface. I rushed up to the platform. Ned was already there.

There was no land in sight. Nothing but the vast open sea. There were a few sails on the horizon, probably boats going out as far as Cape San Roque is search of a favorable wind to take them around the Cape of Good Hope. The sky was overcast, and there was a windstorm in the making.

Ned was fuming, and tried to pierce through that misty horizon. He still hoped that behind all that fog he might catch a glimpse of some land he longed for.

At midday the sun came out for an instant, and the second-in-command took advantage of the improved visibility to take his bearings. The sea was becoming rough. The hatch was closed, and we dived once more.

An hour later, on consulting the chart, I saw that the position of the *Nautilus* was at longtitude 16° 17' west by latitude 33° 22' north, 150 leagues from the nearest land. There could be no thought of escaping, and the reader can well imagine the Canadian's fury when I informed him of our position. As far as I was concerned, I did not take it too much to heart. On the contrary, I felt as if a weight had been taken off my mind, and I was now able to resume my normal routine with relative calm.

That evening, at about eleven o'clock, I received a most unexpected visit from Captain Nemo, who asked me most graciously whether I was tired from having stayed up so late the night before. I told him I was not.

"In that case, Monsieur Aronnax, I should like to suggest a very interesting excursion."

"By all means do, Captain."

"So far you have explored the depths of the sea only during the day and in the sunlight. Would you like to explore these depths in the darkness of night?"

"That would please me very much indeed."

"I warn you, however, this excursion will be tiring. It will be a long one. You will have to climb a mountain, and the paths are not in a good state of repair."

"What you are telling me, Captain, only whets my curiosity. You have only to lead."

"Come with me, then, Professor. We will go and put on our diving suits."

When we got to the dressing room, I noticed that neither my companions nor any member of the crew were to accompany us on this trip. Captain Nemo had not even suggested taking Ned or Conseil with us.

A few seconds later we had put on our suits. Air tanks, filled to the brim, were harnessed to our backs, but the electric equipment was not included. I mentioned this to the Captain.

"We will not need it," he replied.

I thought I had not heard him correctly, but I was unable to repeat my remark, because the Captain's head had already disappeared inside his metal headgear. So I finished arranging my harness, and someone put a spiked walking stick in my hand. A few minutes later, after going through the usual procedure, we set foot on the bottom of the Atlantic, about a thousand feet down.

Midnight was approaching. The waters were pitch-black. However, Captain Nemo pointed to a reddish glow of light shining in the distance about two miles away. What that beacon was, what made it glow, and how it could shine so brightly through those waters, I could not possibly have guessed. Nevertheless, it did light our way, however dimly, but I soon got used to that strange semidarkness, and I realized how useless our own light would have been.

Captain Nemo and I walked together in the direction of that glimmer of light. The flat ground rose imperceptibly. We kept walking along with long strides, helped by our sticks. Our progress was slow, however, since our feet kept sinking into a sort of thick mud and a growth of seaweeds dotted with flat rocks.

As we walked along, I began to hear a kind of pattering noise above my head. Sometimes that noise grew in intensity and became a continuous crackling. I soon discovered what was causing it. It was a very heavy rain, falling and pattering on the surface of the water. Instinctively, I thought I was going to get drenched! Drenched with water, although immersed in it! I couldn't help laughing at that weird idea. However, there was nothing strange about this because when one is in water, wearing a diving suit, one is not aware of the water; one merely feels that he is in an atmosphere denser than that on land.

After we had walked for half an hour, the ground became rocky. Medusae, microscopic crustacea, and pennatules made that soil shine with a faint glow of phosphorescence. I could make out the outlines of heaps of rocks, covered with a carpet of millions of zoophytes and masses of seaweed. I often slipped on this carpet, and without my iron stick I would have fallen more than once. When I turned around, I could still see the light of the *Nautilus* fading in the distance.

Those piles of stone I have just mentioned were laid out on the bed of the ocean with a certain regularity that I found hard to explain. I noticed gigantic furrows which faded away in the distant darkness and whose length could not be measured. There were other details also that I could not account for. I had the impression that my heavy leaden soles as I walked along were crunching a layer of bones that made a dry, crackling sound. What could this vast plain I was treading be? I wanted to ask the Captain, but his sign language, which he used to communicate with his crew on their underwater excursions, was still incomprehensible to me.

Meanwhile, the rosy glow that guided us was growing brighter and lighting up the horizon. I was greatly intrigued by the presence of this fiery beacon under the sea. Could it be an electrical phenomenon? Was I approaching a natural phenomenon unknown to the scientists on earth? Or—the thought occurred to me—did the hand of man have anything to do with it? Could the hand of man be responsible for that conflagration? Was I going to meet, in these depths, the friends and companions of Captain Nemo, living, like him, a strange existence and whom he had come to visit? Would I meet, in these depths, a whole colony of exiles who, weary of the misery of terrestrial life, had sought refuge and independence at the very bottom of the sea? These were the mad, incredible ideas that ran through my mind as I became more and more bewildered by the marvels that unfolded before my eyes. I would not have been surprised to find one of those cities Captain Nemo dreamed of, at the bottom of this sea!

Our path was becoming brighter and brighter. The whitish glow came from the peak of a mountain about eight hundred feet high. But what I saw was just a reflection produced by the crystal clarity of the water. The actual source of this inexplicable light was on the other side of the mountain.

Captain Nemo advanced unhesitatingly through the maze of rocks that crisscrossed the bottom of the ocean. Evidently, he knew this dark road quite well, having often traveled it, so that there was no danger of his becoming lost. I followed him with unshakable confidence. I thought of him as one of those spirits of the sea, and as he walked in front of me I admired his tall stature, outlined against the background of a glowing horizon.

It was one o'clock in the morning when we reached the first slopes of the mountain. But before beginning our climb, we had to walk along some difficult paths through a vast expanse of brushwood. Yes, it was a forest of dead trees, without leaves and without sap, petrified by the water of the sea, dominated here and there by gigantic pines. It was like a colliery still standing, whose trees were still held by their roots in the sunken soil while their branches, like fine traceries cut out of black paper, stood in bold relief against the watery background. Let the reader imagine a forest in the Hartz Mountains, with trees clinging on the slopes of its steep rocks, but completely immersed in a sea of water. The paths were cluttered with seaweed and fucus, among which swarmed innumerable kinds of crustacean. I walked on, climbing over rocks, stepping over fallen tree trunks, breaking seaweed slung between one tree and another, frightening fish that flew from branch to branch. I was so carried away that I felt no fatigue, and followed my indefatigable guide.

What a spectacle! How can I describe it! How can I describe a vision of those rocks and those trees standing upright in those waters, their bases dark and sinister, their tops tinted by shades of red, intensified by the pure reflection of the water? We were scaling rocks that crumbled and let loose stones that crashed down behind us with the muffled rumble of an avalanche. To the right and the left were caves and grottos, hollowed out in the rocks, gloomy and impenetrable to the eyes. Elsewhere there were vast clearings, which seemed to have been created by human hands, and I wondered whether I might not suddenly come face-to-face with some inhabitant of these waters.

Captain Nemo kept climbing up the slope. I did not want to be left behind. I followed with assurance. My stick proved most useful to me. One false step would have been dangerous on those narrow passes flanked on both sides by abysses, but I walked along with a firm step and without feeling the slightest giddiness. Occasionally I would leap across a crevice, whose depth would have made me shrink back had I come upon it in some glacier on land; or I would venture out on some shaky tree trunk spanning a ravine without even looking down, fascinated only by the wild beauty around me. Here and there I could see vast, monumental rocks jutting forward on their craggy, irregular foundations, seeming to defy the laws of equilibrium. From between those rocky fissures, trees sprouted forth like jets under heavy pressure, supporting other trees that in turn supported them. Elsewhere there were natural towers and wide walls that dropped straight down like curtains, or leaned over at an angle that the laws of gravity would have made impossible on land.

I was conscious of this difference due to the density of the water; in spite of my heavy apparel, my copper headpiece, and my leaden soles, I managed to scale slopes of impossible steepness, surmounting them, so to speak, with the agility of an izard or a chamois!

I am aware that the description of this excursion under the sea must sound incredible. However, I am a writer whose business it is to record things that appear impossible, yet are incontestably real. This was not a dream. I saw and felt what I am describing!

Two hours after leaving the *Nautilus*, we had climbed above the tree line, and a hundred feet above us rose the peak of the mountain, whose shadow was projected by the brightly glowing slope on the other side. Here and there, petrified shrubs traced a perilously zigzag path over the mountainside. Shoals of fish rose from under our feet like birds startled out of tall rushes. The rocky mass was pitted with impenetrable winding crevices and grottos, deep caves of unfathomable depth, inside which I could hear frightful sounds of movement. My blood froze whenever I saw a huge antenna barring my path, or a formidable claw closing with a vicious snap in those cavernous shadows! Thousands of little luminous objects sparkled in the darkness; these were the eyes of gigantic crustaceans, crouching in their lairs; giant lobsters reared up like halberdiers, brandishing their claws with a metallic click, while titantic crabs stood ready menacingly, like so many cannons on their carriages; and frightful octopi lashed about with their intertwined tentacles, like a living thicket crawling with snakes.

What was the nature of this strange, fantastic world I did not know? To what order did these articulates belong, which used the rocks for a second shell? Where had creation found the secret of their vegetative existence, and for how many centuries had they lived like this at the very bottom of the sea?

But I could not stop to ponder. Captain Nemo, who was familiar with these terrible animals, paid no attention to them. We had reached a first plateau, where other surprises were in store for me. Here I saw picturesque ruins, which betrayed the hand of man rather than that of the Creator. They were vast heaps of stone that still had the vague outlines of castles and temples, covered with an infinite variety of flowering zoophytes and draped, not with ivy, but with a thick tapestry of seaweed and fucus.

What part of the world was this which had been swallowed by some cataclysm? Who had laid out those rocks and stones which resembled the dolmens of prehistoric times? Where was I? And where had the whims of Captain Nemo led me?

I should have liked to ask him, but since this was not possible, I stopped him and seized him by the arm. But he shook his head, and pointing to the summit of the mountain, seemed to say: "Come on! come on! Keep coming!"

I made a final effort, and within a few minutes we reached the peak, which was some thirty feet higher than all that rocky mass we had just left.

I looked back at the slope we had just scaled. The mountain rose no more than seven or eight hundred feet above the plain, but on the other side, it stood twice as high above the floor of the valley and all that area of the Atlantic. As I looked out into the distance, my eyes took in a vast space lit up by a blazing glow. Needless to say, this was a volcano. Fifty feet below the summit, a large crater vomited forth a deluge of stone and slag and exuded torrents of lava, which dissolved into cascades of fire in the water all around. In that commanding position the volcano, like an immense torch, cast a brilliant light on the plain below, as far as the eye could see.

It is true that this underwater crater threw up lava; but there were no flames, for flames require oxygen found in the air, and cannot exist in water. But streams of incandescent lava can attain a red-white heat which, when coming in contact with water, can successfully vaporize. Streams of these vapors and torrents of lava flowed to the base of the mountain like the eruptions of Vesuvius on another Torre del Greco.*

Down below, before my very eyes, lay the ruins of a submerged city, swallowed by the sea. Its roofs were sunken, its temples demolished, its arches in pieces, its columns on the ground, but its proportions were clearly outlined, reminding me of the stately architecture of Tuscany. Farther on there were the remains of a gigantic aqueduct; here were the encrusted remains of an Acropolis, with the floating forms of a Parthenon; the remains of a quay, also, vestiges of an ancient port on the shore of a vanished sea, which had given shelter to merchant ships and craft of war; farther still, the outlines of crumbled walls and long lines of wide, deserted streets, an ancient Pompeii, buried beneath the sea. All this was what Captain Nemo had brought me to see!

Where was I? Where could all this be? I had to know, regardless of consequences! I felt a sudden impulse to speak, to tear off the helmet I was wearing! But Captain Nemo stopped me with a gesture. He came to me, picked up a piece of chalky rock, walked to a block of black basalt, and scribbled one single word:

ATLANTIS

What a thrill that word gave me! Atlantis, the ancient Meropis of Theopompus, the Atlantis of Plato, the continent whose disappearance had been questioned by Origen, Porphyry Jamblichus, D'Anville, Malte-Brun, and Humboldt, who classed it among the legends, but whose existence was accepted by Posidonius, Pliny, Ammianus Marcellinus, Tertullian, Engel, Sherer, Tournefort, Buffon, and D'Avezac. There it was before my eyes, majestic evidence of its tragic fate! Atlantis, then, was beyond Europe, Asia, and Libya, be-

* A city on the Bay of Naples at the foot of Mt. Vesuvius.—M.T.B.

yond the Pillars of Hercules*; Atlantis, where the Atlantes had dwelled, against whom the Greeks had waged their first wars!

Plato himself was the historian who described the events of those heroic times. His dialogue between Timaeus and Critias was inspired, so to speak, by Solon, the poet and legislator.

One day, Solon was conversing with some elderly sages from Saïs, an ancient city then eight hundred years old, verified by the annals engraved on the sacred walls of its temples. One of the wise old men told the story of another city that was a thousand years older. This first Athenian city—Saïs—nine centuries old, had been invaded and partly destroyed by the Atlantes. These Atlantes, he said, occupied a vast continent, larger than Africa and Asia put together, extending from the twelfth degree of latitude to the fortieth degree north. Their dominion even extended as far as Egypt. They had wanted to impose their rule on Greece, but had to withdraw because of the indomitable resistance put up by the Hellenes. Centuries went by. Then a terrible cataclysm, accompanied by floods and earthquakes, occurred, and within twenty-four hours, the whole continent of Atlantis disappeared beneath the sea. Only its highest peaks, the Madeiras, the Azores, the Canaries, and the Cape Verde Islands, remained above that sea.

Such were the historical memories that the word written by Captain Nemo evoked in my mind. Here I was, by the strangest destiny setting foot on one of the mountains of that continent! With my hand I was touching those ruins thousands of centuries old, contemporary with geological times! I was treading the same ground where the contemporaries of the first man had trodden! My heavy boots were crushing the skeletons of animals of prehistoric times which had basked in the shade of these trees, now petrified!

Ah, why had I so little time! I should have liked to descend the steep slopes of this mountain, explore the whole of this immense continent, which doubtless joined Africa to America, and visit its great antediluvian cities. Perhaps before my very eyes I should see the warlike city of Makhimos, and the pious Eusebes, whose gigantic inhabitants lived for centuries, and who were so powerful that they could pile up those blocks of stone that still resisted the erosion of the waters. One day, perhaps, some volcanic eruption would bring these sunken ruins back to the surface! Numerous underwater volcanoes have indeed been reported in this part of the

* Gibraltar on the European side and Gebel Musa at Ceuta on the African side.—M.T.B.

ocean, and many ships have felt inexplicable tremors as they sailed over these tormented depths. Some have heard rumblings indicating a struggle of the elements going on below, while others have picked up volcanic ash thrown up by the sea. All this area, as far as the equator, is still racked by Plutonian forces. Who knows but what, at some time in the distant future, through the accumulation of volcanic eruptions and of successive layers of lava, these glowing mountaintops may not appear on the surface of the Atlantic!

As I stood there dreaming, trying to fix in my mind all the details of this magnificent landscape, Captain Nemo was leaning on a mossy pillar, motionless and seemingly petrified in mute ecstasy. Was he dreaming of those vanished generations and seeking the secret of human destiny? Was it here that this strange man came to steep himself in memories of the past and relive the life of antiquity!—he who would have nothing to do with the actual world around him? What would I not have given to know his thoughts, to share those thoughts with him and to understand them!

We remained there for a whole hour, contemplating that vast plain illuminated by the brilliant glow of the lava, which at times became surprisingly intense. At times, the vibrations of internal convulsions made the slope of the mountain tremble. Rumblings, emanating from the deep, transmitted clearly by those crystal waters, reverberated with majestic sounds. And then the rays of the moon pierced through the waves and cast their pale shadows on that submerged continent. It was only the dimmest light, but its effect was indescribably beautiful. The Captain rose, and casting one final glance at that immense plain, he motioned for me to follow him.

We descended that mountainside quickly. Once across that petrified forest, I saw the searchlight of the *Nautilus* shining like a star in the distance. We reached the ship just as the first light of dawn was spreading its white glow on the surface of the sea.

Chapter X

COAL MINES UNDER THE SEA

ON THE FOLLOWING DAY, February 20th, I rose very late. The fatigues of the previous day caused me to sleep until eleven o'clock. I dressed quickly. I was anxious to find out in what direction the *Nautilus* was going. The instruments told me that she was still heading south at a speed of twenty miles an hour and at a depth of three hundred feet.

Conseil came in. I told him about our nocturnal excursion, and since the panels were open, he could still catch a glimpse of the submerged continent.

Actually, the *Nautilus* was grazing the plains of Atlantis barely thirty feet above the soil. She was gliding along like a balloon swept by the wind on land. However, in that room, we were more like passengers on an express train. The first objects that passed before our eyes were some fantastically chiseled rocks, forests of trees that had been transformed from the vegetable to the mineral world, whose immobile silhouettes made wry faces beneath the waves. There were also masses of rocks buried under a tapestry of axidies and anemones bristling with long vertical hydrophytes; then blocks of lava strangely contorted, silent witnesses of the furies of volcanic eruptions.

While gazing at that eerie scenery, brilliantly reflected by our powerful searchlight, I related the story of the Atlantes, who had inspired Bailly, from a purely imaginative point of view, with so many charming pages. I spoke of the wars of these heroic people and discussed the question of Atlantis as a man who could no longer doubt its existence. Conseil, however, was distracted and was no longer listening. His indifference to my historical references was evident.

I realized that schools of fish were catching his eye, and when fish swam by, Conseil, thoroughly obsessed by a mania for classification, was completely oblivious to the world around him. When this happened, nothing could be done except to follow him and pursue our ichthyological studies together.

The fish of Atlantis, however, differed little from those we had already observed. There were gigantic rays, fifteen feet in length, possessing enough strength to leap out of the water; sharks of various kinds, among them a glaucus, fifteen feet long, with sharp triangular teeth, so transparent it was almost invisible in the water; brown-colored sargos; prism-shaped humantins, protected by a tubercular hide; sturgeons similar to their cousins in the Mediterranean; trumpet shells, a foot and a half long, brownish-yellow in color with little gray fins, lacking teeth and tongue, which glided by like lithe, supple serpents.

Among the bony fish, Conseil noted some blackish makairas, fifteen feet long, armed with a piercing sword in their upper jaws; bright-colored weevers, known in Aristotle's times as sea dragons, dangerous to catch because of the spikes on their dorsal fins; prickly dolphins, with brown backs, striped with fine blue lines framed in a border of gold; beautiful dorado; moonfish that looked like dishes with a touch of blue, and when the rays of the sun fell upon them, shimmered like silver specks; finally, swordfish, twenty-five feet in length, swimming in schools, with their sickle-shaped fins and their six-foot swords—intrepid animals, more herbivorous than carnivorous—and, like well-trained husbands, they obey the slightest whims of their females.

But while observing these different species of marine life, I did not fail to study the wide plains of Atlantis. Occasionally, capricious accidents in the formation of the rock beneath caused the *Nautilus* to slow her pace, and then she would slip through the narrow gaps between the jutting hills with the grace of a cetacean. If this labyrinth became difficult enough to prevent passage, the ship would rise like a balloon, and having gone over the obstacle, would resume its rapid course a few yards above the floor of the sea. It was an awesome and enchanting voyage, reminding me of a balloon flying through space, except, of course, that the *Nautilus* passively obeyed every move desired by the helmsman.

Toward four o'clock in the evening, the ground, which had for the most part been composed of thick mud with scattered petrified branches, began slowly to change. It became more rocky and strewn with a mixture of basaltic tuff, bits of lava and sulphurous obsidian or volcanic glass. I thought that the mountainous region would soon replace the wide plains and, in fact, as the *Nautilus* sailed onward, I soon saw on the southern horizon a high wall which, it seemed, would block any further progress. Its summit evidently rose above the surface of the ocean. It must have been a continent or, at the very least, an island—either one of the Canary Islands or one of the Cape Verde Islands. Our bearings had not been taken, purposely perhaps, and I did not know what our position was. In any case, such a barrier seemed to me to mark the border of Atlantis, of which we had covered but a small area.

Night fell. It did not, however, interrupt my observations. I was alone. Conseil had returned to his cabin. The *Nautilus* reduced her speed, hovered over the tortuous masses below, sometimes brushing the bottom of the sea as if she wished to come to rest, sometimes rising unexpectedly to the surface. It was then that I caught sight of some brilliant stars shining through the crystal waters; they were, to be more precise, five or six of those stars of the Zodiac that hang on the tail of Orion.

I would have remained much longer at the window, admiring the beauties of the sea and sky, but the panels closed. Just then the *Nautilus* had arrived at the sheer face of the high wall. What would she do to overcome this obstacle? I could not guess. I returned to my room. The *Nautilus* was no longer in motion. I fell asleep with the firm intention of awakening after a few hours' rest.

The next morning, at eight o'clock, I returned to the saloon. I looked at the manometer and realized that the *Nautilus* was floating on the surface of the ocean. Then I heard the noise of footsteps on the platform.

There was no motion, not the usual movement of the waves. I went up to the stairway. The hatch was open. But, instead of the broad daylight I expected, I found we were in complete darkness. No! Not a single star was shining above, and besides, no night had ever been so utterly dark!

I did not know what to think, when suddenly a voice said: "Is that you, Monsieur le Professeur?"

"Ah! Captain Nemo," I replied. "Where are we?"

"Underground, Monsieur le Professeur."

"Underground!" I cried. "And the *Nautilus* is floating on the water?"

"Yes, it is floating on the water."

"But I do not understand!"

"Be patient for a moment, Professor. Our searchlight will soon brighten up the scene, and if you like things to be clear, you will be happily surprised."

I stepped on the platform and waited. The darkness was so intense that I couldn't even see the Captain. I looked straight above me, however, and saw a faint glimmer—something like a dim twilight filtering through a circular opening. Just then there was a blaze of light from our searchlight, and its dazzling beam dispelled that glimmer above me.

That brilliant light blinded me for a moment. When I opened my eyes I saw the *Nautilus*, motionless, floating on a bank jutting out like a quay. It was floating on the calm waters of a lake, enclosed by a circle of walls about two miles in diameter and about six miles in circumference. Its level, as indicated by the manometer, was the same as the level of the sea. There was, no doubt, a channel connecting it with the sea. The high walls, inclining inward from their base, formed a vaulted roof, something resembling an immense funnel turned upside down. At the top, which was about two thousand feet above us, was a circular orifice through which I had seen that glimmer of light—evidently daylight.

Before examining with care the interior of that enormous cavern, before asking myself whether it was the work of nature or of man, I went over to Captain Nemo.

"Where are we?" I asked.

"In the very heart of an extinguished volcano," answered the Captain. "A volcano whose interior was filled by the sea, following some convulsion of the earth. While you were sleeping, Monsieur le Professeur, the *Nautilus* cruised into this lagoon through a natural channel thirty feet below the surface of the ocean. Here our *Nautilus* has a safe, secluded, and mysterious haven, sheltered from all winds and all storms! Is there, on the shores of any of your continents or any of your islands, a haven and a refuge so completely sheltered from the fury of tempests?"

"Indeed," I replied, "you are quite safe here, Captain Nemo. What have you to fear in the heart of a volcano? But didn't I see an opening at the top of this dome?"

"Yes, you saw its crater—a crater once full of lava, vapors and flames, but which now gives us the air we are breathing."

"But where is this volcanic mountain located?" I asked.

"It belonged to one of the numerous small islands which are scattered about this area. Just a rock for your ships, but for us an immense cavern. It was by chance that I discovered it, but fortune served me well."

"Is it possible to come through that crater above us?"

"No, Monsieu⸱ le Professeur. The internal base of this mountain can be climbed, but only up to one hundred feet. Above that, the overhanging walls lean inward and cannot be scaled."

"I see, Captain. Nature serves you well everywhere and always. You are quite safe in this lake, and you alone can visit these waters. But what use is all this to you? The *Nautilus* doesn't need a haven."

"No, it doesn't. Monsieur le Professeur, but it does need electric power—materials to produce that power—sodium! It needs coal to produce sodium, and mines to produce coal. This sea covers entire forests, buried in the geological past, which were transformed into coal. For me, these former forests are an inexhaustible mine."

"And where do you get your miners? Your crew, I presume."

"Precisely. These mines extend out beneath the waves like the coalfields of Newcastle. It is here that, dressed in their diving suits, pick in hand, my men dig out coal. I do not need coal from the mines on the continents. When I burn this fuel to make sodium, the smoke escapes through the crater of this mountain, making it look as if it were still an active volcano."

"Shall we be seeing your companions at work?"

"No, not this time. I am in a hurry to continue our underwater voyage around the world. I have enough reserve here to take care of my present needs. However, it will take a day to get our supply on board, and then we shall be on our way again. If you are interested in exploring this cavern, take a stroll around the lagoon. It's an opportunity. You should take advantage of it, Professor."

I thanked the Captain and went off to find my two companions, who had not yet left their cabin. I invited them to follow me, but I did not tell them where we were.

They came up on the platform. Conseil, never surprised at anything, thought it perfectly natural to wake up under a mountain after having slept beneath the waves. But Ned Land's only thought was to see if there was a way out of that cave.

After breakfast, about ten o'clock, we went down on the bank.

"Here we are on land again," said Conseil.

"I don't call this land," replied the Canadian. "Moreover, we are not on, we are under."

Between the base of the mountain and the waters of the lake stretched a sandy shore, which measured about five hundred feet at its widest point. Along this strand of beach, it was possible to walk around the lake. But the base of the high walls was strewn with jagged rocks and volcanic blocks, and enormous pumice rocks lay in picturesque heaps. All these scattered masses had been smoothly polished by volcanic and subterranean fires, and when the beams of the searchlight fell upon them, they created a resplendent shower of brilliant lights. Mica dust lay along the shore, and when our feet stepped upon it, it also raised clouds of sparks.

The ground rose sharply as we drew farther away from the edge of the water, and we soon reached some long, winding gradients, steep slopes that slowed our progress. We had to walk carefully among these conglomerates, for there was no cement binding them together, and our feet slipped on the glassy trachyte, composed of feldspar and quartz crystals.

The volcanic nature of this huge cave was evident. I pointed this out to my companions.

"Just imagine," I asked them, "what this funnel must have been like when it was filled to the brim with molten lava! When the level of incandescent liquid rose up and spilled over the orifice of this mountain, just like molten iron overflowing the walls of a furnace!"

"I can well imagine what it was like," replied Conseil. "But will Monsieur tell me how this came about and how that furnace was transformed into the quiet waters of a lake?"

"It is very probable, Conseil, that some convulsion of the earth created the channel used by the *Nautilus*. Then the waters of the Atlantic swept into the interior of the mountain. There must have been a terrific struggle between fire and water, a struggle which was won by Neptune. But that was many, many centuries ago, and eventually the submerged volcano was transformed into a peaceful cavern."

"That is all very well," retorted Ned Land. "It's too bad, for our sake, that the channel the Professor is talking about didn't appear above sea level."

"But Ned," replied Conseil, "if this passage had not been underwater, the *Nautilus* would not have been able to enter this cavern. And I would add, Ned, that if the waters had not rushed in, this mountain would still be a volcano. So your comments don't make much sense."

We continued climbing. Our paths became steeper and narrower. We had to jump across deep crevasses that appeared now and then, and at times we had to work our way around overhanging masses of rocks. Sometimes we had to crawl on our knees and slide on our bellies, but with the agility of Conseil and the strength of the Canadian, we overcame all obstacles.

At a height of about ninety feet the nature of the ground changed, without, however, becoming any easier. The conglomerates and trachyte were followed by black basalt. These boulders lay in rugged, craggy stretches in some places, in others they formed regularly shaped prisms, standing like columns supporting the arches of this huge vault—a magnificent example of natural architecture. Then, between these basalt blocks, long streams of hardened lava wound their way, encrusted with bituminous coal, and here and there stretched wide carpets of brimstone. The stronger light of day, pouring in through the crater above, flooded all these volcanic forms with a faint glow, and remained forever shrouded in the heart of the extinguished mountain.

Our upward march, however, soon came to a stop. At a height of about 250 feet, we came across an impassable barrier. The interior cove began to overhang, and our ascent became a circular walk inside the mountain. At this point the vegetable kingdom began to appear, competing with the mineral kingdom. A few shrubs and even a tree sprouted here and there from the crevices in the walls. I recognized some euphorbias with their bitter sap oozing from their trunks; heliotropes, scarcely recognizable as such, with their clusters of flowers drooping and somewhat wilted, since the rays of the sun never reached them; an occasional chrysanthemum grew timidly at the foot of aloes, whose long leaves looked sickly and withered. But between the streams of hard lava I saw some little violets, still lightly scented, and I confess I smelled with delight. Fragrance is the very soul of flowers, and sea flowers, as beautiful as they may be, have no soul!

We had reached the foot of a clump of sturdy dragon trees, which had split the rocks with the force of their vigorous roots, when Ned Land suddenly exclaimed:

"Ah! Monsieur! A beehive!"

"A beehive indeed," I commented, with a gesture of utter disbelief.

"Yes! A beehive," repeated the Canadian, "and bees buzzing around it."

I drew nearer and had to believe what I saw. There, at the mouth of a hole bored in the trunk of a dragon tree, were thousands of these ingenious insects, so common throughout the Canaries, and whose honey is very highly esteemed.

Naturally, the Canadian wanted to collect his store of honey, and it would have been unreasonable for me to stop him. With the spark of his flint, he lit a small quantity of dried leaves mixed with sulfur and began to smoke out the bees. The buzzing slowly subsided, and the hive produced several pounds of fragrant honey. Ned Land stowed it away in his haversack.

"I will mix this honey with the pâté of the breadfruit," he said. "I will offer you a very delicious cake."

"*Mon Dieu!*" exclaimed Conseil. "It sounds like gingerbread to me."

"Forget the gingerbread for the present," I said, "and let us continue with this interesting walk."

At times, when we came to a turn in our path, the whole lake spread out before us. The searchlight lighted up its whole peaceful surface. No waves, no ripples, played on the waters.

The *Nautilus* lay perfectly motionless. On the platform and on the bank, members of the crew were busy working, looking like black shadows, clearly outlined under the brilliant light of the ship.

By that time, we were circling the crater that stood above the first rock that supported the vault. I noticed then that the bees were not the only representatives of the animal kingdom inside the volcano. Birds of prey hovered and dived here and there in the shadows, or flew out from their nests, perched on the crags of the rocks. They were white-breasted sparrow hawks and screeching kestrels. Some fine fat bustards scampered about on the slopes as fast as their long legs would carry them. I leave you to imagine whether the Canadian's eagerness was aroused at the sight of this succulent game, and whether he regretted not having a gun in hand. He attempted to use stones instead of bullets, and after a few fruitless efforts, he finally wounded one of these magnificent birds. He risked his life at least twenty times to retrieve the bird, but in the end the bird joined the honeycombs in his sack.

We then had to return to the shore, since the crest of the cavern could not be scaled. Above us, the yawning crater looked like the opening of a large well. We could now see the sky quite clearly, and I saw clouds, driven by a western wind, grazing the top of the mountain with their misty vapors. This was certain proof that those clouds were not very high, since the volcano did not rise more than eight hundred feet above the level of the ocean.

Half an hour after the latest exploit of the Canadian, we were back on the inner shore. Here the vegetable kingdom was represented by carpets of sea fennel, a small plant in the shape of a parasol, which makes an excellent preserve. Conseil collected a few bundles of them. As for animal life, there were thousands of shellfish of all kinds: lobsters, crabs, prawns, musis, spider crabs, galatheides, and a great number of other shells, such as porcelaines, or cowrie rockfish, and limpets.

Then we discovered a magnificent grotto. My companions and I found great delight in stretching out on its fine sand. The fire had glossed its enameled walls which glittered with their sprinklings of mica dust. Ned Land tapped the walls and tried to figure out their thickness. I could not help smiling. The conversation then turned to his eternal plans to escape, and I thought I could give him some hope without too much of a gamble, since Captain Nemo had only come down south in order to renew his stock of sodium. I surmised now that he would coast the shores of Europe and of America, which would permit the Canadian to have more success than his abortive attempts so far.

We had been stretched out inside that enchanting grotto

for an hour. The conversation, which had been lively to begin with, now began to lag. We were overcome by a certain weariness. Since I saw no reason why I should not take a nap, I let myself fall into a deep slumber. I dreamed—one does not choose one's dreams—that my existence was slowly being transformed into the vegetative life of a simple mollusk and that this grotto was nothing more than the bivalve of my shell.

Suddenly I was awakened by Conseil's voice.

"Wake up, wake up!" cried the worthy lad.

"What is the matter?" I asked, sitting up.

"The water is rising! We shall drown!"

I stood up. The sea was surging into our grotto like a torrent, and decidedly, since we were not mollusks, we had to get out.

In a few moments we were safe above the grotto itself.

"What's going on?" asked Conseil. "Is this a new phenomenon?"

"No, my friends," I replied. "It is the tide. It is the tide which almost took us by surprise, like the hero of Walter Scott! The ocean is rising outside, and following the natural law of equilibrium, the level of the lake is rising also. We have got off with only half a bath. Let us go and change our clothes on the *Nautilus*."

Three-quarters of an hour later, we had finished our circular journey and were on board. The men of the crew had just finished loading the supply of sodium, and the *Nautilus* could have left immediately.

Captain Nemo, however, gave no orders. Was he waiting for the night to creep out secretly through his underwater passage? Perhaps.

Whatever it was, the following day the *Nautilus*, having left her mooring, was sailing on the high seas, a few yards below the waves of the Atlantic.

Chapter XI

THE SARGASSO SEA

THE DIRECTION of the *Nautilus* had not changed. All hope of returning into the European seas had now to be abandoned for the time being. Captain Nemo held a southerly direction. Where was he leading us? I dared not imagine.

That day the *Nautilus* crossed an unusual area of the Atlantic Ocean. Everyone has heard of the existence of this great current of warm water that is known as the Gulf Stream. After leaving the Florida channels, it winds its way toward Spitsbergen. But before entering the Gulf of Mexico, about latitude 44° north, the current divides into two streams: the main one flows toward the coasts of Ireland and Norway, while the second turns toward the south near the Azores; then, touching the shores of Africa and describing a long oval, it flows back toward the Antilles.

This second arm, more like a collar than an arm, surrounds with its rings of warm water a colder area of the ocean—a quiet, tranquil area called the Sargasso Sea, a veritable lake in the midst of the ocean. The waters of the Gulf Stream take no less than three years to travel right around it.

The Sargasso Sea, properly speaking, covers the whole of the submerged part of Atlantis. Some writers have even maintained that the numerous types of weed that are found in its waters arise from the ancient prairies of this former continent. It is more probable, however, that these weeds, algae, and fucus, carried away from the shores of Europe and America, are brought to this area by the Gulf Stream. It was this hypothesis that led Columbus to believe in the existence of a new world. When the ships of this bold explorer reached the Sargasso Sea, they had considerable difficulty in sailing through those weeds, which impeded their progress. The crews of his ships were terrified, and they lost three long weeks crossing it.

Such was the region that the *Nautilus* was now visiting, a veritable prairie, a tight-woven carpet of weeds, of floating fucus, of tropical pokeweed, which was so thick and compact that the prow of a large ship would not have ploughed through it without serious difficulty. Captain Nemo had no desire to engage his propeller in this mass of weed, and kept his ship several meters below the surface.

The name Sargasso comes from the Spanish *sargazo*, which means "seaweed." This weed, also called kelp or berry plant, is the principal constituent of this immense bank. The theory advanced by the learned Maury to explain the presence of these hydrophytes in this tranquil basin of the Atlantic is found in his work, *Physical Geography of the Sea*. The presence of this seaweed, he says, is due to a phenomenon familiar to everybody. If one were to put pieces of cork or fragments of any floating material in a basin of water and a circular motion be given to the water, one will soon see the scattered fragments come together in the center of the liquid surface—that is, where there is the least motion. In the phenomenon with which we are concerned, the basin is the Atlantic, the circular current of the liquid is the Gulf Stream, and the center where all the floating fragments come together is the Sargasso Sea.

I share Maury's opinion, and I had the opportunity to study the phenomenon in this special area where ships rarely sail. Above us floated bodies of all kinds, trapped in the midst of those brownish-colored weeds: tree trunks, ripped from the Andes or from the Rocky Mountains, carried down by the Amazon or the Mississippi; parts of wrecked ships; the remains of keels and ships' bottoms; battered planks, so weighted down with barnacles and shells that they could no longer rise to the surface of the ocean. And time will one day prove Maury's other theory that these materials, accumulated over centuries, will change to mineral form by the action of the water, and will then provide inexhaustible coalfields—a precious reserve that far-sighted Nature is now preparing for the day when men will have exhausted the mines on the continents.

In the midst of this inextricable tangle of weeds and fucus, I noticed beautiful starred alcyons of a pink hue; actinies, which trailed their long mantle of tentacles; green, red, and blue jellyfish; and above all, the large rhyzostoma of Cuvier, whose bluish umbrella shape is bordered with a violet festoon.

Throughout the whole day of February 22nd we remained in the Sargasso Sea, where the fish, lovers of marine plants, and the crustacea find abundant food. The next day, the ocean presented its normal aspect again.

For nineteen days, from February 23rd to March 12th, the *Nautilus*, keeping to the middle of the Atlantic, sailed at a constant speed of one hundred leagues every twenty-four hours. Captain Nemo evidently wanted to complete his underwater voyage, and I had no doubts that his intention, after doubling Cape Horn, was to return toward the southern seas of the Pacific.

Ned Land had, therefore, good reason to be apprehensive. In the midst of these vast seas, with no visible islands, he could no longer think of deserting the ship. There was no way to oppose Captain Nemo's wishes, either. The only thing to do was to accept the inevitable. What could no longer be achieved by force or trickery, I hoped to achieve by persuasion. When this voyage was over, might Captain Nemo not give us back our freedom under oath never to reveal his existence? An oath of honor that we would certainly have kept? We would have to discuss this delicate matter with the Captain. Was I in a position, however, to request this freedom? He himself had definitely declared, from the very beginning, that the secret of his life required our perpetual imprisonment aboard the *Nautilus*. Would not my silence during four months seem to him to be a tacit acceptance of the situation? To return to the subject would probably have the result of merely arousing his suspicions, which might hamper our plans if any favorable occasion were to arise in the future to warrant another attempt. All these reasons troubled my mind. I weighed them and discussed them with Conseil, who was as bewildered as I. All in all, even though I was not easily discouraged, I realized that the chances of ever returning to our fellowmen diminished with every day that went by, above all, at a time when Captain Nemo was heading boldly toward the Southern Atlantic.

During those nineteen days mentioned above, nothing unusual happened. The Captain kept very busy, and I rarely saw him. I would often find books left half open in the library—especially books on natural history. He had, evidently, been leafing through my own work dealing with the mysteries of the deep. It lay open with his comments in the margin, some of which contradicted my theories and my classifications. He hardly ever discussed these matters with me. He seemed satisfied just to revise and correct them. Occasionally I heard strains of melancholy music. He played his organ with a great deal of expression, but only during the night, when the sea was shrouded in darkness and the *Nautilus* in slumber in the vast desert of the sea.

During this stage of the journey, we cruised on the surface for days on end. The sea appeared deserted. We saw a few sailing ships, on their way to the Indies, making for the Cape of Good Hope. One day we were pursued by boats of a whaler, which had undoubtedly taken us for a huge whale of great value. But Captain Nemo did not wish to make these hardy men waste their time and efforts, and he ended the chase by plunging beneath the waves. This incident seemed to interest Ned Land very much. I should not be wrong, I believe, were I to say that the Canadian was very sorry that our ship could not be harpooned to death by those whalers.

The fish Conseil and I saw during this period differed little from those we had already observed in other latitudes. However, we did see some specimens of that terrible genus of cartilaginous fish, divided into three subgenera that comprise no fewer than thirty-two species: striped sharks, about fifteen feet long, whose heads are flat and bigger than their bodies, with a rounded tail fin, and whose backs carry seven wide black bands that run parallel down their backs; there were some perlon sharks, of a cinder-gray color, pierced with seven bronchial openings and provided with a single dorsal fin placed roughly in the middle of their bodies.

Some large seadogs also passed by, a voracious fish if ever there was one. One may well doubt stories told by fishermen, but here are some stories they tell: In the body of one of these, a buffalo's head and a whole calf were found; in another, two tunnyfish and a sailor in uniform; in another, a soldier with his saber; and finally, in yet another, a horse complete with rider. All this, frankly, is not credible. But what is certain is that none of these ever allowed themselves to be caught in the nets of the *Nautilus,* and that I was never able to verify their voracity.

Schools of elegant and playful dolphins accompanied us for days on end. They traveled in groups of five or six, hunting in packs like roaming wolves on land. These, moreover, are as voracious as the seadogs, if one is to believe a professor from Copenhagen who retrieved thirteen porpoises and fifteen seals from the stomach of a dolphin. It was, it is true, a grampus, which belongs to the biggest species known, whose length sometimes measures more than twenty-four feet. This family of dolphins includes ten genera, and those I saw belonged to the delphinian genus. These are distinguishable by their excessively long straight snout, which is four times the length of the skull. Their bodies, measuring ten feet, are black on top, pinkish white on the underside, and are occasionally speckled.

I should also mention some curious examples of fish belonging to the order of acanthopterygii and the family of sciaenidae, found in this sea. Some writers—more poets than naturalists—claim that these fish sing melodiously, and that their voices, when singing in unison, provide a concert equal to, or better than, a choir of human voices. I do not deny all this, but the sciaenidae did not serenade us on our way, much to our regret.

Finally, Conseil classified a large number of flying fish also. Nothing was more curious than to see the dolphins chasing them with incredible precision. However far they flew, whatever direction they took, sometimes even when flying right over the *Nautilus*, these ill-fated fish always found a way to land in the mouths of the dolphins ready to receive them. Then there were also pirapedes and flying gurnards, with their luminous mouths, which at night, after tracing dazzling paths through the air, plunged beneath the dark waters like falling stars.

Until March 13th, we continued sailing in this manner. That day, however, the *Nautilus* undertook some experiments in taking soundings of ocean depths, which interested me very much.

We had traveled almost thirteen thousand leagues since leaving the high seas of the Pacific. Our bearings showed our position to be latitude 45° 37' south and longitude 37° 53' west. It was in the same area where Captain Denham of the *Herald* had sounded over forty-five thousand feet without touching bottom. There, too, Lieutenant Parker, of the United States frigate *Congress*, had not been able to touch bottom with soundings just short of fifty thousand feet.

Captain Nemo decided to take his *Nautilus* to the greatest depth of the ocean in order to check these different soundings. I prepared to take notes of the results of the experiment. The panels of the saloon were opened, and the maneuvers began in this attempt to reach the remotest depths of the sea.

It was out of the question to dive by filling the tanks. Perhaps he could not have increased sufficiently the specific weight of the *Nautilus* for that. Besides, in order to rise to the surface again, it would have been necessary to rid the ship of this surcharge of water, and the pumps would not have been sufficiently powerful to overcome the outside pressure.

Captain Nemo decided to reach the bottom of the ocean by taking a sufficiently long diagonal direction, using the lateral fins, set at an angle of 45° to the waterline of the *Nautilus*. Then the propeller was set to its maximum speed, and its quadruple blade churned the water with indescribable power.

Under this powerful thrust, the hull of the *Nautilus* vibrated like the string of a musical instrument and ploughed its way beneath the waves. The Captain and I, stationed in the saloon, followed the needle of the manometer, which moved rapidly. Soon we had dived below the level where most fish can live. If some fish can live only on the surface of the sea or in the rivers, others, few in number, to be sure, live in great depths. Among the latter I noticed the Hexanchus, a sort of seadog, which has six respiratory openings; the telescope fish, with its enormous eyes; the armored malarmat, with gray fins and black pectorals, and whose pale red breasts are protected by bony plaques. Finally, I saw the grenadier, which, living at a depth of about four thousand feet, bears a pressure of 120 atmospheres.

I asked Captain Nemo whether he had seen fish at still greater depths.

"Fish?" he replied. "Rarely. But in the present state of science, what do we know about this subject?"

"We know, Captain, that on reaching the lower depths of the ocean, vegetable life disappears at a higher level than animal life. We know that where living creatures can still be found, not a single hydrophyte can be found. We know that oysters and some species of scallops live at a depth of over six thousand feet, and that McClintock, the hero of the polar seas, brought up a living starfish from a depth of no less than eight thousand feet. We also know that the crew of the *Bull-Dog,* belonging to the Royal Navy, fished up a starfish from a depth of over fifteen thousand feet, in other words, more than a league down. How can you say, Captain Nemo, that we know nothing on this subject?"

"No, Monsieur Aronnax," replied the Captain, "I should not be so presumptuous. Nevertheless, I should like to ask you, how do you explain the fact that living creatures can live at such depths?"

"I explain it on two grounds," I answered. "First, because there are vertical currents, caused by the differences in salinity and the densities of the waters, that produce a movement which is sufficient to support the rudimentary life of the Encrinidae and the starfish."

"Quite right," said the Captain.

"Secondly, if oxygen is the basic requirement of life, we know that the quantity of oxygen dissolved in seawater increases with depth rather than diminishes, and that the greater the pressure at the lowest levels, the more of it goes into solution."

"Ah! So you scientists know that?" replied the Captain, somewhat surprised. "Well, Monsieur le Professeur, there are solid reasons for believing it, because it is true. I should add, furthermore, that the natatory bladders of fish contain more nitrogen than oxygen when they are caught at the surface, and more oxygen than nitrogen when they are caught at great depths. Which only goes to prove your point. But let us continue with our observations."

My glance fell on the manometer again. The instrument indicated that we were at a depth of about twenty thousand feet. We had been diving for an hour. The *Nautilus* was gliding on her inclined fins, plunging deeper and deeper. The barren waters were magnificently transparent and possessed a diaphanous quality that no paintbrush could ever paint. An hour later, we had reached a depth of over forty-three thousand feet, approximately 3¼ leagues, and there were no signs yet that we were approaching the bottom of the sea.

At about forty-five thousand feet, however, I noticed some blackish peaks rising in the midst of the waters. But these summits could be the peaks of mountains as high as the Himalayas, or Mont Blanc, or even higher, and the depth of their valleys was still undetermined.

The *Nautilus* dived still deeper, despite the powerful pressures it was being subjected to. I could feel its steel plates vibrating at the joints; its bulkheads quivered; the windows of the saloon seemed to bulge under the pressure of the waters. And this solid vessel would have been crushed, without doubt, had it not been capable, as its Captain said, of resisting like a solid rock.

As we brushed past those rocky slopes, lost beneath the waters, I saw a few surviving conchs, some serpulae, some living spinorbes, and specimens of starfish.

Soon, however, these last representatives of animal life disappeared altogether, and, more than three leagues down, the *Nautilus* had dived below the level that marks the limit of marine life, just as a balloon can rise above the zone where breathing is no longer possible. We had reached a depth of over fifty thousand feet—four leagues—and the hull of the *Nautilus* was then bearing a pressure of sixteen hundred atmospheres, that is to say, about twenty-four thousand pounds on every square inch of its surface.

"What an incredible experience," I exclaimed. "To explore the utmost depths of the sea where no man has ever been! Look, Captain, look at those magnificent rocks, those uninhabited grottos, the last refuges of the world, where life is no longer possible! What unknown haunts! What a pity that we can only carry back the memory of all this!"

"Would you like," Captain Nemo asked me, "to carry back something more than just a memory?"

"What do you mean?"

"I mean that nothing is easier than to take a photograph of these regions."

I had barely time to express my astonishment at this new overture when, at the Captain's request, a camera was brought in. Through the open panels the waters, illuminated by the brilliant gleams of the searchlight, spread before us with perfect limpidity. No shadows blurred the crystal clearness of those depths. The sun itself could not have been more favorable. The *Nautilus,* under the thrusts of her propellers, controlled by her inclining fins, stood perfectly still. The camera was leveled at that submerged landscape, and in a few seconds we had a negative of incredible clearness.

That print, still in my possession, is positive evidence. It shows those primordial rocks that have never seen the light of day; those massive blocks of granite, which form the powerful axis of the earth, lying in the lowest depths of the sea; those deep grottos, hollowed out among those rocky masses; all defined in their outlines with incomparable dark clearness, as if painted by the brush of a great Flemish artist. Beyond, a landscape of mountains, an undulating line of shapes and shadows, sleek, black, polished heights, without a trace of moss, without a stain, molded into a fantastic vision and firmly resting on a carpet of sand which sparkled under the brilliant glow of our searchlight.

Then Captain Nemo, after having taken the photograph, said:

"We must go back, Monsieur le Professeur. We must not abuse our power, nor expose the *Nautilus* to such pressures for too long."

"Let us go back up, then," I said.

"Hold on tight."

Before I had time to realize what the Captain had meant, I was suddenly thrown to the floor. With her propeller thrown into gear, her fins set vertically, the *Nautilus* shot up like a balloon in the air and rose with vertiginous speed. She sliced through the watery mass with a high-pitched tremor. Nothing but a blur was visible on the way up. In four minutes she had crashed through the four leagues that separated her from the surface of the ocean, and emerging like a flying fish, she fell back on the water, splashing waves to an incredible height.

Chapter XII

CACHALOTS AND WHALES

DURING THE NIGHT of March the 13th to 14th, the *Nautilus* again resumed its southerly course. I thought that once it had reached the latitude of Cape Horn, it would head toward the west and sail into the Pacific to complete its tour around the world. Nothing of the kind happened; the *Nautilus* continued to sail toward the southern regions. Where was it heading for? To the Pole? This was insane. I began to think that Captain Nemo's rashness more than justified the apprehensions of Ned Land.

For some time now the Canadian had not spoken of his plans to escape. He had become less communicative, almost silent. I could see how heavily this prolonged imprisonment was weighing on him. I could sense that his anger was beginning to tell on him. Whenever he met the Captain, his eyes lit up with a sinister fire, and I feared that someday his natural aggressiveness might lead him to do something rash.

That day, March 14th, he and Conseil came to see me in my room. I asked them why they had come to see me.

"I have a very simple question to ask, monsieur," the Canadian answered.

"Yes, Ned. What is it?"

"How many men do you think there are aboard the *Nautilus?*"

"I couldn't say, my friend."

"It seems to me," Ned Land went on, "that it shouldn't take much of a crew to run this ship."

"I don't think so either. Everything considered, I believe ten men could handle her."

"Well," said the Canadian, "why should there be more?"

"Why indeed?" I remarked. I was staring closely at Ned Land, whose intentions were easy to guess.

"Because," I said, "if my guess is correct, and if I have fully understood the Captain's *raison d'être*, the *Nautilus* is not merely a ship; it must be a place of refuge for all those who, like her commander, have broken off all ties with land."

"Perhaps," said Conseil, "but presumably the *Nautilus* can

only house a certain number of men. Could Monsieur not estimate the maximum?"

"How could I, Conseil?"

"By using mathematics. Monsieur knows the capacity of the vessel, the volume of air it contains. Monsieur knows how much air each man uses with each breath; Monsieur also knows that the *Nautilus* has to rise to the surface every twenty-four hours. Can Monsieur not calculate . . . ?"

Conseil did not finish his sentence, but I realized what he was getting at.

"I understand," I said, "but the calculation you speak of, easy enough to work out, will only give us a very uncertain result."

"Why not try?" Ned Land insisted.

"Well, let us analyze the problem," I replied. "Each man consumes in one hour the oxygen contained in a hundred liters—or three and a half cubic feet—of air. In twenty-four hours, he consumes, then, the oxygen contained in two thousand four hundred liters. We must therefore see how many times two thousand four hundred liters of air will go into the *Nautilus*."

"Exactly," said Conseil.

"Well, then," I continued. "The capacity of the *Nautilus* is fifteen hundred tons, and, since each ton contains one thousand liters, the *Nautilus* contains fifteen hundred thousand liters of air, which, divided by two thousand four hundred—"

I made a rapid calculation with a pencil.

"Gives six hundred and twenty-five. Which indicates that the *Nautilus* could store enough air for six hundred and twenty-five men for a period of twenty-four hours."

"Six hundred and twenty-five!" cried Ned.

"You may be sure," I added, "that if we include all the officers and passengers, it would only add up to one-tenth that number."

"It is still too many for three men!" murmured Conseil.

"Hence, my poor Ned, I can only advise you to be patient."

"And better than patience, resignation," replied Conseil.

Conseil had used the right word.

"After all," he continued, "Captain Nemo cannot sail south indefinitely. Sooner or later, he will have to stop. Who knows? He may even be impeded by an iceberg. He will have to return to well-traveled lanes again, and then we can reconsider Ned's plans to escape."

The Canadian shook his head, ran his hand over his brow, and without replying, left the room.

"Would Monsieur allow me to express an opinion?" said

Conseil. "Our poor Ned always wants what he cannot have. Everything stems from his past life. Everything that is forbidden us is a source of despair for him. His memories oppress him and his heart is heavy. One must try to understand him. What can he do here? Nothing. He is not a scientist like Monsieur; he cannot possibly derive the same pleasure that we do by looking at the marvels of the sea. He would risk all to get back to a tavern back home!"

To be sure, the monotony aboard must have been intolerable for the Canadian, who was used to an active and outdoor life. Incidents that might interest him happened rarely. On that day, however, an incident occurred that reminded him of his past glories as a harpooner.

About eleven o'clock in the morning, cruising on the surface of the ocean, the *Nautilus* came upon a herd of whales. Such an occurrence did not surprise me, for I know that these animals, hunted mercilessly everywhere, have sought refuge in the coldest regions they could find.

The role played by whales in the marine world and their influence on geographical discoveries have been considerable. It was the whale that first led the Basques in their wake, followed by the Asturians, the English, and the Dutch, and taught these mariners how to brave the dangers of the ocean, and led them to both ends of the world. Whales love to frequent the Arctic as well as the Antarctic seas. There are ancient legends that claim that these animals had led whalers to within sixteen or seventeen miles of the Pole. However false the claim may be, it may well happen someday, because in hunting these animals in the Arctic and Antarctic regions, the whalers will reach these two unknown areas of the world.

We were sitting on the platform in a calm sea, enjoying one of those fine autumn days that the month of October offers in those regions, when the Canadian sighted a whale on the eastern horizon. He could not be mistaken. Looking at it carefully, we could see its dark back rising and falling just beneath the surface of the waves, about five miles away.

"Ah!" cried Ned Land. "If I were only aboard a whaler, what a pleasure that would be! It's a very big fellow! Look at the power behind those columns of air and mist he is spouting! Great God! Why do I have to be shut up in this piece of steel!"

"Well, Ned," I replied, "haven't you yet given up your old notions of fishing?"

"Can a whaler ever forget his trade, monsieur? Can a whaler ever forget the excitement of such a pursuit?"

"You have never fished in these seas, have you, Ned?"

"Never, monsieur. Only in the northern seas, in the Bering Strait and Davis Strait."

"Then these southern whales are strangers to you. You have only hunted whales that would never venture beyond the warm waters of the equator."

"Ah! Monsieur le Professeur, what are you trying to tell me?" replied the Canadian in an incredulous tone of voice.

"I am telling you only what is true."

"That is nonsense! Two and one-half years ago, in 1865, I hauled in a whale near Greenland and found a harpoon imbedded in its flesh with the mark of a whaler from the Bering Sea. Now I ask you, how could that whale, after being wounded west of America, come to be killed in the east, if it had not crossed the equator after having either made its way around Cape Horn or around the Cape of Good Hope!"

"I agree with Ned," said Conseil, "and I am waiting for Monsieur's answer."

"Monsieur's answer, my friends, is that whales, depending on their species, remain in their native waters and never leave them. So, if one of those animals came from the Bering Strait to the Davis Strait, it is simply because there exists a passage from one sea to the other, either along the northern coast of America or along the coast of Asia."

"And you expect us to take you seriously?" asked the Canadian, winking with one eye.

"We must believe Monsieur," replied Conseil.

"If that is the case," continued the Canadian, "since I have never hunted in these waters, I don't know the whales that frequent them, is that right?"

"That is what I said, Ned."

"All the more reason for getting acquainted," replied Conseil.

"Look! Look!" cried the Canadian, his voice full of emotion. "She's drawing near! She's coming up to us! She's defying me! She knows I can't do a thing to her!"

Ned was stamping his foot. His hand shook as he brandished an imaginary harpoon.

"These cetaceans," he asked, "are they as big as those of the northern seas?"

"About the same, Ned."

"I've seen some pretty big whales, monsieur. Whales which measured up to a hundred feet in length. I have even heard that the Hullamock and the Umgallick of the Aleutian Islands sometimes measure over a hundred and fifty feet."

"That is somewhat exaggerated," I replied. "Those Aleutian animals are only balaenopterons, with dorsal fins, and like the cachalots, they are generally smaller than the Greenland whales, you know."

"Ah!" cried the Canadian, who had not taken his eyes off the ocean. "She's coming closer, she's coming right up to the *Nautilus*."

Then, continuing his conversation:

"You speak of the cachalot, monsieur, as if it were a small creature. There are, they say, gigantic cachalots. They are very intelligent cetaceans. Some, it is said, dress up with weeds and fucus. They are taken for small islands and fishermen set up camps on them, settle down, build fires—"

"And build houses on them also, don't they?" said Conseil.

"That's right, you joker," replied Ned Land. "Then one fine day the creature takes a notion to dive and all the inhabitants are sucked into the depths of the sea."

"Just like in the travels of Sinbad the Sailor," I retorted, laughing. "Ah, Master Land, it seems that you are fond of tall tales, and those cachalot stories of yours are really amusing! I hope you do not take them too seriously."

"Monsieur le Naturaliste," the Canadian replied in all seriousness. "When it comes to whales one can believe almost anything. Take a good look at the speed of that one! Notice how stealthily she dives. They say that those creatures can speed around the world in fifteen days."

"I would not doubt it."

"But what you undoubtedly don't know, Monsieur Aronnax, is that in the beginning of time whales could swim even faster than they do now."

"Oh, really, Ned! And why was that?"

"Because at that time their tails were crosswise, just like fish, and they could swish the waves from right to left and left to right. When the Lord realized that they were swimming too fast, he twisted their tails, and from then on they have had to beat the waves up and down and, of course, they lost some of their speed."

"You would not be joking, would you, Ned?" I said, repeating an expression used by the Canadian.

"Don't take it seriously," answered Ned Land. "No more than if I told you that there are whales three hundred feet long, weighing a hundred thousand tons."

"That is a lot of weight," I said. "However, we must admit that there are certain whales which grow to a considerable size, since some of them, they say, give us as much as one hundred and twenty tons of oil."

"I know. I've seen them," said the Canadian.

"I believe you, Ned, just as I believe that there are certain whales which attain the size of one hundred elephants put together. Just imagine the effects of such a mass launched at full speed!"

"Is it true," asked Conseil, "that they can sink a ship?"

"A ship! I do not think so," I replied. "Nevertheless, it is said that in 1820, right in these southern seas, a whale rushed on the *Essex* and drove it backward at a speed of over twelve feet per second. Waves entered astern, and the *Essex* sank almost immediately."

Ned gazed at me quizzingly.

"I know," he said. "I was hit once by the tail of a whale, in an open canoe, of course. My companions and I were thrown twenty feet in the air, believe it or not. But that whale, compared to the whale of the professor, was just a young baby."

"Do these animals live a long time?" Conseil asked.

"A thousand years," replied the Canadian without hesitation.

"And how do you know, Ned?"

"Because people say so."

"And why do people say so?"

"Because they know."

"No, Ned, they don't know, but they think they do, and for this reason. Four hundred years ago, when fishermen first began to hunt whales, these animals were larger than those we hunt now. It is assumed, with some logic, we must admit, that the smaller size of today's whales is due to the fact that they haven't had time to reach their full growth. This is what made Buffon say that they could live and did live a thousand years. Do you understand?"

Ned Land did not understand. He was no longer listening. The whale was coming closer and closer, and he was devouring it with his eyes.

"Look!" he cried. "It's not a whale, but ten, twenty—a whole herd of them! And I can't do a thing! Here I am tied hand and foot!"

"But Ned," said Conseil, "why don't you ask Captain Nemo's permission to hunt them . . . ?"

Conseil had not quite finished his sentence when Ned Land rushed off and scrambled below to find the Captain. A few seconds later, both of them appeared on the platform.

Captain Nemo took a good look at the herd of whales frolicking on the waters a mile away from the *Nautilus*.

"They are southern whales," he said. "There is a fortune for a whole fleet of whalers over there."

"Sir," asked the Canadian, "can I have a go at them, even if it is only to remind me of my old trade!"

"What good would it do to hunt them for the sole purpose

of destroying them?" replied the Captain. "We can do nothing with whale oil aboard."

"Nevertheless, sir," continued the Canadian, "you gave us permission to hunt a dugong."

"Then it was a matter of providing some fresh meat for my crew. Here it would be killing just for the sake of killing. I know very well that this is a privilege reserved for men, but I do not approve of these murderous pastimes. The destruction of these harmless and inoffensive creatures, such as the southern and right whales, by whalers like you, Ned, is a crime. You have already depopulated all of Baffin's Bay, and you will exterminate, eventually, a whole class of useful animals. Leave these poor creatures alone. They have enough natural enemies, such as the cachalot, the swordfish, and the sawfish, to contend with, without adding another."

You can imagine the Canadian's face while listening to this lesson in morals. To lecture a hunter such as the Canadian was a waste of words. Ned Land stared at the Captain, and obviously did not understand what he meant. The Captain, nevertheless, was right: the barbarous slaughter and lack of forethought shown by whalers would one day wipe out the last whale from the ocean.

Ned Land whistled "Yankee Doodle" through his teeth, stuck his hands into his pockets, and turned his back on us.

In the meantime Captain Nemo kept his eyes on that herd of cetaceans, and turning to me, said:

"I was perfectly right in saying that these animals had enough enemies without adding men. That herd of whales will soon have a battle to contend with. Do you see, Monsieur Aronnax, those dark spots stirring above the surface about eight miles away?"

"Yes, I do," I replied.

"They are cachalots, dreadful creatures, found in these waters. These murderers travel in packs of two or three hundred, and one is perfectly justified in exterminating them."

The Canadian turned around quickly at the sound of these last words.

"Well, Captain," I said. "There is still time—on behalf of the whales—to—"

"There is no point taking any risks, Monsieur le Professeur. The *Nautilus* will suffice to disperse those cachalots. It is armed with a steel spear which is just as effective as Master Land's harpoon, I imagine!"

The Canadian didn't even deign to shrug his shoulders. "Attack those cetaceans with a spear! Who ever heard of such a thing!"

"Wait, Monsieur Aronnax," said the Captain, "We will

show you a hunt such as you have never seen before. There will be no mercy for those ferocious beasts. They are nothing but teeth and jaws!"

Teeth and jaws! There could be no better description of the macrocephalous cachalot, whose body sometimes measures over eighty feet. The enormous head of this cetacean is about a third of its total length. Better armed than the ordinary whale, whose upper jaw is merely armed with whalebone, this animal has twenty-five large teeth, each about ten inches long, cylinder-shaped and pointed, each weighing over two pounds. In the upper part of this enormous head there are large cavities, separated by cartilages, that contain up to six or eight hundred pounds of that precious oil called spermaceti. The cachalot is a rather clumsy animal, more like a tadpole than a fish, to use an expression by Frédol. It is badly built, being, so to speak, "deficient" along the whole of the left side of its frame, and it can see only with its right eye.

Meanwhile, the monstrous herd was drawing closer and closer. They had seen the whales and were preparing to attack. One could foresee in advance a victory for the cachalots, not only because they are better adapted for attacking than their inoffensive adversaries, but also because they can remain longer underwater without coming up to breathe.

There was barely enough time to go to the whales' rescue. The *Nautilus* submerged beneath the surface of the water. Conseil, Ned, and I took up our places in front of the saloon's panels. Captain Nemo stood by the helmsman to maneuver his ship like an engine of destruction. Soon I heard the throbbing of the propeller increase as we gathered speed.

The battle had already begun between the cachalots and the whales when the *Nautilus* arrived on the scene. The ship was maneuvered so as to split the herd of the attacking enemy. At first, the whales showed little concern at the sight of the new monsters that had attacked them. But soon they were forced to be wary of the deadly thrusts.

What a battle! Even Ned Land, overcome by the excitement of that struggle, kept clapping his hands. The *Nautilus* had become a formidable harpoon in the hands of its commander. Responsive to every whim of its helmsman, it hurled itself against that mass of flesh, splitting it cleanly, leaving behind two writhing halves. It seemed indifferent to the powerful blows of their tails against its hull, nor could we feel the impact of its blows against the monsters. Once it had slaughtered an animal it rushed against another, veering swiftly so as not to miss its prey, moving forward and backward, diving when the creature dived, rising when the creature rose to the surface, striking full on or aslant—cutting, tearing, piercing with that destructive spur in every direction and at any speed.

What a carnage! What noises on the surface of that sea! What sharp hissings and roars those terrorstricken creatures let out! In the midst of those waters so habitually calm, the strokes of their tails churned up swells as if a storm were raging.

That Homeric slaughter continued for an hour, and no escape was possible. On occasions, in groups of ten or twelve, they would try to crush the *Nautilus* with their weight. Through the panels we could see their terrifying eyes and their huge mouths studded with teeth. Ned Land, beside himself, threatened and cursed them. We could feel them clinging to our ship like a pack of dogs holding a wild boar at bay in the brushwood. But the *Nautilus,* with increasing speed, dragged them along or brought then back to the surface, unconcerned with either their enormous weight or their formidable grip.

Finally the horde dispersed, the waves became calm again. I could feel the ship rising to the surface. The hatch was opened and we rushed out on the platform.

The sea was covered with mutilated bodies. Not even a powerful explosion could have split, ripped, and torn those fleshy masses more violently. We were floating amidst gigantic corpses, with bluish backs and whitish bellies, all deformed with enormous protuberances. A few frightened cachalots were seen fleeing toward the horizon. The waves were tinted with red for several miles around, and the *Nautilus* was sailing in a sea of blood.

Captain Nemo joined us.

"Well, Master Land?" he said.

"Well, sir," replied the Canadian, whose enthusiasm had now cooled down. "It certainly was a remarkable spectacle. But I am not a butcher, I am a hunter, and this was just butchery."

"It was a massacre of vicious animals," replied the Captain, "and the *Nautilus* is not a butcher."

"I prefer my harpoon," retorted the Canadian.

"Each to his own harpoon," replied the Captain, looking Ned straight in the eye.

I was afraid that the Canadian might lose his temper and become violent, with serious consequences. But his anger was diverted by the sight of a whale that was floating near the *Nautilus* at that moment. The animal had not been able to escape the jaws of the cachalots. I recognized the black or southern whale, with its flat head. Anatomically it is distinguished from the white whale and the North Cape whale because its seven cervical vertebrae are joined together, and it possesses two ribs more than its cousins. The ill-fated cetacean was floating on its side, its belly ripped open with the bites it had received. It was dead. A little baby whale, which it had not been able to save during the carnage, still hung at the tip of its mutilated fin. Its mouth was open, and the water flowing over its whalebone murmured like the breakers of an undertow.

Captain Nemo brought the *Nautilus* alongside the animal's body. Two of the crew leaped on the whale's side and, not without some surprise, I saw them drawing two or three casks of milk from her breasts.

The Captain offered me a cup of this milk, which was still warm. I could not help showing him the repugnance I felt for this beverage. He assured me that the milk was excellent and that it could not be distinguished in any way from the milk of the cow.

I tasted it and agreed with him. Made into salted butter or cheese, it provided us with additional stock and an excellent change in our usual diet.

From that day on, I noticed with some uneasiness that Ned Land's hostility toward the Captain was becoming increasingly worse. I decided to keep a very close watch on the Canadian.

Chapter XIII

UNDER THE ICE SHELF

THE *Nautilus* HAD RESUMED her steady course toward the south. She was following the line of the 50th meridian at a considerable speed. Was it intended to go as far as the Pole? I didn't think so, for so far all attempts to reach it had failed. Moreover, the season was already very far advanced, since March 13th in the Antarctic corresponds to September 13th in the north, at which time the equinoctial period begins.

On March 14th I noticed floating ice at latitude 55°; these were, however, just thinnish, shadowy blocks, twenty to twenty-five feet long, forming reefs against which the sea broke into foam. The *Nautilus* cruised on the surface. Ned Land, having fished in arctic waters, was familiar with icebergs, while Conseil and I were admiring them for the first time.

On the horizon to the south, a dazzling streak of white appeared. English whalers have given it the name of "ice blink," and however thick the clouds may be, they cannot dim its brightness. This strip indicates the presence of an ice pack, or a bank of ice.

Indeed, we soon came across much bigger blocks of ice, whose brightness varied according to the whims of the mist. Some of these masses had green veins, as though wavy lines of copper sulfate had been drawn through them. Others looked like enormous amethysts, reflecting the sun's rays in a thousand crystal facets, while others, colored by brilliant particles of limestone, looked like great masses of marble, sufficient to build a whole city.

The farther south we sailed, the more numerous and bigger these floating islands became. Polar birds were nesting on them by the thousands. There were petrels, *damiers*, and puffins, deafening us with their cries. Some of them, mistaking the *Nautilus* for the dead body of a whale, alighted on our hull, and we could hear them pecking at its steel plates.

During this voyage through the ice, Captain Nemo spent much time on the platform, observing these desolate regions with attention. Occasionally, the calm expression of his face became animated. Was he thinking that this was his home— that he alone was master of all these polar regions, inaccessible to man? Perhaps. But he did not say anything; he stood motionless, and only emerged from his thoughts when his helmsman's instincts got the upper hand. Then, steering the *Nautilus* with consummate skill, he would avoid a collision with those masses of ice, some of which were several miles long and about 200 to 250 feet high. Not infrequently, they actually seemed to blot out the horizon. When we reached 60° latitude, every passage seemed to have disappeared. But Captain Nemo, after a careful search, would soon find some narrow opening through which he would slip boldly, although he knew very well that the gap would close in behind him.

The *Nautilus*, steered by his skillful hand, advanced through those masses of ice, which are classified with a precision that delighted Conseil. They are classified, according to their shape or size, as icebergs or ice mountains; ice fields, vast, boundless plains; drift ice or floating ice; ice packs, or broken-up fields, called palches when round in shape, and streams when they are long and narrow.

The temperature was rather low, the outside thermometer registering 2° or 3° below zero, or 27° to 29° F. But we were warmly dressed in furs, thanks to the seals and polar bears. The inside of the *Nautilus*, heated by electricity, maintained an even temperature against the severest cold. Moreover, we could always dive down a few fathoms to find a milder temperature.

Had we come here two months sooner, we should have enjoyed continuous daylight at this latitude—nights were even now no more than three or four hours long; but later, night would cast its shadow for six long months over these polar regions.

On March 15th, we passed the latitude of the New Shetland and Orkney Islands. The Captain informed me that large herds of seals had formerly inhabited this area, but the English and American whalers had wantonly massacred both the males and the pregnant females, leaving in their wake nothing but silence and death.

On March 16th, at about eight o'clock in the morning, the *Nautilus*, following the 55th meridian, crossed the Antarctic Circle. We were surrounded by ice on all sides, so that the horizon was totally obscured. Meanwhile, Captain Nemo found one passage after another and continued his progress southward.

"Where is he headed for?" I asked.

"Straight ahead, I should say," replied Conseil. "After all, when he can't go any farther, he will stop."

"I wouldn't be too sure about that!" I replied.

Frankly, I must admit that I was very much pleased with

this new adventure, and I cannot express my delight at the beauty of those strange regions. The ice created the most superb formations, sometimes resembling an Oriental city with innumerable minarets and mosques; sometimes a ruined town, destroyed by an earthquake. The scenery kept constantly changing, varied by the rays of the sun or lost in the gray mists of a snowstorm. All around, we could hear the sounds of ice cracking, crumbling, falling, or the loud rumblings of colliding icebergs, changing the scenery into spectacular and translucent landscapes.

Whenever the *Nautilus* submerged to avoid these upheavals, the crashing sounds echoed through the water with frightening intensity, and when the masses of ice fell back in the sea, they created a turmoil that made the *Nautilus* pitch and toss like a ship caught in the fury of a hurricane.

At times I could not see any way out of this maze, and feared that we were definitely imprisoned without any hope of escaping. But Captain Nemo, guided by his instinct and taking advantage of the slightest opening, found new passages to sail through. He never seemed to err in judging the thin threads of bluish water running through those ice fields. There was no doubt in my mind that he had sailed through these polar regions before with his *Nautilus*.

However, on March 16th, our path was completely barred by the ice fields. This was no mere pack ice, but a vast, continuous expanse, welded together by the cold. But this obstacle could not stop Captain Nemo, and he launched his ship against the ice field with frightful violence. The *Nautilus* drove her way like a wedge into the brittle mass, breaking it up with terrible cracking sounds. It reminded one of those battering rams of ancient times, propelled with incredible force. Blocks of ice were thrown up in the air and rained down around us like hail. Our craft was creating her own channel by brute force. Occasionally she overshot her point of impact, mounting the ice shelf and crushing it with her weight, or else, finding herself hemmed in beneath the ice, would pitch about violently until she had rent wide cracks in it.

Some days we were hit by violent, swirling gales. These brought with them thick fogs that made it impossible to see from one end of the platform to the other. Sudden winds would spring up from every direction, and snow would pile up into such hard layers that it had to be chipped off with a pick. When the temperature dropped below 5° C. or 23° F., all the *Nautilus* would be covered with ice. A vessel with rigging would never have managed it; the ropes would have become stuck in the pulleys. Only a ship driven by electricity, rather than coal, could have faced those high latitudes.

The barometer, under these conditions, remained very low. It even dropped to 73° 5′. Even the compass could no longer be relied on, for its needle would madly move in all directions as we approached the south magnetic pole, which is not to be confused with the South Pole itself. Indeed, according to Hansten, the Pole is situated approximately at latitude 70° and longitude 130°, while Duperré gives the position as 70° 30′ and 135°. We therefore had to take numerous readings of the compass at different points of the ship and strike an average. Often, we had to resort to a rough estimate in tracing our course—not a very satisfactory method in view of our zigzag path through the ice and our continual shift of position.

Finally, on March 18th, after twenty fruitless attempts, the *Nautilus* found itself completely frozen in. What lay ahead of us was neither a patch, nor a stream, nor a field, but an endless solid chain of mountains of ice.

"The great ice shelf!" exclaimed Ned.

I realized that for Ned Land, as for all the navigators who had gone before us, this was the impassable obstacle. Toward noon the sun came out for a moment and Captain Nemo was able to take a fairly accurate bearing, which gave our position as longitude 51° 30′ by latitude 67° 39′. We were already deep into the Antarctic regions.

There was no sign of a sea or water anywhere. Beyond the prow of the *Nautilus* there stretched a vast, uneven plain, littered with a confused mass of ice blocks, with all the haphazard disorder that is typical of a river just before the ice breaks up, but this was on a gigantic scale. Here and there, we could see sharp peaks, slender as needles and rising to a height of two hundred feet; farther on, there was a series of steep grayish cliffs which reflected, like vast mirrors, the rays of the sun, half lost in the mist. In these desolate surroundings, there was an eerie silence, occasionally broken by petrels or puffins flapping their wings. Everything was frozen, including the sounds!

The *Nautilus* has been forced to halt her adventurous course in the middle of the ice.

"Monsieur," Ned Land said to me that day, "if your Captain can move beyond this . . ."

"Yes?"

"He will be a superman indeed!"

"Why, Ned?"

"Because no one can break through this ice shelf. Your Captain may be a superman, but, by heavens, he's not stronger than nature! And where nature sets up her barriers, you have to stop, whether you like it or not!"

"Quite true, Ned. And yet, I should like to know what is behind all that ice. There is nothing more frustrating than to be faced by a wall."

"Monsieur is right," said Conseil. "Walls were just invented to frustrate professors. There shouldn't be any walls anywhere."

"Well," said the Canadian, "everyone knows what's behind that barrier."

"What?" I asked.

"Just ice, lots more ice!"

"You seem to be sure of your facts, Ned," I replied. "But I am not. That is why I should like to take a look at what lies beyond."

"I'm afraid you'll have to give up that idea, Professor," replied the Canadian. "You've come to the great ice shelf, which is good enough, but you won't get any farther; nor will your Captain Nemo and his *Nautilus*. Whether he likes it or not, we'll just have to turn back to the north—to countries inhabited by sensible human beings."

I had to agree that Ned was right. Until ships are built to float over seas of ice, they are immobilized before the great ice shelf.

Indeed, despite all efforts and despite the powerful means employed to dislodge the ice, the *Nautilus* was reduced to immobility. Normally, he who can go no farther is free to retrace his steps; but this was just as impossible as going forward, for the passages had closed up in our wake, and our ship, which was now motionless, would very soon be frozen in completely. And this is precisely what happened at about two o'clock in the afternoon, when fresh ice formed along the hull of the ship with astonishing rapidity. I was forced to admit that Captain Nemo had been more than reckless.

I was then on the platform. The Captain, who had been surveying the position for some minutes, said to me:

"Well, Professor, what do you think about this?"

"I should say we are trapped, Captain."

"Trapped! What do you mean by that?"

"I just mean that we cannot go forward, cannot go backward, and we cannot go sideways, and that is the usual meaning of trapped; at least, that is what we would say on the Continent."

"So, Monsieur Aronnax, you believe the *Nautilus* will not be able to extricate herself, do you?"

"It will be extremely difficult, Captain, for the season is already too far advanced, and you were counting on the ice breaking up."

"Ah, Monsieur le Professeur," replied Captain Nemo in an ironical tone of voice, "you never change, do you! You never see anything but impediments and obstacles! I can assure you that not only will the *Nautilus* break free, but she will go still farther!"

"Farther south?" I asked, looking at the Captain.

"Yes, monsieur. We will go to the Pole."

"To the Pole!" I exclaimed, unable to conceal my incredulity.

"Yes," replied the Captain with cool assurance, "to the South Pole, that unknown region where all the meridians of the earth intersect. The *Nautilus,* as you know, will do whatever I command it to do."

Yes, I knew that. I also knew that this man was bold and incredibly reckless. But to reach the South Pole, more inaccessible than the North Pole, a desolate area bristling with obstacles that the boldest navigators had failed to conquer— this was an utterly reckless venture which only a madman could conceive!

Then the idea struck me to ask the Captain whether he had, in fact, already discovered that Pole on which no man had ever set foot.

"No, monsieur," he replied. "But we will discover it together. Where others have failed, I will not fail. I have never sailed the *Nautilus* this far south. But, as I have already told you, we will continue to move south."

"I should like to believe you, Captain," I said, somewhat ironically. "I believe you! By all means, let us go forward! There are no obstacles for us, of course! Let us smash that barrier! Let us blow it up! And if it resists our efforts, let us put wings on the *Nautilus* and let us fly right over it!"

"Fly over it, Monsieur le Professeur?" replied the Captain calmly. "No, monsieur, not over it, but under it."

"Under it!" I cried.

Suddenly the Captain's plan flashed in my mind. I realized what he meant to do. Once more the incredible powers of the *Nautilus* were going to be used in a superhuman undertaking.

"I see we are beginning to understand each other, Professor," the Captain said to me, a trace of a smile on his lips. "Now you can see the possibility—I should say, the success —of this venture. What is impracticable with an ordinary ship becomes easy with the *Nautilus*. If the mainland of a continent is situated at the Pole, we shall stop short of that land. But if, on the other hand, there is an open sea underneath, then we will reach the Pole itself!"

"Of course," I said, carried away by the Captain's reasoning, "even if the surface of the sea is frozen solid, the lower levels are not. There is a providential law of nature that causes water to expand when its temperature reaches the freezing point, thereby lowering its specific gravity or density. Because of this lower density ice is lighter than water and rises to the surface. Moreover, if I am not mistaken, that part of an ice shelf that rises above the surface of the water is only one-fourth of what lies beneath it. Am I right, Captain?"

"More or less, Professor. For every foot of iceberg above the surface, there are three feet below. Now, since these mountains of ice are no higher than three hundred feet, it follows that what lies below the surface cannot be greater than nine hundred feet, and after all, what is nine hundred feet to the *Nautilus*?"

"Nothing, of course, Captain."

"Furthermore, we can dive even deeper and take advantage of the uniform temperature that exists in the depths of the oceans, and once there, the temperature of thirty or forty degrees below zero on the surface of the ice will not affect us."

"Naturally, naturally," I replied excitedly.

"The only difficulty," Captain Nemo resumed, "will be to remain submerged for several days without renewing our air supply."

"Is that all?" I replied. "But the *Nautilus* has huge tanks; we will fill them up, and they will provide us with all the oxygen we need."

"You are quite right, Monsieur Aronnax," the Captain rejoined, smiling. "But since I do not want you to accuse me of foolhardiness, I am acquainting you with all the possible obstacles that may arise."

"You mean there are other obstacles?"

"Just one. It is possible that if there is an open sea at the South Pole, it may be completely frozen solid, so that we may not be able to emerge to the surface!"

"But you forget, Captain, that the *Nautilus* is armed with a redoubtable spur, which we could drive diagonally through the ice and tear it open, don't you think?"

"Congratulations, Professor, you are full of excellent ideas today!"

"Moreover, Captain," I continued, becoming more and more enthusiastic, "why should there not be an open sea at the South Pole, as there is on the North Pole? The poles of cold temperatures and the poles of the globe do not coincide, either in the Arctic or in the Antarctic, and until we have proof to the contrary, we must assume that in these two regions of the earth there is either a continent or an open sea."

"I believe that, too, Monsieur Aronnax," replied Captain Nemo. "However, I should just like to point out that after having raised so many objections to my plan, you are now destroying all my arguments and are in favor of it."

What Captain Nemo said was true. I was actually going so far as to outdo him in audacity! It was I who was now urging him to go to the Pole! I was outpacing him, outstripping him! How could I be such a presumptuous fool? Captain Nemo knew the pros and cons of the question far better than I, and he was merely amusing himself to see me carried away by my dreams of the impossible!

Meanwhile, he had not lost a moment. He sent for his second-in-command, and the two men entered into a rapid conversation in their incomprehensible language. Whether the other man had been apprised in advance, or whether he found the plan entirely practicable, I don't know; but he showed no surprise.

Impassive as he may have been, Conseil was even more so. When I told this worthy lad that our plans were to press onward to the South Pole, he just greeted the news with his usual "as Monsieur pleases," and I had to be satisfied with that. Ned Land, however, shrugged his shoulders more emphatically than ever.

"Really, Professor," he said, "I can't help feeling sorry for you and your Captain Nemo."

"But we are going to the Pole, Ned."

"Perhaps. But you'll never come back!"

With that, Ned returned to his cabin, to keep from "doing something desperate," as he said on leaving us.

Meanwhile, preparations for this daring venture had begun. The powerful pumps of the *Nautilus* were filling the tanks and storing them under high pressure. At about four o'clock, Captain Nemo announced that the hatches leading to the platform were going to be closed. I cast a final glance at the thick ice shelf, which we were about to cross. The weather was fine, the visibility fairly clear, and the temperature was 12° below zero C.; but since the wind had dropped, this temperature did not seem at all unbearable.

About ten members of the crew—armed with picks—then went out on the sides of the *Nautilus* and proceeded to break up the ice that had formed around her hull. This did not take very long, for the ice was still fairly thin. Then we all went back inside the ship. The tanks were filled with available water, and the *Nautilus* dived without further delay.

I sat in the saloon with Conseil. Through the open panels, we looked out into those lower reaches of this southern sea.

The thermometer was rising, and the needle of the manometer began to fluctuate across the dial.

At about 900 feet, just as Captain Nemo had predicted, we were navigating below the undulated surface of the ice shelf. But the *Nautilus* went deeper still, reaching a depth of 2,500 feet. The temperature of the water, which had been 12° below zero C. at the surface, was now no more than 11°. At that depth it had risen two degrees already. Needless to say, the temperature inside the *Nautilus,* heated by electricity, was much higher. All the ship's movements were executed with extraordinary precision.

"If Monsieur doesn't mind my saying so, I think we will get through," remarked Conseil.

"Indeed we will!" I replied in a tone of deep conviction.

In these open waters, the *Nautilus* headed straight for the Pole, without deviating from the 52nd meridian. From 67° 30′ to 90°, we still had 22½ degrees of latitude to go, about five hundred leagues, or more than a thousand miles. The *Nautilus* was averaging twenty-six knots, the speed of an express train. If we maintained this speed, forty hours would suffice to reach the Pole.

The novelty of the situation kept Conseil and me peering out of the window for a good part of the night. The sea was bright in the rays of our searchlight, but it was deserted. There were no fish in these waters. They use these waters only as a passage from the Antarctic Ocean to the open polar seas. We were moving fast. We could guess the speed by the vibrations of the long steel hull.

About two o'clock in the morning, I retired for a few hours' rest. Conseil did likewise. On my way along the corridor I did not meet Captain Nemo, and I supposed that he was on duty at the helmsman's cage.

The next day, March 19th, at five o'clock in the morning, I returned to my place in the saloon. From the electric log, I could see that the speed of the *Nautilus* had been reduced. We were rising to the surface with caution, emptying our tanks slowly.

My heart was beating fast. Would we emerge to breathe the fresh air of the polar sea?

No! A sudden shock made me realize that the *Nautilus* had struck the underside of the ice shelf, still very thick, judging by the dull sound I heard. We had indeed collided, but it was "an upward collision," as mariners would say, and at a depth of 3,000 feet. This meant that we had 4,000 feet of ice above us, of which 1,000 feet protruded above the surface. Here, then, the ice shelf was higher than it had been where we had submerged. Not a very consoling thought!

Throughout that day the *Nautilus* repeated the experiment, each time, however, striking the icy ceiling above it. Sometimes it struck the ice at 2,700 feet, which meant a total thickness of 3,600 feet, of which 900 was above the surface. This was double the height of the shelf at the point where the *Nautilus* had first dived under.

I took careful note of the various depths, and I was able to obtain an outline of the underside of this chain of icy mountains.

By nightfall, our predicament had not changed. The ice above us was still between 1,200 and 1,500 feet thick. This indicated that the thickness of that wall of ice was decreasing, but what an impenetrable mountain of ice still lay between us and the surface of the sea!

It was then eight o'clock. According to our daily routine, the air inside the *Nautilus* should have been renewed four hours before. However, I was not feeling it too much, even though Captain Nemo had not yet decided to use his reserve tanks.

I slept very uneasily that night, assailed, as I was, by hope and fear. I got up several times. The *Nautilus* continued to grope her way. At about three o'clock in the morning I noticed that we were striking the lower surface of the ice shelf at 150 feet. Only 150 feet of ice separated us from the surface. Gradually the shelf was becoming thinner and turning into an ice field. That mountain of ice was slowly turning into a plain.

I could not take my eyes off the manometer. We were still rising diagonally, moving slowly toward the surface, which we could see glistening beneath the rays of our searchlight. Above, below, and all around us, the ice shelf spread out like a long ramp, which grew visibly thinner as we progressed mile by mile.

Finally, at six o'clock in the morning, on that memorable day of March 19th, the door of the saloon opened, and Captain Nemo appeared.

"The open sea!" he said.

Chapter XIV

THE SOUTH POLE

I RUSHED UP ON DECK.

There it was, the open sea! Except for a few floating icebergs and blocks of ice here and there, there was an endless expanse of sea; a whole world of birds filled the air, while myriads of fish swarmed the water, which, depending on its depth, varied from a deep blue to an olive-green. The thermometer registered 3° C. or 37° F. Relatively speaking, it was as though spring had lain concealed behind that ice shelf whose far-off masses stood outlined against the northern horizon.

"Are we at the Pole?" I asked the Captain with a throbbing heart.

"I do not know," he replied. "We will take a bearing at midday."

"But will the sun be visible through all this mist?" I asked, looking at the gray sky.

"However dimly it may shine, it will be enough for me," replied the Captain.

Ten miles from the *Nautilus,* toward the south, a solitary island rose to a height of over six hundred feet. We were now approaching it cautiously, for there might be reefs beneath the surface of this sea.

An hour later we had reached the island, and two hours after that, we had sailed completely around it. It was four or five miles in circumference, and a narrow channel separated it from a large body of land, perhaps a continent, whose limits we could not see. The existence of this land seemed to lend credence to Maury's theory, for the ingenious American had indeed noticed that between the South Pole and the 60th parallel, the sea is covered with floating ice of enormous dimensions, never found in the North Atlantic. From this, he deduced that the Antarctic Circle encloses vast territories, since icebergs cannot form in the open sea, but only along the coastlines. According to his calculations, the ice masses around the South Pole form a vast cap, whose diameter must be around four thousand kilometers, or 2,500 miles.

Meanwhile the *Nautilus,* for fear of running aground, had

stopped about three cables' lengths from a beach overhung by a majestic formation of rocks. Then the dinghy was launched, and the Captain, with two of his men to carry the instruments, Conseil and I, jumped aboard. It was ten o'clock in the morning. I had not seen Ned Land. Doubtless the Canadian did not want to eat his words in the presence of the South Pole.

A few strokes of the oars brought us to the beach, and Conseil was about to jump ashore, when I held him back.

"Captain," I said to Captain Nemo, "the honor of being the first man to set foot on these shores belongs to you."

"Yes, Professor," replied the Captain, "and if I do not hesitate to tread the soil of this Pole, it is only because, so far, no other human being has done so."

So saying, he sprang lightly on the sand. Clearly, he seemed full of joy. He climbed up to a rock that overlooked a little promontory, and standing there with his arms crossed, his eyes shining, silent and motionless, he seemed to be claiming possession of these southern regions. After five minutes of ecstatic meditation, he turned toward us.

"Whenever you wish, monsieur," he said.

I stepped ashore, followed by Conseil, leaving the two sailors in the dinghy.

The ground on which we stood was a long stretch of reddish volcanic rock, looking as though it were made of crushed brick. It was littered with slag, streams of hard lava, and pumice stones. There was no mistaking its volcanic origin. In some places, tiny curls of smoke gave off a sulphurous odor, indicating that the internal fires had still lost nothing of their power. However, when I climbed a steep escarpment, I could see no volcano within a radius of many miles. We do know, however, that in the Antarctic, James Ross discovered the craters named Erebus and Terror,* still fully active, on the 167th meridian, latitude 77° 52'.

The vegetation of this desolate continent seemed very sparse. Some lichens of the species Usnea melanoxantha spread out on black rocks; certain microscopic plants; rudimentary diatoms, with cells placed between two quartz shells; long purple and crimson fucus thrown up on the shore by the surf, were all the signs of vegetable life in this region.

The coast was strewn with mollusks, mussels, limpets, smooth cockles shaped like hearts, and especially clios, with their oblong membranous bodies and their heads formed of two round lobes. I also saw myriads of arctic clios, each about an inch long, which a whale can swallow a whole

---

* Ross had two ships, named *Erebus* and *Terror*.—M.T.B.

school of in one mouthful. The water near shore was alive with these charming pteropods, veritable butterflies of the sea.

Among other zoophytes, I saw in the deep waters some shrublike corals, the type that, according to Ross, can live in Antarctic seas as far down as three thousand feet. Then there were little alcyonarians, belonging to the species Procellaria pelagica, as well as great numbers of asteroids, peculiar to this climate, including the starfish that studded the soil!

But it was in the air that life was most abundant. Thousands of birds, of all kinds, fluttered and swooped about, deafening us with their cries. Others were crowded together on the rocks, watching us go by without fear and even following close on our heels. These were penguins, which are so swift and agile in the water, where they are sometimes taken for the striped tunny, but so clumsy and awkward on land. They uttered harsh cries, stood about in numerous groups, made few movements, but very loud noises.

Among other birds I noticed the chionis—belonging to the long-legged wading family—as large as pigeons, white, with a short conical beak, a red circle around their eyes. Conseil caught a few of them because, if well cooked, they make an excellent dish. Dark brown albatrosses passed overhead, with a wingspread of about twelve feet, justly called the vultures of the sea; giant petrels, including a species called *quebrante-huesos,** with arched wings, which are great eaters of seals; "damiers," a kind of small duck, with black and white beaks; and, finally, a whole series of ordinary petrels, some white with brown-bordered wings, others blue and peculiar to the south polar seas, and so oily—as I told Conseil—that the Faroe Islanders need only to insert a wick in them and light them!

"If Nature had only provided them with a built-in wick," Conseil remarked, "they would make perfect lamps. But that is expecting too much!"

Half a mile on, the ground was riddled with penguins' nests; these looked somewhat like burrows, so arranged as to make it easy for the female to enter and lay her eggs, and we saw many birds emerging from them. Captain Nemo later on ordered his men to hunt a few hundred of them, for their dark flesh is quite good to eat. These birds, with their slate-colored bodies, shaped like geese, white bellies and yellow bands around their necks, uttered cries that sounded like the braying of an ass. They made no attempt to escape, and were easily killed with stones.

* "Bonebreaker." A large hawk noted as a diver for fish.—M.T.B.

In the meantime the mist had not cleared, and at eleven o'clock there was still no sun. I was afraid it would not appear, for without it we could not take our position. How could we determine whether or not we had reached the South Pole?

When I rejoined Captain Nemo, I found him leaning against a rock, looking up at the sky. He seemed to be annoyed and impatient. But what could be done about it? After all, this powerful, daring man could not command the sun as he commanded the sea.

Midday came and went without the sun having appeared for a single moment. It was not even possible to tell where the sun was behind that curtain of fog, which soon turned into snow.

"Tomorrow, then," was all the Captain said, and we returned to the *Nautilus* through flurries of snow.

During our absence the nets had been cast, and I was interested to see the kind of fish that had been hauled aboard. The Antarctic seas serve as a refuge for a large number of migrants, fleeing from the storms of other regions, only to fall a prey, it must be said, to porpoises and seals. I noticed some southern sea scorpions, about four inches long and a species of whitish, cartilaginous fish, with livid stripes and covered with prickles; some Antarctic chimaera, which have a narrow body three feet long, smooth, silvery-whitish skin, a round head, three dorsal fins, and a horn-shaped snout that curves down toward the mouth. I tasted their flesh but found it without flavor, but Conseil thought it was good.

The snowstorm lasted until the following day. It was impossible to stay up on deck. From the saloon, where I was jotting down the incidents of our excursion to the polar continent, I could hear the cries of the petrels and the albatrosses as they swept to and fro in the blizzard. The *Nautilus* did not remain still, but moved along the coast for another ten miles or so in a southerly direction in that half-light that indicates that the sun is just touching the horizon.

The next day, the 20th of March, the snow had stopped, but it was a bit colder. The thermometer showed 2° below zero C. or 28° F. The mist was lifting, and I hoped that we might be able to take our position that day.

Since Captain Nemo had not yet appeared, Conseil and I were taken ashore. Here, too, the nature of the soil was volcanic. Everywhere there were traces of lava, slag, and basalt, but I was unable to locate any crater that had emitted them. Here, too, myriads of birds filled the sky. However, here they shared their domain with vast herds of sea mammals, which looked at us with their soft eyes. They were various kinds of seal, some of them stretched out on the ground and others lying on floating pieces of ice, while others plunged in and out of the sea. They did not flee at our approach, since they had never had contact with man before, and I reckoned that there were enough of them to supply meat for some hundreds of ships.

"How fortunate it is," said Conseil, "that Ned Land didn't come with us!"

"What makes you say that, Conseil?"

"Because that mad hunter would have killed everything in sight."

"Well, I feel that 'everything' is going a bit far; but I do think that we could not have prevented our Canadian friend from harpooning some of those magnificent animals. That would have upset Captain Nemo, because he does not believe in the useless slaughter of harmless animals."

"And he's right."

"Of course he is, Conseil. But tell me, haven't you yet classified these superb specimens of marine fauna?"

"As Monsieur well knows," replied Conseil, "I'm not very good in this field. However, when Monsieur has taught me the names of these animals—"

"They are seals and walruses."

"Two genera belonging to the family of the pinnipeds," my learned Conseil hastened to add, "order of carnivores, group of unguiculates, subclass of monodelphians, class of mammals, branch of vertebrates."

"Very good, Conseil," I replied. "But those two genera, the seals and walruses, are divided into species, and if I am not mistaken, we shall have the opportunity of observing them here. Let us go."

It was eight o'clock in the morning, we still had four hours before the sun could be observed to any good purpose. I led the way toward a vast bay, set within a semicircle of granite cliffs along the shore.

There, I can truly say that as far as the eye could see, the land and the floating ice were covered with sea mammals, and unconsciously I looked for old Proteus, the mythological shepherd who watched over those immense flocks of Neptune. Most of them were seals. They formed distinct groups of males and females, the father guarding the family, the mother suckling her young, while some of the calves, strong enough to walk, ventured forth on their own a short distance away. When these animals wanted to move, they would draw their bodies together and bounce forward, helped along, somewhat clumsily, by their cumbersome flippers, which, among the lamentin, their cousins, are really forearms. However, it must be said that once in the water where they are thoroughly at home, these creatures, with their flexible spinal column, narrow pelvis, smooth compact fur and webbed feet, swim magnificently. When resting on land, they lie in most graceful positions. The ancients, when they saw the gentle features of these animals, their soft, velvetlike eyes, their expressive look, unsurpassed by that of the most beautiful woman, and their most charming postures, celebrated them in poetry, transforming the males into tritons and the females into mermaids.

I pointed out to Conseil the advanced development of the cerebral lobes of these intelligent creatures. No mammal, with the exception of man, has a greater brain. Moreover, seals can easily be domesticated and trained, and I agree with certain naturalists who think that, properly taught, they could be most useful in helping man to fish.

Most of these animals were asleep on the rocks or on the sand. Among these seals, which have no external ears—unlike otters, whose ears are prominent—I noticed several varieties of stenorhynchae about nine feet long, with white hair, bulldog heads, ten teeth in either jaw, including four incisors in the upper and four in the lower jaw, and two big canine teeth in each jaw shaped like fleurs-de-lis. Among them slithered sea elephants, a kind of seal with a short, flexible trunk. These giants of the species were at least thirty feet long and had a girth of twenty feet; they did not move at our approach.

"Aren't these animals dangerous?" Conseil asked me.

"No," I replied, "not unless you attack them. When a seal is defending its young, its ferocity is terrible, and it is not unknown for them to smash a fishing boat to pieces."

"And they're quite right to do so," added Conseil.

"I quite agree with you."

Two miles farther on, our progress was halted by the promontory which protected the bay from the south wind; the waves foamed as they broke against its vertical rocks. From the other side came the sound of loud bellowing, such as can only be produced by a herd of cattle.

"Well," said Conseil, "a concert of bulls?"

"No," I said, "a concert of walruses."

"Are they fighting?"

"Either fighting or playing."

"If Monsieur doesn't mind, I'd like to see them."

"We must indeed, Conseil."

So there we were, climbing over blackish rocks, where the ground would suddenly crumble beneath our feet, or walking over slippery stones covered with ice. More than once I fell, hurting my back, while Conseil, who was either wiser or more sure-footed, never faltered, and would pick me up, saying:

"If Monsieur would be good enough to keep his legs further apart, he would find it easier to maintain his balance."

When we got to the top of the promontory, I saw a vast white plain covered with walruses. The animals were playing with one another; their bellowing was an expression of pleasure, not anger.

Walruses are just like seals as far as their bodies and limbs are concerned. But their lower jaws have no canine teeth or incisors, while the canine teeth in the upper jaw consist of two long tusks measuring as much as thirty inches in length and twelve around at the base. These teeth are made of a very solid ivory that has no grooves, is harder than that of elephants, and does not discolor so easily; they are much sought after. Moreover walruses are the victims of wanton hunting and killing by man, who will soon exterminate them completely, since the hunters slaughter the young and the pregnant females indiscriminately, destroying more than four thousand every year.

As we passed by these curious animals I was able to examine them at leisure, for they did not stir. Their skin was thick and furrowed and reddish tan in color; their fur was short and sparse. Some of them were thirteen feet long. Quieter and less timid than their northern cousins, they did not post sentries to guard the approaches to their camp.

After observing this colony of walruses, I thought of returning. It was eleven o'clock, and if Captain Nemo found the weather favorable to take our bearings, I wanted to be present. However, I had not much hope that the sun would appear that day. Heavy clouds on the horizon still hid it from us. It seemed as if the sun were jealous, and did not wish to reveal the secrets of this inaccessible part of the globe to man.

Nevertheless, I decided to go back to the *Nautilus,* and we followed a narrow path along the top of the cliff. At half past eleven we reached the boat, which had since brought the Captain ashore. I could see him standing on a block of basalt with his instruments beside him. His eyes were fixed on the northern horizon, near which the sun was describing its long arc.

I took up my position beside him and watched, without saying a word. Noon came and, as on the day before, the sun did not appear.

This was a grave setback, for we had not yet taken our

bearings. If it could not be done during the following day, we should have to give up all attempts to establish our position.

It was the 20th of March, and tomorrow would be the 21st, the equinox, when the sun would drop below the horizon for six months and the long polar night would begin. Since the September equinox it had emerged from the northern horizon, and had risen in long spirals to the 21st of December. At that period, the summer solstice of the northern regions had begun to descend, and the next day it would shed its last rays on those regions.

I expressed my thoughts and fears to Captain Nemo.

"You are right, Monsieur Aronnax," he said to me. "If I cannot observe the sun at its highest point tomorrow, I will not be able to do so again for another six months. On the other hand, since chance has brought us into these waters on the twenty-first of March, it should be easy to determine our position if the sun comes out at noon."

"Why, Captain?"

"Because, when the sun describes such long spirals, it is difficult to measure its exact height above the horizon, and instruments can make serious errors."

"So what do you intend to do?"

"I shall just use my chronometer," replied the Captain. "If tomorrow, March twenty-first, at noon—after taking in consideration the refraction, of course—the sun's disk is cut exactly in two by the northern horizon, then I know that I am at the South Pole."

"That is true," I said. "However, that statement is not mathematically accurate, because the equinox does not necessarily occur at midday."

"That is so, Professor. But the margin of error cannot be more than a hundred yards, and that is good enough for us. So, until tomorrow."

Captain Nemo returned to his ship, while Conseil and I stayed behind until five o'clock, walking up and down the beach, observing and studying. I found no unusual objects except for a penguin's egg, remarkable for its size, for which a collector would have paid more than a thousand francs. It was cream colored, with stripes and markings like so many hieroglyphics—a rare trinket, indeed! I gave it to Conseil to take care of, and the patient, sure-footed fellow, holding it as cautiously as if it had been a precious piece of Chinese porcelain, brought it back intact to the *Nautilus*.

There I put this rare egg in one of the museum's showcases. I had an excellent supper, consisting of a piece of seal's liver, whose taste reminded me of pork. Then I went to bed, not forgetting to invoke, like an Indian, the favors of the sun.

The next day, the 21st of March, I was up on the platform

at five o'clock in the morning. Captain Nemo was already there.

"The weather is breaking up a bit," he said. "I have high hopes. After breakfast, we will go ashore and choose an observation post."

Having made this arrangement, I went to find Ned Land. I should have liked to take him with me, but the obstinate Canadian refused, and I could see that he was becoming more taciturn and more ill-tempered every day. Actually, under the circumstances, I did not mind his refusal, because there were too many seals lying about ashore, and it was best not to expose this thoughtless fisherman to such a temptation.

After breakfast, I went ashore. The *Nautilus* had cruised a few miles farther south during the night. It was now more than three miles out to sea, off a coastline dominated by a sharp peak, twelve to fifteen hundred feet high. The dinghy carried me, Captain Nemo, two members of the crew, and the instruments—a chronometer, a telescope, and a barometer.

During our crossing, I saw numerous whales belonging to the three species peculiar to southern waters: the true whale, or right whale, as it is known in English, which has no dorsal fin; the humpback whale, with a wrinkled belly and large whitish fins which resemble wings; and the finback, a yellowish-brown whale, the liveliest of all whales. This powerful animal could be heard a long way off when it sent columns of air and vapor to a great height, resembling spirals of smoke. These various mammals were frolicking about in herds in these quiet waters, and I realized that this Antarctic basin was now serving as a refuge for whales hunted by the whalers. I noticed also long whitish rows of salpae, a kind of mollusk that live in colonies, as well as an immense jellyfish, which drifted about in the surf.

At nine o'clock we reached land. The sky was growing brighter, and the clouds were scurrying away southward. The mist was rising from the cold surface of the water. Captain Nemo made his way toward the high peak, where he doubtless wanted to make his observation. It was a difficult climb up the sharp-edged lava and the pumice stone, in an atmosphere often filled with sulfur fumes that rose from the crevices. For a man unaccustomed to walking on land, the Captain was scaling the steepest slopes with a suppleness and agility that I found difficult to match, and which would have been envied by a hunter of chamois.

It took us two hours to reach the summit of this peak, which consisted of a mixture of porphyry and basalt. From there, our eyes could see a vast sea that stretched into the northern horizon as far as the eyes could see. Below us were fields of dazzling whiteness. Overhead the sky was a pale blue, without mist. In the north the sun, like a ball of fire, was already sinking below the horizon. Whales playing in the waters below us spouted hundreds of liquid jets that resembled flowers, which spread like fireworks. In the distance, the *Nautilus* looked like a sleeping cetacean. Behind us, toward the south and east, lay an immense expanse of land, a chaotic accumulation of rocks and ice, extending as far as our eyes could see.

Captain Nemo, on reaching the summit, carefully noted our altitude by means of the barometer, for he had to take this into consideration to determine our position.

At a quarter to twelve the sun, like a golden disk and visible now only by refraction, was shedding its last rays over this deserted continent and over these seas never before seen by man.

Captain Nemo, using a special telescope that corrected refraction by means of a mirror, watched the sun sinking below the horizon, moving on a long diagonal path. I held the chronometer. My heart was pounding with excitement. If the disappearance of the semicircle of the sun coincided with noon on the chronometer, then we were at the Pole!

"Noon!" I cried.

"The South Pole!" replied Captain Nemo in a grave voice, as he handed me the telescope through which showed the sun exactly bisected by the horizon.

I watched the last rays of the sun crowning the peak of our mountain, and the shadows gradually rising on its slope.

At that moment Captain Nemo, putting his hand on my shoulder, said:

"Monsieur, in 1600 the Dutchman Gheritk, driven by storms and currents, reached the sixty-fourth parallel and discovered New Shetland. In 1773, on the seventeenth of January, the illustrious Cook, following the thirty-eighth meridian, reached latitude sixty-seven degrees thirty minutes south, and the following year, 1774, on the thirtieth of January, on the one hundred and ninth meridian, he reached a latitude seventy-one degrees fifteen minutes.

"In 1819, the Russian Bellinghaugnit reached the sixty-ninth parallel, and in 1821 the seventy-sixth at one hundred and eleven degrees longitude west. In 1820, the Englishman Brunsfield was stopped at the sixty-fifth parallel. That same year, 1820, the American Morrel, whose accounts are not very reliable, went along the forty-second meridian and discovered the open sea at seventy degrees fourteen minutes latitude.

"In 1825, the Englishman Powell could not get beyond the

sixty-second parallel. That same year, 1835, a simple seal fisherman, the Englishman Weddell, got as far as seventy-two degrees fourteen minutes latitude on the thirty-fifth meridian and as far as seventy-four degrees fifteen minutes on the thirty-sixth meridian. In 1829, the Englishman Forster, commander of the *Chanticleer,* took possession of the Antarctic continent at sixty-three degrees twenty-six minutes latitude and sixty-six degrees twenty-six minutes longitude.

"In 1831, the Englishman Biscoe, on the first of February, discovered Enderby in latitude sixty-eight degrees fifty minutes south; in 1832, on the fifth of February, he discovered Adelaide in sixty-seven degrees latitude, and, on the twenty-first of February, Graham, in sixty-four degrees forty-five minutes. In 1838, the Frenchman Dumont d'Urville was stopped by the great ice barrier at sixty-two degrees fifty-seven minutes south, but took the bearings of the Land Louis-Philippe. Two years later, in a new attempt, he discovered, on the twenty-first of January, Adélie, at sixty-six degrees thirty minutes, and eight days later, at sixty-four degrees forty minutes, Clarie Coast.

"In 1838, the Englishman Wilkes advanced to the sixty-ninth parallel on the one-hundredth meridian. In 1839, the Englishman Balleny discovered Sabrina on the edge of the Antarctic Circle. Finally, in 1842, on the twelfth of January, James Ross, also an Englishman, in command of the *Erebus* and the *Terror,* discovered Victoria Land; on the twenty-third of the same month, he reached the seventy-fourth parallel, the farthest point reached up to that time; on the twenty-seventh, he was at seventy-six degrees eight minutes, on the twenty-eighth, at seventy-seven degrees thirty-two minutes, and on the second of February, seventy-eight degrees four minutes. Later in the year 1842 he returned, reached the seventy-first parallel, but was unable to advance any farther.

"And now, on March twenty-first, 1868, I, Captain Nemo, have reached the South Pole, at a latitude of ninety degrees, and I am taking possession of this part of the earth, an area equal to one-sixth of all known continents!"

"In the name of whom, Captain?"

"Mine, sir!"

Captain Nemo unfurled a black banner, bearing the letter *N,* embroidered in gold. Then, turning toward the sun, whose last rays were faintly rippling on the horizon, he exclaimed:

"Farewell, sun! Retire, O radiant star! Rest beneath this open sea, and let the shadows of the long night fall upon my new domain!"

Chapter XV

ACCIDENT OR INCIDENT?

THE NEXT DAY, the 22nd of March, at six o'clock in the morning, preparations were begun for our departure. The last glimmers of twilight were blending into the night. It was bitterly cold. The stars were shining with unusual intensity. Above our heads the beautiful Southern Cross, the polar star of the Antarctic, glittered brilliantly.

The thermometer registered 12° below zero C. or 9° above zero F., and when the wind blew, it was biting cold. The ice floes were becoming more numerous; the sea was beginning to freeze everywhere, and blackish patches on the surface of the water indicated that fresh ice would soon be forming. Evidently, this southern basin was frozen over during the six months of winter, when it became completely inaccessible. What did the whales do during this period? Most probably, they swam under the ice barrier to look for clearer waters. The seals and walruses, accustomed to living in the coldest climates, however, remained in these icy regions. These creatures instinctively dig holes in the ice fields and keep them open, so that when they are in the water they can always come up to these holes for air; when birds, driven by the cold, have migrated northward, these sea mammals remain the sole masters of the polar continent.

Meanwhile the water tanks had been filled, and the *Nautilus* was slowly diving. When she reached a depth of a thousand feet, she stopped. Her propeller began to churn, and she headed straight north at a speed of fifteen knots. When evening fell, we were sailing beneath the immense icy shell of the ice shelf.

The panels in the saloon had been closed, in case the *Nautilus* would collide with blocks of submerged ice. I spent the day putting my notes in order. My mind was completely occupied with memories of the South Pole. We had reached that inaccessible point without undue effort and without danger, as if our floating craft had been traveling on rails. And now we were actually on our way back. Would our return journey bring as many surprises? I expected it would, for this world beneath the sea is an inexhaustible source of wonders!

During the 5½ months that fate had cast us on board the *Nautilus,* we had traveled fourteen thousand leagues, and on this long voyage, longer than the circle of the earth at the equator, we had been fascinated by many incidents, both strange and frightening: the hunting excursion in the forests of Crespo; our running aground in the Torres Strait; the coral burial ground; the Ceylon pearl fisheries; the Arabian Tunnel; the volcanic eruption of Santorin Island; the millions in Vigo Bay; Atlantis; the South Pole! All these memories, one after another, haunted me in a succession of dreams which disturbed my slumber all night long.

At three o'clock in the morning, I was awakened by a violent shock. I sat up in bed, listening in the dark, when suddenly I was thrown into the middle of the room. Evidently the *Nautilus* had collided with something, had rebounded, and heeled over at an angle.

I felt my way along the walls and corridors to the saloon, which was lit by its ceiling lights. The furniture had been overturned, but fortunately the showcases, whose legs were firmly attached, had stood up to the shock. The pictures on the starboard side were no longer hanging but were flat against the wall, while those on the port side dangled outward so that their lower edges were a foot away from the wall. The *Nautilus* was then lying on her starboard side and, furthermore, completely motionless.

I could hear the sound of footsteps and confused sounds of voices. But Captain Nemo did not appear. I was just about to leave the saloon when Ned Land and Conseil came in.

"What has happened?" I asked them.

"I was just coming to ask Monsieur that," replied Conseil.

"Confound it!" cried the Canadian, "I know very well what's happened. The *Nautilus* has hit something, and judging by the way she's lying, I don't think she'll get out of this as easily as she did in the Torres Strait."

"But at least are we on the surface?" I asked.

"We don't know," replied Conseil.

"That is easy enough to find out," I said.

I looked at the manometer. Much to my surprise, it indicated a depth of 1,080 feet.

"What can all this mean?" I exclaimed.

"We'd better ask Captain Nemo," said Conseil.

"But where can we find him?" asked Ned Land.

"Follow me," I said to my two companions.

We left the saloon. There was no one in the library. There was no one near the staircase, nor near the crew's quarters. I thought Captain Nemo must be in the pilot's cage. It was best to wait. We returned to the saloon.

I shall pass over the Canadian's recriminations without comment. This was a good opportunity for him to let off steam, and I let him vent his ill humor to the full without answering back.

We had remained like that for about twenty minutes, waiting to pick up the slightest sound inside the *Nautilus*. Then Captain Nemo came in. He seemed not to see us. His face, usually so impassive, betrayed signs of anxiety. Silently, he checked the compass and the manometer. Then he went over and placed his finger on a point in the planisphere in the region of the Antarctic.

I did not want to interrupt him. However, when he turned toward me a few moments later, I used an expression that he himself had used in the Torres Strait:

"Just an incident, Captain?"

"No, monsieur," he replied. "This time, it is an accident."

"Is it serious?"

"Perhaps."

"Any immediate danger?"

"No."

"Is the *Nautilus* stranded?"

"Yes."

"How did it happen?"

"Not through our incompetence, but by a trick of nature. There were no errors in our maneuvers. Nevertheless, the laws of equilibrium are what they are; we can defy human laws, but not the laws of nature."

Captain Nemo had chosen a strange moment indeed to philosophize. Moreover, his reply told me nothing.

"May I know, Captain," I asked him, "the cause of this accident?"

"An enormous block of ice, a mountain turned over," he replied. "When icebergs are undermined by warmer waters or by repeated collisions, their center of gravity rises, with the result that they overturn completely. That is what happened. One of these icebergs turned over and struck the *Nautilus*, which was cruising beneath the surface. After striking us, the iceberg slipped under its hull and lifted it with an irresistible force. We are now lying on our side at a higher level."

"But can we not free the *Nautilus* by emptying her tanks and restoring her balance?"

"That is just what we are doing at this moment, monsieur. You can hear the pumps working. Look at the needle of the manometer. It shows that the *Nautilus* is rising, but the mass of ice underneath it is rising with it. Until some obstacle stops this upward movement, our position cannot change."

And, in fact, the *Nautilus* was maintaining her list to starboard. Probably she would right herself when the iceberg stopped rising, but at the moment it was quite possible that we might strike the lower edge of the ice shelf itself, and we might be horribly crushed between the two masses of ice!

I kept thinking over all the possible consequences of our situation.

Captain Nemo did not take his eyes off the manometer. Since the iceberg had turned over, the *Nautilus* had risen about 150 feet, but she was still lying at the same angle.

Suddenly we felt a slight movement of the hull. Evidently the *Nautilus* was straightening up a bit. The objects in the saloon that had been hanging in midair were slowly returning to their normal position. The walls were resuming their vertical position. None of us spoke. With beating hearts, we could see and feel this movement. The floor was once more becoming horizontal beneath our feet. Ten minutes went by.

"We are standing upright at last!" I cried.

"Yes," said Captain Nemo, moving toward the door of the room.

"Well, will we be able to float again?" I asked him.

"Certainly," he replied. "As soon as the tanks have been emptied, the *Nautilus* will rise to the surface."

The Captain went out, and I soon realized that he had given orders to halt the rise of the *Nautilus*. Had he not done so, we should soon have struck the underside of the ice barrier. It was better to remain free in the water between the masses of ice.

"That was a narrow escape!" said Conseil.

"Yes. We could have easily been squashed between those two masses of ice, or at least shut in by them. Then, with no means of replenishing our air . . . Yes, indeed! We had a narrow escape!"

"If that's the end of it!" muttered Ned Land.

I did not want to get into a pointless argument with the Canadian, so I did not reply. Moreover, the panels opened at that moment, and the light from the outside poured in through the panes.

Here we were, thoroughly immersed, suspended in water. Thirty feet away on each side of the *Nautilus* there rose a dazzling wall of ice. Above us, the vast bottom of the ice barrier formed an immense ceiling; below us, the iceberg that had capsized, having slid slowly around, had come to rest at the base of the two lateral walls, and was firmly lodged there. The *Nautilus* was now a prisoner in a veritable tunnel of ice about sixty feet wide, filled with calm water. However, the *Nautilus* could move either forward or backward, then dive several hundred yards deeper, and continue its journey in an open passage under the ice barrier.

Although the light of the saloon had been turned off, the room was flooded with a brilliant light. It was the powerful reflection of the beams of our searchlight playing on those walls of ice. I could not possibly describe the effects of those beams as they fell on those masses of ice cut into every shape and form. Every angle, every ridge, every facet, reflected a different shade of color, depending on the nature of the veins running through it. Imagine a brilliant display of precious dazzling gems, especially sapphires, casting and fusing their jets of blue with jets of green emeralds. Here and there, pale shades of infinite mellowness, mingled with the sparkling fiery glow of diamonds, reflected a light so brilliant that the eyes could not endure it. The rays of our searchlight were intensified a hundredfold, like the rays of a powerful beacon passing through lenticular lenses.

"How beautiful! How magnificent!" exclaimed Conseil.

"Yes," I said, "it is a magnificent sight. Don't you think so, Ned?"

"Yes, it is, confound it!" replied Ned Land. "It's superb, I hate to admit it. I've never seen anything like it. But we may have to pay dearly for this show. And if I must say so, I think we are looking at things God never intended man to see!"

Ned was right. It was too beautiful! Suddenly, a cry from Conseil made me turn around.

"What is the matter?" I asked.

"Monsieur should close his eyes! Monsieur should not look!"

As he said this, Conseil covered his eyes with his hands.

"What is the matter, my boy?"

"I cannot see, I'm blinded!"

Involuntarily, I looked out of the window, but I could not stand the blazing light coming into the room.

Then I realized what had happened. The *Nautilus* had just increased her speed, and all the quiet reflections from the walls of ice had suddenly changed into brilliant flashes of lightning. All those dazzling, fiery reflections had merged together. The *Nautilus*, driven at great speed, was sailing through a sheath of lightning.

Then the panels of the saloon were closed. We had to hold our hands over our eyes, for our vision was affected by concentric lights, caused by the bright rays, and it took some time for our troubled eyes to recover.

Finally, however, we uncovered our eyes.

"Great heavens, I should never have believed it," said Conseil.

"And I still don't believe it!" said the Canadian.

"When we get back on land," continued Conseil, "we'll be so spoiled by all these marvels of nature that we won't think much of all those wretched countries created by the hand of man! No, the world and its inhabitants will no longer be worthy of us!"

These words, coming from the lips of a stolid Fleming, showed how excited and enthusiastic we had become. But the Canadian lost no time in pouring cold water on our enthusiasm.

"The world and its people!" he said, shaking his head. "Don't worry, friend Conseil, we'll never see it again!"

It was then five o'clock in the morning. Suddenly there was a shock at the bow of the *Nautilus*. I realized that her spur had run into a block of ice. It must have been due to an error in maneuvering, for this underwater tunnel, obstructed here and there by ice, was difficult to navigate. I thought Captain Nemo would alter his course and circumvent these obstacles, or else follow the twistings and turnings of the tunnel. In any case, the path ahead could not be completely blocked. Contrary to my expectations, however, the *Nautilus* went into reverse.

"Are we cruising backward?" asked Conseil.

"Yes," I replied. "The tunnel must be blocked at this end."

"So! . . . what do we do now?"

"So," I said, "it is quite simple. We will retrace our steps and leave through the southern end."

In saying this, I wanted to appear more confident than I really was. In the meanwhile, the *Nautilus* was still cruising backward and picking up speed.

"We will be losing time," said Ned.

"A few hours more or less will not matter, as long as we get out!"

"Yes, provided we do get out," remarked Ned.

A few minutes later I walked into the library. My companions sat in silence. I stretched on a sofa, picked up a book, and scanned its pages without thinking.

A quarter of an hour later, Conseil came up to me and said:

"Is that book Monsieur is reading interesting?"

"Very interesting," I replied.

"I can well believe it. Monsieur is reading Monsieur's own book!"

"My own book?"

And indeed I was, for the book I held in my hand was

none other than *The Great Ocean Depths,* and I had not been aware of it. I closed the book and continued to pace up and down. Ned and Conseil got up to go to their room.

"Stay here, my friends," I said, motioning to them not to go. "Let us stay together until we get out of this tunnel."

"As Monsieur wishes," replied Conseil.

Several hours went by. I kept looking at the instruments hanging on the wall of the saloon. The manometer showed that the *Nautilus* was keeping at a constant depth of over nine hundred feet; the compass indicated that she was still heading south; the log showed that her speed was twenty knots, too fast in such a narrow space. But Captain Nemo knew perfectly well that he had no time to lose under the circumstances, for every minute was worth a century.

At 8:25 there was a second collision; this time it was in the rear. I turned pale. My companions came closer; I took Conseil by the hand. We looked at each other questioningly. Our looks betrayed our thoughts more than any words could have done.

At that moment, the Captain entered the saloon. I went over to him.

"Is the route to the south blocked also?" I asked.

"Yes, Professor. When the iceberg turned over, it sealed off all openings."

"So we are trapped?"

"Yes."

Chapter XVI

LACK OF AIR

THUS, all around the *Nautilus*, above and below, there was an impenetrable wall of ice. We were prisoners inside the ice shelf! The Canadian had struck the table with his powerful fist. Conseil was silent. I looked at the Captain, who had recovered his usual impassive demeanor. He had folded his arms, and stood thinking. The *Nautilus* had come to a standstill.

The Captain then began to speak.

"Gentlemen," he said in a calm voice, "in our position, there are two ways of dying."

This enigmatic character had the look of a mathematics professor explaining a problem to his students.

"The first," he went on, "is to be crushed to death. The second is to die asphyxiated. I need not mention the possibility of starving, because the provisions on board the *Nautilus* will certainly outlast us. Let us therefore consider our chances of being crushed or asphyxiated."

"As for asphyxiation, Captain," I replied, "there is no fear of that, since our tanks are full."

"Quite so," rejoined Captain Nemo, "but we have only two days' supply. We have been submerged for the past thirty-six hours, and the air on board the *Nautilus* should be changed now. Within forty-eight hours, our reserves will have been exhausted."

"In that case, Captain, we will have to get out within forty-eight hours!"

"We shall try to do so by cutting through the wall that surrounds us."

"On which side?" I asked.

"That will depend on our soundings. I am going to land the *Nautilus* on the ice below us, and my men, in their diving suits, will attack the iceberg on its weakest side."

"Could the panels in the saloon be opened?"

"No difficulty about that. We are no longer moving."

Captain Nemo left the room. Soon a hissing sound told that the tanks were filling with water. The *Nautilus* sank slowly, and came to rest on the ice at a depth of about 1,200 feet, the level of the lower ice shelf.

"My friends," I said, "our situation is serious, but I am relying on your courage and your energy."

"Monsieur," replied the Canadian, "this is not the time to trouble you with my complaints. I am ready to do anything for the common good."

"Very good, Ned," I said, holding out my hand.

"May I add," he went on, "that I'm just as handy with the pick as I am with the harpoon, and if I can be useful to the Captain, I am at his service."

"He will not refuse your help. Come, Ned."

I led the Canadian to the room where the crew of the *Nautilus* were putting on their diving suits, and informed the Captain of Ned's offer, which was accepted. So the Canadian put on a suit and was ready to accompany his workmates. Each of them had his tank strapped to his back, filled with a large supply of pure air. This was a considerable drain on our reserves, but a necessary one. They carried no lamps, since these were unnecessary in waters brilliantly illuminated by our searchlight.

As soon as Ned had dressed I went back to the saloon, whose panels were open, and standing beside Conseil, I examined the surrounding layers of ice that supported the *Nautilus*.

A few moments later, we saw a dozen members of the crew set foot on the ice, among them Ned Land, recognizable by his height. Captain Nemo was with them.

Before proceeding to break through that ice, he had soundings taken to determine the best direction in which to work. Long soundings were sunk into the side walls, but after fifty feet they still found solid ice. It was pointless to attack the ceiling, since this was the ice shelf itself, which was more than thirteen hundred feet thick. Captain Nemo then took a sounding on the ice underneath. There, thirty feet of ice separated us from the water below. It was then a question of cutting out a piece equal in area to the waterline of the *Nautilus*. This meant the removal of over 6,500 cubic yards of ice, in order to cut an opening big enough for us to dive through into the water below.

Work began at once and was conducted with indefatigable energy. Instead of digging around the *Nautilus*, which would have involved considerable difficulty, Captain Nemo planned to have a huge trench dug about twenty-five feet from the port quarter. Then his men began chipping away at various points of that trench. Very soon, picks were chipping away and large blocks were soon broken away from the mass.

Owing to the strange effect of specific gravity, these blocks, being lighter than water, rose up to the roof of the tunnel, the upper part of which became thicker by the amount removed from the floor. But this was of no consequence, as long as the floor below became thinner.

After two hours of toil, Ned Land came in exhausted. He and his workmates were then replaced by a new team, including Conseil and myself. We were directed by the second-in-command of the *Nautilus*.

The water seemed extremely cold, but I soon warmed up wielding my pickax. I could move very freely, although I was working in a pressure of thirty atmospheres.

When I came in after two hours' work to take some nourishment and rest, I could feel the striking difference between the pure air I had been breathing from our tanks and the air in the *Nautilus*, which was already charged with carbon dioxide. The air in the craft had not been changed for forty-eight hours, so that its invigorating quality was considerably lacking. Meanwhile, after twelve hours' work, we had removed only a layer of ice one yard thick, or about 650 cubic yards. Assuming that we could manage to do as much every twelve hours, it would still take four days and five nights to bring the task to a successful conclusion.

"Four days and five nights!" I said to my companions. "But we only have two days' supply of air in the reserve tanks."

"And do not forget," said Ned Land, "that even after we get out of this infernal prison, we'll still be under the ice shelf and still cut off from the open air."

He was right. Who could possibly tell how long it would take us to get out of that prison? Might we not be asphyxiated before the *Nautilus* could reach the surface of the sea? Was she destined to perish in this icy tomb with all aboard? The situation seemed desperate, but all of us were facing this possibility squarely and all were determined to do our duty to the very end.

As I had foreseen, another yard of ice was removed from the trench during the night. But the next morning, when, clad in my diving suit, I went out to work in a temperature of between 60 and 70 below zero C., I noticed that the side walls of the trench were closing in gradually. This was because the water in the trench not in the immediate vicinity of the men and their work tended to freeze again. Faced by this new and imminent danger, what were our chances of escaping, and how could we prevent this water from freezing and crushing the sides of the *Nautilus* like glass?

I said nothing about this new danger to my friends. What

was the use of running the risk of damping the enthusiasm and the energy they had in this arduous labor of salvation? When I came back on board, however, I mentioned this new danger to Captain Nemo.

"I know," he said in that calm voice that he always maintained, no matter how tragic the situation might be. "That is just one more danger for us, but I do not see what we can do about it. Our only chance to escape is to dig faster than the water can freeze. We just have to get there first, that is all."

Get there first! But after all, I should have become accustomed to his manner of speaking by now!

For several hours that day I wielded my pick with more energy than ever. That task kept up my spirits. Besides, working meant leaving the *Nautilus* and breathing pure air from the tank on my back. It meant leaving the foul, stagnant air of the ship.

Toward evening, another cubic yard of ice had been cut away from the trench. But when I returned on board I was almost asphyxiated by the carbon dioxide with which the air was saturated. If we only had some chemical process to rid the air of this dangerous gas! After all, there was no lack of oxygen. All that water contained a considerable quantity of it if only we had the means to extract it with our powerful batteries and obtain a fresh supply! I had thought of this possibility, but what was the good, since the carbon dioxide expelled by our lungs had filled every corner of the ship! In order to absorb it, we would have to fill receptacles with potassium lye and shake them about continually. But we had no potassium lye on board, and nothing else could replace it.

That evening, Captain Nemo had to open the valves of his tanks and let some pure air into the *Nautilus*. If he had not taken this precaution, we should never have awakened from our sleep.

The next day, the 26th of March, I resumed my work by helping to cut away the fifth yard of ice. The walls on either side of the trench and the ceiling above us were becoming visibly thicker, and it was obvious that they would close in before the *Nautilus* could get away. For an instant I was filled with despair. My pickax almost dropped from my grasp. What was the point of digging if I was bound to die of suffocation or be crushed by this water that was turning to stone, the victim of a torture undreamed of by the most savage tribes? It seemed as if I were held between the formidable jaws of some monster and that they were closing on me inexorably.

At that moment Captain Nemo, who was working hard as well as directing the operations, passed near me. I touched him with my hand and pointed to the walls of our prison. The starboard wall had crept inward at a distance of less than twelve feet from the *Nautilus*.

The Captain understood and motioned for me to follow him. We went on board, and after removing my diving suit, I followed him into the saloon.

"Monsieur Aronnax," he said to me, "we shall have to take some heroic measures, or we shall be sealed up in this water which is solidifying like cement."

"Yes," I said, "but what can we do?"

"Ah," he exclaimed, "if only my *Nautilus* were strong enough to withstand this pressure without being crushed!"

"What do you mean?" I asked, not realizing what he was driving at.

"Don't you understand," he rejoined, "that this freezing of the water could help us? Don't you realize that this very solidification could break up these masses of ice that imprison us just as it can rend apart the hardest of rocks? Do you not feel that this, far from destroying us, could be a means of saving us?"

"Yes, Captain, perhaps. But however powerful the *Nautilus* may be to withstand pressure, she could not withstand the terrible pressure of these masses, and she would be flattened into a sheet of iron."

"I know, Professor. We must not depend on nature to help us. We must depend on ourselves. We must stop that water from freezing. We must find a way. Not only are the side walls closing in, but there is not more than ten feet of water fore and aft of the *Nautilus*. The ice is moving in on us on all sides."

"How much time," I asked, "have we got before the air tanks give out?"

The Captain looked me straight in the eye.

"The day after tomorrow," he said, "the tanks will be empty!"

A cold sweat ran through me. And yet, why should I have been surprised at his reply? On the 22nd of March, the *Nautilus* had dived beneath the open waters at the Pole. It was now the 26th. For five days we had been living on our reserves of air! What air was left had to be saved for the workers. As I write these lines, the vivid memories of how I felt at that time still fill me with terror, and I find it difficult to breathe!

Meanwhile Captain Nemo, silent and motionless, seemed lost in thought. Obviously an idea had occurred to him, but he seemed to be rejecting it, telling himself that it was not possible. Finally, two words escaped his lips:

"Boiling water!"

"Boiling water?" I exclaimed.

"Yes, Professor. We are enclosed within a fairly limited space. Do you not think that streams of boiling water, poured from the pumps of the *Nautilus,* might not raise the temperature around us and slow up that freezing?"

"We must try it," I cried emphatically.

"Yes, Monsieur le Professeur, let us try."

At that moment the outside temperature was less than 7° below zero C., or 19° F. Captain Nemo led me to the kitchens, where huge distilling machines operated to produce drinking water by a process of evaporation. These machines were filled with water, and all the electric energy from the batteries was thrown into the coils immersed in the water. Within a few minutes, the water was boiling. It was then pumped out, while fresh water replaced it in the tanks. The heat developed by the batteries was such that cold water, taken from the sea, had only to pass through the machines to reach the pumps boiling.

Three hours after the process of projecting hot water had begun, the outside temperature was 6° below zero C., or 21° F. One degree centigrade had been gained. Two hours later, the thermometer registered 4° below zero C., or 25° F.

"It is working," I said to the Captain, having carefully followed and checked the progress of the operation.

"I think so," he replied. "At least we will not be crushed. Asphyxiation is our only danger now."

During the night, the temperature of the water rose to 1° below zero C., or 30° F., but the streams of hot water proved unable to raise it higher. But since seawater will not freeze at less than 2° below zero C., I felt reassured about the danger of being frozen in.

The next day, the 27th of March, about twenty feet of ice had been dug out of the trench. Only about twelve feet remained, but that meant another forty-eight hours' work. The air could no longer be renewed inside the *Nautilus,* and during the course of the day, it became worse and worse.

I felt an unbearable weariness was oppressing me. At about three o'clock in the afternoon, this oppressive feeling was overwhelming me. I yawned repeatedly and felt my jaws coming apart. My lungs gasped, seeking that indispensable air that was becoming scarcer. I was seized by a mental torpor. I had reached the limits of my endurance and was all but unconscious. My good Conseil, although affected by the same symptoms and suffering the same discomfort, would not leave me. Holding my hand, he encouraged me, and I could still hear him murmuring:

"Ah, if I could only stop breathing so that Monsieur might have more air!"

To hear him speak like that brought tears to my eyes.

The more intolerable our breathing became inside the ship, the more eagerly we hastened to put on our diving suits to work our shift! Our picks resounded on the icy surface; our arms became weary and our hands blistered, but what did our fatigue matter, or our blisters! Pure air poured into our lungs! We were breathing! We were breathing!

Yet no one attempted to prolong his underwater stint beyond the time allotted. Having done his bit, each man ungrudgingly handed over to his gasping companion the tank that would restore his life. Captain Nemo was the first to set an example to submit himself to this severe discipline, and when the hour struck, he would give his tank to his relief and return to the foul atmosphere on board, calm, unflagging, and uncomplaining as always.

That day the work went on with even more vigor. Only six more feet remained to be cut away. Only six feet were between us and the open water. But the air tanks were almost empty! What little they contained was kept for the workers. Not a breath remained for the *Nautilus!*

When I returned to the ship, I was half suffocated. What a night it was! Words could not describe it. Such tortures cannot be put into words! The next morning, I found it almost impossible to breathe. Not only did my head ache, but I was strangely dizzy, like a drunken man. As for my companions, they were suffering from the same symptoms, and some members of the crew were at their last gasp.

That day, the sixth of our imprisonment, Captain Nemo, finding the work with the picks going too slowly, decided to use the *Nautilus* to crush the remaining layer of ice separating us from the open water. He had managed to retain all his coolness and energy, overcoming physical discomfort by sheer moral strength. He never stopped thinking, planning, acting.

He gave orders to lighten the vessel, so that it was raised from its bed of ice by a change in its specific gravity. When it was floating, the crew towed it until it was directly above the trench we had cut in the ice to correspond to the shape of the *Nautilus*. Then the tanks were filled and the ship settled down at the bottom of the trench.

At that moment the whole crew returned on board, and the double hatch was closed. The *Nautilus* was now resting on a layer of ice no more than a yard thick, which had already been pierced in thousands of places by the soundings.

Then the valves were opened wide and 100 cubic yards of

water poured in (3,500 cubic feet), thus increasing the weight of the *Nautilus* by over 100,000 kilograms, or 220,000 pounds.

We waited and listened, forgetting our suffering and filled with new hope. Our lives depended on this final effort.

In spite of the buzzing in my head, I soon heard the hull of the *Nautilus* vibrate. We began to sink, and the ice was rent asunder with a strange noise like the sound made by tearing paper, and the *Nautilus* dropped through.

"Monsieur will be pleased," murmured Conseil in my ear. "We are getting through."

I was unable to reply. I grasped his hand. I squeezed it with a sudden involuntary burst of emotion.

Suddenly, carried down by her enormous excess weight, the *Nautilus* sank into the water like a cannonball, almost as she might have done had she been hurtling through space!

Then the electric pumps were switched on full to eject water from the tanks, and after a few minutes our dive was stopped. Soon the manometer showed that we were rising. The propeller, turning at full speed, made the ship's hull vibrate to its very bolts as it moved speedily northward.

How long was this cruising under the ice shelf to last before we reached the open sea? One more day? I would be dead by then!

Stretched out on a sofa in the library, I was slowly suffocating. My face was purple, my lips were blue, my faculties paralyzed. I could no longer see or hear. I had lost all notions of time. My muscles were unable to contract.

How many hours went by while I was in this state, I cannot say. I felt that death was approaching. I realized that I was going to die. . . .

Suddenly I regained consciousness. A little air was entering my lungs. Had we surfaced? Had we at last cleared the ice shelf?

No! It was Ned and Conseil, my two good friends, who were sacrificing their lives to save mine. There were still a few atoms of air left in one of the tanks. Instead of breathing it themselves, they had kept it for me, and while they were suffocating, they were giving it to me, drop by drop. I tried to push the tank away from me, but they held my hands, and for a few moments I felt the joy of breathing!

My eyes strayed toward the clock. It was eleven o'clock in the morning; it must have been the 28th of March. The *Nautilus* was traveling at the frightening speed of forty knots, tearing furiously through the waters.

Where was Captain Nemo? Had he succumbed? Had his comrades died with him?

At that moment, the manometer showed that we were only twenty feet below the surface. Only an ice field lay between us and the atmosphere. Could we break through it?

Perhaps! In any case, the *Nautilus* was going to try. I could feel her maneuvering into a slanting position, so that her stern was lowered and her prow raised. This shift in balance had been effected by letting in water. Then, driven forward by her powerful propeller, she charged the ice field from below like a formidable battering ram. She was piercing the ice bit by bit; then she would dive down again and return to the charge at full speed against that mass of ice, which was slowly cracking. Then, with a final onslaught, she hurled herself against that icy surface and crushed through!

The hatch was opened—almost torn open—and waves of fresh air flooded into the *Nautilus!*

Chapter XVII

FROM CAPE HORN TO THE AMAZON

I CANNOT SAY how I got up on the platform. Perhaps the Canadian had carried me there. But I was breathing—I was more than breathing that invigorating air of the sea! My two companions near me were becoming intoxicated with that fresh and pure oxygen. Unlike those who had been deprived of food for a long time and need to exercise restraint and moderation when fed, we were free to breathe deeply and fill our lungs with this fresh air to our hearts' content. The breeze that was blowing filled us with joy and exaltation.

"Ah," said Conseil, "how wonderful it is to breathe this air! Let Monsieur breathe as much as he likes. There is plenty for everyone."

Ned Land did not utter a word. He kept opening his mouth wide enough to frighten a shark. What deep breaths he took! The Canadian was puffing away like a furnace at full blast!

We were soon revived, and when I looked around me, I saw that we were alone on the platform. None of the crew was to be seen, not even Captain Nemo. Those strange men of the *Nautilus* were satisfied to breathe the air circulating inside the ship. None of them had come up to enjoy the fresh air of the sea breeze.

The first words I spoke were words of thanks and gratitude to my two companions. Ned and Conseil had given me an extra lease on life during those last hours of my suffering. Nothing that I could say could repay such devotion.

"Well, monsieur," replied Ned Land, "that's not worth talking about! What praise do we deserve for that? None at all. It was a matter of simple logic. Your life was worth more than ours, so we had to save it."

"No, Ned," I replied, "it was worth no more than yours. Nobody is superior to a good and generous man, and that is what you are!"

"Oh, that's all right! That's all right!" repeated the Canadian, somewhat embarrassed.

"And you, my good Conseil, how you must have suffered!"

"Oh, not too much. If Monsieur will permit me to tell the

truth, I did seem to be short of a few mouthfuls of air, but I think I should have gotten used to it. When I saw Monsieur passing out like that, I didn't have the slightest desire to breathe. It took the wind right out of me—as they say."

Now Conseil felt embarrassed by the banality of his expression and could not finish his sentence.

"My friends," I replied, profoundly moved, "we are bound to each other forever. I am indebted to you—"

"And I intend to take advantage of that," said the Canadian.

"What!" exclaimed Conseil.

"Yes," added Ned Land. "I reserve the right to take you with me when I leave this infernal *Nautilus*."

"By the way," said Conseil, "are we going in the right direction?"

"Yes, we are," I replied. "We are heading towards the sun, and from here the sun means north."

"That may be," Ned Land went on, "but it remains to be seen whether we're heading for the Pacific or the Atlantic. In other words, are we headed towards deserted waters or well-traveled waters?"

I was unable to answer that, and I was afraid that Captain Nemo was more likely to take us back to that vast ocean that touches the shores of both Asia and America. He could then complete his underwater voyage around the world and could return to the seas where the *Nautilus* enjoyed the greatest freedom. But if we were to return to the Pacific, far from all populated shores, what would happen to the plans of Ned Land?

However, before long, this important question would be settled, for the *Nautilus* was moving fast. We soon crossed the Antarctic Circle and were heading for Cape Horn. Toward seven o'clock in the evening on March 31st, we reached the tip of the American continent.

All our recent sufferings were now forgotten, and the memory of our imprisonment under the ice was gradually being erased from our minds. We thought only of the future. Captain Nemo did not appear, either in the saloon or on the platform. The bearing marked each day on the planisphere by the second-in-command enabled me to follow the exact course of the *Nautilus*. That evening it became obvious to me that, much to my satisfaction, we were returning northward by way of the Atlantic.

I informed the Canadian and Conseil of this.

"That's good news," replied the Canadian, "but where's the *Nautilus* going?"

"I could not say, Ned."

"Having been to the South Pole, do you think the Captain would like to go to the North Pole next, and then return to the Pacific through the famous Northwest Passage?"

"I wouldn't put it past him," interjected Conseil.

"Well," said the Canadian, "we'll be parting company with him before then."

"Whatever you may say," submitted Conseil, "this Captain Nemo is a fantastic man, and we will never regret having known him."

"Especially when we've seen the last of him!" retorted Ned Land.

The next day, April 1st, just before noon, the *Nautilus* rose to the surface for a few minutes. We sighted land to the west. It was Tierra del Fuego. It was given this name—the Land of Fire—by the early navigators after they had seen so many columns of smoke rising from native huts. Tierra del Fuego is a very large group of islands stretching out thirty leagues in length and eighty leagues in width, lying between 53° and 56° latitude south and 67° 50′ and 77° 15′ longitude west. The coastline seemed low, but in the distance rose high mountains. I even thought I saw Mount Sarmiento, which rises almost seven thousand feet above sea level, a pyramid-shaped mountain of shale with a very pointed summit. According to Ned Land, if its pointed peak is clear of clouds, it indicates good weather; if it is misty or cloudy, bad weather.

"It is a good barometer, then," I remarked.

"Yes, monsieur, a natural barometer that never failed me when I used to sail through the Strait of Magellan."

Just then, the peak stood out clearly against the sky. This was a forecast of good weather, and as it turned out, a reliable one.

The *Nautilus* then submerged, approached the coast, and cruised along for a few miles. Through the panes of the saloon I noticed long seaweeds and gigantic sea wrack, those varech specimens that may be seen in the open sea around the South Pole. With their sticky, polished filaments, they measured as much as one thousand feet or three hundred meters in length, real cables, thicker than a man's thumb and strong enough to be used to moor ships. Another seaweed known as velp, with leaves four feet long, grew among the coral and covered the seabed like a carpet. It served both as a nest and as food for myriads of mollusks, crabs, and cuttlefish.

What magnificent meals the seals and sea otters were having there, feeding on a mixture of fish and sea vegetables, in the English manner.

The *Nautilus* cruised over this rich and luxurious bed at

high speed. Toward evening we approached the Falkland Islands, whose rugged summits I identified the following day. The water was not deep, and I had good reason to believe that these two islands, surrounded by numerous smaller islands, had once been a part of the lands near the Magellan Strait. The Falklands were probably discovered by the famous John Davis, who gave them the name of Davis Southern Islands. At a later date, Richard Hawkins called them the Maiden Islands, islands of the Virgin. They were subsequently renamed Malouines by fishermen from Saint Malo at the beginning of the eighteenth century, and finally Falkland by the English, to whom they still belong today.

In these waters, our nets brought in beautiful specimens of seaweed, especially of a certain fucus whose roots were loaded with splendid mussels, the best in the world. Geese and ducks landed on our deck by the dozen, and soon took their places in the larder of the galley. As for fish, I noted particularly certain bony varieties belonging to the genus of the goby and, above all, groundlings, about six inches long, flecked with whitish and yellow spots.

I admired, too, numerous jellyfish, and the most beautiful of them all, the chrysaor, peculiar to the seas around the Falklands. Sometimes they were shaped like a very smooth semicircular umbrella, with red and brown stripes and ending in twelve symmetrical tentacles; sometimes they resembled a basket, out of which there trailed, most gracefully, large leaves with long red twigs. As they swam they shook their four leafy arms, while the shock of tentacles on their heads dangled in their wake. I should have liked to preserve some specimens of these delicate zoophytes, but they are like clouds, shadowy phantoms that dissolve and evaporate when removed from their native surroundings.

When the last peaks of the Falklands had dropped below the horizon, the *Nautilus* dived to a depth of sixty or seventy feet and followed the coast of South America. Captain Nemo had not yet appeared.

We remained off the coast of Patagonia, sometimes submerged and sometimes on the surface, until April 3rd. The *Nautilus* passed the wide estuary formed by the mouth of the Plata, and on April 4th we were off the coast of Uruguay, but about fifty miles out to sea. Maintaining a northerly course, we then followed the long, sinuous coastline of South America. We had then sailed sixteen thousand leagues since we had embarked on our voyage in the seas of Japan.

At about eleven o'clock in the morning, we crossed the Tropic of Capricorn on the 37th meridian and passed off Cape Frio. Much to Ned Land's disappointment, it seemed that Captain Nemo did not particularly care for the inhabited coast of Brazil, for we shot past it at breathtaking speed. Neither fish nor fowl, however fleet of fin or wing they might be, could keep up with us, and the wealth of interesting things in those waters escaped our observation.

This speed was maintained for several days, and on the evening of April 9th we sighted the easternmost point of South America, Cape San Roque. But then the *Nautilus* changed course again, seeking at great depths an underwater valley that lies between this cape and Sierra Leone on the African coast. This valley splits into two branches at the same latitude as the Caribbean, and ends in the north in an enormous depression thirty thousand feet deep. At this spot, the ocean bed features a line of sheer cliffs, six miles long, which extends as far as the Lesser Antilles, while, on a line with Cape Verde, another no-less-considerable wall completes the encirclement of the whole sunken continent of Atlantis. The bottom of this immense valley is dotted with a few mountains, which render those depths particularly picturesque. I base my remarks largely on the manuscripts in the library of the *Nautilus,* including maps evidently drawn by Captain Nemo in accordance with his own personal observations.

For two days, those deep and deserted waters were visited by the *Nautiius,* using her fins to good advantage to make long diagonal sweeps, which enabled us to observe at all depths. On the 11th of April, however, we suddenly surfaced at the mouth of the Amazon, a vast estuary whose flow is so great that fresh water may be found for several leagues out in the sea.

We crossed the equator, and twenty miles to westward lay the Guianas, French territory, where we could easily have found refuge. But there was a very strong wind blowing, and a dinghy could not have faced those raging waves. Doubtless Ned Land realized this, for he did not utter a word about escaping. I did not bring up the subject either, for I did not want to push him into an attempt that would inevitably be doomed to failure.

Instead, I took advantage of this delay and spent my time pleasantly engrossed in my interesting studies. During those two days, the 11th and the 12th of April, the *Nautilus* remained on the surface of the sea and its nets brought up a most marvelous variety of zoophytes, both fish and reptiles.

Some of the zoophytes had been dragged up by the chain of the nets. For the most part they were lovely phyctallines, belonging to the actinidian family, and among other species there was the *Phyctalis protexta,* original denizens of those waters, whose small cylindrical body was adorned with verti-

336

cal lines and speckled with red dots, and crowned with a marvelous cluster of tentacles. As for mollusks, these consisted of creatures that I had already observed, such as turitellae; olive-colored porphyry shells with regular intersected lines whose reddish spots stood out vividly against the color of their flesh; bizarre pterocerae, which resembled petrified scorpions; translucent hyalines; argonauts; cuttlefish, excellent to eat; and a certain species of squid, which naturalists of antiquity classified among the flying fish, used primarily as bait for cod fishing.

I noticed several species of fish on these shores that I had not yet had an opportunity to study. Among the cartilaginous fish, "pteromyzons-pricka," a kind of eel, about fifteen inches long, greenish head, violet fins, a gray-blue back, a silvery-brown belly, speckled with bright spots, and the iris of the eye circled with gold, a strange creature that the currents of the Amazon have brought into the open sea, for they are a freshwater animal; a species of tubercled ray with pointed snout, a long thin tail, armed with a jagged spur; small sharks about a yard long, whitish-gray in color, with several rows of teeth curved backward, popularly known as "pantoufliers"; fish bats or vespertilios, shaped like a reddish isosceles triangle about a foot and a half long, with long fleshy pectoral fins which make them resemble bats. However, a horny appendage, set near the nostrils, has given them the nickname of sea unicorns. And finally, some species of triggerfish, the curassavian, whose flecked flanks sparkled with a golden tint; and the capriscus, light violet in color, whose shades glistened like the throat of a pigeon.

I shall conclude this list, somewhat dry, to be sure, but very accurate, with a series of bony fish I observed: passans, belonging to the genus apteronotes, whose body has an unusual, attractive black color, with a blunt snow-white snout and a very long, delicate "lanyard"; odontagnathae, sardines over ten inches long, with their resplendent flashes of silver; a species of mackerel with two anal fins; black centronotae, which are fished with torches, and which attain a length of six feet and have a white, firm, fatty flesh, which tastes like eels when fresh and like smoked salmon when dried; reddish vrasse or lip fish, cousins of the parrot fish, scaly around the base of their dorsal and anal fins; chrysopterae, whose bodies glitter like gold and silver and sparkle like rubies and topazes; gold-tailed giltheads, whose flesh is extremely delicate, and whose phosphorescence betrays their presence in the water; orange-colored giltheads, with long tongues; sciaena, with golden tails; dark acanthopterygians; anableps from Surinam, etc.

337

This should not prevent one from mentioning one more fish, which Conseil has good reason to remember for a long time to come.

One of our nets brought in a monstrous flat ray, weighing about forty pounds, which, if its tail had been cut off, would have formed a perfect disk. It was white underneath and reddish on top with big round dark-blue spots encircled in black. Its skin was glossy and it had a flipper divided into two lobes. Once on deck, it struggled and tried to turn over by convulsive movements, and it squirmed so well that it finally succeeded in reaching the edge of the platform. One more effort and it would have fallen into the sea. But Conseil, who did not like to lose that specimen, ran upon it, and before I could stop him, seized it with both hands.

As soon as he did so, however, he was flung on his back with his legs in the air, half paralyzed and shouting:

"Monsieur! Monsieur! Please help me!"

It was the first time that the poor boy had failed to address me in the third person!

The Canadian and I picked him up and massaged him energetically, and when my poor eternal classifier of fish returned to his senses, he murmured in halting tones:

"Class, cartilaginous; order, chondopterygians with fixed gills; suborder, selachian; family, rays; genus, electric ray!"

"Yes, my friend," I replied, "that was an electric ray that left you in such a deplorable condition!"

"Ah, Monsieur can believe me," answered Conseil, "I'll have my revenge on that creature."

"How?"

"By eating it."

That is exactly what he did that very evening, purely for revenge, because, frankly, that animal was as tough as leather.

The unfortunate Conseil had attacked an electric ray of the most dangerous kind, the cumana. This strange animal, immersed in water, which is an excellent conductor of electricity, can electrocute fish at a distance of several yards, so great is the power of its electric organ, whose two surfaces are not less than twenty-seven square feet in area.

The next day, April 12th, the *Nautilus* approached the coast of Dutch Guiana near the mouth of the Maroni. There we saw several herds of sea cows. They were manatees, which, like the dugong and Steller's sea cow, belong to the sirenian order and live in family groups. These beautiful animals, which are peaceful and harmless, attain a length of twenty feet and weigh at least four tons. I told Ned Land and Conseil that a provident Nature had assigned these mammals an important role. It is these animals, as well as the seals, that graze in submerged fields and eat the vegetation that would otherwise obstruct the estuaries of tropical rivers.

"And do you know," I added, "what has happened since men have almost completely exterminated these useful creatures? The putrified vegetation has poisoned the air, and it is this foul air that is the cause of the yellow fever that ravages these beautiful lands. The poisonous vegetation has accumulated under these torrid waters, so that illness has spread unchecked from the mouth of the River Plata to Florida!

"If one is to believe Toussenel, this scourge is nothing to that which will afflict our descendants when the seas have been depleted of whales and seals. We shall then have our waters cluttered with octopi, medusae, and squids, which will create hotbeds of infection in the absence of those huge mammals whose stomachs were intended by God to keep the oceans clean!"

However, following the law of preservation rather than the theories of Toussenel, the crew of the *Nautilus* killed half a dozen of these manatees. We needed to replenish our larder with this excellent meat, better than beef or veal. There was nothing exciting about this hunt, because the manatees permitted themselves to be killed without offering any resistance. Several thousands of pounds of meat were brought on board to be dried and stored.

In addition, we added to our food supply, from these waters so rich in game, by a strange manner of fishing. The net had brought in its meshes a certain number of fish whose heads ended in an oval plaque with fleshy edges. These were echeneis, belonging to the third family of sub-branchian malacopterygians. Their head plaques are composed of transverse cartilaginous movable plates, between which this creature can actually create a vacuum, enabling it to fasten itself to objects like the suckers of a leech.

The remora that I had observed in the Mediterranean belonged to the same species, but the one we are describing, common in these waters, was an *Echeneis osterchara.* As they were caught, the crew placed them in tubs full of water.

When the fishing was over, the *Nautilus* cruised nearer the coast where a number of sea turtles were asleep on the surface. It would have been difficult to capture these valuable reptiles, for the least sound rouses them, and their hard shell is proof against a harpoon. But the echeneis can capture them easily and with assurance. This animal is as good as a living fishhook and would be a blessing to the most inept fisherman.

The crew of the *Nautilus* attached to the tails of these animals a ring just large enough not to interfere with their movements. They tied one end of a long line to the ring and the other end to the ship.

When the echeneis were thrown in the sea, they immediately swam and attached themselves to the shells of the turtles. Their grip was so strong that they would have to be torn apart before letting go. They were then hauled on board, together with the turtle to which they were attached.

Several cacuans were also caught in the same manner. They were about three feet long and weighed well over four hundred pounds. Their shells were covered with large, thin, transparent brown plates, with spots of yellow and white, which made them rather precious and valuable. Besides, they were as excellent and as delicious to eat as tortoise.

This catch brought to an end our stay on the shores of the Amazon, and at nightfall the *Nautilus* returned to the high seas.

Chapter XVIII

THE SQUID

FOR SOME DAYS the *Nautilus* kept well away from the American coast. Evidently she did not wish to enter the Gulf of Mexico or the Caribbean. It was not that the water in those parts would have lacked depth, since the average depth of those seas is well over 5,500 feet; it was, more likely, that the many islands and the many ships in the area would have made Captain Nemo very uncomfortable.

On the 16th of April, we sighted Martinique and Guadeloupe, about thirty miles away. For a few moments I had a glimpse of their highest peaks.

The Canadian, who had planned to make our escape while in the gulf either by reaching land or by being picked up by one of the many ships that sail between the islands, was very disappointed. To escape would have been perfectly possible if Ned Land could have taken possession of the dinghy unbeknown to the Captain. But since we were out in mid-ocean, that idea had to be given up.

The Canadian, Conseil, and I had a fairly long conversation on this subject. We had been prisoners on board the *Nautilus* for six months. We had traveled seventeen thousand leagues, and as Ned Land pointed out, there seemed to be no reason to think that it would ever come to an end. He made a proposal that I had not expected. He proposed that we ask Captain Nemo point-blank whether or not he intended to keep us on board indefinitely.

Such a step, however, did not appeal to me, for in my opinion this would be useless. Our hopes lay not in the Captain of the *Nautilus,* but only in ourselves. For some time, moreover, he had become more moody, more reserved, less sociable. He seemed to avoid me. I saw him only on rare occasions. In the past, he had enjoyed explaining the wonders of the underwater world to me. Now he left me to my studies and he no longer came into the saloon.

What was the reason for this change of attitude toward me? I had done nothing to reproach myself for. Did our presence on board begin to disturb him? Whatever it was, there was no reason to hope that he would give us our freedom.

I asked Ned to give me time to think the matter over before doing anything, because if this step failed it could rekindle the Captain's suspicions, make our situation very unpleasant, and this would hamper any plan the Canadian had in mind. I may add that we could not possibly use our health as an excuse, for with the exception of that trying ordeal under the ice barrier, the three of us had never felt better. The wholesome food, the invigorating air, the regular hours, and a uniform temperature made us less susceptible to illness. For a man who had forsaken life on land as Captain Nemo had done, for a man who felt at home in the sea, free to come and go as he pleased, who lived and followed paths shrouded in mystery to achieve a goal of his own choosing, an existence such as his was understandable. But we had not broken with humanity, nor had I, who had been doing such interesting explorations under the sea, any wish to have all these studies die with me. I was now in a position to write a definitive work, and I wanted this work sooner or later to see the light of day.

Meanwhile, in the waters of the West Indies, thirty feet or so below the surface, with panels open, how many interesting things passed before my eyes, day after day, things I entered in my notes! Among other zoophytes I observed some "galleys" or Portuguese men-of-war, known as Physalia pelagica, a kind of fat and oblong swimming bladder, with a tint of mother-of-pearl, holding up their membrane to the wind and letting their blue tentacles float like silk threads on the water —lovely medusae to the eye, but corrosive, poisonous nettles to the touch. Among the articulata, there were annelides, or sea worms, about five feet long, armed with a pink horn and equipped with 1,700 organs of locomotion, meandering under the surface, reflecting all the colors of the rainbow in passing. Among the numerous fish, I saw some devilfish, enormous cartilaginous animals, ten feet long, weighing six hundred pounds, with triangular pectoral fins, a slightly humped back, and eyes set at the extreme rear of the head. They were floating in the water like wrecked ships, and sometimes they covered our panels like heavy shutters. There were American triggerfish, which nature has colored only in white and black; a kind of goby with long fleshy bodies, yellow fins, and protruding jaw; mackerel about six feet long, with short sharp teeth, their bodies covered with small scales, belonging to the albacore species. Then we observed swarms of gray mullet, with golden stripes running head to tail, splashing around with their resplendent fins. These masterpieces of jewelry were once considered sacred to Diana and were particularly sought after by wealthy Romans. There was a proverb about them that said, "Let him who catches them not eat them!" Finally, we saw golden pomacanthae, decorated with emerald bands, dressed in velvets and silks, swimming before us like Veronese lords and ladies; spurred giltheads, disappearing swiftly with a stroke of their powerful pectoral fin; clupeidae, fifteen inches long, immersed in their own phosphorescent glow; common mullet, beating the sea with their large plump tails; red coregoni, which seemed to be mowing the waves with their sharp pectoral fin; and silver selenes, or moonfish, worthy of their name, rising on the horizon of the waters like so many moons, reflecting pale rays.

How many other marvelous new specimens I might have observed if the *Nautilus* had not gradually dived down into deeper waters! With inclined fins she took us down to 6,600 and even to 11,500 feet. At such depths, animal life was represented only by sea lilies, starfish, lovely pentacrins with medusa heads, their straight stalks bearing a little chalice, some trochi, some "bleeding teeth," and some fissurellas, or "keyhole limpets," coastal mollusks of a huge species.

On April 20th, we had risen to an average depth of about 5,000 feet. The nearest land was the archipelago of the Bahamas, spread out like so many paving stones, on the surface of the water. There we saw tall cliffs under the water, great perpendicular walls formed by stone blocks arranged like bricks, between which there were dark holes into which the beams of our searchlight could not fully reach.

These rocks were carpeted with large species of seaweed, giant laminariae and the endless fuci—a veritable tangle of hydrophytes worthy of a world of Titans.

In talking about these huge plants, Conseil, Ned, and I naturally fell to discussing the gigantic animals of the sea, for this vegetation was obviously intended as food for them. However, as I looked through the panels of the *Nautilus*, which was now almost motionless, I could see among those long filaments nothing but the principal articulata of the division of branchipodes; long-legged purplish-blue crabs, and clios, or sea butterflies, found in the Antilles.

It was about seven o'clock when Ned Land drew my attention to a great wriggling and squirming movement among those tall seaweeds.

"Well," I said, "those are probably caves inhabited by squids, and I should not be at all surprised to see a few of those monsters."

"What!" exclaimed Conseil, "ordinary squids of the class of the cephalopods?"

"No," I said, "I mean giant squid. But friend Land has probably made a mistake, because I do not see anything."

"I'm sorry about that," replied Conseil. "I should like to come face-to-face with one of those squids I've heard so much about, which can drag whole ships down into the deep. Those animals are called 'krak—' "

" 'Crack' will do," retorted the Canadian sarcastically.

"Krakens," rejoined Conseil, getting his word in without heeding his companion's quip.

"You'll never make me believe that such creatures exist," said Ned Land.

"Why not?" replied Conseil. "We believed in the existence of Monsieur's narwhal, didn't we?"

"And we were wrong, Conseil."

"That's true, but there are people who still believe in it."

"I shouldn't be a bit surprised," I said to Conseil, "but as far as I am concerned, I have decided not to admit the existence of these monsters until I have dissected them with my own hand."

"Does Monsieur mean that he does not believe in the existence of giant squid?" Conseil asked me.

"Who in the devil has ever believed in them, anyway?" exclaimed the Canadian.

"Oh, many people, Ned."

"Not fishermen. Scientists, perhaps!"

"You are wrong, Ned. Fishermen and scientists!"

"But let me tell you," said Conseil, in a most serious tone of voice, "I can remember clearly seeing a large ship dragged down beneath the waves by the tentacles of a cephalopod."

"Do you mean you actually saw that?" asked the Canadian.

"Yes, Ned."

"With your own eyes?"

"With my own eyes."

"Do you mind telling me where?"

"At St. Malo," Conseil replied, without batting an eye.

"In the harbor, I suppose?" Ned Land asked ironically.

"No, in a church," replied Conseil.

"In a church!" cried the Canadian.

"Yes, my friend. In a painting that represented the squid in question!"

"That's a good one!" said Ned Land, laughing. "Monsieur Conseil is pulling my leg, monsieur!"

"As a matter of fact," I said, "he is right. I have heard about that painting. But the subject is based on a legend, and you know what legends are worth when it comes to natural history! When it is a question of monsters, there is no limit to the flight of the imagination. Not only has it been alleged that these squids could drag ships down beneath the waves, but a certain Olaüs Magnus mentions a cephalopod one mile long that looked more like an island than an animal. Another tale relates that the Bishop of Nidros one day set up an altar on a large rock; once the Mass was over, the rock began to move and returned to the sea. That rock was a giant squid."

"Is that all?" asked the Canadian.

"No," I replied. "Another bishop, Pontoppidan of Berghem, also speaks of a squid on which it was possible to maneuver a regiment of cavalry!"

"Those bishops of old were pretty good at telling tall tales," said Ned Land.

"Lastly, the naturalists of ancient times referred to monsters whose mouths were as big as a gulf. They were too big to pass through the Straits of Gibraltar!"

"Well, can you beat that!" exclaimed the Canadian.

"But is there any truth in all these tales?" asked Conseil.

"None, my friends, at least for those which exceed the bounds of probability and become fables or legends. However, the storytellers require at least a pretext, if not a real cause, for their tales. It cannot be denied that there exists a species of octopus and cuttlefish of great size, but they are not as big as the whales. Aristotle reported seeing a squid five cubits long—that is, over ten feet in length. Our fishermen often see some whose length exceeds five feet. The museums of Trieste and Montpellier have some skeletons of octopi measuring over six feet. Furthermore, naturalists have calculated that if one of these creatures were only six feet long, it would have tentacles twenty-seven feet in length, which is quite a formidable monster."

"Do fishermen fish for them these days?"

"If they do not fish for them, sailors nevertheless come across them. One of my friends, Captain Paul Bos of Le Havre, has often told me that he met one of these huge monsters in the Indian Ocean. But the most astonishing incident, which makes it impossible any longer to doubt the existence of these gigantic creatures, happened a few years ago, in 1861."

"What happened?" asked Ned Land.

"Well, in 1861, northeast of Teneriffe, at about the same latitude as we are at this moment, the crew of the dispatch boat *Alecton* saw a monstrous squid swimming near it. Captain Bouguer approached the creature and attacked it with harpoons and gunfire, but without much success, since the bullets and harpoons just passed through the soft flesh as they might have done through a soft jelly. After several fruitless attempts, the crew succeeded in passing a slipknot round the body of the mollusk. The knot slipped down the rope as far as the caudal fins and stopped. An attempt was made to haul the monster aboard, but its weight was so great that the rope cut through the body and severed its tail. The creature, minus its tail, disappeared under the water."

"Well, at least we have some facts," said Ned Land.

"An indisputable fact, my good Ned. Not only that, but it was actually suggested that this animal be called 'Bouguer's squid.' "

"How long was it?" asked the Canadian.

"Wasn't it about twenty feet long?" said Conseil, who, standing at the window, was again examining the rugged outlines of the cliffs.

"Precisely," I replied.

"And wasn't its head crowned with eight tentacles that splashed in the water like a nest of snakes?"

"Quite right."

"And weren't the eyes huge and set near the top of the head?"

"Exactly."

"And wasn't its mouth just like an enormous parrot's beak?"

"Indeed it was, Conseil."

"Well, if Monsieur doesn't mind my saying so," Conseil said calmly, "if what I'm looking at is not Bouguer's squid, it must be one of its brothers."

I looked at Conseil, and Ned Land sprang toward the window.

"What a horrible monster!" he exclaimed.

I looked also. I could not repress a feeling of repulsion. Before my eyes there wriggled a terrible monster, worthy to figure among all the legends of these creatures.

It was a squid of colossal dimensions, about twenty-five feet long. It was moving backward at great speed in the direction of the *Nautilus*, peering through enormous blue-green eyes. Its eight arms, or rather, its eight tentacles, set in its head, which is why it is called a cephalopod, were twice as long as its body, and swirled about like the hair of the Furies. One could distinctly see the 250 suckers on the inner surface of its tentacles, shaped like semicircular capsules. Sometimes these air holes, or suckers, would stick to the panel of the saloon, creating a vacuum. The mouth of that monster—a horny beak, shaped like that of a parrot—opened and closed with a vertical motion. Its tongue, also horny in texture and armed with several rows of sharp teeth, vibrated in and out between the blades of those shears. What a fantastic creature of nature! A bird's beak in a mollusk! Its tapering body, bulbous in the middle, formed a fleshy mass that must have weighed forty to fifty thousand pounds! Its color changed with incredible speed from a livid gray to a reddish brown, depending upon the mood of the beast.

What was irritating that monster? Doubtless, it was the presence of the *Nautilus*, more formidable than it, on which neither its suckers nor its jaws could gain any hold. And yet what fabulous monsters these squids are, what vitality the Creator has given them, what vigor in their movements, propelled as they are by three hearts!

Chance had brought us into the presence of this animal, and I did not want to miss the opportunity to make a careful study of this specimen of a cephalopod. I overcame the horror with which its appearance filled me, and taking a pencil, I began to draw it.

"Perhaps this is the same monster that got away from the *Alecton*," said Conseil.

"No, it can't be," replied the Canadian. "This one is intact. He hasn't lost his tail!"

"That does not mean anything," I interjected. "The tentacles and tails of these creatures can grow again by a process of regeneration, and Bouguer's squid must certainly have had time to grow a new tail in the past seven years."

"Anyway," said Ned, "if this isn't the one, perhaps it's one of those over there."

Indeed, other squids were appearing at the starboard window. I counted seven of them wriggling around the *Nautilus*, and I could hear them grinding their beaks against the iron plates of our hull. We could not have wished for more.

I continued my work. The monsters were sticking so close to us that they scarcely seemed to be moving, and I could have traced an outline of them on the windowpane. Furthermore, our speed was quite slow.

Suddenly the *Nautilus* stopped, and a shock made her whole structure tremble.

"Have we run into something?" I asked.

"If that is the case," replied the Canadian, "we are free again, because we are floating."

The *Nautilus* was certainly afloat, it is true, but she was no longer moving. Her propeller was no longer beating the water. A minute went by, and then Captain Nemo, followed by his lieutenant, came into the saloon.

I had not seen him for some time, and he seemed depressed. Without speaking to us, perhaps without having seen us, he went to the panel, took a good look at the squids, and said a few words to his second-in-command.

The first mate left the room. Soon the panels were closed and the ceiling lights came on.

I went over to the Captain.

"That is a curious collection of squids," I said in a non-committal tone, like some amateur who had just been looking through the glass in an aquarium.

"Yes, indeed, monsieur," he replied. "We will soon come to grips with them."

I stared at the Captain, scarcely believing my ears.

"Come to grips with them?" I repeated.

"Yes, monsieur. The propeller has stopped, and I imagine that the horny jaws of one of these animals are wrapped around the vanes—which is preventing us from moving."

"What do you propose to do?"

"Surface and massacre these vermin."

"A rather difficult thing to do."

"That is true. Our electric bullets are powerless against that soft flesh, because they do not find enough resistance to explode. But we'll have a go at them with our axes."

"And with a harpoon, sir," added the Canadian, "if you'll permit me to help."

"I accept your offer, Master Land."

"We will go with you," I said, and following Captain Nemo, we made our way toward the central staircase.

There, about ten or twelve men, armed with boarding axes, were all ready for the attack. Conseil and I each took an ax, while Ned Land took a harpoon.

The *Nautilus* had surfaced by then. One of the sailors, at the top of the steps, was unscrewing the bolts of the hatch. But hardly had the bolts been freed when the hatch shot up with great force, obviously pulled up by the suckers on a squid's tentacle.

Immediately one of those long tentacles came sliding through the opening like a serpent, while twenty others flailed about overhead. With one blow from his ax, Captain Nemo cut through the formidable tentacle, which slithered squirming down the steps.

We pushed forward, one behind the other, to get onto the platform. Two other tentacles came snaking down through the air, grabbed the sailor standing in front of Captain Nemo, and pulled him upward with irresistible force.

Captain Nemo gave a shout, and rushed on deck. We rushed behind him.

What a scene! The poor man, in the grip of that tentacle, held fast by its suckers, was dangling in the air at the mercy of that enormous arm. He was gasping, choking, and kept shouting: "Help! Help!" I was astounded to hear these words *spoken in French!* So I had a compatriot on board, perhaps several! I shall remember his heartrending cry to the end of my days!

The poor fellow was lost. Who could save him from that powerful grip? Nevertheless, Captain Nemo had rushed at the squid, and with one blow of his ax had hacked off another of its tentacles. The second-in-command was battling furiously with other monsters, which were climbing up the sides of the *Nautilus*. The whole crew was battling furiously. The Canadian, Conseil, and I were also sinking our weapons into that fleshy mass. A strong smell of musk filled the air. It was horrible!

For a moment, I thought that the unfortunate man entangled in the clutches of the squid would be freed from those powerful suckers. Seven of the eight tentacles had been cut off. The remaining one brandished its victim, dangling in the air, like a feather. But just as Captain Nemo and his lieutenant plunged at it, the animal threw up a jet of black liquid, which these animals secrete in a sack of the abdomen. We were blinded by it. When the black cloud had cleared away, the squid had disappeared, and with it my unfortunate fellow countryman!

With what incredible fury we attacked those monsters! We fought like men possessed! Ten or twelve of those creatures had now swarmed over the deck and sides of the *Nautilus*. We hurled ourselves pell-mell into that mass of truncated tentacles that squirmed like serpents all over the platform, in the midst of a deluge of blood and black ink. Like Hydra's head, those slimy arms seemed to grow back almost instantly. Ned Land's harpoon plunged and pierced the greenish eyes of those creatures, but my bold companion was suddenly thrown on his back by the tentacles of a monster he could not avoid.

Why had my heart not stopped beating with emotion and horror? The huge jaws of that monster had opened over Ned Land. The poor man was about to be cut in two. I sprang to his aid, but Captain Nemo was quicker than I, and with one blow buried his ax between the two formidable jaws of that creature. Saved by a miracle, the Canadian sprang to his feet and plunged his harpoon into the triple heart of that monster.

"I owed you that!" said Captain Nemo to the Canadian.

Ned bowed his head without answering.

The battle had lasted a quarter of an hour. The monsters, defeated, mutilated, or slaughtered, finally gave way and disappeared beneath the waves.

Captain Nemo, spattered with blood, stood motionless beside the searchlight, gazing at that sea that had just swallowed one of his companions. Tears streamed down his cheeks.

Chapter XIX

THE GULF STREAM

NONE OF US WILL EVER FORGET that horrible scene which took place on the 20th of April. When I wrote about it, immediately after its occurrence, I was still under the influence of violent emotions. I went over its details later on and read it to Conseil and the Canadian. They agreed that the facts were accurate, but they thought I had failed to convey the emotional drama of the situation. But to describe such scenes adequately, one would require the gift of the most illustrious of our poets, the author of the *Travailleurs de la Mer,* Victor Hugo.

I described how Captain Nemo had wept as he gazed at those waters below him. His sorrow had been deep and sincere. This was the second companion he had lost since we had come aboard. What a horrible death! His friend had been crushed, stifled, and torn into pieces by the powerful arms of that monstrous squid, crunched by its iron jaws. Never would he lie in a peaceful grave with his companions in those tranquil waters of that coral cemetery!

The cry of despair uttered by that unfortunate victim in the midst of that battle had torn my heart. That poor Frenchman, forgetting the strange language used on board, had turned again to the language of his country and his mother, to express a last desperate call for help! Among the crew of the *Nautilus,* bound body and soul to Captain Nemo and, like him, having renounced all contact with mankind, there was a fellow countryman of mine! Was he the only Frenchman in that mysterious brotherhood, obviously made up of men of different nationalities? This was another insoluble problem that constantly haunted my mind!

Captain Nemo returned to his room, and I did not see him again for some time. How sad, how depressed and irresolute he must have been, if I were to judge from his ship, of which he was the moving spirit and which faithfully reflected his every mood! The *Nautilus* was no longer keeping to a set course, but was drifting here and there, like a corpse at the mercy of the waves. Although the propeller had been disentangled and freed, it was scarcely used. The Captain cruised at random, unable to tear himself away from the scene of that last fight, from those waters that had swallowed one of his men!

Ten days passed in this manner, and it was not until the 1st of May that the *Nautilus* took a definite course toward the north, after having sighted the Bahamas at the mouth of the Bahama Channel. We were now following the largest current in the sea, a veritable river that has its own banks, its fish, and its own temperature. I mean, of course, the Gulf Stream.

This is a current that flows smoothly in the middle of the Atlantic, without its waters becoming mixed with those of the ocean. It is a salty stream, saltier than the surrounding sea. Its average depth is three thousand feet, and its average width is 60 miles. In some places, its current flows at a speed of about 2½ miles an hour. The constant volume of its waters is greater than that of all the rivers in the world put together.

The true source of the Gulf Stream, discovered by Commander Maury, its point of departure, if you will, is situated in the Bay of Biscay. There, its waters, which are still low in temperature and somewhat colorless, begin to take form. The stream flows south along Equatorial Africa, is warmed by the torrid rays of the tropical sun, crosses the Atlantic, reaches Cape San Roque on the Brazilian coast, and splits into two branches, one of which flows into the warmer waters of the Caribbean. Then the Gulf Stream, whose task it is to restore the balance between the extremes of temperature and to mix the tropical with the northern waters, begins its stabilizing role. Brought to a white heat in the Gulf of Mexico, it flows northward along the American coast as far as Newfoundland, is deflected by the cold current from the Davis Strait, then resumes its oceanic route by following a rhumb line, and divides into two branches in the region of the 43rd parallel, one of which, helped by the northeast trade winds, returns to the Bay of Biscay and the Azores, while the other, after having warmed the waters around the coast of Ireland and Norway, meanders up to Spitsbergen, where its temperature drops to 4° centigrade, or 40° Fahrenheit, and empties into the polar seas.

It was in this ocean current that the *Nautilus* was now navigating. On leaving the Bahama Channel, which is thirty miles wide and more than a thousand feet deep, the Gulf Stream flows at about five miles an hour. This speed decreases steadily as it goes north, and it must be hoped that this regular trend will persist, for should its speed and direction be changed, the climate in Europe would undergo an upheaval of incalculable consequences.

At about midday, I was on the platform with Conseil. I was initiating him into the mysteries of the Gulf Stream. When I was through with my explanations, I asked him to put his hands in the water.

Conseil obeyed, and was very surprised to feel no sensation of cold or heat.

"The reason for that," I told him, "is that the temperature of the Gulf Stream, as it leaves the Gulf of Mexico, differs very little from that of the human body. The Gulf Stream is a vast distributor of warmth, which enables the coast of Europe to be continually decked in green. If one is to believe Maury, the heat of this current, if it were fully exploited, would supply enough warmth to prevent a river of molten metal as big as the Amazon or the Missouri from solidifying."

At that moment, the speed of the Gulf Stream was about seven feet a second. Its current is so different from that of the surrounding sea, and its waters are so compressed, that they actually rise higher than the surrounding ocean, so that there is a difference in level between it and the cold sea. The waters of the Gulf Stream are dark in color and rich in salts; their pure indigo color makes them stand out from the green water surrounding them. So clear is the line of demarkation that the *Nautilus*, when she was level with the Carolinas, had her prow in the Gulf Stream while her propeller was still beating the water of the Atlantic.

This current carried with it a whole world of living creatures. Argonauts, so common in the Mediterranean, were to be seen in great numbers. Among the cartilaginous fish, the most remarkable were rays, whose tails formed almost one-third of their bodies, which were shaped like huge diamonds about twenty-five feet long. There were also small sharks, about a yard long, with large heads, short round muzzles, and several rows of sharp teeth, whose bodies seemed to be covered with scales.

Among the bony fish, I noticed some gray wrasse peculiar to those waters; a certain kind of black gilthead whose iris shone like fire; sciaenidae, or croakers, a yard long, with large snouts set with many little teeth, which uttered soft cries; black centronotae, which I have already mentioned; dolphins, or blue coryphenes, speckled with gold and silver; parrot fish, veritable rainbows of the ocean that can rival the most beautiful tropical birds in color; blennies with triangular heads; bluish rhombs, or garfish, without scales; toadfish, with yellow stripes shaped like a Greek T; masses of little gobies with brown-spotted bodies; dipterodons with silver heads and yellow tails; several species of salmon; gray mullets with slender bodies, shining with a soft light which Lacépède dedicated to his wife; and finally, a lovely fish, the American horseman, covered with medals and ribbons, which is found in the waters of that great nation where medals and ribbons are so little esteemed.

I must add that during the night, the phosphorescent waters of the Gulf Stream rivaled the electric glow of our searchlight, especially during the stormy weather that was constantly threatening us.

On the 8th of May we were passing Cape Hatteras, parallel with North Carolina. The breadth of the Gulf Stream at that point is seventy-five miles, while its depth is about seven hundred feet. The *Nautilus* continued to cruise aimlessly. There seemed to be no supervision on board. Indeed, I had to agree that under such conditions, there seemed to be every chance of a successful escape, since these inhabited shores would have offered easy refuge. The sea was crisscrossed continually by numerous steamers plying between New York or Boston and the Gulf of Mexico, and frequented day and night by little coastal craft that called at various points on the American coast. There was therefore every hope of being picked up, and the opportunity to escape appeared to be good, in spite of the thirty miles separating the *Nautilus* from the coast of the United States.

But an unfortunate circumstance made the Canadian's plans impracticable. The weather was very bad. We were approaching an area where storms are frequent, the home of waterspouts and cyclones, caused by the Gulf Stream itself. To brave a sea that was often whipped into turmoil, in a fragile dinghy, was to risk certain death. Even Ned Land agreed. Nevertheless, he was champing at the bit, tortured by a furious nostalgia that only an escape could cure.

"Professor," he said to me that day, "this business has got to come to an end. I want to be clear about all this. Your Captain Nemo is leaving the land behind and sailing towards the north. But let me tell you that I had enough of the South Pole, and I won't follow him to the North Pole."

"But what can we do, Ned, since an escape is out of the question at present?"

"We must reconsider my last plan. We must speak to the Captain. You didn't say a word when we were in your home waters, but now that we are in mine, I'm going to talk. When I think that within several days the *Nautilus* will be off Nova Scotia, where a large bay opens toward Newfoundland—the St. Lawrence empties into this bay and the St. Lawrence is my river, a river that flows by Quebec, my home town; when I think of this I am overcome with fury and my hair stands on end. No, monsieur, I'd rather jump in the sea! I can't stand this any longer. I'm suffocating!"

Obviously the Canadian was at the end of his patience. His energetic temperament could no longer put up with this long imprisonment. His face was changing day by day; his mood was becoming worse. I realized that he must be suffering, for I too was beginning to feel homesick. Nearly seven months had passed without our having any news from the outside world. Moreover, Captain Nemo's self-imposed isolation, his changed attitude, especially since the battle with the squids, his silence, all this made me see things in a different light. I no longer felt the same enthusiasm as I had felt at the beginning. One had to be a Fleming like Conseil to accept such a situation and live in surroundings reserved for cetaceans and other inhabitants of the deep. Really, if that worthy young man had been equipped with gills instead of lungs, he would have made an excellent fish!

"Well, Professor?" asked Ned Land, when I did not reply.

"Well, Ned, do you want me to ask Captain Nemo what his intentions are regarding us?"

"Yes, monsieur."

"Even though he has already made it clear to us?"

"Yes, I want to be certain once and for all. Speak only for me and me alone, if you want to."

"But I do not see him very often. He avoids me now."

"All the more reason to go and see him."

"All right, Ned. I will ask him."

"When?" insisted the Canadian.

"When I see him."

"Monsieur Aronnax, do you want me to go and look for him?"

"No, let me do it. Tomorrow—"

"No, today," said Ned Land.

"All right, then, today," I replied. I did not want him to spoil everything for all of us.

The Canadian left me. Once I had decided to ask the Captain, I determined to do so at once and have done with it. I prefer to have things done rather than leaving them to be done.

I returned to my room. I could hear Captain Nemo's steps in his own cabin. I must not lose this opportunity to broach the matter. I knocked at his door. There was no answer. I knocked again and turned the knob. The door opened.

I entered. The Captain was there, bent over his work table. He had not heard me. Since I was determined not to leave without having questioned him, I walked straight up to him.

354

He raised his head suddenly, frowned, and said to me somewhat rudely:

"What are you doing here? What do you want?"

"I want to speak to you, Captain."

"But I am busy, Professor. I am working. Why not grant me the same freedom I grant you—the freedom to be alone?"

This reception was not very encouraging. But I was determined to be patient and see the matter through.

"Captain," I said coldly, "I have already spoken to you of a matter that I can no longer put off."

"What matter, Professor?" he replied ironically. "Have you made some discovery that has escaped my attention? Has the sea revealed some new secrets to you?"

Evidently we were not thinking of the same thing. But before I could reply he showed me a manuscript, lying open on his table, and said to me in a more serious tone of voice:

"Here, Monsieur Aronnax, we have a manuscript written in several languages. It contains a summary of all my studies on the sea. God willing, it shall not perish with me. This manuscript, signed by me, including the story of my life, will be sealed in a small, unsinkable container. The last man of us all to survive on board the *Nautilus* will throw it into the sea, and it will drift wherever the waves may carry it."

Signed in his own name, with his life's story written by himself! Did this mean that his secret would one day be revealed? But, for the moment, I only saw this as an excuse for broaching the subject.

"Captain," I replied, "I find it impossible not to approve this idea of yours. The fruits of your study must not be lost. But the means that you employ seem to me primitive. Who can tell where the winds may blow your container and in whose hands it may fall? Could you not find a better solution? Could not you, or one of your men—?"

"Never, Professor," said the Captain emphatically, interrupting me.

"But I and my companions are prepared to treat your manuscript in confidence, and if you will give us our liberty—"

"Your liberty!" exclaimed Captain Nemo, getting up.

"Yes, Captain, and that is precisely what I have come to talk to you about. For the past seven months we have been on board your ship, and I want to ask you today, in the name of my companions and myself, whether it is your intention to keep us here forever."

"Monsieur Aronnax," said Captain Nemo, "I will tell you today what I told you some months ago: Whoever enters the *Nautilus* must never leave her."

"But this is slavery that you are imposing on us!"

"Call it whatever you like."

"But everywhere a slave has the right to regain his liberty! Any means he may use to escape are justified!"

"Who has ever denied you that right?" replied Captain Nemo. "Have I ever tried to bind you with an oath?"

As he spoke, the Captain looked at me and folded his arms.

"Monsieur," I said, "let us go back once more to a subject which is somewhat painful to both of us. Let us discuss and settle it once and for all. You know very well that I am not the only one concerned in this matter. You are well aware that my studies here are of deep interest to me. They are not only a great pleasure and diversion for me, but also a passion that can make me forget everything else. Like you, I am not a man who is seeking recognition and renown. I can live in obscurity and, like you, nurture only a frail hope that some-day in the future the fruits of my labors may be discovered by means of a hypothetical 'container' entrusted to the haz-ards of the winds and the waves. I can and do admire you. I can even follow in your footsteps with pleasure, but only in the aspects of your life which are understandable to me. There are, however, other aspects which we find difficult to understand and are unable to share. On occasions, we have been touched to the heart by your sorrows. On others, we have been stirred by your deeds of genius and courage. On these occasions we have had to suppress even the slightest token of sympathy and admiration which a human being feels in the presence of something noble and good, whether it come from friend or foe. It is the feeling that we are alien to all that affects you closely that makes our situation somewhat unacceptable and impossible even for me, but especially for Ned Land. Every man, for the very fact that he is a man, deserves some consideration. Have you ever asked yourself what a love of liberty or hatred of slavery can do to engender vengeance in a man like Ned Land? Have you ever thought what he might think, what he might try or attempt to do?"

I paused. Captain Nemo got up.

"Ned Land can think, try, or attempt whatever he wishes. What does it matter to me. It is not I who sought him out, nor am I keeping him on board for my pleasure! As far as you are concerned, Monsieur Aronnax, you are a man capa-ble of understanding everything, even silence. I have nothing more to say. Let this be the first and the last time for you to come and discuss this matter with me. I will refuse to utter another word on this subject."

I withdrew. From that day on, our situation was very tense. I reported this conversation to my two companions.

"Now we know that we can't expect anything from *him*," said Ned Land. "The *Nautilus* is approaching Long Island, and we'll make a break for it, no matter what the weather is like."

The sky was becoming more and more threatening. Signs of a hurricane appeared in the sky. The whole atmosphere was turning into a grayish-white color. On the horizon, layers of cirrus and cumulus clouds were gathering, accumulating like mountains in the background, while low clouds sped by swiftly around us. The waves rose higher and higher, swelling into long, rough breakers. The birds disappeared except those lovers of tempests, the petrels. The barometer dropped noticeably, indicating an extreme tension in the air. The mixture in the storm glass was decomposing rapidly due to the electric energy that saturated the atmosphere. All the elements were ready to unleash their fury.

The storm broke on the 18th of May, just when the *Nautilus* was sailing off Long Island, only a few miles from the entrance to the New York harbor. I can describe this fury of the elements, for instead of taking refuge in the depths of the sea, Captain Nemo, by some inexplicable whim, decided to brave the storm on the surface.

A very strong wind was blowing from the southwest at almost forty miles an hour. By three in the afternoon it had reached a speed of fifty miles an hour, the speed of a tempest.

Captain Nemo, imperturbable despite the storm, had taken up his position on the platform. He had had a rope fastened around his waist and had himself tied fast, so that he could stand up to the monstrous waves. I had done the same, my admiration divided between the storm and that incomparable man who could brave it.

The raging sea was swept by great billows of clouds, which dipped in the waves as they passed. I could no longer see those smaller intermediate waves that form in the hollow of large ones. Nothing was visible except those murky undulations, whose crests were so compact that they never broke. They kept getting higher and higher, urging each other on with fury. The *Nautilus*, sometimes lying on her side, sometimes standing up like a mast, rolled and pitched frightfully. At about five o'clock, the rain began to come down in torrents, but neither the wind nor the sea abated. The hurricane was now blowing at a speed of about 150 feet per second, or about one hundred miles per hour. At such a speed it can overturn homes, drive roofing tiles through wooden doors, tear iron gratings, and move twenty-four-pound cannons. But the *Nautilus,* in the turmoil of that storm, justified the comment of an eminent engineer who stated that "there is no well-constructed hull which cannot defy the sea!" Our ship was not a solid, sturdy rock which the storm would have demolished. It was more than that. It was rather a spindle built of steel, with neither masts nor rigging, mobile and maneuverable, which could brave the fury of the sea with impunity.

Meanwhile, I carefully examined those raging waves. They measured as much as fifty feet in height and up to five or six hundred feet in breadth, and they were running about fifty feet a second, about half the speed of the wind. Their volume and their force increased with the depth of the water. Now I realized the role that these waves play in the scheme of nature. They capture air and force it down to the bottom of the sea, where its oxygen nurtures life. Their pressure, it has been calculated, can rise to as much as 6,500 pounds per square foot on any surface they strike. In the Hebrides, waves like this once moved a block of stone weighing 84,000 pounds. In the hurricane of the 23rd of December, 1864, after having destroyed part of Tokyo, the waves traveled across the Pacific and broke on that same day against the shores of America!

The intensity of the storm increased with the coming of night. The barometer fell to twenty-eight inches, just as it had during the cyclone that struck Réunion in 1860. As night was falling, I saw a large vessel struggling painfully along the horizon. It was moving at reduced speed, trying to stay afloat. It was probably one of those steamers that ply between New York and Liverpool or Le Havre. It soon disappeared in the darkness.

By ten o'clock that night, the sky was on fire. The heavens were streaked with flashes of lightning. I could not take the dazzling flashes, but Captain Nemo stared them in the face, appearing to inhale the soul of that tempest. The air was rent by horrible noises, made by the crashing of the waves, the howling of the wind, and the claps of thunder. The wind seemed to come from all directions, and the cyclone, rising in the east, whirled north, west, and south, moving counterclockwise, just the opposite of storms in the Southern Hemisphere, whose winds move clockwise.

Ah, that Gulf Stream! How well it justified its name of King of the Tempests! For it is the cause of these formidable cyclones, created by the difference in temperature between its waters and the layers of air above them.

The rain was followed by showers of fire. Raindrops were transformed into sparkles of lightning. One would have thought that Captain Nemo, seeking a death worthy of him, sought to be struck by lightning. With a fearful pitching movement the *Nautilus* reared in the air, with her spur pointed upward like a lightning rod, with flashes of lightning shooting from it.

Completely exhausted, I crawled on my stomach toward the hatch, opened it, and went down into the saloon. The storm was then reaching its greatest violence. It was impossible to stand up inside the *Nautilus*.

Captain Nemo came in at about midnight. I heard the tanks of the *Nautilus* being filled slowly, and she sank gently below the surface.

Through the open panels of the saloon I saw large fish, frightened by the storm, shooting by like ghosts through the fiery waters. Some of them were struck dead by lightning before my very eyes!

The *Nautilus* kept submerging. I thought it would find calm waters at a depth of 50 feet, but I was mistaken. The storm above was churning too violently for that. We had to dive down to 150 feet in the bowels of the sea before we found peace.

How quiet, silent, and peaceful it was there! Who would have thought that a frightful hurricane was unleashing its fury on the surface of that sea at that very moment!

Chapter XX

AT LATITUDE 47° 24′ AND LONGITUDE 17° 28′

THE STORM had driven us eastward again, and all hope of escape on the shores around New York, or on the St. Lawrence, vanished. In his despair, poor Ned had withdrawn into himself, and like Captain Nemo, sought solitude. Conseil and I no longer left each other.

I have said that the *Nautilus* had been driven eastward. To be more exact, I should have said northeast. For some days it cruised aimlessly, sometimes on the surface, sometimes submerged, in the midst of those fogs so dangerous to sailors. Those fogs are caused primarily by melting ice, which saturates the atmosphere with moisture. How many ships have been lost in these waters while seeking to reach the uncertain and dim lights on the coast! How many calamities these heavy fogs have caused! How many wrecks occur on those reefs whose noisy breakers are drowned by the winds! How many collisions take place in spite of lights, foghorns, and bells!

For this reason the seabed of this area looked like a battlefield, a burial ground, where lay all the victims vanquished by the sea. Some were already old and encrusted; others, more recent, still reflected the glare of our searchlight on the iron and copper of their hulls. How many of those ships had sunk with all hands on board, including immigrants, around those points marked dangerous on the mariners' charts: Cape Race, St. Paul Island, Belle Isle Strait, and the estuary of the St. Lawrence! Just in the past few years, how many victims have been entered in the funeral annals of the Royal Mail, of Inman and of Montreal: the *Solway*, the *Isis*, the *Paramatta*, the *Hungarian*, the *Canadian*, the *Anglo-Saxon*, the *Humboldt*, and the *United States*, all run aground; the *Arctic*, the *Lyonnais*, sunk by collisions; the *President*, the *Pacific*, the *City of Glasgow*, fate unknown; dismal remains, among which the *Nautilus* cruised as if passing in review a parade of the dead!

On the 15th of May, we reached the southernmost tip of the Grand Bank of Newfoundland. This bank is the product of alluvia, or huge masses of organic matter, brought either from the equator by the Gulf Stream or from the North Pole by the countercurrent of cold water that skirts the American coast. There are also huge masses of rocks, dropped there by the breaking up of the ice. It is also a vast ossuary of fish, mollusks, and zoophytes that have perished there by the million.

The depth of the sea is not very great at the Grand Bank, no more than a few hundred fathoms at most. But toward the south there is a deep depression, a pit about ten thousand feet deep. Here is where the Gulf Stream widens and spreads. It loses both its speed and some of its warmth and becomes virtually a sea.

Among the fish that the *Nautilus* frightened away as she cruised along, I would mention the *Cyclopterus lumpus*, or lumpfish, three feet long, with a blackish back and an orange belly, which gives other fish a seldom-followed example of marital fidelity; a large unernack, a kind of emerald moray, excellent to eat; karracks, with big eyes in a head shaped like that of a god; blennies, oviparous like the reptiles; black gobies or gudgeons, about an inch long; grenadiers with long tails and a brilliant silver sheen—all fast-swimming fish that had ventured far from their northern seas.

The nets also brought up a hardy, bold, vigorous fish with strong muscles and armed with pricking nettles on its head and spurs on its fins, a real scorpion, six or ten feet long, and a deadly enemy of blennies, codfish, and salmon. It was the bullhead of the northern seas, with a brown, gnarled body and red fins. The men of the *Nautilus* had some trouble with this animal, which, thanks to the formation of its gills, can prevent its lungs from drying when exposed to the open air and can thus live for some time out of the water.

Just as a reminder, I will cite bosquians, little fish that follow ships for a long time in the northern seas; sharp-snouted bleaks, peculiar to the North Atlantic; hogfish; and finally, the gadidae, represented by their main species, the cod, which I was able to observe in its favorite waters, the inexhaustible Grand Bank of Newfoundland.

One could well call the cod a mountain fish, for Newfoundland is just that, a submerged mountain. As the *Nautilus* made its way through massive ranks of the cod, Conseil could not restrain himself:

"What! Are those cods! But I thought cod were flat, like flounders or soles."

"How naïve can you be!" I cried. "Cod is only flat at a grocery store, where they are opened and spread out. But in the water, they are as spindle-shaped as mullets and perfectly built for speed."

361

"I believe whatever Monsieur says," replied Conseil. "But what masses! What swarms!"

"Well, my friend, I can only say that there would be many more if it were not for their enemies, the hogfish and man! Do you know how many eggs have been counted in one single female?"

"Let us be generous," replied Conseil. "Five hundred thousand?"

"Eleven million, my friend."

"Eleven million! I refuse to believe that unless I count them myself."

"Go ahead and count them, Conseil. But it would be quicker to believe me. Remember that cod is fished by Frenchmen, Englishmen, Americans, Danes, and Norwegians, who catch them by the thousands. They are consumed in prodigious quantities, and if it were not for their astounding fertility, the seas would soon be stripped of all supply. In England and America alone, five thousand ships manned by seventy-five thousand fishermen are engaged in cod fishing. Each ship has an average catch of forty thousand, which adds up to a total of twenty-five million. We have the same figures from Norway."

"All right," replied Conseil. "I'll take Monsieur's word. I won't count them."

"You will not count what?"

"Those eleven million eggs. I should like to point out one thing, however."

"What is that?"

"If all those eggs hatched, four female cods could supply England, America, and Norway."

As we moved across the bottom of the Grand Bank, I could clearly see those long fishing lines, each carrying two hundred hooks, which every boat puts out by the dozen. Each line was held down by a small grappling anchor and held up at the surface by a string tied to a cork buoy. The Nautilus had to do some skillful steering to get through that underwater network.

We did not stay long in these crowded waters. We cruised north toward the 42nd parallel, off St. John of Newfoundland and Heart's Content, where the Atlantic cable ends.

Instead of continuing northward, the Nautilus then turned east, as if she wished to follow the plateau on which the telegraphic cable was laid, where numerous soundings have given an accurate map of the ocean floor.

It was on the 17th of May, about five hundred miles from Heart's Content, at a depth of about nine thousand feet, that I first saw the cable lying on the ocean floor. Conseil, whom I had not forewarned, at first thought it was a gigantic sea serpent, and was ready to classify it, following his usual methods. However, I set him straight, and to console him for his blunder, I gave him some details about the laying of the cable.

The first cable was laid during the years 1857 and 1858. But after having transmitted about four hundred telegrams, it ceased to function. In 1863, the engineers constructed a new cable, measuring over two thousand miles in length and weighing 4,500 tons, which was loaded aboard the *Great Eastern*. But that attempt also failed.

The *Nautilus*, on May 25th, submerged at a depth of 12,500 feet, passed over the very spot where the break in the cable had occurred, ruining the earlier project. This spot was 638 miles from the coast of Ireland. At two o'clock in the afternoon, it was noticed that communications with Europe had been interrupted. The electricians on board decided to cut the cable before bringing it to the surface, and at eleven o'clock in the evening they had recovered the broken part. They repaired it by splicing it; then the cable was let down once more. A few days later, however, it snapped again, but this time it could not be recovered from the ocean depths. The Americans did not lose heart, however. The audacious Cyrus Field, promoter of the enterprise, who was risking his entire fortune, announced a new series of bonds, which were immediately bought up. Another cable was manufactured, with greater care this time. The bundles of electric wires were insulated with a casing of gutta-percha, which, in turn, was protected by pads of textile materials and all inserted in a metal casing. The *Great Eastern* set sail again on the 13th of July, 1866.

This time everything went well. However, a strange thing happened. On several occasions, as they unrolled the cable, the electricians noticed that nails had been driven into it with the object of damaging the core. Captain Anderson, his officers, and his engineers met to discuss the matter, and posted a notice stating that if the culprit were discovered on board, he would be thrown into the sea without more ado. From then on, there was no repetition of the incident.

On July 23rd, the *Great Eastern* was only five hundred miles from Newfoundland when she received a telegram from Ireland stating that an armistice had been signed between Austria and Prussia after the Battle of Sadowa. On July 27th, in a thick fog, she reached Heart's Content. The enterprise had been brought to a successful conclusion, and the first message young America sent to an old Europe consisted of these wise words so rarely understood: "Glory to God in Heaven. Peace on earth to all men of good will."

I did not expect to find the cable in its original state, such as it was when it had left the factory. That long serpent, covered with shells and encrusted with foraminifera, was, however, still embedded in a kind of rocky cement that protected it from mollusks that might bore into it. There it lay, peacefully, sheltered from the movement of the sea and subjected to a pressure favorable to the transmission of the electric impulse that travels from America to Europe in thirty-two hundredths of a second. Doubtless, this cable will last indefinitely, for it has been noted that the sheath of gutta-percha is improved when immersed in salt water.

Moreover, on this well-chosen underwater plateau, the cable is never lowered at depths that will cause a break. The *Nautilus* followed it to its lowest depth, 14,500 feet down, where it lay without any danger of breaking. Then we approached the spot where the accident had taken place in 1863.

The floor of the ocean in that place consisted of a valley about seventy-five miles wide, and deep enough to contain Mont Blanc without its peak rising above the surface. This valley is closed off to the east by a perpendicular wall of about 6,000 feet.

We reached this point on the 28th of May, and the *Nautilus* was no more than a hundred miles from Ireland.

Did Captain Nemo intend to sail northward and head for the British Isles? No. Much to my great surprise, he turned south toward European waters. As we sailed around the Emerald Isle, I caught a glimpse of Cape Clear and the Fastnet lighthouse, which lights the way for thousands of ships leaving Glasgow or Liverpool.

An important question now occurred to me. Would the *Nautilus* venture into the English Channel? Ned Land, who had reappeared as we approached coastal waters, kept asking me questions. I did not know what to tell him. Captain Nemo was nowhere to be seen. Having permitted the Canadian to catch a fleeting glance of the shores of America, was he going to show me the coast of France?

Meanwhile, the *Nautilus* continued south. On May 30th, she cruised within sight of Land's End, between the southernmost tip of England and the Scilly Isles, which we left to starboard.

If he intended to enter the Channel, he would have now to veer sharply to the east. But he did not do so.

Throughout the day of May 31st, the *Nautilus* kept cruising in a series of circles, which intrigued me. She seemed to be searching for a certain spot and was having difficulty in locating it. At midday, Captain Nemo himself came out to take our bearings. He paid no attention to me and he seemed to be more depressed than ever. What could be the reason for that depressed mood? Was it because he was approaching European shores? Was he moved by memories of his forsaken land? What did he really feel? Was it remorse or regrets that moved him?

This thought occupied my mind for a long time, and I had a presentiment that fate would soon betray the Captain's secrets.

The next day, June 1st, the *Nautilus* continued to cruise around in circles. It was obvious that she was looking for a definite spot in the sea. Captain Nemo measured the height of the sun, just as he had done the day before. The sea was calm, the sky clear. About eight miles to eastward, a big steamer was outlined against the horizon. She flew no flag and I could not tell her nationality.

A few minutes before the sun passed its zenith, Captain Nemo took up his sextant and peered through it with great care. The sea was perfectly calm and facilitated his task. The *Nautilus* lay motionless, neither rolling nor pitching.

I was still on the platform when the Captain finished his observations. I heard him say only a few words:

"This is it."

Then he went down the hatch. Had he seen the ship, which was now altering its course and seemed to be speeding toward us? I could not say.

I went back to the saloon. The hatch was closed, and I heard the sound of water hissing into the tanks. The *Nautilus* began to submerge straight down, vertically. Its propellers had stopped turning.

A few minutes later, it stopped at a depth of about 2,700 feet, and lay motionless on the bed of the sea.

Then the lights of the saloon were switched off, the panels were opened, and through the panes I could clearly see the sea, brilliantly lit by the beam of our searchlight for a radius of half a mile.

I looked to port, but could see nothing but an endless expanse of tranquil water.

To starboard, in the distance, however, my attention was attracted by something large and bulky, suggestive of ruins buried beneath a coating of whitish shells, resembling a mantle of snow. On taking a closer look at this mass, I thought I could make out the warped structure of a ship, stripped of its masts, which must have sunk downward. The wreck had certainly occurred a long time ago. To be so encrusted with calcareous matter, it must have lain on the ocean bottom for many, many years.

What ship was it? Why had the *Nautilus* come to visit its tomb? Had something other than a shipwreck been the cause of its disappearance beneath the waters?

I was just wondering about this when the Captain, who was standing next to me, said in a slow measured voice:

"This ship was once called the *Marseillais*. She was launched in 1762 and her armament consisted of seventy-four guns. On the thirteenth of August, 1778, under the command of La Poype-Vertrieux, she fought courageously against the *Preston*. On the Fourth of July, 1779, she took part in the capture of Granada in the squadron commanded by Admiral d'Estaing. On the fifth of September, 1781, she participated in the Battle of Chesapeake Bay, with Count de Grasse. In 1794, the French Republic changed her name. On April sixteenth of the same year, she joined at Brest the squadron of Villaret-Joyeuse, which had been ordered to escort a convoy of wheat from America under the command of Admiral Van Stabel. On the eleventh and on the twelfth *Prairial* of the year II, this squadron encountered some English ships. Today, monsieur, is the thirteenth *Prairial,** the first of June, 1868. Seventy-four years ago to the very day, at this very spot, at latitude forty-seven degrees twenty-four minutes and longitude seventeen degrees twenty-eight minutes, this ship, after putting up a heroic fight, having lost all three of her masts, with water pouring into the holds and a third of her crew out of action, preferred to be swallowed by the sea with her three hundred and fifty-six men rather than surrender. With her flag nailed to the poop, she disappeared beneath the waves to the cries of 'Long Live the Republic!' "

"The *Avenger!*" I exclaimed.

"Yes, monsieur, the *Avenger*. A wonderful name!" murmured Captain Nemo, crossing his arms.

* "The month of pasture" (May 20–June 18), the ninth month of the French Revolutionary calendar, 1793 to 1805.—M.T.B.

Chapter XXI

A HECATOMB

THE CAPTAIN'S strange manner of speaking, the unexpected appearance of that spectacle, the story of that patriotic ship, first related in cold words, but becoming increasingly emotional toward the end, the mention of that name *Avenger*, whose significance did not escape me, had a profound effect on me. I could not take my eyes off the Captain. He stood there, his arms stretched toward the sea, his ardent eyes fixed upon that glorious wreck. Would I ever know who he was, where he came from, or where he was going? Perhaps. More and more I was becoming aware of the man in him as distinct from the scientist. I was beginning to realize that no ordinary misanthropy had caused him and his men to seek refuge in the *Nautilus*. It was, rather, a deep hatred, monstrous or sublime, a hatred that would never diminish. Was this hatred still seeking vengeance? I was soon to know.

In the meantime, the *Nautilus* kept rising slowly to the surface, and the confused outline of the *Avenger* gradually receded into the background. A slight roll of the craft soon told me that we had come to the surface.

Just then a muffled *boom* was heard. I glanced at the Captain. He stood motionless.

"Captain?" I asked.

He did not reply.

I left him and went up on the platform. Conseil and the Canadian were already there.

"Where did that explosion come from?" I asked.

I looked in the direction of the ship that I had previously seen. It had drawn closer to the *Nautilus* and was coming toward us at full speed. Six miles now separated us.

"A cannon shot," replied Ned Land.

"What kind of ship is it, Ned?"

"Judging by her rigging and the height of the masts," replied the Canadian, "I should say she's a man-of-war. I hope she attacks this infernal *Nautilus* and, if necessary, sinks us!"

"Friend Ned," rejoined Conseil, "what harm can she possibly do to the *Nautilus*? Can she attack us underwater, or bombard us at the bottom of the sea?"

"Tell me, Ned," I asked, "can you recognize the nationality of that ship?"

The Canadian knitted his eyebrows, lowered his eyelids, and peered intently at the ship.

"No, monsieur," he replied, "I cannot tell what nation she belongs to. She's not flying any flag. But she's certainly a warship, because she has a long pennant fluttering from her mainmast."

For a quarter of an hour, we continued to watch the ship speeding toward us. But I could not believe that from that distance she could have sighted the *Nautilus*, still less have identified it as a submarine.

Soon the Canadian told me that she was a big warship, with two armor-plated decks and a ram. Dense smoke was pouring from her twin funnels. Her sails were so closely furled that they merged with the outline of the yards. She was flying no flag at her mast. She was still too far away for me to make out the colors of her pennant, which was floating in the breeze like a light ribbon.

She was approaching rapidly. If Captain Nemo allowed her to come in close, we might yet have a chance to escape.

"Monsieur," said Ned Land, "even if that ship comes within a mile of us, I intend to jump into the sea, and I suggest you do the same."

I made no reply to the Canadian's suggestion, but continued to watch the ship, which kept looming larger and larger. Whether she was British, French, American, or Russian, she would surely welcome us on board if only we could reach her.

"Monsieur would do well to recall," Conseil suggested, "that we have had some experience in swimming together, and he can rely on me to tow him towards the ship, should he decide to follow our friend Ned."

I was about to reply when a puff of white smoke appeared in the bow of the warship. A few seconds later, there was a splash in the rear of the *Nautilus*. A heavy shell had landed in the water. A moment later we heard the sound of cannon.

"Great heavens! They're firing at us!" I cried.

"Good luck to 'em!" muttered the Canadian.

"Well, they certainly do not take us for shipwrecked sailors, clinging to their boat."

"If Monsieur doesn't mind— Well!" said Conseil, brushing away water that had been sprayed over him by another shell. "If Monsieur doesn't mind my saying so, I think they've recognized the narwhal and are firing at it."

"But they must have seen by now that there are men here!" I exclaimed.

"Perhaps that's exactly why they are firing!" retorted Ned Land, looking at me.

Then it dawned on me. Of course, everyone now knew what the supposed monster had turned out to be. In its encounter with the *Abraham Lincoln,* when the Canadian had struck the *Nautilus* with his harpoon, Captain Farragut had realized that the supposed narwhal was, in fact, a submarine, far more dangerous than a monstrous whale.

Yes, that must be the case. Doubtless, everywhere at sea, this fearful engine of destruction was being pursued.

And indeed one can well imagine how frightful the *Nautilus* could be if Captain Nemo were using her as a weapon of vengeance!

During that night in the Indian Ocean, when he had locked us up in a cell, had he not attacked a ship or other? Had not that man who was now buried in the coral cemetery been a victim of a collision provoked by the *Nautilus?* Yes, of course, that must be it. A part of Captain Nemo's mysterious existence was becoming clear. If his identity was still unknown, the nations that had joined in their pursuit of him at least knew they were no longer pursuing a phantom, but a man who had sworn an implacable hatred against them!

All that appalling past came to my mind, and I realized that instead of meeting friends on board that warship that was speeding toward us, we would only meet merciless enemies.

In the meanwhile, more and more shells fell around us. Some, on hitting the water, ricocheted and were lost in the distance. None hit the *Nautilus.*

The warship was now only three miles away. Despite all the violent cannonading, however, Captain Nemo did not once appear on the platform. Yet, if one of those shells had made a direct hit on the hull of the *Nautilus,* it could have been fatal.

Just then the Canadian spoke up.

"Monsieur," he said, "we've got to do everything we can to get out of this. Confound it! Let's signal! Perhaps they will realize that there are some decent men on board!"

Ned Land took out his handkerchief, and was about to wave it, when he was struck by a blow of an iron fist and, in spite of his great strength, fell on the deck.

"You fool!" cried the Captain. "Do you want me to nail you on the prow of the *Nautilus* before it rams that ship?"

Captain Nemo was terrible to hear, and even more terrible to look at. His face had grown so pale that his heart must have stopped beating for a moment. His pupils had contracted frightfully. He was no longer speaking, he was roaring. He had bent down and with his strong grip was twisting the Canadian by the shoulders.

Then he suddenly let go, and turning toward the warship, whose shells were raining around him, he shouted:

"Ah, you know who I am, ship of an accursed nation! I do not need to see your colors to recognize you! Look, I am going to show you mine!"

And walking on the front part of the deck, he unfurled a black flag similar to the one he had planted at the South Pole.

Just then a shell struck the hull of the *Nautilus*, but obliquely. Instead of piercing it, the shell bounced past the Captain and was lost in the sea.

Captain Nemo shrugged his shoulders. Then, turning to me, he said curtly:

"You and your friends get down below."

"Captain," I exclaimed, "you are going to attack that ship?"

"I am going to sink her, monsieur."

"You wouldn't do that!"

"I shall do so," Captain Nemo replied coldly. "Do not presume to judge me. Fate has let you see what you were not supposed to see. We have been attacked. Our answer will be terrible. Get down below."

"What ship is that?"

"You do not know? So much the better! At least her nationality will remain a secret to you. Down below!"

The Canadian, Conseil, and I had no alternative but to obey. About fifteen sailors from the *Nautilus* were now standing around their Captain, gazing with implacable hatred at the ship that was bearing down on them. They all seemed to be stirred to their very souls by the same need for vengeance.

As I was going down, another shell grazed the hull of the *Nautilus*, and I heard the Captain shout:

"Keep firing, you senseless ship! Squander your harmless shells! You will not evade the spur of the *Nautilus*! You will perish, but not where you are now! Your remains must not lie amidst the glorious remains of the *Avenger*!"

I returned to my room. The Captain and his second-in-command had remained on the platform. The propeller began churning. The *Nautilus*, speeding away, was soon beyond the range of the shells. The pursuit continued, however, and Captain Nemo was satisfied just to keep his distance.

Toward four o'clock in the afternoon, unable to contain the impatience and anxiety that was consuming me, I returned to the central stairway. The hatch was still open. I ventured up on the platform. The Captain was still pacing nervously up and down. He kept looking at the ship, now five or six miles to leeward. He kept stalking around like a wild beast, drawing her eastward, permitting himself to be pursued. But he was not attacking. Perhaps he had not made up his mind yet.

I wanted to intervene one last time, but no sooner had I spoken to Captain Nemo than he bade me be silent.

"I am the law, I am justice!" he said to me. "I am the oppressed, and there is the oppressor! It is through him that all those whom I loved, cherished and venerated, perished: my country, my wife, my children, my father and mother! Everything I hate is there! Not another word from you!"

I took one last look at the warship, which was coming on at full steam, and rejoined Ned and Conseil.

"We must escape!" I cried.

"Good," said Ned. "What's the name of that ship?"

"I do not know, but whatever it is, it will be sunk before nightfall. Whatever happens, it will be better for us to sink with her than to become accomplices in an act of vengeance whose justice we cannot assess with fairness."

"I agree with you," Ned Land replied coldly. "Let's wait for nightfall."

Night came. A deep silence reigned on board. The compass indicated that the *Nautilus* had not changed its course. I could hear its propeller churning through the waves at an even speed. We were still on the surface, rolling gently from side to side.

My companions and I had decided to make a dash for it as soon as the other ship was close enough to hear us or see us, for the moon, which would be full within three days, was shining brightly. Once on board that ship, even if we could not prevent the blow that threatened her, we could, at least, do everything that circumstances would permit. Several times I thought that the *Nautilus* was getting in a position to attack. But she was apparently content to let her adversary draw near, then would suddenly resume her flight.

Part of the night went by without incident. We watched for the chance to act. We were too excited to talk much. Ned Land wanted to jump in the sea then and there, but I persuaded him to wait. I was of the opinion that the *Nautilus* would attack the warship on the surface, and this would make it not only possible but easy to escape.

At three o'clock in the morning I felt very uneasy and went up on deck. Captain Nemo was still there. He was still standing beneath his flag, which fluttered above him in a light breeze. His eyes remained fixed on the ship. The deep intensity of his gaze seemed to draw it closer, to hold it spellbound, to make it follow him more surely than if it were towed.

The moon was now crossing the meridian. Jupiter was rising to the east. In the midst of this tranquil scene, sea and sky vied with each other in peaceful serenity. It seemed as if the sea were offering the moon the most beautiful mirror it had ever had to reflect its beauty.

As I gazed at the serene tranquillity of that night, the thought of the hatred that was brewing in the bowels of the almost imperceptible *Nautilus* made my whole being shudder.

The ship was only two miles away now. She had drawn closer. She kept following that phosphorescent glow that revealed the presence of the *Nautilus*. I could see her green and red riding lights, and the white light of her lantern hanging from the foresail. A dim glow, reflected from her rigging, indicated that the boilers had been stoked up to the utmost. Showers of sparks, ashes, and red-hot cinders of coal escaped from her funnels, glittering like so many stars in the darkness.

I stood there until six o'clock in the morning. Captain Nemo appeared not to notice me. The ship was only a mile and a half away, and as the first rays of dawn appeared, her cannonade began again. The moment could not be far off now when the *Nautilus* would attack its enemy and my companions and I would leave forever that man whom I did not dare to judge.

I was about to go below in order to alert my friends when the second-in-command came up on the platform, followed by several sailors. Either Captain Nemo did not see them, or he did not wish to see them. Certain steps were then taken that might be described as clearing the decks of the *Nautilus* for action. These steps were quite simple; they lowered the iron railing around the platform and pushed the pilot's cage and that of the searchlight down into the hull until they were flush with the deck. Nothing now protruded from the surface of the long steel cigar-shaped vessel that might hamper her movements.

I returned to the saloon. The *Nautilus* was still on the surface. The light of day came filtering down through the water. Through the movements of the waves, I caught the occasional red glint of the rising sun shining through the panels.

That terrible day of the 2nd of June had dawned.

At seven o'clock the log indicated that the *Nautilus* was slackening its speed, and I realized that it was letting the other ship draw closer. The sound of gunfire grew louder; shells splashed through the water around us with a strange hissing sound.

"My friends," I said, "the time has come. Let us shake hands, and may God be with us!"

Ned Land was resolute, Conseil was calm, and I was so nervous I could hardly control myself.

We entered the library, and just as I was pushing open the door that led to the central stairway, I heard the hatch close suddenly.

The Canadian sprang to the steps, but I stopped him. A familiar hissing sound told me that water was filling the tanks, and a few moments later, the *Nautilus* dived a few yards below the surface.

I knew what this maneuver meant, but it was too late to do anything about it. The *Nautilus* had no intention of ramming the warship through her impenetrable armor above the surface. It was going to ram her, but below the waterline, which did not have this protection. Once again we were prisoners, compelled to witness the grim drama that was about to take place. But we scarcely had time to think. We had all taken refuge in my room, and we looked at each other, speechless. I fell into a deep stupor; my mind stopped thinking. I was in that painful state of suspense that precedes a frightful explosion. I waited and listened, straining my ears, for only my sense of hearing was alive.

The speed of the *Nautilus* had increased perceptibly. She was gathering momentum. Her whole body quivered. Suddenly I uttered a cry. I had felt a light shock. I could now feel that powerful steel spur penetrating. I could hear sounds of rattling and scraping. The *Nautilus*, propelled forward by her powerful momentum, plowed right through the body of that ship, just like the needle of a sailmaker goes through a canvas.

I could stand it no longer. Frantic and bewildered, I rushed out of my cabin into the saloon. Captain Nemo was there looking through the port panel, silent, cold, and implacable!

The huge mass of the ship was sinking. The *Nautilus*, in order not to miss a single detail of its tragic fate, followed it down into the abyss. Thirty feet away from me I could see water pouring with thunderous noise into its gaping hull. Soon the double line of cannons and bulwarks came into view, followed by the deck covered with black shadows running in every direction. As the water kept rising, those wretched victims rushed up the shrouds, clung fast to masts, or writhed in the water—a human anthill suddenly invaded by the sea.

I stood there tense, unable to move. Struck with horror, my hair standing on end, my eyes wide open, breathless and speechless, I, too, kept looking, held spellbound before that panel by an invisible power.

The huge ship sank slowly. The *Nautilus* followed it, watching its every movement. Suddenly there was an explosion. The compressed air within the hull had blown the decks up in the air as if the powder stores had caught fire. Beneath the force of that explosion, the *Nautilus* swerved. Then that unfortunate ship sank faster. Its top masts, crowded with victims, appeared, followed by its spars, which were bent beneath the weight of men clinging to them, and finally, the top of its mainmast. Then the dark mass, with all its victims, disappeared beneath the sea, swallowed by a whirlpool of churning waters.

I turned toward Captain Nemo. That satanic judge, that veritable archangel of hatred, stood there, still watching. When it was all over, he walked to the door of his stateroom, opened it, and disappeared. I followed him. On the far wall, beneath the paintings of his heroes, I saw a portrait of a woman, still young, with two small children. Captain Nemo stood looking at them for a few moments, stretching his arms toward them. Then, falling on his knees, he burst into deep sobs.

Chapter XXII

CAPTAIN NEMO'S LAST WORDS

THE PANELS HAD CLOSED on that frightful scene, but the light in the saloon had not yet gone on again. All was darkness and silence inside the *Nautilus*. We were leaving that place of desolation at a prodigious speed, at a depth of a hundred feet. Where were we going? North or south? Where was Captain Nemo fleeing after his horrible vengeance?

I returned to my room, where Ned and Conseil sat in silence. I felt an insurmountable horror for Captain Nemo. Whatever he might have suffered at the hands of men, he had no right to punish them in such a manner. He had made me, if not an accomplice, at least a witness to his vengeance! And that was too much!

At eleven o'clock the electric light went on again, and I went into the saloon. It was deserted. I consulted the various instruments. The *Nautilus* was fleeing northward at twenty-five miles, sometimes on the surface and sometimes at a depth of thirty feet.

Glancing at the chart, I saw that we were sailing off the mouth of the English Channel, and that our course was taking us toward the northern seas at an incredible speed.

We were traveling so rapidly that I could scarcely catch a glimpse of the long-nosed sharks, the hammer sharks, and the spotted dogfish that frequent these waters, not to mention the large sea eagles, the swarms of sea horses, looking like knights in a game of chess, the eels, writhing along like squids in fireworks, armies of crabs, fleeing sideways with their pincers crossed on their shells, and, lastly, schools of porpoises, which vied with the *Nautilus* in speed. However, there was no question of observing, studying, or classifying these creatures just then.

By evening, we had covered two hundred leagues across the Atlantic. Dusk fell, and the sea was shrouded in darkness until the moon rose.

I returned to my room. I could not sleep. I was troubled by nightmares. That tragic scene of destruction kept recurring in my mind.

From that day on, who could tell in what region of the North Atlantic the *Nautilus* was sailing? But always through these northern mists and always with such speed! Had we skirted Spitsbergen or the Novaya Zemlya? Did he sail through those unknown waters of the White Sea, the Kara Sea, the Gulf of Ob, the Archipelago of Liarrov, or the unexplored coasts of Asia? I could not say. Time went by, but there was no way of calculating, since all the clocks on board had stopped. I had the impression that night and day, as happens in polar regions, no longer followed their natural course. I felt as if I were being led into an eerie world, where the overwrought imagination of Edgar Allan Poe would feel at ease. Any moment I expected to see, like the fabulous Gordon Pym, "a shrouded human figure, much, much larger in its proportions than any dweller among men, lying athwart that waterfall that bars access to the Pole!"

I calculated, but I may be mistaken, that the *Nautilus* sped on this hazardous course for fifteen or twenty days. I do not know how long this voyage would have lasted if a catastrophe had not occurred to put an end to it. Neither Captain Nemo, nor his second-in-command, nor any member of the crew, had been seen for one single moment during this voyage. The *Nautilus* cruised almost continuously underwater. Whenever it emerged to the surface, it was only to renew its supply of air. The hatches would then open and close automatically. Our bearings no longer appeared on the planisphere. I did not know where we were.

I should add that the Canadian, at the end of his strength and his patience, no longer appeared either. Conseil could not get a word out of him, and he was afraid that in a fit of loneliness and melancholy, Ned might commit suicide. He looked after him constantly, with care and devotion.

One can well imagine that under such conditions, our situation was no longer tolerable.

One morning—I cannot say on what day—in the early hours of dawn, I had finally fallen into a troubled and morbid slumber. When I awakened, I saw Ned Land leaning over me, and I heard him whispering:

"We are going to escape!"

I sat up.

"When?" I asked.

"This evening. All supervision seems to have disappeared on the *Nautilus*. Everyone seems dazed. Will you be ready, monsieur?"

"Yes. Where are we?"

"We're within sight of land. I caught sight of it through the mist this morning about twenty miles to the east."

"What coast is it?"

"I don't know, but whatever it is, we'll take refuge there."

"We will, Ned! We will make a dash for it tonight, even if the sea swallows us."

"The sea is rough, and there's a strong wind blowing. But

I'm not afraid of tackling twenty miles in that light dinghy. I've managed to store some food and a few bottles of water without the crew's knowing about it."

"I will follow you."

"Furthermore, if I'm caught, I'll defend myself to the death."

"We will die together, Ned."

I had made up my mind. The Canadian left me. I went up on the platform, but the sea was so rough that I found it difficult to keep on my feet. The sky was overcast and threatening, but since there was land out there on the misty horizon, we simply had to escape. Neither a day nor an hour was to be lost.

I returned to the saloon, fearing, yet somehow hoping, that I would meet Captain Nemo, inwardly uncertain as to whether I ever wanted to see him again. What could I say to him? Could I hide that involuntary revulsion I felt toward him? No, it was best to avoid him, it was best to forget him! And yet . . . !

How long that day seemed, the last I was to spend on board the *Nautilus!* I remained alone. Ned Land and Conseil avoided talking to me for fear of betraying our plan to escape.

At six o'clock I dined, although I was not hungry. I forced myself to eat against my will, since I wanted to conserve my strength.

At half past six, Ned Land came into my room.

"We won't see each other again before we leave," he said. "At ten o'clock, the moon won't have risen yet. We'll take advantage of the darkness. Come up to the dinghy. Conseil and I will be waiting for you."

The Canadian went out, without giving me time to reply.

I wanted to check the direction of the *Nautilus*. I went into the saloon. We were traveling in a north-northeasterly direction, at prodigious speed, at a depth of about 150 feet.

I took one last look at all those wonders of nature, at that wealth of art treasures assembled in that museum, and at the unrivaled collection, destined one day to perish at the bottom of the sea with him who had collected it. I wanted a final crowning impression of all that fixed in my mind forever. I remained there for an hour, basking in the light emanating from the ceiling, and reviewing all those resplendent treasures gleaming in their showcases. Then I returned to my room. I put on my heavy sea clothes, collected my notes, which I stowed carefully on my person. My heart was beating fast and I found it impossible to keep cool. Certainly my excitement and uneasiness would have betrayed me to Captain Nemo.

What could he be doing at this moment? I listened at the door of his room and heard a footstep. The Captain was there. He had not yet gone to bed. At every sound he made, I

377

thought he would appear and ask me why I wanted to escape! I was in a continual state of alarm, intensified by my own imagination. So overwhelming was my feeling that I began to wonder whether it would not be best to walk boldly into the Captain's room, look him straight in the eye, and have it out with him!

This was the idea of a madman. Fortunately, I controlled myself and lay down on my bed to relax and quiet my mind. My nerves calmed down somewhat, but my overexcited mind recalled the whole period of my existence on board the *Nautilus:* all the incidents, happy or unhappy, that had occurred since my disappearance from the *Abraham Lincoln,* the hunting expeditions underwater, the Torres Strait, the Papuan savages, our running aground, the coral cemetery, the tunnel under the Suez, the Santorin Island, the Cretan diver, Vigo Bay, Atlantis, the ice shelf, the South Pole, our imprisonment beneath the ice, the fight with the giant squids, the storm in the Gulf Stream, the *Avenger,* and that horrible scene of the ship sinking with all its crew! All these events flashed before my eyes like a series of backdrops in a theater. In such strange settings, Captain Nemo stood out like a colossus. His qualities stood out boldly and assumed superhuman proportions. He was no longer my equal, but the king of the water, the genie of the seas!

It was then half past nine. I held my head in my hands to keep it from bursting. I closed my eyes. I did not want to think anymore. Another half hour to wait! Another half hour of nightmare which could drive me mad!

Just then the soft, mellow sounds of organ music reached me, a vague, melancholy harmony accompanied by an indefinable melody. It was like the mournful cry of a soul seeking surcease from the sorrows of the world. My whole being was enraptured and, scarcely breathing, I, too, was lost in a musical ecstasy that was carrying him beyond the confines of this world. Then a sudden thought of terror struck me. Captain Nemo was not in his room, but in the saloon, the room I had to cross in order to escape! How was I to avoid a final meeting! If he were to see me, he would perhaps talk to me! A single gesture from him could destroy me, a single word could bind me on board forever!

Ten o'clock was about to strike. The time had come to leave my room and rejoin my companions. This was no time to hesitate, even if Captain Nemo were to rise before me. I opened the door cautiously. It seemed to me, as I turned the handle, that it creaked loudly. But perhaps the noise was a figment of my imagination!

I crept across the dark corridors of the *Nautilus,* stopping at every step to calm the beating of my heart.

I reached the door at the angle of the saloon. I opened it quietly. The saloon was in complete darkness. I could hear the soft strains of the organ. Captain Nemo was there. He did not see me. Even with the full light on, I do not believe he would have seen me, he was so ecstatically absorbed in his music.

I crawled along the carpet, taking care not to make the slightest noise that would betray my presence. It took me five minutes to reach the door leading into the library, at the opposite end of the room.

I was just going to open it when a sigh from Captain Nemo riveted me to the spot. I realized that he was getting up. I could even see him, for a few rays of light from the library filtered through into the saloon. He came toward me, silent, with his arms folded, gliding like a specter across the floor rather than walking. His chest was heaving with deep sobs, and I could hear him murmuring these words, the last that I ever heard him utter:

"Almighty God! Enough! Enough!"

Could this be an expression of his remorse escaping from this man's conscience?

Bewildered, I rushed into the library. Then, up the central stairway, along the upper corridor to the dinghy. I reached it through the hatch that had already given access to my two companions.

"Let us go!" I cried. "Let us go!"

"At once!" replied the Canadian.

The compartment in the hull of the *Nautilus* was first sealed off on the inside by means of a wrench, which Ned had with him, and the same tool was used to open the outside hatch. Then the Canadian proceeded to unscrew the bolts that fastened the dinghy to the hull.

Suddenly a noise was heard inside the craft. Voices calling out to each other excitedly. What was the matter? Had our escape been discovered? I felt Ned Land slip a dagger in my hand.

"Yes," I murmured, "we shall know how to die!"

The Canadian had stopped working. One word, repeated twenty times, one terrifying word, told me what was causing that commotion on board the *Nautilus*. It was not us that the crew were excited about!

"The maelstrom!" * they cried, "the maelstrom!"

---

* A whirlpool in the Lofoten Islands, two contiguous island groups within the Arctic Circle in the Norwegian Sea. Their cod and herring fisheries are the richest in the world. The treacherous tidal currents are a constant danger to the fishing craft that come to fish here. The maelstrom, greatly exaggerated by both Verne and Poe, is south of Moskenes Island.—M.T.B.

The maelstrom! Could we possibly hear a more frightening word in a most frightening situation? Were we in those dangerous waters not far from the Norwegian coast? Did this mean that the *Nautilus* was about to be dragged down into the whirlpool at the very moment when we were leaving her in the dinghy?

It is well known that the tidal currents between the Faroe and Lofoten Islands rush together with irresistible violence, forming a whirlpool from which no ship has ever escaped. Towering waves converge here from all points of the horizon. These waves form a vortex, rightly called the "navel of the ocean," whose power of suction may extend as far as ten miles around. Not only ships, but whales and white polar bears from the far north, are swallowed by it.

It was here, then, that the *Nautilus*, unintentionally—or perhaps deliberately—had been brought by her Captain. The submarine was now spinning around and around in a radius becoming smaller and smaller. The dinghy, too, as long as it was lodged in the side of the *Nautilus*, was being whirled around at a breakneck speed. I could feel it whirling around. I felt that sickly feeling caused by rapid circling movements. We were in a state of extreme terror. Our circulation stopped, our nerves no longer felt, we broke out in a cold sweat, like that of an agonizing death. What a din around our frail dinghy! What roars were heard, echoing from miles around! What a noise the waves made as they crashed against the sharp rocks on the bottom of the sea—there where the hardest objects are shattered, where the trunks of trees are worn down to look like "hairy furs," as the Norwegians say.

What a predicament! We were tossed about like a frail cork. The *Nautilus* kept struggling like a human being. Her muscles of steel creaked. Sometimes she stood straight up on end, we with her!

"Hold on," shouted Ned. "Hold on! Screw the bolts down again! If we stay with the *Nautilus* we may yet be saved!"

He had scarcely finished speaking when we heard a loud cracking sound. The bolts had been wrenched from their sockets and the dinghy torn from its compartment. We were hurled into the middle of the whirlpool like a stone hurled from a sling.

My head struck an iron rib of the dinghy, and under the shock of that blow I lost consciousness.

Chapter XXIII

CONCLUSION

AND SO OUR VOYAGE BENEATH THE SEAS ENDED. What happened during that night, how the dinghy escaped the fearful swirling waters of the maelstrom, how Ned Land, Conseil, and I managed to emerge safely from it all, I cannot say. But when I regained consciousness, I was lying in a hut of a fisherman on one of the Lofoten Islands. My two friends, safe and sound, were beside me, holding my hands. We embraced each other with joy.

For the moment, it is impossible for us to think of returning to France. Communications between the north and the south of Norway are far from good, so I have to wait for a steamship that runs twice a month from North Cape.

It is here, among these good people who have given us shelter, that I am revising the story of our adventures. It is perfectly accurate. Not a fact has been omitted, not a detail exaggerated. It is the faithful account of an incredible expedition in an element as yet inaccessible to man, but which progress will, no doubt, one day reveal to him.

Will the world believe me? I do not know. But, after all, it does not really matter. All I am doing now is asserting my right to speak of those waters under which, in the space of less than ten months, I covered twenty thousand leagues, and of that voyage around the world that revealed to me so many wonders in the Pacific and Indian Oceans, the Red Sea, the Mediterranean, the Atlantic, and the North and South Polar Seas.

What happened to the *Nautilus?* Did she succeed in escaping from the powerful grip of the maelstrom? Is Captain Nemo still alive? Is he still lurking beneath the waters, bent upon revenge, or was that last hecatomb his final act of vengeance? Will the waves one day wash up on shore his manuscript, containing the story of his life? Shall I ever know what his real name was? Will the nationality of the last ship he sank give us a clue to the nationality of Captain Nemo?

I hope so. I also hope that his powerful craft managed to escape the most dangerous whirlpool of the sea, and that the *Nautilus* survived where so many other ships have perished!

If such is the case, if Captain Nemo still inhabits the ocean —his country of adoption—may all hatred have abated in his fierce heart! May the contemplation of so many marvels extinguish in him the spirit of vengeance! May the judge in him disappear, and may the scientist in him continue the peaceful exploration of the sea! However strange his destiny be, it is also sublime. Did I not experience and understand his destiny? Did I not live that unnatural existence for ten whole months? So, to that question, asked six thousand years ago by the Book of Ecclesiastes: "Who has ever fathomed the depths of the abyss?" two men, among all men, have the right to reply: Captain Nemo and I.

PENGUIN POPULAR POETRY

Published or forthcoming

The Selected Poems *of:*

Matthew Arnold
William Blake
Robert Browning
Robert Burns
Lord Byron
John Donne
Thomas Hardy
John Keats
Rudyard Kipling
Alexander Pope
Alfred Tennyson
Walt Whitman
William Wordsworth
William Yeats

and collections of:

Sixteenth-Century Poetry
Seventeenth-Century Poetry
Eighteenth-Century Poetry
Poetry of the Romantics
Victorian Poetry
Twentieth-Century Poetry

PENGUIN POPULAR CLASSICS

Published or forthcoming

PENGUIN POPULAR CLASSICS

Published or forthcoming

PENGUIN POPULAR CLASSICS

Published or forthcoming

PENGUIN POPULAR CLASSICS

Published or forthcoming

Charles and Mary Lamb	Tales from Shakespeare
D. H. Lawrence	The Rainbow
	Sons and Lovers
	Women in Love
Edward Lear	Book of Nonsense
Gaston Leroux	The Phantom of the Opera
Jack London	White Fang *and* The Call of the Wild
Captain Marryat	The Children of the New Forest
Herman Melville	Moby Dick
John Milton	Paradise Lost
Edith Nesbit	Five Children and It
	The Railway Children
Francis Turner Palgrave	The Golden Treasury
Edgar Allan Poe	Selected Tales
Sir Walter Scott	Ivanhoe
	Rob Roy
	Waverley
Saki	The Best of Saki
Anna Sewell	Black Beauty
William Shakespeare	Antony and Cleopatra
	As You Like It
	Hamlet
	Henry V
	Julius Caesar
	King Lear
	Macbeth
	The Merchant of Venice
	A Midsummer Night's Dream
	Othello
	Romeo and Juliet
	The Tempest
	Twelfth Night